Ls

The Summer of Secrets

ALISON LUCY

Canvas

Constable & Robinson Ltd
55–56 Russell Square
London WC1B 4HP
www.constablerobinson.com

First published in the UK by Canvas,
an imprint of Constable & Robinson Ltd., 2012

A copy of the British Library Cataloguing in
Publication data is available from the British Library

ISBN 978-1-78033-498-1 (paperback)
ISBN 978-1-78033-519-3 (ebook)

Printed and bound in the UK

1 3 5 7 9 10 8 6 4 2

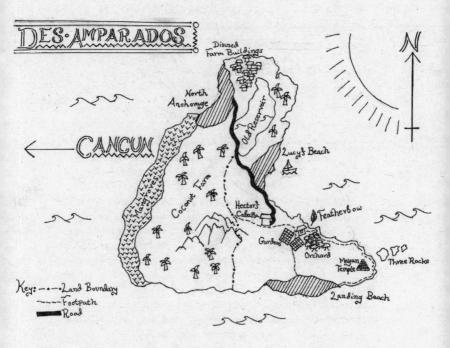

DES·AMPARADOS

N

Disused Farm Buildings

North Anchorage

Old Reservoir

← CANCUN

Lucy's Beach

Coconut Farm

Hector's Cabaña

Featherbow

Gardens

Orchard

Mayan Temple

Three Rocks

Landing Beach

Key: ·—·—· Land Boundary
‒ ‒ ‒ Footpath
▬▬▬ Road

1

Cancún, Mexico, 1989

Mexico was Danny's idea. Harriet was unsure at first – they had bought a house and were trying to make it beautiful – but she came around. 'It's the Caribbean,' she told everyone. 'Totally unspoilt.' It was expensive, but they saved money on their wedding where they could because they wanted to have tales to tell of their exotic honeymoon and to have memories to carry them through the trials of married life ahead.

The look on Harriet's face when she caught her first glimpse of Mexico made Danny's gamble worthwhile. The sun was setting and the Caribbean sea took on the pinks and purples of the sky above, the islands dotted in the endless ocean like buttonholes, the towering hotels of Cancún glinting with the promise of modern luxury in the timeless blue. A delighted gasp escaped from her cupid's bow mouth and her sharp eyes melted at the edges, softening the angles of her face so that she looked more radiant than ever. Danny wondered once more how he had persuaded such a beauty to marry him.

'It's gorgeous,' she said.

'You're gorgeous.'

She rewarded him with the kind of smile he lived for, the kind of smile that made other people suppose that although Danny might be a little bit rough around the edges – his grey eyes were too serious for his boyish face and his thick sandy hair refused to conform to anything approaching a style – he could still make Harriet happy. He had asked her to marry him so that he could spend the rest of his life conjuring more smiles just like that.

The plane came in with a fierce bump and the roar of heavy brakes. The force of the landing pinned them back in their seats. His heart beat a rapid tattoo until they came to a complete stop. Harriet was shaken, her smile had faded, but the cabin crew seemed unfazed as they prepared the doors for opening and they disembarked.

The newlyweds shrank away from the armed police who patrolled Cancún Airport smiling and chain smoking Delicados, their AR-15s hoisted under their arms. They were bombarded by offers of taxis and hotels and stood firm at the official taxi rank, accepting a price only slightly above what they felt was fair.

Danny liked that his new wife held his hand for the entire journey to their honeymoon hotel. 'It's an adventure,' he said.

She stared out of the window as the sleek new taxi carried them down the main boulevard. 'An adventure?'

'A few years ago there was nothing here,' he said, 'not even an indigenous community to resettle, just bugs and dunes, and now look. Don't you think it's amazing they could build a whole resort, a whole city, in the boring part of nowhere?' The sky was gathering darkness, and the dust from the construction outside the arrivals hall coated the back of his mouth.

'It'd better not be boring, Danny,' she said, and pinched the soft flesh of his thigh.

'Look!' He pointed out of the window to where the aqua Caribbean Sea fluffed over grey rocks to dance on the pale sand and her spirits were once more revived.

Cancún was a Mexican success story. Within a decade it had an airport, a handful of top-class hotels with planning granted for many more, a highway, and mile upon mile of beaches to rival the very best in the world. Within twenty years it was as if it had always been there and people started to forget that less than a lifetime ago it was a dangerous swamp called *Kan-Kun*, or 'nest of snakes', and that danger was still everywhere.

'Welcome to paradise,' said Harriet. 'Watch you don't trip over the locals.'

Danny started to wind down the car window but their driver tapped the air-conditioning vents on the dashboard of the taxi and Danny stopped fiddling. They raced past slender palm trees in the centre of the road, planted in earth that was pristine and free of weeds. The white-painted concrete bollards, the very road beneath their wheels was shiny and new. Above them a frigate circled and Danny wondered if the lonely bird was confused by all this change.

Their hotel had made a small effort to blend in with the natural surroundings, but it was a monster of concrete and steel and no amount of tropical planting could disguise that. They were checked in without too much ceremony. Harriet told the reception staff that they were on their honeymoon. 'Why did you do that?' he said as he unlocked the door to their third-floor lagoon-view room. The night had closed in and he could barely make out the dark outline of the inky water.

'It makes it less bizarre. Can you believe that we're married?' she said. 'It doesn't feel real.'

Their room was simple and clean, pretty tiles covered the floor and continued halfway up the wall. He was gripped by the odd sensation that it should be the middle of the night.

'It feels real to me,' he said. 'Come here, Mrs Featherbow.' He locked the door behind them and pulled her onto the bed.

Later that same night they emerged with jet-lagged hunger and walked down to the beach, hoping to find some authentic Mexican food but settling for a burger and fries from the hotel bar. They talked about finding a nightclub. In the corner a group of Mexicans were gathered watching a televised poker game from Las Vegas. She saw him staring at them.

'Gambling is illegal in Mexico, Danny.' There were no casinos in Cancún. It was one of the reasons she had agreed to come. She put a hand on his arm and willed him to turn back to her. If they could make it through a fortnight without having an argument about gambling, then it could still be the honeymoon of her dreams.

'I know it is,' he said. 'But they play cards everywhere.'

'No, *you* play cards everywhere.'

'They're watching a bit of sport on telly, Harry, don't get so tetchy.'

'Don't call me Harry.' She finished off her burger in silence and didn't suggest another drink. The possibility of going to a nightclub was not mentioned again.

He came back downstairs after she had fallen asleep. Just as he crept from their bed back home if there was late-night sport on the television. She was a deep sleeper, his new wife, and would sleep anywhere. It was the most laid-back thing about her.

He spoke to the men with his schoolboy Spanish and got invited to a card game by pretending he was richer and more drunk than he was. He returned to the hotel room several hours later, up three hundred dollars, and when Harriet asked him why he was exhausted the following day he spent most of the money on distracting her by buying a solid gold necklace with a small pendant; a star of gold and a creamy, iridescent opal in the shape of a crescent moon.

And so their honeymoon continued. By day Danny was an attentive new husband: they stayed in bed late and went to bed early; spent the time in between on the beach, eating in the restaurant, drinking cocktails at sunset. But at night Danny crept downstairs to seek out the illegal card games that ran the length of the Hotel Zone until at last it was 4 a.m. and he was sitting around a table with seven high rollers and a straight flush in his poker hand.

'Your wife doesn't mind you playing cards on your honeymoon?' asked one man.

'If she did, I wouldn't have married her,' said Danny, instead of admitting that he was scared of the very thought of what his wife would do if she found out that he was unable to control his addiction.

Over the course of his week, Danny had amassed almost two thousand dollars. When his grandmother taught him to play poker, she had pronounced that Danny was born lucky. He played cards whenever he could for the rest of his life and soon realized that luck had nothing to do with it.

His straight flush came at a pivotal moment in the game. The two biggest spenders were still in the hand: a Mexican hotel guy and a Canadian builder. The Canadian dropped out as soon as the amounts became dizzying, which left Danny and the hotel guy, whose name was Paco.

'Raise,' he said, and pushed his cash into the centre of the circle.

Danny was fairly certain by now that Paco had a full house. He would lose. The question was: how much? Danny needed to draw him in. He needed to use the skills that he could never use back home in his regular Friday night game because the guys he played against knew him too well. They had all been in the same school, found jobs in the same town, and lived with the same small disappointments and vast dreams. They knew who he was. Here he could be anyone. There was only one person in Cancún who thought that he would never make much of himself and she was sleeping in the hotel room upstairs.

He stared directly into Paco's eyes almost like a dare.

'Call,' said Paco.

The tension in their corner of the bar stepped up a notch. A few of the hotel waiters had gathered, watching, and he prayed that the game would not be noticed and shut down just when it was getting interesting. He flipped over his straight flush and Paco made a sound as if he had been punched. 'Fucking gringo,' he said. But there wasn't any menace behind his words. Danny smiled and raised his eyebrows, pulling all the money in the pot towards him and calculating there must be close to four thousand American dollars. In addition to the fifteen hundred he still had rolled up in the pocket of his trousers. And the traveller's cheques.

Maybe his grandmother had been right. Perhaps he was lucky after all.

'Another hand?' said Paco, riffling through the cards and being gracious in defeat. Paco had been working on a coconut farm offshore when they started to construct Cancún. He had set himself up as a human resources hot-shot and found people from all over to work in the bars and hotels. He was rich man on the Yucatán Peninsula; he could afford the chance to win his money back.

'One more hand,' said Danny. He had never had so much cash on him in his life. He could feel the burn in his pocket. He wanted to get it back upstairs before he did something stupid.

But it was too late. The euphoria of his last win clouded his judgement and he went in for too much too soon and before he knew it he was facing up in the final round of betting and there was nothing he could do except bluff his way to a possible recovery. His pair of sevens probably wouldn't beat whatever Paco was holding.

The Mexican went along with it for a while and the amounts started to climb.

Danny's better judgement begged him not to throw good money after bad, but he did anyway, as if in a fever dream, listening only to the surge of endorphins that made him take illogical risks. Win, lose, it barely mattered – it was the rush of the gamble itself that he couldn't live without.

'Raise,' he said, putting everything that he had won back on the table again to join the enormous pot there. Real money. His money. Their money. For richer or poorer. 'All in.'

Paco leant back in his chair, studying Danny's face. 'You don't have anything,' he said. 'I want to call. But you've cleaned me out.' He pulled some keys out of his pocket. 'You want my car?'

'I fly home to England in three days. Why would I want a car?'

Please fold, he willed. *Put down your cards, go home, have sex with your wife. We should all go home.* England shone brightly in his mind, more brightly than he remembered, and suddenly he wanted nothing more than his own bed, his own job, and all the safe, solid things he had built his life around.

'Maybe you don't go back,' suggested Paco. 'Maybe you stay here in Cancún and drive around in my car.'

'If you want to call me, call me. If you don't, then fold.'

'You take a – what is the word? – an IOU?'

Danny laughed. 'You take the Mick?' It was lost in translation. 'No, *amigo*. Cash is king.'

'You seem very confident,' said Paco. He tapped his

cards on the surface of the table. 'I have an idea. I own a house, a little beach house, on Des Amparados. The island with the big coconut farm?'

'That's not a beach house,' the Canadian chipped in, amused. 'Don't listen to him. It's a shack, and if the land was good for growing anything it would be part of the farm and it isn't.'

'It's a valuable piece of real estate, Danny. I'm serious. It may not be worth much right now but in a few years . . . There's only way one this city is going and that's up and up.'

'Okay,' said Danny.

'Okay?'

'Yeah, why not?'

Danny's heart was pounding and the bitter taste of adrenalin flooded his mouth. He was about to bet four thousand dollars on a hunch he had that Paco was trying too hard to win. He recognized the trace of a confident desperation that he was trying so hard to hide. It was a mirror. They were playing the same game, both trying to scare the other off the pot, which likely meant they both had the same hand. He just wanted to get on with it. Suddenly his pair of sevens didn't look so bad. Everybody in the bar knew what was going on by now. The amounts being counted in thousands, the talk of cars and farms and houses. He felt like a gangster. He had to see what Paco had. He had to play until the very end.

'Call,' said Paco.

What would they do, Danny wondered, if he grabbed the money, more than ten thousand dollars in non-sequential bills, and ran? He breathed.

'A pair of sevens,' he said.

The men watching each beat of the game unfold with undisguised intrigue swivelled their heads towards Paco.

'Shit,' said Paco. 'I thought you had nothing.'

Danny shrugged. 'A pair of sevens, that's nothing.'

Paco turned over his hand. Some random cards. The highest was a queen.

'Nope,' said the Canadian cheerfully. 'A pair of sevens wins the night.'

Danny exhaled with a puff of air strong enough to lift some of the notes on the table, ruffling the money that now belonged to him.

And a shack on a beach somewhere. He couldn't roll it up and stuff it in the pocket of his trousers. How would he explain that one to Harriet?

He would take a look.

A beautiful house. Just like she always wanted.

The shallow metal hull of the small fishing boat trembled as the engine opened up, taking the thud of each rolling wave as the prow lifted and fell, splattering them all with spray.

'You still haven't told me where we're going,' said Harriet.

'It's a surprise,' said Danny. 'Relax.'

At first the island was no more than a dark green mass on the horizon, but as they drew nearer it became more clearly defined, an expanse of palm trees stretching across for five miles or more. A thin line of rocks was obscured by the hazy rainbows above the curling surf and so the waves appeared to roll directly onto the trunks of the palms as if the trees were growing out of the ocean. To the south of the vast island the same limestone rock bed swept upwards to become cliffs, and then broke into three jagged rock formations, each progressively smaller, thrusting out into the distant sea.

Paco seemed prepared to honour his end of the deal and considered it to be a deal between men. He said nothing of cards in front of Harriet. He had taken Danny aside as Harriet boarded. 'We'll cruise over to Des Amparados, you see what you think. If you feel cheated then we can talk,' he promised. 'I am not a cheat.'

Their boat pulled past another headland and then drew into a deeper cove, sheltered by the currents so that the water was as still as glass and the silvery sand was clean and soft. The boat lulled in the shallows and Danny jumped out, his first steps ungainly and waterlogged, jarred by the feel of solid ground after forty minutes at sea. His senses were filled with a feeling of space, the air was clear and fresh, the light that tumbled through the palms and onto the sand was sharp and crystalline. Two white butterflies collided above him.

Harriet clambered from the boat and looked around in confused wonder.

'This way,' said Paco, leading them off the beach and into the trees, brushing invisible flakes of sand from the shoulders of his white suit, and felt profoundly glad that he no longer worked picking coconuts.

They walked for a long time, through the trees and ferns at the edge of the beach, the sound of insects humming loudly in Danny's ears, and the heat pressing down

11

on them with an almost physical heft; then they climbed, until at last they emerged into a clearing where a small wooden shed was built on a bluff overlooking the vast ocean that stretched out to the east without end.

'That's it?' said Danny.

'That's it,' said Paco.

Extruding from the modest home were two dramatically unfinished wings of painted concrete block, dazzling white in the hot afternoon sun. Behind them was the view back towards the city of Cancún and its ever-changing skyline.

'Parts of the house need to be completed, as you see,' said Paco, with a shrug towards the beautiful dancing waves, 'but, you know . . .'

Harriet, who had been struggling in her hugely inappropriate wedges and was breathless and something close to scared, felt an insect on her shoulder; when she turned to flick it away she saw something that made her scream. The sudden noise disturbed a pair of egrets and they flew off in the direction of the sun.

Standing a few feet away was a shirtless man with a long beard and skin like leather. He had a bucket in his hand and looked as if he might have been shipwrecked here a hundred years ago, were it not for the old Sony Walkman that he had strapped to the waistband of his shorts. He ripped the headphones from his ears when he saw Harriet scream. A silver earring in his left ear winked in the sunlight.

'*Lo siento*,' he said. 'I am sorry.'

'This is Hector,' said Paco. 'Hector watches the place for me.' He spoke to Hector in rapid Spanish, their conversation dragged on, and after a while both men were laughing.

'Where the hell are we?' said Harriet. 'Is your friend thinking of buying this place? What's going on Danny?'

'Do you like it here?' said Danny.

'There's nothing here,' said Harriet.

'But do you like it?'

She shrugged. 'It's okay.'

'It's ours,' he said.

Her brow furrowed as she started to understand. 'Oh, Danny, what have you done?'

'I played poker,' he said, and rushed to apologize as her face fell. 'I know, I know, I said I wouldn't do that any more, not once we were married, but I couldn't sleep.' There was no need to tell her that he had been up every single night. This was Cancún, it was 1989, he wanted to have some fun. 'And I won, Harry, I won big. Ten thousand dollars almost.'

'Ten thousand dollars? Jesus, Danny, what if you'd *lost*?'

'I didn't though. I won. Ten thousand dollars and this.'

'What do you mean: this?'

'The house.'

'Danny, come on. Be serious.'

'I am serious. You're always going on about being bored back home. We could live here . . .'

'Live here? In a shed? Danny, are you mad? What are you talking about, live here?'

'You say you want me to change.'

'I mean get a new job or stop wearing trainers, stop playing cards, not live on the other side of the world.'

13

'A holiday home, then. Come on, Harriet. Open your mind.'

'Open my mind? Danny, for the love of God, listen to yourself. Can we leave? Can we just leave now please?'

She didn't say a word all the way home and then later, after they had gone to bed incredibly early, he lay awake for a long time and so did she. He wanted to reach out to her but he didn't know how. And she was his *wife*.

Eventually her breathing slowed and he slipped from the bed.

It wasn't very late. Instead of heading straight for the nearest poker game, he approached one of the hopeful old men who lingered across the street from the hotel with their old Ford cars as big as boats. Some had the word 'taxi' crudely painted on the side; most didn't bother.

'Food?' said Danny and made a knife and fork gesture with his hands. The old man smiled but seemed confused. Danny wished that he spoke more Spanish. '*Tacos? Burritos?*' he said, hoping that he had pronounced it right. 'Good food, yes? Not hotel food, Mexican food.'

The old man nodded firmly and heaved open the back door of his car, whisking a spotless handkerchief from his pocket to brush away nonexistent crumbs. He gestured towards the broken window and was embarrassed that it didn't close. Danny jumped in, undaunted.

They drove away from the lights of the Hotel Zone, down a stretch of deserted coast road and into a small grid of streets that were lined with plain single-storey buildings, identical, one after another. Then he saw signs of life emerging like spring. Children playing in the dark streets, a house that had been painted a brilliant jade green, then another in crimson, another in white, with a border of hand-painted pink flowers; another strung with paper chains as if it was Christmas. More children, so many children, women standing in doorways with babies on their hips, old men sitting on the concrete benches at the side of the road.

He heard the shouts of children and some distant music and his senses sparked. They stopped and the smell of roasting corn hit his nose and his mouth watered instantly. The house, and Harriet's reaction to it, seemed unimportant. What was important was eating that smell, putting that inside him to see if it filled up the emptiness within.

At the side of the road a man stood behind a rattling old cart. He was juggling two pans over a single gas burner. The house behind him seemed to overflow with people, one or more in every window, children running in and out of the front door, circling the taco stand and laughing.

Danny got out of the car and watched in wonder as his chef twisted a lump of dough down onto a sizzling pan to make a thin wheat tortilla the size of a child's hand and smearing it with dark grey beans which turned into paste at the merest touch of the back of his knife. Then he sizzled strips of ugly chicken thighs with onions and peppers in another pan before daubing it with a muddy sauce, wrapping the whole little tortilla parcel up and starting the process all over again. It took three minutes at the

15

most. Danny bit down on the sweet, moist chicken and his mouth skittered with excitement. The melting beans were the perfect counterpoint to the yielding meat and the crunch of the well-seasoned vegetables. In a couple of bites it was gone. He heard the scrape of metal behind him and saw an old woman wrestling with a chair for him and immediately he stood to help her but she would not let him. She was embarrassed that he would try.

She stood back and watched as he ate another, like a mother would watch her toddler, and gradually a small crowd started to gather, surrounding him in a respectful, curious circle, smiling and offering the occasional culinary suggestion. Would he like a squeeze of lime? Some roughly torn herbs? Radishes sliced so thin you could see through them? A block of white cheese that could be crumbled like chalk. He took these things with a clumsy '*Gracias*' and felt self-conscious. He resolved to learn proper Spanish if he ever came back to Mexico.

A table was produced, a pile of napkins for his greasy fingers, and he searched for the words or gestures to ask for hot sauce. 'Chilli?' he tried and the chef laughed, producing a small dried chilli and crumbling it into the pan. The next taco was spicy and he wafted his hand in front of his mouth to indicate his approval. '*Picante*,' said the chef and Danny repeated the word – 'Pea-can-tay' – to the obvious approval of the crowd. He enjoyed a good curry back home as much as the next Englishman; he could take more than a little heat. A small boy came running over with a bottle of hot sauce, no lid, a thick crust of dried goop around the neck. He tasted it and his tongue wilted, but seconds later he wanted some more.

His head was spinning and his taste buds danced. He saw his taxi driver sitting down outside the house opposite, talking animatedly with a woman who wore Nike Air on her feet and a baby on her hip. Two teenage girls giggled when he caught their eye. They were both beautiful. Everyone was beautiful. He remembered what his guidebook had said about there being no indigenous community here before the hotels came and, startled, he realized that all of these people were new here just as he was. No wonder the houses looked so uniform and clean – they were little more than a decade old; the very streets they stood on had been built on sand, and everyone here – the old men, the women, the children, the chef who was turning out these delicious morsels faster than he could eat them – were all here searching for something. Tears came into his eyes and the people watching him thought it was the chillies.

After he could eat no more, he pulled the pack of cards from his top pocket and saw the faces of the gathered men spark with interest.

When he got back to the hotel he slipped his key into the door and tried to make as little noise as possible as he pushed open the door.

Harriet was awake. She was packing a bag. She had been crying, he could tell from the way her eyes were swollen and her lips were dry and cracked.

'What is it?' he said. 'What's going on?'

She just looked at him and shook her head. A kitten-lick of fear scraped the back of his neck.

'Danny,' she said finally, and her voice was as tender as a recent wound. 'I'm leaving.'

'What do you mean?' His stomach turned. 'I don't have to keep the house, Harriet. Don't let one stupid idea ruin our honeymoon.'

She choked out a strangled half-laugh. 'It's not the house, Danny.'

'The cards? I'm trying babe, I swear to you I'm trying.'

'Did you win tonight?'

'I couldn't sleep,' he protested. 'I went out for food.'

'Did you win tonight?'

He considered lying but she knew him too well. He nodded. 'I always win,' he said in a half-whisper. But she looked at him with disgust and he felt like a loser. 'Give me one more chance,' he said. 'Please? Come on.'

'It's too late,' she said. 'It's not the house. It's not even the cards. That's not it.'

'Then what?'

'I'm in love with someone else,' she said. 'I've been in love with someone else since last summer. I'm leaving you.'

His chest hurt and his vision started to narrow until looking into his wife's face was like looking down the barrel of a rifle. The silence was unbearable.

And it felt as though he had been shot.

2

Catalina hoisted her drowsy child onto her hip and pushed her hair back from her face with her free hand. She pinned the raven curls back more tightly and left the hotel through the kitchens, past the dominoes and cigarettes of the busboys. If Catalina wanted to flout the hotel policy by bringing her son to work with her, that was none of their business.

Catalina thought about going home to her mother every day. Tonight, as ever, only the sound of sea stopped her from getting on the stinking train and heading back to Veracruz. When she heard the sea she felt lucky. She trained her ears towards the surf but what she heard instead of their gentle lull was the sound of voices raised in anger. Two of the voices spoke Spanish. But a third man was speaking English, the same word over and over again.

'*Please.*'

She looked down the beach where the white line of breaking water caught the light of the moon. She saw their shadows and knew that the foreigner was begging them to stop. He was on the floor and it looked as if his ankles were lashed together, maybe his arms too. She drew a little closer and could see that they were piling sand and rocks into his pockets and into a sack by his feet.

'Hey!' She put little Ray down in the sand with his bag and marched towards the men. 'What the hell are you doing?'

The larger of the two men looked up and shooed her away with a quick insult, but she was not deterred. As she drew closer she could tell that they were little more than teenagers. 'Untie that man,' she demanded. If this fight broke out between a Mayan and an immigrant labourer, Catalina would have tried harder to hold her tongue. This was not the local violence of the streets, this man was a tourist. He was the money that would keep this part of their country afloat. Hurricane Gilbert had cost Cancún dearly last year, and now it was 1989 and the economic downturn was starting to bite.

'We won't hurt him,' said the second assailant. 'We are only trying to frighten him.'

Catalina immediately translated this for the man on the floor so that he would no longer be frightened. She had been taking every language class the hotel offered and her English was pretty good.

Both the Mexicans turned towards her with angry faces. One called her a whore and the other spat on the floor.

She stood with her hands on her hips and her feet firmly planted, shoulder-width apart. 'Go!' When they looked at her they were both reminded of scoldings from their mothers and muttered to each other before aiming a final kick at the weeping man with his face in the sand.

She stood strong until they were out of sight, but the moment they were gone she raced back to Ray, who was entirely unconcerned by the brief drama. She took him with her back to the man on the floor and together they untied his ankles. Ray thought it was some kind of game.

'Thank you,' slurred the foreigner, '*gracias*.' He was very drunk. He tried to twist his own arms out of the loose rope around them but got into a tangle and thrashed around so much that Ray started to laugh.

'Be still,' she said.

'Is your mum always this stern?' asked the man, and pulled a face. Ray laughed, even though he barely knew any English and he couldn't have understood.

'Only with fools who drink too much,' she said.

Her tone subdued him and he sat there quietly until he was free.

'Which hotel are you staying at?' She would point him in the right direction and then leave him to it.

'No hotel,' he said. 'An island.' He pointed out into the dark ocean. 'I have a boat. Somewhere.'

'You are drunk,' she said. 'You need a hotel.'

'No hotel. Don't need one. Here . . .' He fumbled at his waistband and pulled out a small cotton bag on a string; from this he produced a wad of pesos and another of American dollars. Her eyes widened. She had never seen so much money before in her life.

'My name is Danny,' he said. 'Help me get home?'

They went to Punta Juarez. She found a friend of hers who was happy to let her borrow his boat, for a price.

21

For a few more pesos his wife was happy to watch Ray while he slept, and soon Catalina set off into the inky blackness with the stranger who promptly fell asleep across the planks at the bottom of the boat. They crossed the choppy waters towards a string of lights on the little island. He said that he owned it, so she knew beyond all doubt that he was rich. The moon came out from the clouds and she could see his face more clearly. He was handsome. More handsome than he had looked when he had cowered on the sand, believing every threat those thugs made.

She opened the throttle and let the boat skip over the waves, her spirits lightened by the thrill of the unexpected. She had never been out on the water at night. But then, she had never rescued a man before.

She pulled around the island to the safe cove on the north-eastern side, raised the engine from the water and paddled in as close as she dared. Then she climbed back in and wrapped his coat around her legs and sat next to The Englishman, reading her paperback romance until eventually he stirred.

He looked up with bleary eyes which immediately filled with tears. He scrambled to his feet, the boat tipped wildly, he yelled and then he grabbed on to her for balance and then they locked eyes and his disappointment registered plainly on his heartbroken face. The boat rocked and then steadied. 'You're not her,' he said. 'I thought . . .' He slumped back into the boat. 'But you're not.'

She dropped her paperback. 'I'm Catalina,' she said. 'I brought you home.'

'Home?'

She smiled awkwardly, not knowing if her English was exact enough. 'You live here?'

'Do you smoke?' he asked.

She shook her head.

'I don't either. I thought I might try it.' He laughed gently. 'I think I'm still fairly drunk, Catalina. I never had tequila before.'

He jerked up suddenly and started patting at his waistband. She wished he would stop his sudden movements. She realized that he was looking for his money bag and pulled it out of her own pockets. 'I was keeping it for you,' she said defensively, handing it back.

They were sitting next to each other now, on the pontoon seats at the side of the boat.

'Did I pay you for the ride?'

She nodded.

'Did I pay you enough?'

She nodded. The half-moon reflected a ribbon in the sea, rippling like a bridal train.

'And I said I wanted to come here?'

'Des Amparados. We all know it. It has coconuts and a Mayan ruin, but nobody comes.'

'Why not?'

'I don't know. Bad fishing, maybe?'

'I'm Danny,' he said. 'Three days ago my wife left me.' He stood up and jumped over the edge of the boat into six inches of water. The motion upset the boat again and Catalina was knocked sideways.

He stood disconsolately, looking down at his feet. 'I should have taken off my shoes.'

'Is she coming back?' She held out her hand so that he could help her over the edge and together they dragged the boat up onto the sand.

'It's my own fault,' said Danny. 'The whole time she was seeing another man. Our neighbour.'

'So how is that your fault?'

'Because I'm an idiot. I like playing cards for money. She hated it and I knew she did and I didn't do anything about it.'

He spotted a coconut lying a few yards away on the beach and took a short run at it before booting it towards the ocean. It wasn't much of a kick and his shoulders slumped as it landed short of its target. He kicked the sand instead and thrust his hands into his pockets.

'She said that marrying me has made her understand her heart's desire more clearly. Her heart's desire! Where was her *heart* when she was in bed with the man across the street? Hey? Where was her heart?'

'Take it easy,' said Catalina. 'She can't hear you.'

'She wants a divorce. She wants the house. Her parents lent us the money, she always brings that up. I hate the house, she can have the house. I never want to see that house again for the rest of my life. I didn't want the house in the first place.' He kicked the side of the boat and Catalina's heart lurched. Even good men are capable of bad things when they are angry.

He was ranting. 'Do you think she went back there or do you think she went to him? How long's the flight? Do you think they're . . .' – he choked – '. . . celebrating? She said it started last summer. Do you think that means last summer or the summer just gone?'

24

He was talking so fast now that she couldn't keep up with his English. She kept her face neutral but her hand, busy twisting the hem of her skirt on her knees gave her away.

He stopped and she could hear the sound of his breath as he came back to earth. His eyes glanced at her white knuckles. 'I'm scaring you,' he said.

'Yes.'

Her body was riddled with nerves. Nobody had made her feel this way since Ray's father. Oh, she knew that being turned on by the outdated machismo was a betrayal of the modern Mexican woman, but she didn't care. Catalina's life was hard work. She liked to be pushed around. Of course, Ray's father had left town the minute she revealed she was pregnant, but this man would never do that. He was a good man, an Englishman.

Danny looked out at the veil of stars laced across the sky above him. She felt the heavy eye contact break with a snap.

She didn't want him to look at the damn stars. She had seen the same stars every night of her life, but not once had she been on a strange island under the moonlight with a heartbroken millionaire. She stood up and smoothed down the front of her skirt, wondering if he could tell that it was a maid's uniform. Wondering if he would care.

She walked over to him and placed her hand on the side of his face. His eyes were still wild with anger and she licked her lips. 'You can kiss me if you like,' she said.

He stared at her. She knew that she was beautiful. She didn't know that she was the exact opposite of the woman that broke his heart. Dark and sultry where Harriet was so blonde and cool.

He kissed her.

She put everything she had into it, grazing her breasts against him and letting her head fall back into his cradling hand. When he pulled away she let out a small, calculated sigh and kept her eyes closed for the count of three. If he was looking at her when she opened them then she knew that she was in with a chance. One. Two. Three.

Her eyes popped open and met his unfocused gaze, before he pushed himself on her for another kiss. Harder this time. Both his hands were on her shoulders. The rough touch of his jaw as his kisses fell to her neck made her arch her spine in delight.

'You see those rocks out there?' whispered Catalina, pointing at the jagged limestone formations to the east and then taking his hand. 'They are the last of Mexico. Beyond them there is Cuba and then there is nothing. Those rocks are the first place in Mexico to see that every day brings a new dawn. The Mayans built a temple there, covering the rock in honour of the Goddess Ixchel, so that she would have the pleasure of the sun's freshest rays on her body. Doesn't that sound romantic?'

They kissed again, and soon they were starting to undress each other with a lazy, exhausted calmness, and in the first of the gentle silver light, feeling close to God, Catalina did the only thing she knew that made men love her.

He was quick, angry, almost vengeful.

The moment that it was over he called her a mistake.

He wouldn't stop apologizing. The stillness of the

dawn exploded in his frantic explanations. She scrambled for her clothes, ashamed of her nakedness, the coquettish flirt deserting her in the face of such obvious regret.

'I'm still married,' he said, holding his head in his hands. 'Christ, my head.' The excuses tumbled out of him: he was drunk, he was upset, he didn't know what he was doing.

'You could just say thank you.' She snapped her bra closed and pulled on her skirt. It rasped against her sandy skin as she forced it over her hips. It never happened like this in the romance novels she loved so much.

'Here,' he said, pushing something at her. 'I want you to have this.' His face was ashen. 'I don't want it. I feel terrible.'

It was the bag with his money in. She had counted it, of course she had, and knew that there was something close to ten thousand dollars in there. But if she took his money then she really was no better than the women who clustered on the streets around Lopez Portillo, earning dollars on their backs.

But how could she not take it? It was the kind of money that her family could only dream of back when she was a girl.

She couldn't look him in the eye when she reached out for the bag and tucked it deep inside her clothes. She felt the rough stitches of the bag against her skin, and thought of it as her own cilice. She reached up to kiss his cheek then turned and ran. He called her name once but he did not come after her.

Catalina climbed out onto the rocks. The small pile of boulders there looked unimpressive until you were close enough to see that each grey stone had been placed with such precision that not a single shaft of sunlight entered the womb-like interior. Women worshipped Ixchel – the goddess of the moon and fertility – when they wanted to get pregnant, or wanted strength during childbirth, or needed to commune with the women in their lives that they had lost.

Catalina knelt at the entrance of the miniature temple and prayed. She thought of her mother back in Veracruz and how ashamed she would be of her daughter selling her body. She couldn't send this money back to her: it was immoral. She prayed for guidance.

Then she prised one of the sacred rocks out of place, took the cotton bag from her waist and buried the bag and its money in the damp earth before putting the rock back on top.

When she got back to her boat Danny had disappeared. She left without him.

Danny stumbled through the trees, blind with shame. The sun climbed higher in the sky and by the time he reached Hector's *cabaña* on the edge of the property he had recovered his thoughts, the day had come, and those few moments of madness in the dawn with Catalina were already starting to take on a dreamlike quality.

The old man was sitting on a stool in the shade, pinching the flowers from a springy young tomato plant. 'Welcome back,' he said.

'I'm hungry,' said Danny, scratching his beard and trying to think more clearly. Hector crossed over to the

28

crude outdoor kitchen and ladled huge bowls of simmering rice soup, rich with chicken stock, and scattered it with chopped lettuce. He warmed some torn stale tortillas in a pan with tomatoes, salt and a slug of golden oil, filling the air with a waft of garlic when he stirred it. Immediately Danny felt a little bit better.

'Where did you learn such good English, Hector?'

'I'm from Belize,' he said. 'We are all English there. I haven't been back for many years.'

Danny asked for his story and Hector told him how he had been one of the first crews to tackle the jungle, to cut through a road so that the rest of the city of Cancún could be built. 'At night we had to sleep buried up to our necks in sand or be eaten alive by mosquitoes. We all buried each other.'

'Who buried the last guy?' said Danny.

'What?'

'If you all buried each other, who buried the last guy?'

Hector scratched his beard. 'I don't know. I suppose he must have got bit.'

The two men sat in silence and ate the rest of their meal.

'I think I might stay here for a while,' said Danny.

'You should,' said Hector. He crossed to the dark, rickety shelves at the back of the *cabaña* and tipped out a jam jar full of coins and buttons. He searched through them until his fingers closed around a small steel medallion of a saint.

'St Joseph,' he said, and pressed the metal disc into Danny's hand. 'The patron against doubt and hesitation, the forgotten father of all hopeless cases. A gift for you.

29

They say that when you buy a house you should pray to him and he will bless it. This is a special place, Danny. I dream of a day when everything is as it could be. The land calls to me and asks me to make it so. St Joseph will help you to build your home.'

3

When he thought about going back to England, Danny felt tightness in his chest and a sense of doom. Better to be here, where the slate was as clean as the air. He swung his legs up over the side of the bed and onto the damp floor. He regarded his face in the mirror with some surprise. The Mexican sun had left its mark on his pallor and a four-day beard made him look like some kind of hippy, a leftover relic from an era of free love and happiness. He decided not to shave.

Danny let the island heal him. He bathed in the ocean, he bathed in the sun. He picked out pages from the Spanish paperback that Catalina had left behind and used it to improve his Spanish. Hector made him a big lunch every day; always the same thing, the soup and the chilaquiles, which they ate in his palapa kitchen. He stopped wearing shoes. He did not sleep, not properly. He would lie in his bed and feel himself drift closer and closer to it, but at the last moment he would pull back, as if he was afraid of falling.

He made small improvements to the house and tried to tame the garden. He cut back some of the undergrowth and built shady palapas over the concrete blocks. On Hector's advice he extended the covering of thatched leaves out across the back of the property to make a covered terrace that stretched all the way to the white bougainvillea that might one day trail across it. He hammered a strong nail into the solid wood of the door frame and he hung the small medallion of St Joseph on it and let the saint guide his hand as he tried to build the house of his dreams. When a day's work felt done he liked to sit on the porch and watch the lights of Cancún flicker and kid himself that he would never have to go home.

He named the house Featherbow in his mind and was proud of it in a way that he had never been proud of anything before. He decided that he would get a sign so that all who came here would know that it was his.

The rest of the island intrigued him. His own holding was a postage stamp compared to the coconut farm, which stretched all the way up to the northern coast. Hector had said very little when asked about it, only that the nuts were harvested four times a year by a crew from the mainland. If he climbed up to the highest point, before the cliffs fell away to the sea, he could sometimes see right down across the middle of the island and make out a tan-coloured pick-up truck lumbering across the trenches cut between the endless rows of palm trees. Sometimes at night he could smell burning. There was no fence between the farm and the boundaries of his own land. He wondered if he should build one, or if that would be a terribly English thing to do.

One day he saw a white sailboat glide into the next bay along. He watched and waited and when the boat failed to emerge after an hour or more he decided to go exploring and use the presence of day trippers as his excuse, should he turn out to be trespassing beyond his boundaries.

At first the going was simple. The rocky eastern shore was easy enough to walk, and to scramble across where necessary. The tide was turning favourably out to sea and he knew that he would be safe. But gradually the walking got less and the scrambling more until he was clinging, almost vertical, to a cliff face and realized that he could go no further. The only problem was that he was not sure he could climb back down again either. He found a better toehold and assessed his situation. He felt like a fool for getting into a fix but then he spotted a twisted tree branch a couple of yards up where the land did appear to level out and with an enormous grunt he threw up his left arm and pulled the rest of his body up quickly. He collapsed, pumped with the effort, and rolled over to stare at the blue sky above him. He felt a million miles from any life he had ever known.

Then he heard the sound of a woman's laughter.

He sat up and looked down into the next bay along. The sailboat was bobbing at anchor and on the white sand beach a small group of people clustered around a stooped palm tree. The focus of all their attention was a woman sitting on the low-slung trunk of the palm, swinging her feet. Behind them were bags and blankets and a crate of cheap Mexican beer.

He wasn't sure whether to approach them; he wasn't sure if the beach they were on even belonged to him or if he had already gone further than his own land. But as he stood up his feet caused a minor landslide and the group in the bay turned to look up at him.

The woman raised a slender arm to shield her face from the sun and the silver bangles that she wore reflected the light and momentarily blinded him.

'Hello! Are you lost?' she shouted.

Danny was captured at once by the lightness of her tone. It sounded as if she was on the brink of laughter. Until everything fell apart and went bad it always seemed as if she was privy to some infinitely amusing joke. As if she alone knew that life was to be enjoyed, to be relished. It was all there in her very first greeting.

He waved a casual hello, as casual as it was possible to be when meeting by chance on a remote island, and clambered down to join them.

The woman was called Lucy. She was the indisputable leader of their little gang of five, Lucy and four jovial young men, all exhilarated from a day's sailing in the Mexican Riviera. They pronounced him marvellous. They didn't seem to notice or care that he wasn't like them – moneyed and carefree – and continued talking about people he didn't know and places he had never been to, assuming that he would be able to follow the conversation.

She would have been considered beautiful if only seen in a still photograph, but she was as mercurial as the glittering surface of the sea and just as compelling.

He told them that he owned a house around the bay and looked at Lucy for her reaction. She had seemed simultaneously impressed and nonchalant, her almond-shaped eyes widening just a fraction before she pulled on a pair of sunglasses and lay down along the length of the tree trunk, relaxing her slender limbs so that she looked as comfortable as a snake stretched out in the sunshine.

'You'll join us for lunch?' she said, with only the merest hint of enquiry, as if she was stating a fact.

'Yes please,' he said, regardless of whether or not he sounded like a sycophant. He wanted to be near her. Maybe some of that blithe spirit would rub away his troubles.

He could barely take his eyes off her for the rest of the afternoon. She quickly bored of sunbathing and organized a makeshift game of quoits which she promptly won. One of the men made her a crown of frangipani flowers as a prize. When one of the men asked her to sing, she launched into a bawdy dance-hall tune without hesitation, making them laugh and accepting their good-natured criticism of her terrible singing voice.

'You try then,' she commanded, and they fell over themselves to do her bidding.

He wanted to know if she was sleeping with any of the men, and for a few moments in the sun with his eyes closed he imagined she was sleeping with all of them, expertly, and that's why they so clearly adored her.

She stripped down to a bikini and announced that she was going for a swim and for a while they all just watched her until she bored of that too and started back towards them. She walked as if she was a single chord away from dancing.

'Remarkable, isn't she?' said one of her friends. His name was Sawyer. He was a lot younger than the rest of

35

them, at eighteen, and he didn't talk as much as the other two.

Danny nodded.

'You're her type, you know,' said Sawyer. 'Better watch out, Luce likes a bit of rough.'

'I'm married,' said Danny.

'Really? Where's the missus?'

'Back home.'

Sawyer raised a boyish eyebrow and grinned. 'Like I said. Watch out.'

'Watch out for what?' said Lucy, returning to the group and batting Sawyer across the head with her sun hat.

'Watch out for you,' said Sawyer. His brown eyes twinkled with mirth.

Danny thought she might be embarrassed, but instead she sat down in the sand behind him and wrapped her damp legs around his waist and her arms around his chest so that he felt as if he was trapped in the most pleasurable deadlock he could imagine.

'I'm harmless,' she said, and then wrestled him down onto the ground, twisting so that she sat shamelessly astride him. He blushed.

'You're scaring him, Lulu,' shouted one of the other two.

'Then he scares too easily,' she said.

When it started to get dark, he wondered briefly how he would find his way back home, but then after a brief twilight the moon rose, full and splendid, and it didn't really get dark at all. The mood of the cavorting friends softened as the men drank more of the beer and turned melancholic.

'Only a few more weeks,' said one of them. 'Then it's back to the real world.'

'Don't,' groaned another. 'What say we just don't go back?'

'I like it,' said Lucy. 'We'll live on the boat, eat tropical fruit and catch fish.'

'Trade seashells for gold.'

'I'll have babies,' she said, 'lots of babies. And when we grow old, we can live in a cave by the sea.'

They were quiet for a little while, contemplating the future.

Under that moon he fancied that he grasped a fundamental truth, that happiness was found in moments like this – strangers by a campfire under the stars – and that all the choices, those life choices he kept getting so magnificently wrong, meant nothing.

'Nothing at all,' he said aloud.

'What's that?' asked Lucy. 'What did you say?'

'Nothing,' said Danny and then he laughed. 'Do you feel like a swim? I never swam at night before.'

'Idiots. You'll freeze,' said Sawyer.

'Sawyer thinks I take too many chances,' said Lucy.

'It's called risk addiction, Lucy. I might be young but I know when to be cautious; it keeps me in the game.'

Lucy stuck her tongue out at Sawyer like a schoolgirl and took Danny's hand in hers. They padded across the sand down to the water and he let the waves crash into his legs as they waded deeper into the chilling embrace of the sea. She broke free of him and swam a few yards out. He followed. He was not a strong swimmer and was glad when she stopped and faced him, treading water.

'This has been a quite perfect day,' said Lucy, tipping her head back to let the water smooth her hair off her face. In the moonlight her face glistened wet and clean; she looked like a siren sent to enchant him.

'So what happens now?' he said.

'Guy and Leo will drink too much and have an argument which Sawyer will have to settle. Alex will fall asleep. And I will bemoan the lack of a decent glass of chilled Sancerre.'

She made everything sound as if it could be so simple.

They fell asleep next to the fire, under a pile of blankets so big and so scattered that it was impossible to tell if they were sharing. In the middle of the night she pushed herself back into the comforting shape of his sleeping form and, without waking, he curled an arm around her waist and pulled her closer. His mouth found the tenderest point of her bare shoulder and he kissed her there.

He heard her whisper as if it was inside his dream. 'Are you sleeping?'

His eyes snapped open. He kissed her shoulder again and she trembled. 'No,' he said. Her buttery soft skin felt like heaven under his lips. He brushed her shoulder with the tips of his fingers and realized that she was naked beneath the blankets. His hand continued, over and under, until he felt the gentle swell of her curves and the little bump of her hipbone.

Everybody else was sleeping soundly a small distance away. He could only hear the lap of the ocean and her hot sweet breath as she turned into him. He kissed her fiercely, losing himself, and when she climbed on top of him and arched her back her long, loose hair trailed across the tops of his thighs and he caught sight of her like that, offering herself to him and to the stars, and she looked like a goddess.

Afterwards she flipped onto her back, breathless, and he did the same, and they both lay there panting, gazing at the chaotic, star-scattered sky.

After a while she could speak again. 'I didn't plan to seduce you,' she said.

'Are you sorry?'

'No, I'll probably do it again tomorrow,' she said.

'Where did you come from?' he said.

'What do you mean?'

'How did you know I needed you?'

Lucy propped herself up on her elbow, draping herself over him with such casual familiarity that he wondered if perhaps she could feel as certain about their connection as he did. It was more than sex, it was the island: it had enchanted them both.

'Keep watching the stars, Danny,' she said. 'There are patterns up there to help you find your way.'

When he woke up the next morning, Sawyer and the rest of the men had gone; the boat had disappeared and it was just him and Lucy.

'Where is everyone?'

He was not unhappy that they had the beach to themselves. The memory of last night was ever present in his mind and could do with refreshing.

'They had to take care of some business,' said Lucy, waving her hand airily.

39

He didn't think to ask what kind of business it could be, out here in the middle of nowhere, and instead he threw himself into the day with Lucy. The thought of going home stabbed at his mind again; home where everyone would have to watch as his marriage was dismantled. Why couldn't life be like Lucy – uncomplicated, happy and free?

He showed her his house. She loved it.

Harriet's reaction faded in the force of her obvious delight. 'You could put another room here,' she said. 'And this could be the master bedroom so every morning you could see the sunrise.' She danced around the space as if the walls were already built and it was a ballroom and not a shack on the edge of a cliff.

He made a mental note of everything she said and then threw a rug on the tiled floor and made love to her in the old stone kitchen.

Later, when the heat became too heavy to bear and dusk brought out the mosquitoes, they swam together out as far as they dared before the currents of the open sea tugged at their bare legs like a warning.

'Stop!' he yelled. 'It's too dangerous.'

Lucy swam further out then turned back to him, flicking sea water into his concerned face. 'Scaredy-cat,' she teased, but she swam back in all the same.

When dark fell and cloaked them in secret shadows, he thought to ask about her friends and the yacht.

'They'll be back,' said Lucy. 'They wouldn't leave without me. It's my boat. Maybe they're back already.'

'Okay.' He didn't move.

'Are you scared of me, Danny?' she said.

40

What could he say? She was like an angel fish, flitting around in the shallows, impossible to see closely for even a moment, impossible to hold. She terrified him.

'What is this?' he said. 'I have to know, what is this we have here?'

She grinned. 'This is love, Danny. Don't you recognize it?'

It was impossible to tell whether or not she was joking. He felt his heart twist like an anxious pair of hands.

'Do you play cards?' he said.

'Only for money,' she replied, quick as a bounce. And they went inside.

In the middle of the night he woke up, certain he had heard something. Beside him, Lucy stirred.

'Did you hear that?' he said.

'Go back to sleep.'

The following morning her friends were back. He watched her barrel into their embraces and cavort from bear hug to bear hug. He remembered with a sharp pang that he was not with her, they were. He felt her slipping away like sand in an hourglass. She belonged to them. But then Sawyer called out to him and dragged him in to the general back-slapping that accompanies a gang reunited. Was it possible he had a gang? He invited them all up to Featherbow for breakfast and went ahead to warn Hector.

At breakfast, Lucy fetched drinks for everyone and was up and down to the kitchen. She was the finishing touch that the house had been lacking and with Lucy there it truly felt like a home. He raised his juice glass and shouted '*Amigos!*' and they all laughed and raised their glasses, except Hector, who had filled his plate and tucked himself in at the far end of the table.

'So where have you guys been?' said Danny. He caught the moment's pause and the odd look that passed between Alex and Guy.

'Taking care of business,' said Sawyer. He too sensed the tension and tried to diffuse it by giving Hector an ill-advised compliment. 'Cool earring, man.' The silver hoop had a small white tooth on it. 'Is that a shark's tooth?'

Hector said something in Spanish and Alex looked rattled. Lucy had mentioned something about him speaking fluent Spanish.

'What was that?' said Danny.

Hector looked up. 'I said, there is only one business out here. When are your friends leaving?'

Danny frowned. He didn't like the atmosphere that had descended. He didn't understand it.

'There's a storm coming in from the Atlantic. We leave straight after breakfast,' said Alex.

'Good,' said Hector. His face was tight and unforgiving.

Danny started to apologize for Hector's rudeness and then realized what Alex had said. They were leaving. She was leaving. But it didn't really matter. He waited until they were alone and then he asked her to stay.

'My life is very complicated,' she said. 'You can't imagine.'

'It could be simple, here with me.'

'I've had a beautiful time,' she said. 'I'll never forget it.

But I like my life, Danny. I like my stupid, complicated life exactly the way it is.'

He looked out to sea and wondered what on earth he was supposed to do now if Lucy was not the answer.

'But I love you,' he said, stumbling over the words, crying in a way that he hadn't cried since his parents died, and all the sadness he'd felt then came rushing back in like the inexorable tide. 'All my life I have been pretending and with you I don't have to. You feel it, you must feel it. I think we are supposed to be together. You can't leave. You can't.'

Thick gulps came from his swollen throat as he pleaded with her to stay. He fell to his knees. He begged. His desperate grey eyes were the exact colour of the thick line on the horizon before a storm at sea.

'Don't,' she said. 'Please.' She looked away, embarrassed for him.

He stumbled to Hector's *cabaña* after their boat was out of sight. Hector came out with a gun in his hand.

'It's me,' said Danny. He stared at the glint of the gun and thought it looked quite beautiful. 'I just needed someone to talk to. I'm sorry, I'm so sorry, I'll go.'

'Sit down,' he said.

'She left,' said Danny.

'I know.'

'Why did you hate her?'

Hector sighed and put the gun down on the table. He pulled the door closed behind him, righted the chair that Danny had overturned and helped him to sit down.

'Lucy was lovely,' said Hector. 'But her friends were drug dealers.'

'You know them?'

'I have seen them before. You don't know this island like I do.'

'So tell me.'

Hector looked at him and then went back inside and he came back out with a bottle of cheap Sauza and two shot glasses. He poured them both some of the golden tequila. Somewhere out in the early morning there was a screech, a bird or an animal or something, and the sound made Danny's teeth clench. The wind shook the palms and dried leaves floated onto the ground like dark snowflakes.

'The cocaine is from Colombia,' said Hector, knocking back his drink. 'It has been passing this way for many years. Long before they called this place Cancún. The coconut farm? That's no farm. It's a cover. You think they will stop now that the city has reached the sea? No way. They will pay off the police. It makes it easier for the drug dealers, all the people passing through the airport, the highways. The shipments are controlled. Your friends, they are taking risks you don't understand. They are buying directly before it reaches the port. To sell. It is an incredibly stupid thing to do. They are stealing from the dealers and from the police. From both.'

'Those guys? Leo, Guy, Alex? Sawyer? You're wrong.'

'I don't think so,' said Hector.

The tequila hit him hard. He wished that he could concentrate on what Hector was saying but it sounded absurd. And somewhere out there among the coconut palms there came another screech. He shook his head rapidly and licked his dry mouth. He didn't like what was happening in his head. It was more than just the tequila.

Hector shrugged. 'There is crime everywhere. But Mexico is not England, it is not America. There are poor people here, poverty you can't imagine, and with poverty comes crime.'

'So why do you stay?'

'The island,' he said. 'The dirty side of this place makes it more beautiful, like a woman with a scar so you know that she has lived, so that you know she is not hiding behind cosmetics, so you know that she is real. It is the most beautiful place on earth.'

'I used to think so,' said Danny. 'But either the island is cursed or I am.'

'Things have gone wrong for you, *compadre*,' said Hector. 'That is true. Maybe you will not grow here after all.'

Danny pushed his tequila aside. 'I have all the papers from the bank to transfer the ownership of this mosquito hole,' he said, spitting out the last word. 'I should give it to you: at least you love the place.'

'You love it. Deep in your heart.'

Hector patted his chest and Danny had a sudden certain feeling that if he were to do the same there would be only a hollow sound where his heart should be. He was the tin woodsman from *The Wizard of Oz*; he was a robot from *Star Wars*, he was nothing. He had no family. Harriet had been it for him and that wasn't love at all. Lucy had felt like love. *Lucy.*

'Is there anyone you love, Hector?' he asked. 'That you know for sure you love?'

'I love my son.' He pulled a photograph from his pocket. At some point it had been folded in half so that a cracked line wounded the little boy from ear to ear. 'He lives in America with his mother. He's older than that now.'

'This is your son?'

'Luis.'

Danny took the photograph and saw an address scrawled on the back. The boy was not smiling. He looked into the camera lens as if he was looking at a spot on the horizon with deep concentration. The boy was handsome and when Danny looked for a family resemblance in Hector he realized that Hector was not as old as he had once thought. Without his beard, without the suntan, they might even be the same age. Hector had love. Danny had nothing.

'Do you see him often?' said Danny.

Hector laughed softly and looked off towards the low morning sun. 'I have only seen photographs,' he said. 'It is my one true regret, Danny.'

'Why don't you find him? Make it right.'

'I am a coward.'

Danny knocked back what was left of his tequila. 'I mean it. This house. Featherbow. You should have it. Harriet will divorce me. She can't force me to sell this place if it isn't mine.'

'You are drunk.'

'Not yet,' said Danny. 'And before I am I will put your name on those papers and I will sign them. For you.'

'What about when you have children of your own?' said Hector, humouring him.

'That's true,' said Danny. 'That is very true.' He swallowed to try and focus his thoughts. It was the tequila. He wasn't used to it. 'So if I have children the island goes to them, when you die. Deal?' He tried to imagine a world where he was a father, but he could not. To be a father there must be a mother and for there to be a mother he would have to fall in love again and he had had enough of love. He had had enough of everything. Suddenly, giving Hector the island he loved seemed the answer to everything. If only he would accept it then Danny could start over. Alone. The way that it should be. The way it was always meant to be. Trying to love people had been his downfall.

He stuck out his hand and Hector shook it.

'Go back to the house,' said Hector kindly. 'You'll feel better tomorrow.'

'I think tomorrow I might be leaving,' he said. He pushed back his chair. 'Do you want to stay on as caretaker? I like what we did with the terrace. You could do some work on the house. I have about two thousand dollars left: you could have it.'

'Money as well as the house?' said Hector, smiling indulgently, for he had grown fond of the Englishman. He knew how it felt to have nowhere that you particularly want to go.

Back on his side of the property, Danny started to pack his things into a suitcase. Just one suitcase; Harriet had taken the other when she left him. He included the paperback that Catalina had left behind, for he had grown fond of its hopeful story. Finally he thought of Lucy and began to wonder if it had been real. Any of it.

Or if any of the women had loved him, even if only for a moment.

Harriet
Catalina
Lucy.

He fell back across his bed and the heat and the gentle shushing of the waves gradually overcame him until he was fast asleep.

He woke with a start, certain that he had heard a gunshot. He sat bolt upright and heard another one. It was coming from the direction of the garden and Hector's shack. He jumped from the bed, still fully clothed, and started running towards it. The sound of a man's voice shouting made Danny drop to the ground, suddenly aware of the risk he was taking, and he started to crawl forward on his hands and knees, lost in the ferny undergrowth. He knew that Hector had a gun. Perhaps he was using it to shoot quail with some buddies from the mainland. As he got closer he could see the tan pickup they used on the farm parked in what could conceivably be called Hector's driveway. Next to it was a gleaming vintage Indian motorbike, chilli-pepper red, spotlessly clean and totally out of place on this island. The keys were in the ignition and the old-fashioned chrome mudguards reflected dazzling silver pinpricks of the searing noon sun.

He slithered round the back of Hector's *cabaña*, on his belly now, keeping as low as he could. He could see a shadow moving about inside the shack. But he couldn't see if it was Hector and he couldn't see a gun. He pressed himself down into the sandy earth, keeping perfectly still, tasting gravel, praying that this brush with death would pass him by. The moisture that was left in his mouth drained into the soil and he felt his vision narrow alarmingly; he closed his eyes tight as a knot of dread closed over his heart. He began to have a silent conversation with God. This could not be the end.

It was not Danny's life that flashed before his eyes but the dazzle of Lucy's smile when she told him this was love.

The sound of the final gunshot echoed across the island.

4

Megan

On her return from Mexico, Harriet discreetly continued the love affair with her neighbour Tony, and convinced him that the child she was carrying was his. So what? Nobody would know for sure. If her soon-to-be-ex-husband Danny made a fuss – well, she would cross that bridge as and when it needed to be crossed. Marrying him had been her first mistake and she was determined that it would be her last.

When he failed to return home she felt relieved, and then eventually annoyed, but soon Megan was thrust into the world, reluctant and vocal. Tony, Harriet and Megan became the Watkins family and even the people who had danced at his wedding started to forget about Danny Featherbow.

They looked for him once when they talked about getting married. But he was nowhere to be found.

Megan Watkins was eleven years old when she found out the truth about her father. Her mother and the man she had up until that point believed to be her dad were having one of their arguments. There was a taxi waiting outside the house. It had pulled up and then the argument had started. That had never happened before.

'*What about Megan?*' said Harriet.

Megan heard her own name and she edged a little closer to the banister and strained to hear. She chewed on the end of one of her pigtails. It was difficult to make out some of the words because her mum was all weepy and breathless, the way she sometimes pretended to be when she wanted people, Megan, to do as they were told and they wouldn't. In response her dad was unwavering and his voice carried well.

'What about her?' he said. 'I love the kid but let's not fool ourselves a minute longer. She's not mine.'

Her pigtail jammed in her throat and she struggled to breathe.

'From the day she was born she had the look of Danny,' he continued. 'As long as I was with you, I was happy – glad, delighted – to raise her. I care about her, but I'm not giving you money for a girl who isn't mine.'

'This is why you didn't marry me,' said Harriet, and Megan heard the spark of a lighter and smelt the unmistakable stench of a rare indoor cigarette. 'Because you knew then that one day you'd leave us.'

'I didn't marry you because technically you're still married to someone else.'

They both heard a small scream and turned immediately to the stairs, where Megan stood with her china-doll face pale and fragile, her huge grey eyes luminous and as wide as the sky. She turned and ran to her bedroom.

A few moments later she heard the front door close, quietly, and the taxi drive away. She heard her mother go into the kitchen and pour a glass of water, drink some, then put the glass down by the side of the sink. She heard a nose being blown. Then the sound of her mother's footsteps climbing up the stairs. When they reached the half-landing they tripped the sensor pad that Megan and her best friend in the world Connor had installed under the carpet on the stairway. A tiny red LED light blinked on in Megan's bookcase, or what she and Connor preferred to call 'Mission Control'. They had found a book in the library that told them how to do it.

Her mother pushed open the bedroom door. She always hovered in the doorway of Megan's room when she spoke to her.

'I suppose you hate me now,' said Harriet.

'I hated you anyway,' said Megan.

'Well then, it shouldn't make much difference,' snapped Harriet.

'Where's . . .' She didn't want to call him Dad, no way, but for a brief moment she couldn't remember his name. What was it? She was an idiot. The pause was stretching out too long and she would look stupid. Her dad's first name, the liar's name, popped into her mouth. '. . . Tony?' It sounded foreign on her tongue, as if she was referring to a new person about whom it would seem she knew nothing. They were all liars.

'He's gone,' said Harriet. 'For a little while at least.'

'Who's my father?'

'Do we have to do this tonight?' Harriet sighed, and picked up the silver hairbrush on the pink dressing table that was never used and never dusted, twisting it over in her hand, turning up her nose slightly, and then putting it back. She glanced around at the stacks of books, at the maps and old travel posters Megan had used to cover up the pretty yellow wallpaper they thought that she would like.

Megan's chest was hurting, tense from trying not to cry. Tony was gone. They used to joke that he was the only thing standing between Megan and her mother killing one another.

'You deserve a proper explanation,' said Harriet. 'But not tonight. It's very late; you have school in the morning.'

It was just after nine. That wasn't late unless you were six years old. 'Tell me his name,' said Megan.

'Sweetheart, it's very complicated.'

Megan squeezed her mouth together tightly. The inside of her nose was burning and she could feel her lips trembling. 'Tell me his name.'

'Danny. Danny Featherbow.'

'Do you know where he is?'

'The last time anybody saw him was in Mexico.'

'Where in Mexico?'

'An island; he bought a house on an island called Des Amparados. It's near Cancún. But that was before you were born.'

'Was it a nice house?'

Her mum's brow creased and then she was remembering and she smiled. 'He liked it – Danny, your father. It was on the eastern side of the island, nothing to see for miles; it felt like the end of the world to me.'

'So what happened?'

'Sweetheart, we looked for him, but either he doesn't

want to be found or he can't be found. A few years ago he was declared legally dead.'

'Why?'

'What do you mean?'

'Why then? Who declared him dead? What? Somebody just decided and then – wham – that's it, game over for you Danny Featherbow?'

Another long pause. This time Harriet and Megan just stared at each other without knowing how to comfort each other.

Her mother turned away first and in a flash of insight Megan realized that her mother didn't like to look at her because she looked like him, like Danny.

'Okay.' Megan arranged her pillows and turned off her bedside light. 'And you'll tell me the rest tomorrow?'

'There really isn't very much to tell . . .' She changed her tone and spoke with as much warmth as she could muster. Megan was so difficult to love, so hidden and calm. Sometimes Harriet wished she could be more like that. 'Yes, I will,' she promised. 'I'll tell you tomorrow.'

She watched her mother standing in the doorway for a few more seconds, then turned to face the wall. 'You can go,' she said.

Megan crept out of bed and waited at the top of the stairs, until she heard the faint 'ding' of the telephone receiver being picked up, shortly followed by the muted sounds of her mother's voice. Of course Mum wouldn't be able to leave it longer than fifteen minutes before telephoning someone to talk all about it. One of her irritating friends probably, none of whom had any idea how to have a conversation about anything but their own stupid dramas.

Megan went back into her bedroom and pulled out the kitbag she had stashed there months ago, a survival kit in case of a nuclear war after they had scared themselves silly reading Raymond Briggs's *When the Wind Blows*. She wondered if she dared to creep downstairs for her thick winter coat, but decided it wasn't worth the risk and instead settled for her woolliest jumper and a raincoat with a hood.

She wrote it all down on a scrap of paper before she forgot. *Des Amparados. Cancún. Mexico*. Beautiful exotic words that made her think of butterflies and palm trees and made her almost forget about words like *liar*. Almost.

She pushed open her bedroom window and jumped down onto the flat roof of the little porch that Tony had constructed for the front door. Then she shimmied down onto the dustbin – dangling for one exhilarating moment in mid-air – and jumped into the dark passageway that led to the back garden. She crept into the back garden, hopped over the fence into next-door's allotment and from there onto the pavement of Highland Crescent, neatly avoiding the front windows of everyone in their cul-de-sac, her own mother included.

She wished that Connor were here to give her the high-five she so richly deserved but settled instead for breaking into a sprint through the park towards the train station, where she went straight to the machine and bought a one-way ticket to Stansted Airport.

There was enough money in the survival kit to buy a bottle

of water and an egg sandwich in case she got hungry in the night. Megan and Connor often came to the airport to muck around, playing Air Hockey in the arcade bit and sitting on the wall just outside the south-west end of the departures terminal watching the planes take off. It was one of their favourite places. She knew a quiet spot in arrivals where she could bed down, cover her head with a coat, and if questioned say that she was waiting for a flight at the crack of dawn. She was tall for her age and fairly sure she looked a lot older than eleven. She read an article once about a man who lived at the airport; maybe she could do that. Or maybe if she was able to get in touch with Connor they could come up with a plan to get them both on an aeroplane so that she could fly far away from her mother and all her stinky lies. To Mexico obviously. Duh.

She barely slept. As soon as the airport started filling up again in the morning, she moved on from her uncomfortable makeshift bed and browsed in the shops, wishing that she had enough money to buy something else to eat. She thought about how she could sneak onto a plane. She went into a bookshop and found a book about Mexico and tried to match up some of the exotic place names on the departure board to the names of cities in there.

Security questioned her shortly after eleven o'clock. By then she was scared and very tired. It only took one phone call to match up this stray with the missing girl in Colchester and, within a few minutes, Megan was in the back of a police car heading for home.

Her mum put on a good act for the police: all concern, no anger. Connor was there too. He had been grilled by his own parents when Megan was discovered missing and immediately gone out on his bike to look for her, and when he ran out of places to look he'd gone straight round to her house to check her room for clues. That was where he was when she was found. He almost made her laugh by pulling a mock serious face when the policeman got all stern and talked about warnings and being lucky that nothing bad had happened. Nothing bad? Was he for real?

After the police left and Megan's mum went to telephone everyone and tell them the hunt was over, Connor demanded every detail of her adventure. She watched his baby blue eyes widen with disbelief as she told him how she had stayed out all night on her own.

'There's an island in Mexico,' she said. 'One day we can live there together, you and I. It's mine. My dad's gone, and he's not my dad,' she said.

'Come again?'

'I bet your parents know. I bet everyone on the street knows. No wonder people look at me funny.'

'They look at you funny because of your ugly face,' said Connor, and she swiped him.

Now that she had been found, the sickening feeling in his stomach had totally disappeared. 'If you ever do that again . . .' he said.

'What?'

'If you ever run away,' said Connor, 'take me with you.'

5

Esmeralda

Esmé was anticipating La Quinceañera, her fifteenth birthday, with mortal dread. Her mother, Catalina, had been looking forward to the ceremony for months and invited half of Cancún. Her friends, most of them also nearly fifteen, could not wait for their own special day, the day that would see them make the transition from girl to woman and become of marriageable age. They saw marriage as a way of finally being free of their fathers. But Esmé had no father and sought no liberation in binding herself to a man for the rest of her life and therefore had no desire to be married.

She awoke on the morning of her fifteenth birthday and seriously considered killing herself.

She was so disappointed that the day she had been dreading had finally dawned that she could barely look at herself in the mirror. Her spooky grey eyes were never the same shade twice and today they were dark and fierce, like gunmetal. She dressed resentfully, cursing her bad luck to be born poor and Mexican. She would wear the dumb dress as she was expected to do, she would wear the tiara, she would even wear the crazy shoes, but it would be a cold day in Cancún before she would smile about it. Her wild hair swirled like a storm about her head and she touched it fleetingly, not knowing where to begin, and decided just to leave it hanging loose and dishevelled. She was heavy handed with the kohl and lipstick, ensuring that her knockout beauty had an angry edge today. Her looks hadn't helped her to escape her destiny. She snapped a bra over her nineteen-fifties chest, and then, after a moment's hesitation, she left her underwear in the dresser drawer. It was the only act of defiance left open to her.

La Quinceañera began with the formal Catholic mass downtown. Her mother was blisteringly anxious, her brother Ray was still drunk from the night before and Esmé was dazed and reluctant. The three of them left their two-room house downtown and crammed into a neighbour's taxi, festooned with ribbons. The trip to the church took less than five minutes; really they could have walked it, like they did every Sunday. The taxi pulled up and her family scurried inside. She heard a murmur of approval from the gathered guests and pictured her mother stopping to say hello to a dozen people before reaching her seat on the first pew, the pride of place. All the friends that she had chosen to compose her court were waiting for her in church dressed as if they were going to the prom. Esmé stood outside and wished that she had thought to secrete a pack of cigarettes somewhere in the yards of sugar pink netting that made up her gown so that she could have a smoke.

She chewed at her fingernail instead.

Everybody would notice that she wasn't being walked up the aisle of the church by her father as was traditional, but instead by her brother. This whole day was a joke.

The bells in El Christo del Rey began to chime and her brother grabbed her arm and smiled. 'Are you excited?' he said.

'I would rather be at my own funeral.'

She was almost crying when the priest removed the ribbon from her hair and replaced it with a tiara, marking her as a princess in the eyes of God. People who noticed them assumed that her tears were of happiness.

When she walked back outside the dark church into the dazzling light, the sun flared in her eyes and made little red dots over her vision like spots of blood. The cars that sped past on the dusty town street tooted their horns when they saw her emerge on the steps. She winced under the barrage of sound.

'Smile,' hissed her mother. And so she smiled.

Afterwards, at the party, she was finally able to sneak away with her friend Carmen, who lit a cigarette, passed it to her and told her that she looked amazing. 'Did your mum make your dress?' said Carmen.

'It was hers for her own fifteenth,' said Esmé. She was wondering how her mother had managed to keep it safe and dry all these years when they barely had enough room to breathe and tropical storms had destroyed their little house twice in the time that they had lived there.

'I love family traditions,' said Carmen. 'How romantic. You have to keep it for your own daughter.'

'I plan on burning it.'

Carmen giggled. Then she stopped giggling because she realized this was Esmé they were talking about and if Esmé said she was going to burn her dress then she probably meant it.

'I'm giving up smoking,' said Esmé suddenly, rebelling in her own way by ditching a predictably rebellious habit. 'Let's go.' She ground out her last cigarette with the sole of her flat shoe. She hated wearing flats. They made her body look ordinary. She was only wearing them because tradition dictated that La Quinceañera's father swap them for heels before the first waltz, yet another unwelcome reminder that the free days of childhood had drawn to a close. It didn't seem to make any difference that she'd been wearing heels for years, nor that she had no father to make the gesture. It was what was done, and so it would be what her mother wanted.

'Your mum looks so happy,' said Carmen as they walked back into the hall. Esmé watched her mother across the room talking to a man (of course) and looking fresher than most of the hard-working Mexican mothers. Catalina had long been admired but to everyone's surprise this had not translated into marriage. Of course, as a single mother of two separately fathered children she was far from a prize, but her grace and beauty should have overcome this disadvantage. Esmé thought that the men could smell her desperation because, though they came to call often, Catalina's boyfriends rarely stayed for very long.

Catalina saw Esmé and her friend and she trotted over, all bounce and nervous excitement. 'It's time,' she said. She smoothed down the sides of Esmé's dress and tucked back a stubborn curl of her daughter's glossy black hair. 'You look very beautiful. I am proud. Are you ready?'

It was Esmé's last chance to run but she nodded, swallowing back the sick feeling that rose in her throat, and her mother motioned for the band on stage who immediately broke into '*Sobre los Olas*'. It was the most famous waltz in the world that everyone thought was from Vienna but had been composed by Rosas in Mexico City. She had never been to Mexico City. She doubted very much that she ever would.

Esmé and her mother toured the room, kissing cheeks and thanking everyone for coming until at last they climbed onto the stage, where the throne – a wing-backed chair decorated with gold ribbons and cream silk – sat waiting. Esmé sat down and met the sympathetic eyes of the room with something approaching defiance. She lifted her foot and let her mother change her shoes. She stood up and took her mother's hand and squeezed it until she could feel the bones of her knuckles, then she walked the three lonely steps down to the dance floor, her new heels tapping out her descent.

The gathered guests clapped with a gathering rhythm and then started to cheer and slap their hand on the tables as Miguel Santos, one of the *chamberlanes* in her Quinceañera court stepped forward and formally asked her to dance. In her heels she was taller than him but she tried not to mind. This was Miguel; she had known him for ever. He did well at school and was good to his grandmother. Last summer she had started letting him hold her hand under the cedar tree in the main plaza and so everyone – all their friends and neighbours, everyone – knew that Esmé and Miguel were together. A few nights ago she had let him touch her breasts. He had dropped the heaviest of hints about what was going to happen tonight. He had as good as said the words.

Miguel took her in his arms and they waltzed across the dance floor in perfect time. She was actually glad that both their mothers had forced them to practise. The watching crowd was a distraction, tapping teaspoons onto the rims of their beer bottles and juice glasses in a rattling crescendo that was half a beat out of time. She felt dizzy and closed her eyes briefly. She let him lead without trying to pretend that they were equals. Miguel was a man and she was a woman. That was just the way that it went.

With a final flourish the band wrapped up the waltz and segued into a boisterous folk song designed to get everybody dancing.

Miguel bowed in front of her and then, to her horror but not to her surprise, for this was exactly what he had been hinting at all along, he produced the thin gold band from the inside pocket of the tuxedo he had borrowed from his father. Then he got down on one knee and asked Esmé to marry him.

Just as she knew he had planned.

A couple of grandmothers sobbed. Everybody nodded and smiled at each other because they were a very good

63

match and Miguel would inherit his father's car service and Esmeralda was a good little housekeeper, hadn't she been keeping house all these years for her uppity mother? The sense of approval in the room was overwhelming.

Esmé wanted to scratch at the sleeves of her dress, rip it off, do something terribly shocking that would wipe the satisfaction from their faces.

The crowd waited, already thinking of the wedding it would be. Today was a good party, possibly a great party, but the wedding would be duty bound to surpass it. Miguel waited, on bended knee.

Security. That was the word her mother used when she talked about marrying a solid, respectable local boy like Miguel. Someone who would stick by her no matter what. As if security was more important than freedom.

And because Esmé had nobody in her life to tell her that it didn't have to be like this, that she was free to say and do whatever she liked, and be whoever she truly was, because she did not know any of this, Esmé looked down at the ring in her sweetheart's trembling hand when he asked her to marry him and she said yes.

6

Claudia

Claudia knew from a young age that she was not the same as other children. Her pale blonde prettiness was remarkable, and her tendency to daydream was often commented on. She lived with her grandfather instead of her parents. But Claudia knew she was different because she liked being on her own. A succession of nannies pushed her on girls her own age and she politely pretended that she liked playing with them. All through school she played nice. But by the time she was twenty-one years old she was through with pretending. She just didn't know it yet.

By the time she was twenty-one, Claudia's pale blonde prettiness had translated into butterscotch tones of youth and vitality, with an old soul looking out from her untroubled blue-grey eyes and a supple mouth that was often pursed in quiet contemplation. In another country, Claudia might have been overlooked, but in Mexico she stood out.

'Claudia? Hey, we're talking to you.' Three young women were staring at her, identical dark cascades of hair, identical expressions of disbelief that they were being kept waiting for a response.

It must be strange to consider yourself so important.

Soon they would insulate themselves from the horrors of the world by marrying well and living in a gated community. Literally as well as figuratively.

Claudia could not say what she had been thinking about exactly, only the way that the towering green plane tree standing outside the entrance to the exclusive Bosques de las Lomas fitness centre cast a constantly shifting shadow through the frosted glass of the double doors. And how very peculiar it was that a tree growing outside this building in the best part of Mexico City could be the same species as a tree on a dark London side street close to where her mother, Lucy, would be fast asleep by now.

'Sorry,' she said, thinking of all the times she had already apologized today. She said sorry to her grandfather for swearing at the breakfast table when they were discussing moving some of his petrochemical factories to Uruguay, to her driver for being late to meet him at the north entrance, to her personal trainer when she failed to answer him and she hadn't the faintest clue which muscle group they were discussing, let alone what question she had been asked.

'Sorry,' she said one more time to her friends, leaning against the wall as if she was weary, and she silently vowed not to apologize again before sunset. It wasn't even as if she meant it.

The leader of the gang of three, four if you included Claudia, which was debatable, was a fierce Bolivian girl called Camille. 'I was just saying if you want to come back to my house for dinner that would be okay,' she said. Claudia and the others had all been students together at Mexico City's prestigious Olivios School and had known each other since kindergarten; in the years since they left school they had been mostly friends, on and off.

'Great,' said Claudia, feigning enthusiasm. 'Brilliant.'

'We need to work out what Debs is going to say in her email.'

'What email?'

'The email she's going to send Andreas. God, haven't you been listening at all?'

'Sorry,' said Claudia. And then grimaced.

'What's wrong?' asked Debs.

'Nothing,' said Claudia. 'And I'm not sorry.' She turned back to watching the shadows dance and wondered if they had planted the plane tree when the building was new or if they had built the city block around an existing tree. It was very large. Could a tree grow that large in a hundred years? And why did trees keep growing whereas human beings stopped, quite soon, and then stayed that way?

When a tree was cut down in the forest, could anyone hear it scream?

Camille and Debs exchanged a glance with the third, Mika, who wondered if all posh English women were as distracted and as impolite, and why the combination wasn't at all repelling.

'Let's go,' said Camille, and the four of them swept out through the doors and down the steps. Lesser mortals scattered in their wake. Debs was wearing stilettos that clacked as loudly as tap shoes. A few miles away, downtown Mexico City sweltered in a smudged skyline.

'Hang on a minute, okay?' Claudia darted across the parking lot and knocked on the tinted window of the town car that was waiting to take her home.

'I'm going home with one of my friends,' she told her driver.

'Which friend?' The driver was older, near to her grandfather's age. He was one of her favourites.

'Camille Lapage?' she said.

'I know,' he said, nodding. Everybody knew Camille Lapage. Her father was CEO of a Forbes 500 company and one of the richest men in Mexico. 'I will pick you up from Santa Fe after dinner?'

'Thanks,' said Claudia, and bounded away to join her so-called friends. Perhaps she would have a good time. She dragged her focus to the matter at hand. What *should* Debs say in her email? It was so hard to care.

They were waiting for her in Camille's Mercedes A20. The top of the convertible was up, it always was, and she wondered why she bothered to buy that model as she clambered into the back next to Mika. 'Okay,' she said.

Camille started the engine and the car's sound system launched into her preferred hip-hop. All four of them sang along as they wheeled through the city streets, aware of everybody looking at them, basking in their fortunate lives and never questioning – why them? A black people-carrier discreetly followed the Mercedes. Camille had bodyguards everywhere she went, but by now they had all grown used to the silent shadows. Claudia tipped back her head and craned her neck to see out of the window.

The high white clouds raced past as the car gathered speed and headed west of the city.

Her friend's family lived in a typically wealthy Santa Fe neighbourhood. More like a technology town in the United States than a province of Mexico City. A series of empty, well-manicured roads leading up to imposing gates, behind which a handful of mansions shared the peace of mind that only comes with decent twenty-four-hour security. Of course Camille still lived with her parents. None of them had climbed onto the property ladder, yet all they had to do was ask. Later her father would commute home by helicopter and land on the helipad outside, beyond the decking and the pool.

The girls dumped their coats in the vast hallway, helped themselves to snacks from the fridge, and then camped out in Camille's luxurious bedroom suite, writing draft after draft of an email to a randy young man called Andreas that Debs would probably never have the courage to send anyway. Claudia kept occupied with a pack of cards, trying to teach herself how to do a Russian shuffle, pulling a card at random now and again and assigning it mystical value, and she was only half listening to the painfully long discussion about whether Debs should sign the note Debs, or just D, or even Deborah ('it's more mature').

'Christ, does it really matter?' she snapped, dropping the cards into her lap.

Camille frowned and actually crossed herself, which Claudia thought was verging on ridiculous.

'Of course it matters,' squealed Mika, who was so scared of getting dumped by her friends she was constantly overcompensating with enthusiasm. 'The ending of something is the most important part.'

'Really?' said Claudia. 'Let's all remember that you said that so when Andreas dumps her again it won't feel so bad.'

Debs coloured. 'You think he's going to dump me?'

'I don't know,' said Claudia, exasperated. 'And neither do you. But I know that if he is going to finish things between you then it's going to be because he wants to have sex with Jeanette Randolph and not because you signed your note "D" and put three kisses instead of one.'

'Claudia!' admonished Camille. 'Stop it.'

'Can't you just talk to him?' said Claudia. 'Is that impossible? You let him stick his penis in you, couldn't the pair of you manage to have a conversation? You're twenty-one Debs, not fourteen. And on top of everything else, this is boring.' For a few seconds the only sound was Notorious B.I.G. 'Can't we at least change the music?'

'Andreas likes this,' said Debs, defending the choice.

'He's not here, is he?' said Claudia. 'He's probably round at Jeanette's listening to the remix and sticking his tongue in her mouth while you're over here taking love advice from Camille, who has slept with fourteen people, none of whom she ever saw again, and Mika, who's been with the same guy since she was nine years old.'

'Claudia, that's enough.' Camille was no longer smiling.

'But don't you see? You're a catch, Debs. You're clever and you're funny, and pretty too, but a love affair is not about an email. You'll spend five hours writing it, he'll

70

spend five seconds reading it, and you'll still have exactly the same problems.'

'It's not a love affair,' said Debs. 'I'm just going out with him, that's all.'

'Really? Does he know that?'

'I think you're being cruel and I don't know why.' Debs hovered somewhere close to tears. 'What do you know about sex?'

Claudia blushed. The problem with holding onto friends from childhood is they know exactly what you've done – or haven't done, in Claudia's case.

'You're a virgin,' said Debs. 'So what gives you the right to have an opinion?'

'I've had boyfriends, Debs. Just because I didn't sleep with them doesn't mean I don't know my way around a man.'

'You're pathetic,' said Debs. 'This holding out for a hero thing is getting embarrassing.'

'You ever think maybe what I know about sex is the reason why I'm waiting? You *know* Andreas is never going to call you again, you know it. He's a joke and in a few months you'll agree with me. The only reason you care so much right now is because he's seen you naked.'

'I love him.'

'That desperate feeling, the anxiety? That's not love,' said Claudia. 'That's shame. If you loved him it would feel fantastic.'

'It's my house,' said Camille, 'and I'd prefer it if we all got along. Maybe we should leave the email for a little while and talk about something else.'

A silence descended and the atmosphere in the bedroom

71

was as thick and unpleasant as the city air in the height of summer. Mika opened her mouth to speak but then closed it again, like a goldfish. Camille pretended she was immune to the heavy mood by trying to find an album for them to listen to, but her search soon turned frantic and betrayed her anxiety and the pause in the usual chatter was pronounced.

Claudia relished the chance to hear herself think, to hear herself breathe, and she closed her eyes briefly and hated that they spent all their time indoors because of the crappy urban air, and felt the mass of a city that went on for miles and miles closing in on her.

'I have to go.' She stood up abruptly, letting the pack of cards she had been playing with fall from her lap. 'I'll be back in a little while,' she said, knowing that she wouldn't.

It would be hours before her driver arrived. Again she wished that she had her own car but her mother wouldn't allow it. Though she wasn't sure what gave her mother the right to insist on anything when she lived mostly on the other side of the world. But insist she did. She insisted that Claudia went to the right school but seemed more concerned with her enrolling in a country club than enrolling in a university; she insisted that Claudia call her 'Lucy' and not 'Mum' or worse 'Mom'; she insisted that she loved her daughter when clearly she did not.

Claudia grabbed one of the immaculate bicycles from the side of the multiple garages that kept the Lepage motors safe at night and she pushed off down the driveway, powering her feet into the pedals as she flew out onto the quiet road. Then she was off, her feet churning, sailing past the gatehouse and down the twisted roads that led down into the valley below. She could feel the late afternoon sun on her exposed face and it glittered on the frame of the bike, explosions of fairy lights that made her feel as if she was riding away from terrible danger on an enchanted bicycle and if only she could think of the magic words the tyres would lift from the earth, take to the skies and they would be flying.

She didn't know which way she was going but it was easy to follow the road's gentle gradient until it barely became necessary to move her feet on the pedals. She wondered if Camille and the others were sitting waiting for her to come back or if they had already decided to give her the cold shoulder for a while and drop her from the circle, and drop her name from their vocabulary. That was the way that Camille worked. She didn't get attached; friendships were dispensable, she was like a little society psychopath.

I need better friends.

The slope pulled up again briefly and after a few miles her legs began to ache from the effort. It felt good. Then she was freewheeling down again, the wind gusting her blond hair back from her face. A few yards in front of her the road filtered into a bigger highway so she veered to the right and trundled down underneath the bridges. The surface that raced beneath the tyres was becoming more level and the bike slowed. She passed a shop on her left, and then another, and then the buildings began to crowd the sides of the roads and the wide boulevards slithered away from their manicured landscaping as they led to the edges of the *villa miseria,* the slum.

She applied the brakes and the bike slid to a stop, kicking up a cloud of dust from the street. Buildings tottered on weak foundations, walls made out of slabs of terracotta with thick mortar oozing out between floors as if it was still wet and the house had been built just the day before.

Two young boys sprang from a doorway and stared at her. She smiled down at them, exhilarated, her cheeks rosy and her hair wild. She spoke to them in her lightly accented Spanish and they started giggling. A young woman a year or two older than Claudia shouted to them from the same doorway and the boys ran back inside.

It was quiet. There was nobody left on the streets and Claudia felt a flicker of apprehension, bordering on fear, but she was so relieved to feel something, anything, that she savoured it. She breathed in the polluted Mexico City air that they were all so afraid of but she did not die. In fact, she felt more alive than she had in months.

A sudden 'hey' startled her. She turned and saw the voice belonged to a young man who had appeared on the road behind her. He had blond hair, like hers, and burnished brown skin. She shielded her eyes from the sun behind him, a sun which made him shimmer at the edges, indistinct, an apparition in gold.

'If you were thinking of it,' he said, 'I wouldn't.'

'Thinking of what?'

'Of going any further.' He jerked his thumb towards the *villa* and shook his head. 'This isn't on the tourist maps.'

'I'm not a tourist,' she said. 'I was born in Mexico City.'

What would her friends say if they could see her now? If they could see where she was? The wrong side of the bridge, talking to a long-haired guy with frayed jeans and dirty feet shoved into a pair of flip-flops. 'I'm a *defeña*,' she said firmly, meaning she was born in the city, and not the more derogatory *chilanga,* meaning a mere resident. 'I can go where I like.'

She willed herself to push off and cycle away into the tangled streets of the *villa* before he could warn her again, but her body wouldn't listen to her mind's command. She stared at him and her heart started to pound. What was happening? He had the longest eyelashes that she had seen on a man, and his skin was a darker gold than his flaxen hair. His gaze was so intense that it took all of her courage to hold it.

She was of English stock through and through. She had self-control. It was one more thing that set her apart from these impassioned Latinos. She wouldn't know how to flirt if she wanted to. 'I go where I like,' she repeated.

'I don't doubt it.' He offered his hand. 'My name is David,' he said.

'Claudia.'

'You want to see the *villa*, Claudia? I will take you. But not today. Another day you can come with me. You can meet my sisters. Not dressed like that and not with your bike.'

'It's not my bike,' she said.

His eyes glittered as he teased her. 'You stole a bike?' he said.

'Sort of.'

She felt his goofy grin reflected across her own face and for a while they both just stood there, staring at each other. He had a small scar on his right cheekbone. She felt a shift inside her, as if the mechanics of her body had unlocked a chamber which was brimming with possibility. Suddenly flirtation seemed a distinct likelihood.

'Are you hungry?' he said.

Her mouth watered and she felt ravenous. For something to eat or for something to eat with him, she wasn't sure which, but she nodded and managed to say 'why not?' without her voice trembling and he took the bike from her and pushed it while they walked back the way she had come, then left, then right, until she had no hope of finding her way back to Camille's again without him.

'Do you know where we're going?' she said.

'Are you lost?'

'Utterly,' she said.

Without meaning to she told him everything. She told him about the argument she had just had with her friends. About her dreams and how stifled she felt living with her elderly grandfather.

'Your parents died?' he said gently.

'My mother lives in England. My father died before I was born.'

'You must miss both of them,' he said.

'I miss having parents,' said Claudia. 'My mother didn't handle being pregnant very well; it was a very brief love affair, and being a single mother didn't fit in with her lifestyle. She wanted to have me adopted.'

'What happened?'

76

'My grandfather, her father, wouldn't hear of it. He insisted on adopting me himself.'

'Did they tell you all this?'

'She did. Lucy, my mother. She's very . . . unconventional.'

'So your grandfather is a hero?'

She smiled. 'Who knows? Perhaps I would have been better off with two parents who loved me?'

'But your grandfather is a rich man?'

'Very,' she said, grinning. 'Which is nice. What about you? Do you have a girlfriend?'

'No,' he said, grinning.

'Are you lying?'

'I never lie,' he said.

'Never?'

'Never.'

David lived nearby with his own parents and his sisters. When he spoke about them he kept referring to a day in the future when she would meet them and she was pulled along by his certainty. They stopped outside a bright café with window boxes spilling scarlet geraniums and wild garlic. David propped her bike against the wall and they sat at a table in the shade. She ordered *una lagrima*, warm milk with a teardrop of coffee, and they talked some more. She told him that she was scared of horses; he told her that he wanted to be a politician.

'Wow,' she said. 'Truly?'

'What? You don't think someone like me can be a politician, is that it?'

'I didn't say that.'

'It's what you were thinking though?'

'I don't know anything about politics.'

'If someone poor like me went out for PRD in Mexico City, then perhaps many more poor people would vote. What is the point of having compulsory voting if it's not enforced? The problem is you can only win elections if you are rich. Social equality in Mexico is a myth.'

He moved his hands when he talked and she longed to touch the skin on his face and see if it was as soft as it looked. To touch the places where the sun had kissed the tips of his eyebrows.

'How old are you?' he said.

'Twenty-one.'

'And you live where, San Angel?'

'Close, Coyoacan.'

'There was a local election in your district four months ago. Did you vote?'

'I don't remember. I don't think so.' She had never voted in her life but didn't want to admit it.

'I doubt it. Only seventeen per cent of people your age did. You think I can't get enough people your age to vote for a guy like me in a little local election like that?' He grinned, sensing that he was getting too intense for her. 'I mean, look at me.'

He was right. He didn't look like a politician, he looked like a pop star.

'Not to mention all the people in this country that aren't registered to vote because they think they'll get in trouble with zoning or the tax department for living the way that they do. And this is democracy? They say a poor man cannot be elected to government office in a capitalist

78

model. I don't believe that,' he said. 'I will never believe that. And I want to prove it.'

He smashed the palm of his hand down onto the table between them, and her coffee cup rattled.

She was shaken. 'I think you can do whatever you want,' she said.

'Okay,' he said.

The force of his belief drained from him slowly until he was relaxed and smiling again and she was left wondering if she had imagined his intensity. 'Okay what?'

'Just okay.' He checked his watch. 'Do you want to see something beautiful?'

He threw some coins on the table and asked the barista to keep an eye on the bike. Then he grabbed her hand and they ran.

The feel of their hands meshed together raced up her fingertips, through her arm and up through the base of her neck, exploding into her mind with a surge of joy. The world rushed in and everything was more sparkling, prettier than she had seen before, from the hard cobbles beneath her feet to the scorching sky above. And his hand, clasping her hand, a perfect fit. They ran. She was laughing as he pulled her after him, her head whirling and her heart thrilled, and she heard the whisper of her soul for the first time in her life as they pelted through the twisting narrow streets of a residential neighbourhood until at last she heard the unmistakable sound of tango music.

They rounded the next corner into a graceful square, lined at each end with jacaranda trees heavy with amethyst blossom. In the middle of the square stood a bandstand and a four-piece band played a tango. On the grass in front of them a large number of elderly couples were dancing in the sweet scented air. She watched them shuffle around to the sound of the music, their feet moving together, their eyes never parting and, as the rhythm cascaded over the old romantics, those eyes were as bright and keen as the eyes of far younger lovers.

'Our generation knows nothing of romance,' he said. 'Not yet.'

She stepped into his arms and they danced in the shadows at the edge of the square until the music finished and she was clinging to him, hoping that she could dance with him until she grew old.

She looked up at him and he traced the curve of her jaw with his fingertips and she hoped that he found her beautiful. They said she was beautiful – her friends, her grandfather – and sometimes she felt beautiful, and loved how her blond hair and her strange grey eyes highlighted her foreignness, but David would know beauty. More than she did.

When he kissed her it was as if the music started to play once more. And when he stopped she was surprised to find that it had not.

This was why she sometimes felt so lonely. She had been waiting for him.

A few days later, just as he had foreseen, David took her into the *villa* to meet his mother and his sisters. His father was at work. His three sisters volunteered at a woman's collective within the slum, helping with health and welfare issues. His mother looked after other people's children so that the parents could go out to work. They all sat down to lunch together and when they pushed her she told them a little bit about her life, but she was embarrassed by its abundance.

'Don't be,' said David. 'We are all born under the same fate. I could have been you, you could have been me.' He slurped from a bowl of thin pork stew. 'I am sure you would have coped.'

She said nothing, dipping her spoon back into the richly spiced broth. She was glad she had chosen to wear simple cut-offs and a plain black vest top instead of something pretty to try and impress him.

In the afternoon they went with his sisters to a small tin-roofed building in the heart of the *villa*. 'Most of the women who live here are too busy raising their children to go out and look for work,' he explained. 'But many of them can sew, like my sisters. Our priest set up this collective so that they could sell what they make. Our links to the church keep us out of the grips of the corrupt politicians.'

'There is no corruption in the church?' she said. 'I heard different.'

'This is Mexico,' he said. 'There is corruption everywhere. Bribery is the liar's only way to a truth.'

The collective made simple cotton dresses in a rainbow of colours. Light, elegant, wrapped across the waist with a crossover belt of plaited ribbon, Claudia could see instantly that they would be a hit with the Mexico City women she knew, and their mothers too. She reached out to touch the fabric, a dress of livid purple, and saw that it was actually two layers of thinly woven cotton, one on top of the other, each one gossamer light and ideal to wear in the sultry city heat. 'These are beautiful,' she said.

Maria smiled. 'The cotton comes from a sister collective in Chiapas, the design from a woman in Corrientes. We sew them here. We send some to a company in Italy. Also to Brazil.'

'England?'

'It is cold in England.'

'Not always,' said Claudia, and she thought of picnics in meadows and wild swimming during the high summers. The design of the dress was a little bit like the tea dresses people wore during the forties. She had seen films. An older England.

'I could . . . I mean, my mother lives in England, perhaps I could help you. I think these would sell there.' She reached out for another dress that was the warm honey colour of the stone cottages in Gloucestershire.

David was nodding. 'That's exactly what we need, someone to help with the international side of things. You speak English.'

'And French,' said Claudia.

'David,' said Maria, 'I am sure Claudia is very busy. You must have things to do, surely, like . . .' She let her sentence hang unfinished, unsure of what girls like Claudia did all day. She had friends who worked out in the big houses. There was a saying in Mexico that labour was so cheap, anyone could be a queen for twenty dollars. Some of her best friends might be Claudia's housemaids one day soon, and they would be the lucky ones. Domestic positions were highly sought after, the food was better and you were less likely to lose fingers than you were on a *maquiladora* assembly line.

'I want to go to university,' said Claudia.

'You're still a student?' Maria shot her brother a dirty look across the rack of dresses. 'Do your parents know you are hanging out with my brother?'

'I know that plenty of the women you work with will be no older than me,' said Claudia. 'Just because I went to school and they had babies doesn't mean they belong and I don't.'

'Your age has nothing to do with why you don't belong,' said Maria. She slammed the coat hangers up to one end and started briskly straightening each item. 'You want to work for us because you feel sorry for us? Because you have nothing else in your life to feel good about? Or because you want David to like you?'

She had been destined to meet him, she knew it. 'Can't it be for all those reasons and still be something worth doing?' she said.

'It's too late, Maria,' said David. 'I already like her.'

Claudia felt a rush as though the sun had just emerged from a cloud.

'You're sure?' Maria was amused by the identical expressions of love-struck bliss and by the fact that her presence was clearly no longer required.

'I'm crazy about her,' said David.

A laugh of pure joy bubbled forth from Claudia and they gripped each other's hands, welded together by the certainty of a shared experience, reassured to see their own hope reflected in another person's eyes.

'God help us all,' said Maria.

For the next few weeks, Claudia juggled her studies and

her increasing devotion to David with her role at the Women's Centre, Centro Mujeres. A name she had suggested to go with their brand-new website.

'None of these women have a computer,' he said, eyeing the demo on her laptop with suspicion.

'A website is not for them. Not directly. It's for the buyers. For the press.' Her fingers flew confidently over the keys. She had always found computers easy, much easier than people.

'What press?'

'A press release. It's fine, I'll ask my mother, she'll know what it should say.'

'Slow down, okay?' said David.

She was wearing one of their own dresses; they were all she ever wore now. She had one in every colour, and her tall, elegant frame was the best advertisement for the simple wrapover style. She paid for them out of her own money and wished she could do more.

'I see these women now, David, when they come in for the Tuesday meeting. They know me and I know them. I know they need this. You don't give people dignity by opening soup kitchens or throwing money at them. This is a special place. I don't want to slow down.'

'I mean, slow down . . .' He took her hands from the computer keyboard and pulled her to her feet then kissed her palms, first one and then the other. 'When you get excited like that it makes the hairs on the back of my neck stand up. Here, feel.'

They kissed, her shoulders dropped and she tipped back her head, twisting her fingertips into the downy hairs at the base of his neck. He traced the line of her collarbone with his free hand and tipped the other strap over the edge with his thumb then leant her back against the desk. It was a long kiss and by the time it was over she was panting with excitement.

'I don't want to wait any more,' she said, the words coming from a place deep in her throat.

He groaned and pulled himself away. 'We can't do this here.'

'It doesn't matter. We can lock the door.' She reached out to pull him back into her embrace but he resisted with a reluctant shake of his head.

'You should come up to the hills,' she said impulsively. She was ready. 'It's so beautiful there at night. Will you?' She caught his strange look. 'What? What is it?'

'Have you told your grandfather about me?'

She hesitated. 'It doesn't matter, he's away. But, yes, I mentioned you. This is . . . I mean, we are serious, aren't we?' She avoided his eyes and busied herself shutting down the computer, and he didn't say anything until she had nothing left to do and nowhere else to look.

Once his eyes held hers, they would not let go, and she felt herself falling deeper under his spell. By the time he moved in to kiss her again she was trembling with the effort not to throw herself at his feet.

'Tonight,' she whispered. 'Come home with me tonight.'

The sun was setting by the time they reached the suburbs. The huge ranch-style house was set back from the road at the end of a twisting driveway. David whistled when he saw the size of the place but she did not regret bringing him here. Someone like David wouldn't judge her by the good fortune of her birth. They parked up and walked inside.

'You're sure your grandfather's not here?'

'He's away. Buenos Aires, I think.'

'Tell me about him,' he said.

They reached her sitting room and she pushed the doors open onto the balmy night. The muslin drapes drifted in the breeze, keeping the biting insects of the suburbs at bay. The noise from the cicadas was louder out here. Later, if it was clear, there was a chance they could see stars.

'We don't spend much time together. He has his own part of the house. This is my bit, the deck and this porch, the rooms upstairs. When it's warm like this sometimes we eat out here and it feels like he is just visiting.'

'You're not close?'

'I think we are in a way. He has treated me like an equal since I was two years old. I can ski and sail and ride a horse. We can talk freely. But the only things he taught me about love were learnt by listening to old Frank Sinatra albums.'

'I can teach you everything about love,' he said. 'If you let me.'

She led him up the stairs to the first floor and a bedroom at the very end of the hallway. It was gigantic, stretching across the entire west wing. It was sparsely decorated with very little furniture but several interesting works of art on the walls. A huge skylight meant that the night sky fell onto the double bed against the wall at the far end.

David took a pair of candlesticks down from the shelf above the bed. 'Do you have matches?'

'I . . . it's not my room. It's my mother's, but she hasn't been back for months. It's the most beautiful room in the house. It's wasted.' She stretched out her arms and turned in a lazy circle, waltzing with some unseen muse in the airy space.

'Okay,' said David, watching her long slender limbs in their supple dance. It was a while before he remembered the candlesticks in his hand, so taken was he with her odd grace. 'Do you think she'd have matches?'

'Have a look,' said Claudia, waving him towards the dresser. 'Knowing my mother she'll have everything. You'll probably find some weed and a bottle of gin if you look hard enough.' She flopped onto the bed and stared up out of the skylight.

David found some matches and lit the candles. He returned to the drawers and replaced some of the things he had moved. 'Is this you?' he said, holding up a photograph of a woman with a little girl.

She walked over and took it from him, looking over his shoulder at the collection of photographs he had unearthed. 'We probably shouldn't be going through her stuff,' she urged.

'Is that your mum? She's . . .'

'It's okay, you can say it.'

'She's beautiful.'

Claudia stared at the photograph and wished she could remember the day it had been taken because they had been together and they both looked happy. Her mother looked impossibly elegant, but then Lucy always did when she was in public. People said they looked similar, and it was true they had the same pale blonde colouring and shared tall, supple figures. But Lucy liked her beauty to shine out, whereas Claudia always aimed for the shadows.

'Who's Danny?' said David.

'What?' Everything she had been thinking about fell away and she stood motionless to let the name reverberate.

'This postcard from Danny. *Love Danny*. Who's Danny?' David was holding a postcard from Las Vegas.

Her heart galloped. 'I'm not sure.' She took the postcard from him and tried to act nonchalant. 'Actually, my father was called Danny.'

Beautiful places make me think of you, love Danny.

She sat down on the edge of the bed. The postcard had the famous 'Welcome to Fabulous Las Vegas' sign against a backdrop of palms and impossibly blue skies.

'My mother has spent her life chasing after blue skies and palm trees,' she said. 'And so I think, was that what was so important? Was that what she wouldn't give up to raise a child? Blue skies?' She traced the handwriting with her fingertips. Danny closed the loops on his gs and ys just as she did.

She stared at the date on the smudged postmark, did a little mental arithmetic, and was confused. It was dated less than ten years ago and sent with an American stamp. But her mother had told her that Danny died before she was born.

'What is it?' said David. 'What's wrong?'

'It must be a different Danny,' she said.

She looked at the address. It had been sent to London but ended up here, packed in a bag with family photographs.

Was there a possibility that her father might still be alive?

'My father was younger than I am now when he died,' said David, taking the postcard from her and putting it aside. He stood at the side of the bed and tenderly picked up her legs underneath her knees. With a flick of his wrists he had pivoted her onto the bed and was laying her down, pushing her legs open with his so that he could lie on top of her. 'When you live longer than your own father, it makes you hungry. You want things more.'

He kissed her throat, breathing in the smell of her perfume as she buckled beneath his touch.

'Tell me what you want,' she whispered, excited by her desire for him. 'Tell me.'

His kisses fell lightly and haphazardly onto her shoulders and the dips and hollows of her neck and shoulders until she was trembling at the thought of his next kiss before it touched her. He tugged the knotted ribbon at the front of her dress and pulled it loose, unfolding her like a gift-wrapped package.

She pushed her arms out of her dress while he pulled at her underwear. Her hips rose and fell and when they fell his hand was there, his thumb pressing softly into her and making small determined circles so slowly that her hips rose and fell again before she could stop them and he started to kiss her breasts while all the time letting her press up into him. 'I want you,' he murmured.

Was this the moment she was supposed to tell him she was a virgin?

He sensed a flicker of hesitation and pulled back,

flipping a condom from his back pocket. 'Don't worry. But I like it slow, I like to do it right.'

The candles, the skylight, it was all perfect. This was what she had been waiting for, not a furtive romp in the back of a schoolboy's car, or a drunken one-night stand with one of the guys from one of the bars. And her body was alive in a way it had never been with any of those guys, her nerve endings screaming at her, demanding that she touch him again. If she told him she was a virgin he might want to stop.

7

After six years of marriage, Esmé knew that only a fool would believe anything her husband said and therefore she must be a fool *mayor* to have married him.

'Esmé?' he yelled. His whiny voice ricocheted through the cramped apartment. Esmé ignored him. She pulled herself up onto the deep kitchen windowsill by the sink where the late morning sun streamed in so fiercely it made the pans on the dish rack hot as if from the stove. Esmé perched her bottom on the windowsill and tipped back her head, elongating her slender neck and letting her damp hair lick the space between her shoulder blades, combing through the heavy locks with her fingers. The rays dried her hair and warmed the base of her spine, melting the tension there.

'*Esmeralda?* Honey?'

He probably wanted her to sit on his lap and coo while he told her how clever it was to buy this unit in an urbanization just outside the city limits while they were still so cheap. She hated it. At least up here on the sixth floor they didn't have to worry about mosquitoes.

'Didn't you hear me yelling?' asked Miguel as he

wandered into the kitchen and came over to her. He lifted up her bare feet and pulled himself in between her legs so that her skirt lifted almost to her hips. He tucked it down modestly, as if a neighbour might see but there were no neighbours. Most of the apartments were empty and she wondered if that was why she felt lonely. With a sigh she linked her ankles behind his back and found a smile. Outside, the only sound was the dull throb of the highway.

'What you doing today?' he said. 'What you up to?'

She shrugged. *Washing my hair?*

'Do you want to visit your mother?'

'Yes!' she said, delighted. Her legs gave him a little squeeze.

'I gotta check in with Ray.'

'Ray? Why do you have to see my brother?'

'We're doing business,' said Miguel.

Esmé pictured what little money they had fluttering from Miguel's weak fists into Ray's greedy clutches and she hoped that when that inevitably happened Miguel would at last let her get a job.

'Come on,' said Miguel. 'Get ready.'

She looked down at her floaty skirt and her tiny white vest top. 'Do I not look ready to you?'

'Put something on here,' he said, gesturing in the general direction of her low-cut neck. 'Folk are going to be driving, they need to concentrate on the road.'

'I'm covered up,' she protested.

'Just put something on, a scarf or whatever, will you?'

'A scarf? Jesus, Miguel, I remember when you liked the way I look.' She pulled a T-shirt from the stack of laundry on the counter and layered it over the white vest. It looked okay, it looked better than okay. Esmé could wear pretty much anything and still be a bombshell.

'I like the way you look still. I just don't want every other punk in town liking it too, okay?'

'Better?' she asked.

'Thanks, honey.'

Esmé trailed after her husband and wished that they could love each other a little better.

Esmé hugged her mother and kissed her on both her cheeks. 'Mama, you are too thin,' she said, linking her arms behind the elder woman's narrow waist to prove her point. 'Let me make you a quesadilla.'

'No cheese,' said Catalina.

'Have you ever known me to make a quesadilla without cheese?'

'No.'

'Then why do you ask me that now?'

'Where's Miguel?' said Catalina, looking for her son-in-law. She looked out into the pretty flowered street where the neighbourhood kids idled away the remainder of the day, watched by elderly couples on stone benches in the shade.

'He's waiting on the corner,' said Esmé, just as Ray came out of his room, slicking back his hair with his manicured nails and acknowledging her presence with a curt nod of his head. 'Hey,' he said.

'Kiss your sister,' snapped Catalina. 'And tell her *bufón* husband that if he doesn't come in and say hello next time, I'll send all the hotel guests to Condor Taxicabs across the street.'

'See you later, Ma,' said Ray. 'Relax.'

'Relax? Relax, he tells me. Who can relax when you have a twenty-six-year-old son doing God only knows what to pay the rent.'

'At least your son is paying it,' said Ray. 'Enough shouting, okay? Think what the neighbours will say.'

'Ha! Like I care what they think,' said Catalina. 'Go on, go. Will you be home for dinner?'

'I don't know, Ma. I'll try.'

Esmé looked at the jacket her brother was wearing, far too thick for the heat of the day, and wondered what he was hiding. She found herself hoping that it was a knife and not a gun. 'What are you talking to Miguel about?' she asked.

'He didn't tell you?'

She shrugged and Ray laughed.

'Why are you laughing?'

'Because it's funny to see you end up with a guy like Miguel. He should be one of the richest men in Cancún by now, but you let him make all these stupid mistakes. When I think of the way you used to boss me around when you were a kid.'

'I never bossed you around,' said Esmé, but that just made him laugh harder. She shouted after him. 'Don't be fooled, Ray,' she yelled. 'My husband is smarter than he looks.'

Her mother rapped her sharply across the knuckles with the back of her hand.

'Ouch,' said Esmé. 'What's that for?'

'For lying,' said Catalina. 'Miguel is exactly as smart as he looks and he looks like an idiot.' She checked the time on the big old clock that hung on the wall. 'Come on, Esmeralda,' she said. 'We're going out for lunch. There's some people I want you to meet.'

Her mother had another new boyfriend. This one was slightly older, wearing a pale linen suit and expensive shoes like a proper Mexican gentleman, but he couldn't quite pull it off and had crooked base notes floating off him like bad cologne. After all, he must have a fatal flaw, otherwise why would he be interested in her mother? He stood up as the women approached the table.

'At last we meet,' he said. 'Your mother talks about you constantly, and I've seen pictures of course, so it's wonderful that you could do this.'

'She kind of sprung it on me,' said Esmé. 'It certainly wasn't my idea.'

'This is Carlos,' said Catalina, willing her daughter to be courteous with a flick of the stern eyes that she mistakenly imagined might have an effect on how Esmé behaved. Her mother had plenty of boyfriends, and every time she began a new affair she believed with an unshakable faith that this time would be the real deal. That this one would be the one who would save her. Who would save them all.

'I don't need anyone to save me,' Esmé would say. 'I intend to save myself.'

Her mother would laugh cruelly, remembering when she used to feel the same way. 'And how is that plan working out for you so far, Esmeralda?'

'I'm twenty-two,' she would say, 'not forty.' A vicious dig at her mother's tender spot. 'I have time.' And yet time had a habit of dripping like water from a leaking faucet, gathering in wasted puddles while your back was turned.

Lunch with Carlos was going okay until he mentioned London and a cloud fell over her mother's expression. 'He does a lot of business there,' she explained.

'More so than here these days,' he added. 'Europe is exploding.'

'What is it that you do?' asked Esmé. He looked like just another corrupt middle-manager, but the mention of international travel piqued her interest.

'Electronics,' said Carlos. 'We make casing for electronic components and ship them overseas.'

'You own the company?'

He nodded and seemed amused by her unguarded surprise. 'Your daughter is very protective of you,' he said to Catalina, reaching over to place his hand over hers. 'You must be very proud of her.'

'Esmé is my jewel,' said Catalina. 'Tell me, Carlos, have you ever seen a more beautiful child? I know that I'm not supposed to say that, being her mother and all, but if her own mother can't call her beautiful, then who can?'

'I would think everyone calls Esmé beautiful,' he said. He smiled across the table and Esmé held his gaze. He was right. Being called beautiful meant nothing to her now. After all, where had it got her? If this was the end of her journey, then she would rather have been born ugly.

Carlos noticed the flicker of defiance and dropped his eyes back to his meal.

'Has your mother told you about her plans?' he asked casually.

Catalina paled and started fussing with cutlery she had not used. 'Are you okay?' asked Esmé. Underneath the table she pressed her knee against her mother's knee.

'I haven't said that I'll go,' said Catalina.

'Go where?' said Esmé. 'What's going on?'

'I have asked your mother to come with me to London. We have offered her a job there.'

'I haven't said I'll go,' repeated Catalina.

'But you want to?'

'What is left for me here? You and Ray don't need me any more. When Carlos is in London I miss him.'

'I am there half the time and here half the time. I think Catalina would be more comfortable there.'

Esmé looked at Carlos again. There was something about him she definitely did not like. Her mother must sense it too, or why was she hesitating? Esmé would say yes in an instant if she was given an opportunity to start again.

'You could visit her,' said Carlos. 'Have you ever been to Europe?'

'I'm married,' said Esmé. 'My husband would never allow me to go without him.'

'And we are *not* married,' said Catalina, waving her ringless finger in his face. To be forty years old and unmarried carried a heavy stigma in Mexico. They said that Catalina's generation would be the last one to feel the same kind of pressure, but as long as girls were still getting engaged at La Quinceañera it was clear that things were only changing for the rich. Her mother was as desperate to marry as she had been for twenty-five years, since her own first waltz ended with nothing but applause.

'I don't see why people have to move anywhere,' said Catalina, with one of her silvery laughs. 'I don't know why we all don't just stay living where we're living but have nicer things.'

'What do you think, Esmé?' said Carlos, probing her with a stare that she did not like.

'Catalina should do as she pleases.' She struggled with an uncomfortable jealously that was seeping into her thoughts. Her mother had a chance to get out.

'What about you?' said Carlos. 'What pleases you?'

Any other man, any other place, and she would be sure that he was hitting on her. But with her mother sitting across the table, would he really be that dumb?

'Dessert,' said Esmé, and they ordered some.

On the way home her mother begged her not to tell Ray about Carlos.

'Why not?' said Esmé.

'They know each other. Through work. Ray wouldn't like it. It would be like I was dating one of his buddies.'

'They're buddies?'

'Not exactly. I don't think they like each other very much. Carlos owed him some money maybe, I don't know the details. I'll tell him, but just in my own time, okay?'

'Will you go to London?' said Esmé.

'I want him to marry me,' said Catalina simply. 'If I let him buy me an air ticket to London he might think that's enough.'

'You could pay for your own ticket.'

'Ha! Right. To the moon and back.'

Ray and Miguel were drinking beer and celebrating when they got back to her mother's apartment. 'Your brother has given me a job,' said Miguel proudly.

'You already have a job,' said Esmé. 'The car stand.'

'You're always saying the car stand doesn't make enough money.'

'I know,' said Esmé. 'I think you should run it differently: work there better, not less.'

'What do you know, sis?' said Ray. 'Don't listen to her, buddy. You have to move with the punches, isn't that right?'

'He's right,' said Miguel. 'The bar is a better gig.'

'A better investment,' said Ray.

'Investment? You're giving him money?'

'A mutual investment,' said Ray. 'The car stand against the bar.'

Esmé stood with her hands on her hips, her grey eyes wide with steely disbelief. 'A second-generation going concern against a stupid dream of my brother's? And you let him talk you into this? Are you an imbecile?'

Miguel shifted his feet, embarrassed that his wife would talk to him this way in front of Ray.

'Why don't you run down to the store for some more beer, sweetheart?' he said. His eyes pleaded with her to hush her mouth. She didn't want to but she contained her fury and dutifully she held out her hand for some money. It took a few minutes to walk to the store. She could have driven but she needed to clear her head and she hated to waste gas.

She came back with cold beer – not icy cold but a lot colder than her temper.

Watching him drink beer with Ray while they watched the wrestling on the television made it feel almost as if she had never left home.

Before the rainy season was over, Miguel had sold his share of the car stand to one of his brothers and invested everything they had in Ray's bar, a nondescript place that was popular with some of the shadier residents of downtown Cancún. There was never any trouble, but whenever she went there she felt bad vibrations and wanted to leave. It was exactly the kind of place she would expect her mother's boyfriend to drink but she had never seen Carlos there.

Miguel worked longer hours than he had at the car stand and for less reward. He stopped talking about new ideas and seemed more settled.

One evening, just as they were going to bed, he grabbed her by the waist from behind and started nuzzling at her throat.

Even as she squirmed he was whispering into her ear. 'It's time. A little baby, my love, I want us to be a proper family.'

She could only think of a baby with him as the final nail in her coffin. 'I have a proper family,' she said. 'And they both drive me nuts.'

'Then when?'

'I'm twenty-two years old, Miguel, we have plenty of time.'

'My little sister is younger than you and she already has two.'

Esmé wanted to tell him that his little sister was an idiot who had married a man for his money, and not much at that, and who was now trying to hang on to him by firing out successive children in the hope that one day she would have a cute one.

'Your sister was born to be a mother,' she said.

'And what is it that you were born to be?'

'I don't know,' she said. 'I think that's the problem.'

She slept badly that night and was relieved when the first light of dawn meant that she could give up trying. She slipped out of the bed, careful not to wake him, grabbed the laundry sack and made her way out of the apartment and down the stairs.

There was a huge laundry room in the basement of their building. Esmé had never seen a soul in there, save for a pair of persistent cats that were sometimes curled up in the nook between the last machine on the left and the pointless tumble dryer. Was there a Mexican woman alive who would choose to dry wet washing in a hot metal drum in this dingy room rather than under the heat of their nation's sun?

She bit down on the orange she was eating for breakfast, dodging the drips of juice that slipped down her chin. She liked to get the laundry out of the way early so that after she took Miguel downtown to the bar she could watch *telenovelas* on Channel 8 all morning before thinking about dinner. Last night's conversation weighed on her mind. A baby was the next step. It was what everyone was waiting for.

The washing machine ended its cycle. She hauled out the heavy wet sheets and traipsed upstairs. She kicked open the fire door and emerged blinking onto the vast roof. As far as Esmé was concerned, the roof was the building's best feature. On a clear day, though they happened less and less, she could see all the way to the ocean. Even the crisp smell of the fresh laundry lifted her spirits. Up here her frustrations at the way her life was turning out lost their cruel edges and she felt hopeful that things would change, that one day she would find her way out. If she had a baby she would never escape. But escape meant money.

When she got back downstairs, Miguel had finished his breakfast and was helping himself to more coffee from the pot on the stove.

'You'll be late,' she said.

'Just a little bit late won't matter.'

'Let's go.'

They drove most of the way in silence. She pulled up outside the bar and deposited Miguel on the kerb. 'I'll be back at ten,' she said.

'Why don't you let me drive myself?'

'I told you why. I want the truck. You don't need it.'

'What if I want to go somewhere?'

'What if *I* want to go somewhere, hey? Like to get steak for your dinner or to go see your mother?'

'You never go and see my mother,' he said.

'She never invites me.'

'She knows you don't like her.'

Esmé shrugged. 'Whatever. I'll be back at ten.'

As she pulled away he yelled after her. 'You look good driving the truck, honey.'

She saw two tourists, Americans probably. There seemed to be more tourists here every day, so many that they were spilling down the backstreets into places they had never explored before. They heard Miguel shout and they looked at her and smiled, excited to be in this place, maybe even thinking that she was lucky to live here. To sit in her tower and dream of running away. The tourists receded in her rear-view mirror.

She drove on and as she did she noticed that a new building was going up quickly. It looked like another small hotel, and a taco stand near the bus stop now had its menu written out in English too. She saw a woman from the *casa de huespedes* struggling with a load of wet sheets. With added tourism, perhaps the bar could work. Except with Miguel and Ray in charge it was doubtful. She had some ideas for it but they never listened to her; the only women that pair ever listened to were their mamas. Ray needed to sever all his connections with the minor criminals who kept this part of Cancún under their thumbs. She knew that he would be paying protection money somewhere and that pissed her off. If he would only open up his bars to the tourists, the potential for trouble would be eradicated overnight. The police hated trouble in the tourist spots and so the shady mafia types would be sure to give the place a wide berth. The only problem was that Ray still hero-worshipped the petty

103

criminals that were hell-bent on keeping some parts of Cancún to themselves and would do whatever they told him to do, believing that their custom was somehow more valuable to him than hard American dollars.

It was dumb. And now Miguel was invested and that made her invested too. Which was the dumbest thing of all.

It was a blistering day. The laundry would dry in no time. And that's when Esmé had the idea. Miguel had made it very clear that he would not be happy for his wife to work for someone else. But he had said no such thing about working for herself. She made a U-turn in the middle of the road and pulled up outside the next hotel that she saw.

All those tourists.

She knew the bigger hotels would have industrial machines or outside contracts for their laundry, but these modest places were still struggling to cope with the new business. If she could just get them to trust her.

She started small. Her first contracts were from family homes that were doubling up in their bedrooms so that they could rent out the spare space to tourists, broke college kids who would sleep anywhere once they had finished partying at Coco Bongo. They wrecked the sheets too. Esmé tried not to look at them as she piled them into machine after machine down in the basement of her building, propping up the cardboard signs she made for each of her customers by the relevant machine and setting them off at fifteen-minute intervals so that when each one finished she was able to get upstairs, hang the sheets out on the roof and be back down ready for the next one. After a few weeks she was racing up the stairs, in the shape of her life, and had rigged up a small television in the laundry room so that she didn't have to miss a single moment of her *telenovelas*.

The new business fitted seamlessly into the fabric of her life. She dropped off Miguel, picked up the laundry, came home, did it, and dropped it off before she picked him up. He had no idea.

'You seem happier,' he said. 'Is there something you want to tell me?' He thought they were trying for a baby. She hid her birth-control pills in the same place as she hid her money.

As she grew in confidence she began to approach some of the bigger guest houses and eventually a hotel, offering to undercut their existing laundry service, being friendly even when she was getting the brush-off, until eventually word of her professionalism spread and by peak season that year every washing machine in the basement was in action and she had enlisted the help of another woman in the neighbouring block. If the building administration noticed the hike in electricity consumption, they didn't act on it. She asked Miguel if she could take a course in bookkeeping so that she could help him at the bar, and because arithmetic made him nervous he agreed. Esmé found a place off Madero Plaza that taught life skills to women and signed herself up. Six weeks later she knew all she needed to know about keeping track of her money. Slowly her nest egg grew.

Every day, except Mondays when Miguel didn't work

and the housekeeping staff knew not to expect her, she worked hard: sweaty, physical labour that made her sleep better than she ever had before. She was at her happiest when she was standing on the roof, looking at line upon line of dazzling white sheets that might as well have been dollar bills.

'You should go,' she said to her mother as they sat at the kitchen table being ignored. She had enough money for two air tickets out.

'What?'

'You should go to London to visit Carlos. To see what else there is to the world. And I should come with you.'

8

Megan stood under the shower and turned on the water. It cascaded, hot and fierce, over her bad mood. She washed her short, choppy hair and scrubbed herself clean, the accumulated dirt of her weekend swirling down the plughole. Her toes were black from walking across the grass with bare feet. The smells of the festival that clung to her – the smoke and the beer and the falafel truck they had favoured – would be washed away with the mud. She was exhausted. And unless she was remembering things about last night in the wrong order, she had also been very recently, very publicly, dumped by a dick drummer.

She stepped out of the shower and saw that she was noticeably thinner than she had been four days ago – Marlboro lights and Jack D, the diet of the rock gods. She liked the way it made her look, like the lead singer from a cool indie band or something. Even without her make-up, her short dark pixie cut could never make her look like a boy, not with her delicate features, those fragile cheekbones and supple lips that were always pink as if she had been biting them. She pulled on her underwear and was about to put on a clean dress when the door opened and a blast of cold air hit her between the eyes, shortly followed by her mother's accusatory tones.

'You disappear for four days and you don't even say hello? What on earth is wrong with you, Megan?'

'Mum! Get out!' Megan hurled the nearest thing to hand towards the door, her toothbrush, but Harriet caught it deftly and gasped, staring in utter horror at the tattoo of ivy and roses and dragonflies trailing across her daughter's hip.

'Megan!'

She was busted. Surely it had only been a matter of time? She sucked in her stomach, so that at least her mother couldn't criticize her for being fat, and looked down at her beautiful tattoo. It had been quite small to begin with, but she had been back to the tattoo parlour three times and still she wasn't sure that she was finished. It had been easy to hide it from her mother: they were not that close.

'What have you done?' whispered Harriet.

'I take it you don't like it?' Megan pulled on a cherry red tea dress covered in tiny skulls and nonchalantly picked up a pair of tweezers from the side of the bathroom sink, plucking the rogue hairs from her skinny eyebrows. 'You know, Mum, for a Class-A bitch you're not very rock and roll.'

'That's *it*,' said her mother, and made a lunge for Megan, grabbing her roughly by her shoulder and forcing her to turn around and face her. For one rather exhilarating moment, Megan thought she was about to slap her. 'I will not have you treating me like this.'

'Like what?' said Megan.

'Like you do,' said her mother and her voice trembled with emotion. 'As if I'm the problem.'

'You ever think maybe you are?'

She let go of her and put the toothbrush back on the edge of the sink. 'I only have one problem, Megan. You. It's always been you.'

'Well, sorry for ruining your life.'

'It's too late for sorry.' Harriet was almost crying and for a brief moment Megan felt a pinprick of guilt pierce her thick skin. 'You have to go.'

'What?' said Megan.

'I can't live with you any more. I lie awake at night and worry when you don't come back, and then when you do come back I can't wait for you to leave. It's been over a year since you left university, you've said nothing about getting a job. What do you plan to do, Megan? Just turn up every couple of days when you need a hot shower and a hot meal? Turn up, call me a Class-A bitch and then leave?' She grabbed the shower head from the floor of the shower and rinsed off the scum that Megan had left, and then picked the wet towel up off the floor too.

'Are you kicking me out?'

'I think I am, yes.'

'Will you pay my first month on a new place?'

Harriet nodded. The fight slithered out of her now that she had said her piece. She regretted grabbing hold of Megan like that, but it had been years coming.

'And a deposit?'

'Christ, Megan . . .'

'Forget it, I'll go. I'll go now, shall I?' Megan marched across the hallway to her room and started opening up her drawers, but then she realized that everything she needed was still in her backpack from the festival. She had to throw in a couple of extra things for effect, anyway.

Her mother stood in the doorway shaking her head. 'Meg, don't throw a tantrum. You're an adult. I get it. There's a better way to do this.'

'I think you're wrong. I think this is the best way. Quick and painful.' She pulled the rucksack closed and zipped the final zip. 'Don't worry. I have plenty of friends, they'll be fine with it.' She picked her jacket up off the floor and put it on. She struggled with one of the sleeves because it had turned inside out and she felt her face go hot and red. She needed air.

'Will you go to Zane's?'

'We split up.' Saying it out loud made it too real – it was painful. 'Happy? Would you like to say I told you so?'

'Where will you go?' Harriet reached out for her daughter but Megan flinched as if she was a stranger.

'Don't,' she said bitterly. 'Please don't. You can't throw me out on the streets with one hand and then try to break my fall. You want me gone, fine, I don't want to be here, so that's easy. Don't make it hard for me by acting like a mother.'

'I don't know another way to act,' said Harriet. 'That's who I am, since the day you were born.' She reached over and smoothed down the front of her daughter's black leather jacket, brushing away imagined imperfections. 'Believe it or not, I am trying my best.'

Megan snorted. 'Shut up and get out of my way.'

She pounded down the stairs and went straight to the drawer in the kitchen where they kept cash on hand in an empty wallet. Mostly fivers, one twenty. Just seventy pounds. It would have to be enough.

'Megan, stop. This is getting silly.'

She shoved the wallet in her back pocket and walked to the front door where she stuffed her feet into her heaviest, blackest boots. 'It's okay, Mum. It's for the best.' She kissed her mum on the cheek but when she went to hug her Harriet stiffened, so Megan backed away quickly and stomped out into the night.

She knew she would leave home one day. She just hadn't thought it would be like this.

She had lied to her mother. She did not have plenty of friends. Many of them had been Zane's friends and her reaction to the break-up had been a little crazed. Most of them would be scared of her now, even if they didn't have loyalty issues. Which left old friends from uni, none of whom she had seen since the day of her last exam – even those that lived in town, consumed as she was by love of Zane. So that only left Connor.

She called him and asked him to meet her at the café they used to camp out in for hours on rainy weekends, and he did. When he walked in, he saw her sitting on a hard wooden chair staring vacantly at the empty cup of coffee on the table. Her black-rimmed eyes looked huge and tough in her dainty childlike face. The air smelt of fried food.

'So this is where you've been hiding,' he said.

'I go to all the classy spots,' said Megan.

Connor sat down next to her. 'You need a place to stay?'

She nodded rapidly, her eyes filling with inexplicable tears, staring dead ahead at her empty cup. 'I need a place to live,' she said.

He was a man now, she realized. When had he grown so much taller than her? When had his sensible nature transformed from being boring to being comforting? He was as handsome as he had always been, the best-looking boy in school. In time he would forget his childhood friend and move on to fragrant blondes who would make his life easier, instead of a retro brunette with witchy pale grey eyes who had a habit of complicating things.

'I'm glad you called me,' he said. 'I'm glad I'm still the person you call.'

'Mum kicked me out.'

'I guessed that. You can stay with us for a bit.'

'Just a couple of nights,' she said. 'Perhaps a week. I'll figure something out.'

His parents were out. Connor still had the bed they slept in together when they were children. He kept the room very dark; he found it hard to sleep if there was light in the room, and so for as long as she could remember Connor's bedroom at night had been exciting. She climbed in next to him and buried her face in his neck. He hugged her tightly for a while and then they started kissing. His kisses were nothing like Zane's. Zane just kissed her with his mouth, whereas when Connor kissed her it felt like a connection that went far deeper. She liked the way his hands roamed over her shoulders. He stopped kissing her and she snuggled back into his shoulder.

'Do you think this is why they stopped letting us have sleepovers?' she said.

'Something like that,' he said.

They never really discussed the kissing thing. It was just something they did. It started when they were twelve or thirteen and never really stopped. Only kisses, nothing more, and though it had been months since they'd last seen each other, it was understood that they would pick up the kissing again.

'What do you think you'll do?'

'I might travel,' she said.

'You'll need money,' he said.

'I'm going to sell my necklace.' Her fingers went to the pendant at her throat, a gold star and a creamy iridescent opal in the shape of a crescent moon.

'You can't sell that,' he said. 'You love it.'

'It's only a necklace. There's that shop on the high street. They said they'd give me two hundred pounds.'

'That won't get you very far.'

'I've got another seventy.'

'Megan, you can't run away when things get a little bit tough.'

'Why not?' she said. 'Seriously? Why not?' The pitch of her voice tightened. 'I need a job, I need a place to live. Why does it have to be round here?'

'It's just not what people do,' said Connor.

'Since when were we people?'

'We?'

'You could come with me,' she said.

He didn't say anything and she wished that she hadn't asked. She felt their easy closeness strain at the edges and remembered too late that she had nowhere else to go tonight and she must take care not to get into an argument.

'I've got my own stuff, Megs,' he said quietly. 'College and whatever.'

'I was *kidding*! God, you're such a loser.'

Eventually Connor fell asleep. Megan lay awake and listened to him lying next to her until his steady breath started to sound like breaking waves, so that when she finally fell asleep she dreamt of the sea and the secret dream that nobody knew, not even Connor.

Mexico.

9

Claudia slipped the postcard from Las Vegas between the pages of her journal. Every night before she went to sleep she looked at it again and wondered if her father might still be alive. She decided that if she was to dream about him then it would be a sign. But she never did. She wondered if that was a sign of something else instead but she couldn't decide what. For once she actually wanted something from her mother. The truth.

'Why don't you call her?' suggested David. 'Why do you have to go all the way out there?' He was mildly sulky. She loved that he was distraught at the idea of them being apart. She loved everything about him. He had transformed her from a spoilt girl with an empty life into a woman in control of her own destiny. And her destiny was wrapped up in him.

'But I always do. If I didn't see my mother every year I am sure she would forget what I look like.'

'But what about me?'

'You won't forget what I look like. If you like, I could give you a photograph.' Her blue eyes simmered.

'What kind of photograph?'

'Use your imagination.'

He kissed her. 'Make me a promise, little Claudia. When you come back, we will never spend another night apart.'

'I promise,' she whispered.

She would stay for as long as it took to get some answers. And then she would return. After all these years of feeling like a scarlet poppy in a field of pale gold corn, at last somewhere felt like home.

They spent their last night together before she left at a hotel in Colonia Roma, a downtown neighbourhood of faded glamour and Cuban music. She was dreading the moment when it was time to say goodbye to him. She did not know how she would find the strength to let him go, even for just one day. As Camille Lepage might say, she was sick in love. Even leaving him, as awful as it was, had a romantic urgency that she was fast becoming addicted to. A break would do them both good and then afterwards, when she got back, then they would probably get engaged.

Her mother would hate it. She would say he was after her money. But if he was after her money he would have chosen another girl who would have all the social connections to launch him into the political career he was passionate about. He would be an incredible force for good in the Federal District, taking everything they worked on to the next level. They could do it together.

She took him to see a timba band in a smoky cellar bar and they drank Argentinean Malbec and whispered sweet nothings through the piano solos. Later on they danced, oblivious to the rest of the patrons, her head on his shoulder, trying to breathe in the essence of him and hold it in her senses for the separation ahead.

He came to the airport to see her off and when they called her flight she started to cry.

'Don't,' he said. 'It's one summer. You'll make contacts for the centre,' said David. 'For our future.'

It was a word they used all the time now, as if the future was taken care of. Perhaps that was why she was drawn to the past. The postcard from Las Vegas was tucked into the pages of her journal like a secret she kept to herself.

'All those rich friends of your mother's with nobody to love,' he said. 'They'll take one look at that beautiful smile and take out their cheque books.'

She laughed through her tears and he kissed away what was left of them. When the plane took off she wondered if he was down there watching the trail it left across the sky.

Her mother never met anyone at the airport. Her version of a warm welcome was to arrange to have one hundred pounds in cash waiting at the British Airways desk. That would pay for a black cab to the flat in Pimlico where Lucy had lived since she was eighteen.

Even though it was summer, the cool evening air still came as a surprise after the oppressive heat of Mexico City. It felt more like spring. She asked the cab to drop her at the bridge, so that she could walk along the Thames past Lupus Street and the dark green spaces of St Saviour's.

117

The Pimlico flat had small high windows and views of the river from the enormous kitchen. The furnishing was rich and expressive, filled with curios from many travels and an art collection of pieces that were clearly chosen more for romantic appeal than value. If Lucy hadn't been her mother, Claudia suspected that she would have liked her very much, but sadly as a mother she was a disaster.

It took her less than three minutes to make a comment about her daughter's weight.

'You're so thin!' said Lucy, pinching her hip. 'Skin and bone.'

'I was too fat at Christmas,' said Claudia lightly, 'so you must have missed the moment I was perfect. What a shame.'

She was not in the habit of making smart remarks and Lucy was momentarily astonished. There was something new in her daughter's eyes, a quiet confidence, and no doubt she would soon learn the reasons for it. She bounced over Claudia's sarcasm with her habitual lightness 'Never mind, I'm sure you looked wonderful. Let's eat.'

'Out?' Claudia had not inherited her love of cooking from her mother. She couldn't remember the last time her mother had fixed her anything that wasn't a drink.

'Of course out. I hope you kept the taxi waiting.'

What might she have inherited from her mother if she had been raised properly by her rather than her being this arbitrary presence, like a cool, if thoughtless, aunt? A drink problem, possibly, and an irresponsible attitude.

'That's a sweet dress,' said Lucy, casting her eye over one of the wrap dresses that Claudia was wearing, a dark

118

indigo colour that looked striking against her pale skin and blond hair. It wasn't a compliment exactly because she made 'sweet' sound rather sour, but Claudia jumped on it and started to explain about the Women's Centre and the work she was doing there.

'I'm sorry,' said Lucy, missing the point entirely, 'I should have given you a while to freshen up and change your outfit.'

Over dinner at her mother's favourite restaurant in Mayfair, they talked about the usual things: school, Pappy and the mutual acquaintances they would see over the summer period. After they ordered dessert, Claudia mentioned the postcard that she had found in her mother's bedroom.

'In my room?'

'I hope you don't mind.'

'Not really.' Lucy held out her hand and after a pause she clearly deemed to be too long she clicked her fingers. 'Well, give it to me then. How long is this going to take?'

Claudia carefully removed the postcard from its place in her journal and passed it to her mother. She studied her face for a reaction and was convinced she saw a flicker of something that looked like longing.

'Sweetheart, I don't remember ever seeing this post-card before. I'm sorry. I have a lot of friends.'

'Friends called Danny?'

'Is everything okay? Are you and Pappy getting on over there? He says you are, we speak all the time. He says you are doing wonderfully well and that you've been involving yourself with charity work. A centre? For children, is it? He tells me you are happy? Are you happy?'

'Danny was my father's name. You told me he died.'

119

'No darling, I told you he might have died.'

'But you didn't.' Her voice climbed a pitch, and with a breath she brought herself back under control. It wouldn't do to act like a child. 'I would remember something like that. You told me he died before I was born.'

'That's not what I said. Is that what I said?' Lucy fanned herself with the postcard and then put it down on the table to pick up her glass. She took a sip of wine and seemed revived, then she went to put her glass back on the table. Claudia's hand darted out to snatch the post-card away before her mother could use it as a coaster. She tucked it back into her journal and placed her hands in her lap, forcing herself to take measured breaths and remain calm in the face of such offence. 'I don't want to get into who said what.'

'Thank Christ,' said Lucy. She grinned.

'But this postcard was sent to Oxfordshire. I found it at Pappy's. Why take it all that way to Mexico City if you can't even remember who it's from?'

'I can assure you that neither of those things was out of any sentimental attachment to your father. It's not from him.'

'So you're saying that Danny, my father, may or may not be dead, but that this postcard isn't from him?' She knew she was very close to losing her internal battle to stay calm and measured. She wanted to breathe but it seemed impossible.

'Oh, who knows what I'm saying?' snapped Lucy. 'I thought you didn't want specifics. You want to try and find your father, be my guest. I have no idea what happened to him. We met on an island in the Yucatán. I tried

120

to get in touch with him when I found out I was pregnant and I was told there had been an incident on the island and he'd died.'

'How can you be so casual about it? This is my father. You had a baby with him. You had sex with him. Is that what you mean by knowing a lot of people? You're a tramp, basically?'

'Maybe I am, but I'm still your mother.'

'Oh please, just barely.'

Lucy sighed deeply. 'Must we have this argument every time we see each other?'

'No mother, today we are having a different one. You tell me as much as you can remember about Danny, and I'll take it from there.'

'What were you doing going through my private things?'

'We were looking for some matches.'

'We?'

She didn't want to tell her mother about David like this, not in the midst of a row. It was wrong, all wrong, that her mother's first impression of the man she would soon marry would be a picture him riffling through the drawers in her bedroom. It would cheapen their commitment. It would cheapen him. She was aware of what Lucy would say if she knew her daughter was in love with a man from the slums. 'A friend,' she said.

'Why did you want matches?' There was a mischievous tone in her mother's voice, as if she knew she had won a point in a game.

Claudia hung her head. For all her mother's faults she was irresistibly playful. 'To light candles.'

Lucy winked. 'Very romantic, yes?'

'Yes, very. It was a few months ago now. His name is David.'

There was a long pause, during which their desserts were served.

'Do you want to tell me about him?'

'You first, Mother.'

'Call me Lucy,' she said, and ordered another bottle of wine. 'Danny? We met in Mexico, like I said. An island near Cancún.'

'What was it called?'

'I don't remember.'

Claudia paused briefly in her interrogation and looked for the flicker of a lie in her mother's eyes. The problem was that their smoky black flashes made it look as though she was lying all the time.

'What were you doing in Cancún?'

'A holiday. Sailing.'

'Who with?'

'Leo, Sawyer, a couple of others, you don't know them.'

'Sawyer Stone?'

Lucy nodded.

'I know Sawyer. Would he remember anything, do you think?'

Lucy finished off her dessert. 'Darling, I doubt he would even remember Mexico. He was only about eighteen, a baby. He's been in the army an entire lifetime since then. You have to understand what it was like in those days: it was one island paradise after another. It was wonderful.'

'I know, you told me, and having a child would have

ruined it all. Was he the same, Danny? The same as you, Mother?'

'Lucy,' she corrected again. She pushed aside her bowl and drummed her fingers on the table, the way she always did after a meal, a ghost of the cigarette smoker she used to be. 'I didn't know your father very well. When I found out I was pregnant, I looked for him, but he'd gone.'

'But the postcard!' She pushed it back into the conversation. 'How do you know this isn't from him? How do you know? How can you be so sure? How do you know?'

Claudia was shouting, she couldn't stop herself. Lucy recoiled, mortally embarrassed. Across the room, a young woman her own age was staring at them, completely ignoring the older man at her table to shamelessly watch Claudia's futile struggle to hold back her tears. Two old ladies stopped their conversation to look across.

She was making a scene. She heard David's voice in her head, his soft reassurances, his love for her, and gradually her thoughts calmed and her anger settled. 'It isn't that you don't know, *Lucy*,' she said, through gritted teeth. 'You don't care.'

She pushed her chair back from the table and stumbled blindly to the toilets where she gripped onto the edges of the sink and wondered if she was about to throw up. A wave of nausea broke over her and then subsided.

She quickly tidied up her face. Her mother hated being left alone for too long in restaurants almost as much as she hated people who made a scene. Claudia was guilty of both.

As it turned out, she need not have worried. When

123

Claudia went back out to the restaurant her mother had left.

Later that night she stole through her mother's address book as furtively as if she was riffling through her wallet until she found the old name that she was looking for. If her mother wouldn't give her any answers, then she would keep looking until she found someone that could.

Outside Saywer Stone's stark warehouse conversion, she asked the black cab to wait in the fine drizzle. She wasn't confident of her ability to find another way to get home. Simply getting to this odd part of London had been exhausting. Hidden away behind the river, miles from her comfort zone, with nothing but his address on a slip of paper. And this she tucked close to her heart as if it was the only key to her past. She tightened the belt on her trench coat and hopped out onto the damp street to peer at the long list of names next to a panel of bells until she saw it. One word. Sawyer. At last. Her knees felt weak.

She rang the bell but there was no answer.

Her eyes darted from the idling cab, back to the bell. She pressed it again. Still nothing. Just as she was about to give up and go home, the intercom crackled.

'What?'

'Um, I'm looking for Sawyer Stone.'

'And what?'

'And I'd like to speak to him.'

'Go ahead.'

'Sawyer? Could I . . . can't I come in?'

'It's a bad time.'

She pulled herself in closer to the wall to allow a group of men to pass her on the street. They laughed. But they weren't laughing at her; it took her a moment to realize that.

'Please,' she said. 'My name is Claudia, my mother is Lucy Egerton.'

Silence.

Then, 'Hang on.'

Her knees buckled with relief. A buzz and she pushed open the door. She gave the taxi driver a cheery wave and then worried that he would take that as a sign to leave. She panicked until she remembered she hadn't given him his fare and he would be highly unlikely to leave without that.

Sawyer was waiting for her in his open doorway and buttoning up his shirt. His feet were bare and there were damp curls of his hair clinging to his forehead, dark hair, flecked with stubborn grey. She wondered if he had just climbed out of the shower. He filled the doorway easily; he was over six foot tall with muscles that gave him bulk and substance. He was the kind of effortlessly handsome older man who breaks hearts without meaning to. She remembered that Lucy told her he had been to war, on the front line, and she wondered if that was where the hostile look in his eyes came from, or if he was just angry all the time. He glared at her with stern brown eyes and a casual air of authority. She wondered if he knew that looking as if he would crush anyone who got in his way was undeniably attractive to any woman who ever had a hero fantasy.

'Has something happened to Lucy?'

'She's fine,' said Claudia, and then when it became clear that he expected her to state her business on his doorstep, she told him she wanted to ask him about Mexico in the eighties.

'Do you remember a man by the name of Danny Featherbow?'

He shook his head, then asked if Danny was the Jamaican guy from Acapulco, and then shook his head again. 'Sorry,' he said, and shrugged. He wandered over to the enormous fridge against the bare brick wall and took out a bottle of water.

'You're sure?' she pleaded. 'It was near Cancún, an island. I'm not sure of the name; maybe if you had some time to think about it?'

He finished almost the entire bottle in one long, satisfying swig. 'Do you want something to drink?'

'No, thank you,' she said, automatically polite. He grinned. His brown eyes twinkled, distracting her. But his smile made her feel on edge, not as though she was wasting his time, exactly, but as if she was wasting her own. Pity, that's what it was, he pitied her.

'Did Lucy say that I would remember him?'

Claudia's despair was etched into the fixed lines of her face as she pulled herself back from the brink of tears. She was tired. She was tired of dead-ends and feeling jealous of people that had met her father and resentful that they couldn't remember a single thing about him.

'No,' she said. 'Lucy made it pretty clear that you were a boatload of rich kids who were so wrapped up in your own good time you didn't care about anyone else.'

'Excuse me?'

'He was my father. Danny was my father. And nobody can tell me anything.'

'What do you want to know?'

'Who he was, what he was like, if he was a good man. I want to know what happened to him. And if he's still alive I want to know where he is.'

Sawyer chuckled and she felt like slapping him. He saw the anger flicker across her face and his laughter stopped. 'I'm sorry,' he said. 'But if I'm your best hope, then you're going to have to scale that down.'

'I just want to know more about him than his name.'

'You're talking about a moment in time over twenty years ago. What do you expect? You want Lucy or me to tell you your father was a good man? Fine. Yeah, sure, I remember him, real nice guy, the best. No idea what happened to him.'

'Don't patronize me.'

'Then don't stand in my home looking at me like it's my fault your past is not the pretty little picture you want it to be. It's that way for everyone. I don't remember him, I barely remember the name.'

She grasped at the chink in his protestations. 'So you knew his name? When I said it? You said you barely remember it, so that means you do remember it a little?'

He stared at her. Then his eyes flicked to a clock on the wall and she knew that she had lost him.

'Let it go,' he said. 'Your own mother couldn't tell you the things you wanted to hear and I'm guessing she knew a whole lot more about him than I did. They were lovers. She was crazy about him.'

'I know my mother, Mr Stone. That doesn't have to mean very much.'

'It's just Sawyer,' he said. 'Or Major, perhaps, but not Mr Stone, okay?'

She was sick of people who were more concerned with the way they were addressed than the question that was being asked. She was sick of all of them.

'Sorry to trouble you, *Sawyer*. I'll leave you to your afternoon.'

She might not like this man but she still didn't want him to see her cry. She spun on her heels and cursed herself for caring so much about Danny, when nobody else seemed to care about him at all.

The black cab was waiting for her and the cabbie grinned when she re-emerged. She knew that it might make her pathetic but she was grateful for his smile. She slipped into the back seat. 'Where to, love?' he said, reasonably.

'I don't know.'

The fare continued to click and climb and he didn't seem at all perturbed that she sat frozen in the back seat, tears sliding down her face, searching her handbag for a tissue.

Then a hammering on the window made her heart stop, and there was Sawyer, still without shoes, holding up his hands in a gesture of peace. She opened the window.

'Des Amparados,' he said.

'What?'

'Des Amparados, that was the name of the island where we met Danny. You have a pen?'

She produced one from her bag and he grabbed her wrist and wrote it on the back of her hand like a tattoo. 'Thank you,' she whispered.

'A life tip: Don't expect too much, kid,' he said. 'You'll only be disappointed in the end.'

'I can live with disappointment,' she said. 'I can't live with low expectations.'

'Suit yourself. Good luck.' And then he was gone.

She took a deep breath and pulled herself up straight. 'Marylebone,' she said.

Claudia caught the train back to the place she still couldn't think of as home, daydreaming of islands in the sun and a man who could be her long-lost father.

She arrived home later that evening and immediately told her mother that she didn't think much of her friends.

'Really? Sawyer said he liked you.'

'You spoke to Sawyer?' said Claudia.

'He called me after you left. I think he was annoyed that I had let you drop in on him like that.'

'You make it sound like he had something to hide.'

'Don't be so melodramatic,' said Lucy. 'It isn't like he's my greatest friend. I've barely seen him all year – a quick hello at a mediocre party – and we haven't been together, just the two of us, forever. Was he helpful at all?'

'Not in the slightest.' She didn't want to tell her mother she had discovered the name of the island. For now it was her secret.

She paid a visit to Stanfords, the map shop in Covent Garden, where she studied charts of the Yucatán coast. Not all of them named the little speck out to the east of

Cancún beyond Isla Mujeres. But eventually she found one that did and there it was, the same name he had given her, Des Amparados. She searched through every guidebook in the shop but none of them mentioned it, the little lost island.

The summer drifted from one dull party to another, and she contented herself with dreams of a paradise where her father still lived. She liked to imagine him fishing. Or staring at the night sky, seeing the same moon she saw. It took her weeks but eventually she came to realize that if she wanted to find out more about Des Amparados and Danny Featherbow, then she would have to go there.

After a hot August day spent losing a tennis game to her mother and a man she clearly had designs on, making small talk with his odious son, Claudia decided that she'd had enough.

'I'm going back to Mexico next week,' she said.

'Don't be silly, darling, we've got the reception at the Royal Society. After that, we'll see.'

There was a small stack of letters on the table on the hallway. The cleaner must have put them there. The one on top had a Mexico City postmark on a pale cream envelope.

'I want to go home,' she said.

'You seem to forget that I'm the one who pays for your ticket.'

'So what are you saying? You'll keep me here against my will?'

She dropped her bag on the table and ripped open the envelope, taking out the letter folded inside.

'Don't be silly, but perhaps you'll think twice before you . . . Sweetheart? Sweetheart?'

Claudia was staring at the letter in her hand and her face had gone sickly pale. A newspaper cutting fluttered to the floor. A wedding announcement: an aspiring politician and a young heiress had got married in Mexico City. David had married Camille Lepage.

10

Megan had told many lies to her mother and so when she told her the story about a flat-share above the delicatessen in the High Street, she almost believed it herself. She felt momentarily sad that she wouldn't be living with the fictional 'Tricia', a newly trained hairdresser from Colchester. And then she remembered the truth and grinned.

'It's two eighty a month,' she said, 'plus deposit.' By Saturday she would be partying on her very own beach next to Mayan ruins. 'And what about next month and the month after that?' said Harriet.

'That's the best thing!' said Megan. 'Tricia has lined me up with a job at the salon where she works! It's on reception, so I won't be cutting hair, don't worry.' Perhaps she should tone down the joviality a touch – she hadn't been this friendly towards her mother in years. 'Part-time at first, but that will cover my rent if I'm careful and the manager guy that I met said there might be more hours as and when. Otherwise I can just get a bar job.'

'It might be harder than you think. You don't have any bar experience.'

'I worked at loads of bars during university. I just never told you because I thought you might stop sending me money.'

'Megan!'

'Come on. Seriously, after rent and books and food I had about four quid left to play with. What kind of experience would I have had with that?'

Harriet frowned. 'And now you get to work as a part-time receptionist. I'm so glad I sacrificed three more years of my life for your continuing education.'

'Are you going to give me the money or not?'

They glared at each other. Megan backtracked through the conversation and tried to work out where her plan to be soft and smiley had derailed. But Mum was reaching for her chequebook, so who cared? Different method, same result.

'Three sixty all together,' she said. Then: 'I really appreciate it,' as an afterthought.

'This is a loan, Megan,' said Harriet. 'I expect to be paid back at some point.'

Whatever.

She met Connor for a goodbye drink. She chose a pub near an industrial estate at the edge of town. She was annoyed when they asked her for ID at the bar, even though they did that everywhere.

'You can't blame them,' said Connor. 'You still look about thirteen, it doesn't matter how much of that stuff you paint on your eyes.'

'It's only because I'm short.'

'Okay, baby-face, whatever you say.'

She punched him on the shoulder and then handed him his pint.

'Why this place?' asked Connor.

'You'll see, I hope.'

'How cryptic.'

They found a table and before long they were laughing about the first time they got drunk together at fourteen and added Ribena to every cocktail to sweeten the harsh taste of alcohol.

'I can still hear you squealing: *don't throw up, oh God, don't throw up*,' he said.

The carpet in the Watkins' front room had been a very pale cream; the booze churning in his belly was deep, sugary purple. It was ghastly and hilarious. But the moment she held most clearly from that night was later, when the room stopped spinning, they stopped laughing, she had slipped out of her bra and lay back across the carpet with her shirt undone, closing her eyes so that she couldn't see him staring. She wondered if he was remembering that night too, and she pushed down a tickle of excitement. She coughed.

'And you didn't throw up,' she said, dragging her attention out of the past and allowing the warm memory to remain. 'So it worked.'

'I would never have thrown up,' he said. 'I knew that if I threw up on your mother's cream carpet there was no way you would have let me kiss you.'

Her good mood evaporated with a hiss of displeasure. 'Why do you have to do that?'

'Do what?'

'We were having a good time. I'm leaving on a jet plane. The whole bit. Do you wish I wasn't going?' She was confused. In his bedroom things were dark and easy, sweet and warm. Out in the real world he made her feel weak and unsettled. It was a good idea to leave town before things between them got more complicated than they already were.

'No. I think you should go. I think it will be an adventure.'

'Then stop – ' she grasped for the right word and when she found it she rolled her eyes – 'stop flirting with me.'

'Okay. But can I say one last nice thing?'

'If you must.' She took a swig of her beer and looked off to the side, like an uninterested French girl.

'I flirt with you because I love you. It's the same reason that I kiss you. I know the score: you have Mexico and I have my masters; we're young. When we get together, properly together, you and me, it'll be a big deal, a forever thing. You know that too, why else would you be running away?'

'How do you know about Mexico?'

'You told me. Don't you remember? You told me you were the rightful owner of an island and that one day you would go there and claim it. I think that's when it started really.'

'When what started?'

'The love.' His eyes were serious and laughing all at the same time, and she wondered if he'd slipped a depth charge into her beer because suddenly she felt kind of drunk.

She took another sip of her drink. 'Is that it? You done?'

His soaring confession over, his confidence plummeted. 'I suppose.'

'You love me?' she said.

'Let's say that I do.'

'And I love you too?'

'Do you?'

The world capsized and she lurched towards the truth. She liked the way that she was around Connor, but that's because she felt as though she was still an eleven-year-old kid who loved life and not the messy grown-up she had become. She had to change. First her teachers, then her tutors, and always her mother; all of them telling her that she needed to transform herself, to be someone different.

Connor was looking at her as if she was crazy. 'You're telling me this is a one-way thing? Me and you? And I'm supposed to believe that? Come on, you feel it. We're in love. We're mad about each other. This is real.'

'You're dreaming,' she said.

'Ouch,' he whispered. 'She cuts me down.' He grinned and she wanted to kiss him and the moment lingered between them, humming softly, and then drifted by.

Connor loves me.

He loves me.

He looked away first, glancing down.

'You sold your necklace,' he said at last.

Her hand flew to her naked throat. 'Yeah, just today, that place on the high street. I . . .' She broke off and sprang upright in her chair, craning for a better look at the man who had just walked in. 'Look,' she said, and pointed. 'It's Alan Watkins.'

'Your dad?'

136

She was surprised to feel sad. Nostalgic for her fabricated past. 'No, not my dad, is it? But yeah.'

'I haven't seen him for years,' said Connor. 'Did you know he'd be here?'

'He still works at the cable place,' said Megan. He looked like he had when he lived with them, when she thought she was his, with small differences. A little softer around the edges where he had put on some weight. Less hair. The same pair of glasses. 'I kept tabs,' she said. 'Figured there was a good chance he'd still have the same Friday night ritual.'

'He looks old,' said Connor, and he was right.

'I'll be back,' she said, and she slipped from her seat. Her head was light from the way that Connor had been looking at her and she walked slowly, trying to recall his exact words. If she had known that this particular conversation was finally going to happen then she never would have brought him here tonight. She was nervous enough already at the prospect of fleecing her old man.

She walked over to the crowded bar and placed herself next to Alan Watkins. She hated it when people sat at a busy bar, getting in the way, while others were trying to get served. He looked basically the same, older like Connor had said, but there was something else different about him and it took her a minute to realize she had never seen him wearing jeans before. Eleven years they had lived in the same house and not once a pair of jeans.

She tried to look stunned when she saw him. 'Dad?' she whispered, her voice catching on the single syllable.

He saw her and winced. 'Megan? Good God, kid. How are you?'

She smiled her most vulnerable smile. 'Sorry, I shouldn't say Dad. What should I . . . should I call you Alan?'

'What are you doing in a pub?'

'Having a drink,' she said, and grinned. 'How are things? I heard you got married?'

'Yeah.' He shifted on his stool and his relief was palpable when the barman asked for his order and he had a minute to collect his thoughts. He turned back, having clearly decided that forced joviality would get him through. 'What about you, love? How have you been? How's your mum?'

When she was about eight years old, Megan had sometimes cried herself to sleep because she had the distinct impression that her father, this man she thought was her father, didn't like her very much. That there was nothing she could do that would make him love her. At the time they had told her she was being silly. It was possible, she supposed, but it was also possible that his love was a lie right from the start. Something else entirely bridged the space between them now. Curiosity. Impatience even. And mistrust.

'Mum's fine thanks, I'll tell her you asked.'

'Send her my best. And how are you?'

'I finished uni,' she said. 'And I'm about to go away for a bit. Travelling. Latin America. I did Spanish A level.' There was no need to tell him she had failed the written part of the exam and barely scraped into a bad university with her two dismal passes. She felt absolutely no guilt for bending the truth; it was nowhere near as bad as what they had done to her. Nothing could be as bad as that. Finding out the way she had, it was a wonder she wasn't even more messed up. So she had a few issues. So what?

'Good for you,' he said. 'I thought about you a lot, you know. It wasn't right that you got caught up in it all, it wasn't right. Here, let me buy you a drink.'

She hesitated, or at least pretended to. 'Okay then,' she said. 'Half a lager, please. Cheers.'

His pint arrived; her drink was ordered and served; money was exchanged. He seemed almost surprised to see her still there when the business was completed.

'So where are you off to then?' he said. His smile was fixed, the corners of his mouth started to strain.

'It all depends on money. I've been saving really hard and I'll try and live cheaply while I'm out there. I want to do some volunteering, children or maybe animals, you know? Work on my Spanish. I think it will be good for me, and Mum needs a break from my drama.' She tapped into the part of him that would surely remember the tension at home.

A few more sips of his pint, and good old Alan was reaching for his wallet, still stuffed with twenties like it always had been, and tucking a fold of notes into her hand, patting it closed and telling her he was sorry about everything.

She acted as if she was moved, kissed his cheek when she thanked him, and she waited until she was back at her table with Connor to count the money.

'Two hundred,' she said. 'Prick.'

He squeezed her hand underneath the table. Perhaps he was the perfect person to bring, after all.

'Anyone else to try and fleece?' asked Connor.

139

'Only you, amigo,' she said, her eyes sparkling with triumph. With the money from her mum, and Alan, the sale of her beloved necklace and her album collection, she felt rich. And very excited.

'Let's do a shot of tequila,' she said impulsively.

'Let's not,' said Connor. 'You're already fairly drunk. Let's get home so that you don't spend the first day of your brand-new life feeling like death.'

'The man makes a fair point.'

Her eyes sought out Alan one last time at the bar as they walked out. She saw him staring into space, drink in hand. She wondered if he might be thinking about her.

The cold air hit them with a sobering slap. 'This time tomorrow I'll have sunscreen on,' she said.

'You can't stand sunscreen.'

'I can't stand you either,' she said, 'but that doesn't stop me.'

'Here.' He shoved something into her hand. 'It's only fifty quid,' he said. 'Maybe enough to keep the wolves from the door for a night or two if you get stretched.'

She pushed it back at him. 'Don't be silly,' she said, 'I can't take your money. Spend it on a haircut.'

'Come on, Megs.'

'Really,' she said. 'I won't need it. Thanks, but you keep it.'

'You're sure?'

They faced each other in the dark street and he shuffled his feet. 'So this is goodbye?'

'Don't get pathetic,' she said. She flinched when he drew her into his arms. They had never kissed in the open before. Even though the night was dark and there

140

was nobody around, it still felt brazen. Almost as if they were a couple. If they were a couple they would kiss this way all the time. They would be one of those sickening couples that couldn't keep their hands off each other and spend parties absorbed in conversation rather than mingling and in the end they would stop going to parties and they would stay at home and kiss, and kiss, and kiss.

She pulled away sharply. 'Take it easy,' she said, stuffing her hands in her pockets. She was grateful for the darkness. A blush had stolen across her cheeks and she was confused. 'I'll . . .' But she couldn't say it.

'I'll miss you too,' he said.

On the train to the airport she cried and cried.

11

There was a moment on the flight to Mexico when Megan thought that they might crash. The plane dropped abruptly and the empty plastic cup on her tray table bounced into the air and she could have sworn she saw it levitate in the gravitational pull before it toppled onto its side. The fasten seat belts sign pinged on. The crew passed through the cabin with cold efficiency, their neutral expressions impossible to read, but she felt the atmosphere in the plane turn as the assorted package tourists gulped back what was left of the free booze and gripped more tightly onto the armrests. She found her own thoughts turning towards what kind of legacy she would leave and how her mother would have to be grateful for her tattoo when it made it easier to identify her daughter's body. Shortly after this morbid thought pattern, the seat belt light went off and the moment had gone. She waited for a sense of relief but none came. Dying in a plane crash would have been the most glamorous thing she had ever done.

The cab driver was not the type to open the door for his fares. 'Where to?' he said.

She looked blank.

'Which hotel?'

'I want to go to the beach.'

'Huh?'

'*La playa?*'

'Which hotel?'

Behind her, a middle-aged American and his wife were struggling with their luggage and having an argument about the trolley they had left behind. The taxi driver looked over Megan's shoulder and evidently considered them a better fare. 'Which hotel?' he shouted at them. There was a sharp retort across the street as a shuttle bus narrowly avoided a collision with a tour group.

The American responded promptly. 'The Fiesta Plaza, how much?'

'Twenty-three dollars, flat fare, tip extra.'

The man started thumbing through a guidebook but his wife, still struggling with the wheels on their suitcase, gave him a shove and told him just to get in the goddamn car.

Megan was buffeted to the back of the queue and stepped away. Twenty-three dollars plus tip? If it was that much for the cabs, then how much was it going to cost for a hotel? Why had she been so set on the romance of spontaneity, keen to blow into town like the warm Caribbean wind and see which way she drifted? An island? She was an idiot. Twenty-three dollars for a cab? For one thing she didn't have any dollars – she had changed all her money into Mexican pesos at the Post Office yesterday before her flight. It had made her feel incredibly efficient. They were in Mexico, why were they asking for dollars? This

143

was Mexico, right? She hadn't stumbled off the plane in a layover airport with a huge Latino population, had she?

She hailed the next cab in line.

'Twenty-three dollars,' said the driver. 'Tip extra.'

'I know,' she said and, when he looked confused, '*yo se.*' In her clunking Spanish she asked if there was a bus stand and, after sucking the air through his teeth to demonstrate his displeasure, he told her that there were two, a short walk away, on the same side of the road. Close inspection revealed that one bus went to the 'hotel zone' and one was an express that went 'downtown', and though really she would do well to find a place to sleep, she figured it was still early and surely there might be places to stay downtown too. She hoisted her backpack onto her shoulders and climbed aboard the bus.

Mexico. At last. She was so close now and yet something was holding her back from making the final leg of her journey across the sea to the island. Because she was afraid of what she would find. Better then to find a cheap place to stay and get settled, rather than scudding onto the island like a ballistic missile and demanding her legacy.

She wasn't being cowardly, just sensible.

The uniformed bus driver had a feel for speed. It was hot on the bus and she loved it. They whipped down a highway that offered tantalizing views of the sparkling waters between mammoth hotel complexes that were distinctly styled to each have its own brand identity – and yet all somehow looked the same: concrete stacks of superior doubles and junior suites. On the near side of the road were a few low-rise shopping complexes and behind them an inky lagoon. She grabbed onto a metal handrail when they raced round a corner to stop herself from sliding off the leatherette seat. The bus didn't stop for a while and when finally it did the hotels had disappeared and they were in a big industrial area that felt as if it was in the middle of nowhere.

Nevertheless the passengers disgorged and Megan was obliged to follow suit. The prospect of adventure kept a smile plastered on her face and when she stepped from the bus she could feel the heat from the street rising up through the rubber soles of her flip-flops. She looked around. There was a Walmart, more buses, which fed off to God knows where, and a deserted playground. This was downtown? She followed the biggest group blindly, tagging after them like the lost lamb she was, until eventually they pitched up outside a large warehouse with a sign made of corrugated steel, which said Mercado 28.

Again, she questioned herself. Why not just go to the island? Wasn't that why she was here?

There were a few tired market stalls on the street outside, selling everything from batteries to lipstick. She ignored them and followed the crowd inside and was immediately enveloped in the noise and colour of one of Cancún's chaotic indoor markets. Her hand went to her throat, and she was reminded again that she had sold her necklace. Only now did she realize she had a nervous habit of touching her pendant for reassurance.

She felt a long way from home.

When she went to the island, what then? She would be better off enjoying everything Cancún had to offer.

She wandered among the rows of traders, hitching her rucksack higher onto her shoulder and inhaling the scent

145

of hot fried *buñuelos* that were being nimbly rolled in sugar before being bagged up in tens and sold for pennies. She bought some. They were still hot and when her teeth cracked through the delicate, crispy veneer the soft dough inside steamed, filling her mouth with sweet warmth. She saw a stall festooned with brightly coloured sarongs and thought about buying one but figured she could always come back tomorrow when she knew what she was doing.

The next row of stalls was jewellery, out of reach under glass-topped tables. She lingered over a pendant of freshwater pearls, and decided that when she got herself settled she would buy herself a new necklace. Was it getting late? She should have thought to buy a watch.

She found a stall that sold pure coconut oil, solid white putty that made her smell like a Bounty bar. She rubbed it on her hands and kept lifting them to her face so that she could smell them.

When she stopped to buy a bag of irresistible yellow tomatoes, she asked the trader the time and promised herself she would leave shortly, find a place to stay and get some rest; she could explore another day.

Panic gripped her. Where was she going to sleep?

Dragging herself away from the spectacle of Mercado 28 before she was seduced by the smell of barbecuing meat that had tickled her nose, Megan wandered the streets looking for a hotel that she could afford.

To begin with she was too picky and lost valuable time expecting decent plumbing and bug-free rooms, when it became obvious that even the newest building within her price range would still feel rough around the edges, a combination of city decay, salt water and the ever-present dust from construction in a resort that was constantly evolving. So she shifted her focus to the older and more charming buildings that clustered around the bus station, but by now it was getting late and those that had vacancies would stretch her funds. She had enough for a month, maybe six weeks if she was careful.

The sun started to slip from the sky and she reviewed her options while she sat at a roadside café and ate eggs with flat tortilla pancakes and a rich tomato sauce, lively with herbs and chilli. She couldn't remember why she hadn't gone to the hotel zone, or why she had wasted all that time at the market, or really why she hadn't booked a place to stay in advance. She paid up and started pounding the streets, slightly more frantic this time, but still confident. After all, what was more fun: looking for a bedsit in Epping before going down to the Job Centre or walking under this dazzling sky and feeling free?

Eventually, just as the last dregs of positivity were ebbing away, she saw a small sign tacked up on the balcony above an establishment that, had it been a little earlier in the afternoon when she still had hope, she would have crossed the street to avoid.

Aquilar – To Rent.

It was a great idea. Why was she looking at hotels anyway? An apartment, that was what she needed. A place to live, not a stopgap. *Did you hear about Megan Watkins?* people would say. *She lives in Mexico now.* She might never go back.

147

She pushed open the door of the place downstairs and was already thinking of buying one of those retro drop-leaf tables she had seen at the market, and learning how to make Cancún-style eggs in her very own kitchen.

It was a neighbourhood bar full of middle-aged Mexican men and they all turned to look at her.

She gave them a wide, tight-lipped smile and nodded her head. Not one of the sullen expressions so much as flickered.

Nice crowd.

There was a man behind the bar, his gaze curious. He had liquid eyes like hot black coffee and his hair was long enough to be pulled back in a short ponytail, his body mean enough to get away with skinny black jeans and still look tough. He was younger than his customers, late twenties, probably, and she was fairly certain that if she got to know him she would find out he once played guitar in a garage band. Her knicker elastic slackened in his presence but then she remembered that she hadn't been to sleep in twenty-four hours and could probably do with a shower.

'*Buenos dias,*' he said as she approached him and there was an unmistakable twinkle of amusement in his eye. The bar was immaculate, the dark wooden bar rail was gleaming and she could see her reflection in the black marble countertop. She ordered a beer and it was icy from the fridge but without the wedge of lime she had been led to expect. She felt his eyes probe every curve of her tired, hot body as she tipped her head back to drink from the bottle. In the corner a television blared out a soccer match that nobody seemed to be watching.

148

Every time she caught his eye he smiled a lazy half-smile that was loaded with suggestion. She wondered what Mexican men were like in bed.

She asked about the rooms above the bar. He didn't reply immediately and she was confused. Was her Spanish really that bad? 'Do I need to speak to the owner?'

'I am the owner,' he said.

'Then what is it?'

'Those rooms are not for tourists.'

'Who are they for then?'

'Normally, forgive me, they are for prostitutes.'

'Oh.' She might have blushed but she hoped not. He was extremely handsome, too handsome, like a soap-opera star. 'I am not a prostitute.'

'You are a tourist.'

'Does that get me a discount?' she said, reaching for the joke with her limited vocabulary and feeling a burst of pleasure when he grunted in an approximation of a laugh. 'I am very quiet,' she added.

'Come back tomorrow,' he said. 'I will have Miguel show you around.'

'Tomorrow is no good.'

'You do not like to wait?'

'I do not like to wait.'

'Then you will not like Mexico.'

He reached behind the till and took a ring of keys down, then pushed open the bar and walked through to her side, closing it behind him. He started towards a door set into the far wall. When she didn't follow, he looked over his shoulder and gave a sharp whistle and flick of his head. 'Let's go.'

She downed the rest of her beer and scurried after him. In the bar the men remained impassive, even as she waved them goodbye.

It was perfect. So it had once been a knocking shop, so what? The mattress was brand new and still packed in plastic and the rest of the place had been cleaned so thoroughly that the scent of bleach lingered faintly, merging with the fresh breeze that had blown in as soon as he opened the shutters onto the balcony and the street below. And the price for the week was something like the hotels had been asking for a single night. He seemed surprised when she asked if she could take it for a whole month and she considered enquiring about a job, but figured that with only half a dozen patrons in his bar he didn't need anyone else to look after them.

'My name is Megan,' she said.

'Ramon Vega,' he said. 'Ray.'

She reached out a hand to shake his, but he picked up hers and kissed the back of it softly, keeping eye contact that made her feel peculiar. She gave him a good chunk of her money and waved him out of the door. She watched him go. His lean body was encased in threads that most Englishmen would consider to be a size too small, but on Ray they looked just right. She had a thing about thin men. She liked to wind herself around her lovers and that was impossible unless they were slender. Luckily, current fashion ensured there were enough emaciated rocker types around to keep her happy – even in Mexico, it seemed.

150

There were clean sheets in the wardrobe and she made up the bed, scrubbed herself fresh in the lukewarm but powerful shower, and fell almost immediately into a deep and untroubled sleep.

Some time later she woke up and it was dark. She could hear music and the occasional burst of laughter through her open window. She got out of bed and padded across the cold tiles to close the window and then she went back to sleep until morning.

The next day she was up ridiculously early. She took a long shower, put on one of her flowery summer dresses, a studded leather belt and her boots, then she went downstairs to the bar. It was closed and there was no sign of Ray. She wondered if he lived nearby and what his place was like. She stepped out into the weak morning sun and walked all the way down to the ferry port near Punta Sam, where the fisherman gathered. It was lively there, even just after dawn; she enjoyed watching the sea birds scrapping over bits of fish left over by the fleet, and hearing the occasional good-natured arguments between the deckhands and the men dragging ropes on shore.

She called one over to her and finally said the name that had been on her lips since the moment she arrived. Since the moment she heard it spoken to her over a decade ago.

'Des Amparados?'

He looked confused. Perhaps it was her accent.

'An island.'

'You want to go to an island? I know a nice island. Mujeres, Contoy, I know all of them. You want to go to Cozumel?'

'Des Amparados.'

'There is nothing there.'

Back in her room, on the small table next to the window, rested a giant pickle jar stuffed with red tropical flowers and waxy green leaves. There was a note. *Welcome to Cancún*, it said.

It was still very early but to Megan's surprise the bar was packed and another guy was making coffee at the big machine behind the bar. He was not remotely grungy like Ray; he looked like a preppy college student, clean-shaven with pristine dark hair, the sort of hair that looks as if a comb is pulled through it several times a day. He nodded when she came in, and continued serving one of the many men who swarmed around sipping coffee and chewing on the hard, sweet rolls that came with it. She enjoyed watching them.

'You're Megan?' he said when he was able to serve her.

'How did you know?'

He grinned and fetched her a coffee. 'Ray said you were cute,' he said.

'Cute?' It was not a word people often used to describe Megan Watkins, despite her pocket-size proportions. 'You're Miguel?'

'At your service,' he said.

The loud chatter made conversation impossible but

she perched herself at the far end of the bar with her coffee and sipped it slowly until the crowd thinned. She liked the dark wood panelling on the walls and the ornate skylight in the centre of the ceiling. There was a mezzanine gallery made of the same glossy wood as the panelling. That would be a great place to stage some live music, if it was safe.

'I'm looking for Ray,' she said. 'Is he around?'

'He usually gets in around eleven,' said Miguel. 'You want to wait?'

'I'm not good at waiting,' she said. Although that wasn't strictly true. She had waited far longer than she'd thought to get over the water to the island.

'Then you won't like Mexico,' he said.

'So I'm told.'

'Any message?'

'No,' she said, 'it's okay. Well, actually, maybe if you see him you could just tell him I said thank you. He'll know what for.'

'For the flowers?' said Miguel. He wouldn't meet her eyes; he just kept polishing an invisible spot on a glass.

She paused for a moment and when he finally looked up he looked like a guilty schoolboy. 'You left them, didn't you?' she said.

He nodded. 'I didn't mean anything, I'm married. To Ray's sister. I just thought it would be nice. A young girl like you, arriving here on her own, no boyfriend, no husband. I saw them, and if my wife were here I would have bought them for her, or I should have – maybe if I brought her flowers once in a while she'd be here, but she's away with her mother, and I miss her, I guess.'

'I like them very much. You are very sweet to think of me. Your wife is a lucky woman.'

Miguel looked down to his feet, and thought about the woman he loved and wondered where she might be. He then rubbed his hands together and focused on the woman in front of him.

'So what are your plans while you are here?'

She grimaced.

'That bad? You want to talk about it?'

'Not really,' she said, and then she sighed. 'I came to Cancún for a reason; it's not just a holiday.'

'You came to find someone?'

'Why do you say that?'

'I don't know. The way you walk with your eyes all around. You are someone who is searching. There is nothing to see in Cancún, not really; people come for the party, they come to relax. If it was something inside, you would seek a spiritual high down in Tulum or in Peru – somewhere else, not here. So it must be a person.'

'I am not searching,' she said. 'I know where he is.' She didn't want to explain about the house, but she was impressed by his intuition. She was searching. Miguel was right.

'So why have you not found him yet?'

'I think I'm afraid that if it doesn't work out I will have nothing. At least now I have the *possibility*.'

'You have hope.'

'Yeah. I have hope.'

'I know you are afraid,' he said. 'I can tell. But what is hope without end except an empty dream? What is a question without an answer?'

'But what if the answer is no?'

'The last thing to die is hope. And hope is not easily killed.'

Back home, Megan spent a lot of energy pretending that nothing scared her, but here nobody knew anything about her and yet this bartender had spotted her fear straight away. Instead of teasing her, he was trying to be a friend. She started to wonder if she had been wasting that energy all along and what she could have done with it.

'Miguel, did anyone ever tell you you're a pretty clever guy?'

'No,' he said dolefully. 'Never.'

Just then the swing doors opened, crashing into the walls, and Ray arrived back, carrying several cartons of cigarettes under his arms. She saw Miguel frown as Ray stopped at a table and offloaded a carton and money changed hands.

'What's wrong?' she said.

'Black-market cigarettes. It's risky being so bold, that's all.'

Ray saw her waiting there and came over. 'Sweet Megan,' he said. 'You smoke?'

'I gave up,' she said.

'Smart move. You want another coffee? On me.'

'Sure,' she said.

He put the pile of cartons on the bar and raked a hand through his collar-length hair, leaning into her personal space and making her feel all woozy. 'And tonight you and me, we'll have dinner, okay? A beautiful girl like you shouldn't be up in her room alone at night. I know some fun places.'

155

She looked at Miguel, almost as if she was asking him for permission.

'She's too good for you, Ray,' said Miguel. 'And will you please put those cigarettes out back before you get us into trouble?'

'So who should our Megan be with, huh? Some gringo? A gangster? You? I don't think so. Megan, sweet Megan, I would be honoured if you would let me take you out to dinner.' He swept down in a deep bow and she was charmed. Her chat with Miguel had turned her pensive mood on its head. What harm could it do to have dinner?

'Okay.'

Miguel groaned. 'Don't say I didn't warn you, Megan.'

'A beautiful woman and a fine dinner: what could be better?' She laughed and he looked confused. 'Forgive me,' he said. 'In Mexico women like being told that they are beautiful.'

'In England too,' she admitted. His eyes were like granite, and only his thick black eyelashes stopped them from being too hard. When she looked at him directly she had the sense of being pulled into them, as if into a dark tunnel. The candour of his stare stripped her back to her most base desires. Passion bubbled into her as if she was simmering under the hot Mexican sun. He was playful with his flirtation, but she could tell from the heat in his gaze how much he desired her.

She decided that he was probably an excellent kisser. In no time at all, if he kept up the bad-boy charm that she found so hard to resist, she would probably find out.

12

Esmé's flight out of Mexico was full of English tourists on their way home, whose scorched faces were the same pink colour as the scales of the snapper they served at the fancy places by the beach. As they taxied to the runway, Esmé noticed her mother threading her rosary through her fingers. She would have reached over to reassure her but she could not be sure that her own hand would be steady. Neither of them had ever been on an aeroplane before, but it seemed apparent that the thing to do was to ignore the safety demonstration and look miserable. The engine roared and they both tensed but nobody else on the plane seemed to react and so it must be normal. Then they were moving and ground was falling away from them as they took to the skies. Below them the ocean sparkled and the islands off the coast of Cancún were pinpricks of bottle green in the blue.

'Are you surprised he let you go?' said Catalina.

'Miguel knew what would happen if he did not.' Somewhere down there her husband was content to be behind a bar that he now co-owned. And he knew that his wife thought it was a colossal mistake. 'Maybe I'll like it here,' said Esmé. 'Who knows? Maybe I will stay with you.' She pushed back her long dark hair and met her mother's gaze with a spark of defiance flashing in her smoky eyes.

'Esmé, no! It would be lovely to have you close but please, please don't mess things up with me and Carlos. He's going to ask me to marry him, here in London. I know he is. I told him you were coming to help me get settled, that's all. I can't land him with my whole family.'

'I could take care of myself,' said Esmé.

'You have a husband already,' said Catalina. 'You would never leave him.'

'Don't be so sure,' said Esmé, and picked up the magazine from the handy little pocket on the back of the seat in front of her. It was full of adverts for perfume and things like that. Miguel had never bought her perfume. He said that he didn't like her to wear it, but she had suspected he was just being cheap.

'You would never,' repeated Catalina. 'What are you saying. A *divorce*?' She dipped her voice, horrified, as if using the word alone would brand their family a failure. 'Miguel is such a hard worker. He can give you the life you've always wanted.'

'I am twenty-two years old and this is the first time I have been on an aeroplane. What makes you think this is the life I have always wanted?'

Carlos collected Esmé and her mother from Gatwick Airport. Catalina was even more skittish than usual,

158

telling him tiny details of their uneventful flight and admiring his rather mediocre car.

Esmé pretended to sleep and listened to her mother and Carlos talk about her plans for the next few months.

'I want to see Mayfair,' said Catalina firmly. 'Like in Monopoly.'

Esmé opened her eyes. 'You live near there, right Carlos?'

'I moved,' he said. 'A bigger place, more room for my *princessa*.'

Catalina simpered and Esmé sighed, looking out at the drab streets as they passed shop after shop, each one more miserable than the last. The roads in England were tiny, with single-lane traffic sometimes only moving in one direction at a time if a parked car did not leave enough room. They moved forward at a pedestrian pace. Even though the streets were clogged with cars, the sidewalks were still crammed with people, struggling with the weight of plastic bags, wrestling with umbrellas as it started to rain. What stolen pleasures would there to be had in a place as cold as this? What would rouse the early morning spirits and melt away the tensions of the day?

After an hour or so, Carlos pulled off the road and behind a tall brick building, square and flat with lots of windows. A small apartment building that was saved from despair by some lawn and tall trees that kept the worst of the rain off them once they were out of the car and walking up the pathway to the front door.

Catalina grabbed hold of Esmé's arm as if she was afraid of the wet and windy night. 'Are we here, do you think?' she whispered.

'Where are we exactly?' asked Esmé.

'Dulwich,' said Carlos. 'Margaret Thatcher used to live here.' The women looked blank. 'Margaret Thatcher? Prime Minister of Great Britain? Very famous?'

'Where does the Queen live?' asked Catalina.

'Not far,' he said, and pushed open the front door of the apartment building, leading them into a big lobby with two staircases heading up in opposite directions. Esmé wanted to take off her shoes to see what it was like to walk barefoot on such a thick carpet, but Carlos walked briskly ahead and they exchanged a glance, then both followed him mutely.

His apartment was huge, with an open-plan living space looking out over a grassy park. It had polished wooden floors, a pair of matching red leather sofas and an entertainment system that took up one entire wall. The kitchen surfaces gleamed; the stainless steel appliances sparkled. Catalina looped her arm around her boyfriend's waist.

'It's gorgeous,' she squealed.

'It's nice,' said Esmé. She averted her eyes while Carlos and her mother kissed but looked back in time to see the look of desire that passed between them. She had a sudden longing for home. Not that crappy little apartment she shared with Miguel in the suburbs, but the quiet, shady plazas and the vast ocean views of her hometown.

'I thought Esmé might be happier in her own space while she is with us. There is an empty apartment just across the hall.'

'You own the neighbouring apartment?'

'We own the building,' he said smoothly.

The apartment across the hall was far smaller, and had none of the mod-cons that Carlos had in his apartment, but Esmé had never lived alone and the prospect of so much uninterrupted time delighted her.

'You'll be okay?' she said. Her mother was sprawled on one of the sofas flicking through the endless channels on the flatscreen television and she looked up incredulously when Esmé asked the question.

'I'll be fine. Sleep well.'

The next day the skies were grey again, except this time it was a watery silver that invited her to dive in. London. She shivered with delight. After an entire lifetime spent within the same state, she could barely contain her glee.

She had no idea where she was heading and there were rows of identical houses in every direction, so she picked a street at random and after a few twists and turns found a busy parade of shops that looked nothing like the England of her imagination. It was full of black faces, women with tiny babies strapped to their backs, wearing colourful African prints. The shops displayed exotic vegetables and every cut of meat imaginable, along with shiny red fish that could have been pulled from the clear waters of the Caribbean that morning. The road was choked with traffic. She saw a series of red double-decker buses with advertisements on the side; it was only those and the other signs she saw written in English that assured her she was indeed in London and not some other place.

This did not feel right.

Her hand went to the pocket where she had stashed her money, the hard-earned pesos she had converted into British pounds before she left. She was hungry, but when she looked at the prices in the window of a café she hesitated. It seemed like ever such a lot of money and the food was unfamiliar to her. She so wanted to be adventurous, but to her shame, after half an hour or so wandering the streets, her enthusiasm faded and she found herself sitting in the window of McDonald's eating a cheeseburger. Her energy slumped and she was quite miserable to realize that the quiet disappointment she felt on her first day in London was almost identical to the way she felt at home most of the time. What did that mean? That Mexico was not the problem; Miguel was not the problem? If these feelings of dissatisfaction and sadness could not be chased away with drastic change, then they must be a part of her soul, not her circumstances. She should go home, run back to the sea and the sun and learn to love her life. Catalina spent her whole life looking for a man like Miguel, loyal and handsome; and ended up with Carlos, wealthy and hollow. What made Esmé so sure that she could do any better?

It shouldn't be about a man, she decided. It would be Miguel or nobody. At least not for a while. She knew that England was like America, and even parts of Mexico: young women could and often did live alone or with groups of friends, not with their mothers and then their husbands. She could learn to live like that.

But even after just one night sleeping alone she missed the feel of naked skin against her own. Miguel was a good lover. She had nothing to compare him with, of course, except the movies and the love songs, but they had plenty of sex and she was not sure she could be alone, physically, for any length of time. Where would that desire go if she didn't feed it? She pictured her passion seeping out of her like resin, and hardening, until she had nothing to offer a man except gritty determination.

Making the break out of Cancún had not changed her, it had only changed her perspective; and the view from here did not look good.

Esmé found her way back to the apartment easily. Her mother was waiting for her in the lobby, pacing the green carpet so forcefully she might have worn it down.

'Where have you been?' demanded Catalina. 'Carlos was terrified. We both were.'

'I went for a walk.'

'On your own?'

'No, Mum, with The Beatles. Of course on my own.'

'Carlos says this is not a good area if you don't know your way around.'

'Not good?'

'Not safe.'

'Nice neighbourhood your boyfriend brought us to, isn't it?'

Carlos came down the stairs in time to catch Esmé's last words. 'It's up and coming,' he said. 'Most of it is perfectly safe – desirable, some would say, but I was worried about you.'

'I need a key,' she said.

'Of course. I'll get one cut. We try to keep the door

double-locked. And if you have any valuables, there's a safe in my apartment.'

'Our apartment,' said Catalina.

'Come on, Carlos,' said Esmé, grinning – he really did seem genuinely concerned about her welfare and he made her mother very happy – 'You really think I'm the kind of girl who has valuables?'

'Then this afternoon we need to go shopping,' he said.

Catalina clapped her hands together and Carlos held her gaze while gesturing for Esmé to lead the way upstairs, a gentlemanly move that cemented her feeling that perhaps he wasn't a bad guy after all.

But a second later she was fairly sure it wasn't an accident when his palm skirted the curve of her ass.

She called her husband. As strange as it felt to dial the numbers and think of the telephone ringing in Ray's bar three thousand miles away, it would have felt more strange not to. Her brother answered.

'It's Esmé,' she said.

'How's our mother? That guy treating her good?'

'What do you care?' said Esmé. Ray had made it very clear that he did not like Carlos at all. A business deal between them had gone bad in the past, he said, but knowing a little about both of them, Esmé knew there was probably legitimate grievances on both sides. Besides, Ray had issues with people all over town. It was part of the reason his business would always struggle.

'You want to speak to Miguel?'

'Is he there?'

'He's outside, banging one of the cocktail waitresses. Can I get him to call you back?'

Esmé smiled. 'Like you guys would ever get so busy you'd need a cocktail waitress. Just tell him I called. We got here. It's all good, okay?'

'That asshole Carlos treating you right?'

'I think it's serious, Ray. You might end up calling him Daddy.'

'Like hell,' said Ray. 'Just look out for her, okay? He might not keep his promises.'

'That's why I'm here,' she said.

'She's my momma, you get that?'

'Yeah, Ray. I think I do. Now go back to watching your TV.'

'Don't mind if I do.'

The problem with Ray and Miguel both was that they'd been spoilt by their mothers. Either that or they were born lazy.

Esmé took the bulk of her cash and her passport into the apartment across the hall.

As her mother moved a mirror and span the combination lock to open the safe behind it, Esmé could not conceal her surprise. 'He trusts you.'

'Carlos? Of course he does. Sweetie, we were up most of last night talking. He wants me to help him in the business.'

'What do you know about engine parts?'

She reached out her hand for the cash and passport. 'Another business. He has a temp agency too, setting up offices and hotels with summer staff.'

'A temp agency?'

'He asked me to take care of some of the books for him, the money stuff. I told him I could do it. Will you help?' Catalina closed the safe and spun the lock.

'Is he paying you?'

'Yes. Not much at first, but how much do I need? He hasn't asked me to pay rent or anything. He's not going to.' She carefully replaced the mirror in front of the safe and stood back, pleased with herself for not breaking the mirror or forgetting the combination, while still hoping that London would be a place where she made fewer mistakes.

Within a couple of days, Esmé had found the best places to shop in the neighbourhood; she bought cocoa butter for her permanently dry skin, and ingredients that reminded them both of home: heavy shoulders of lamb and tiny fiery chillies, limes cheap enough to buy by the handful. She rubbed the lamb with cumin seeds and tamarind, left it in the oven all day, and cut through the rich results with a dressing of green tomato pulp and fresh coriander. It became that she would rather spend the day rooting through the markets of south London than cut across town and see the sights. She had seen Buckingham Palace and Big Ben, imposing buildings that left her cold. She had been on a red double-decker and on an underground train that made her uneasy. She didn't want to shop incessantly and she had nobody to eat dinner with, so after a while she stopped going into central London at all and the days of her stay drained away. One evening she stood in her small kitchen, giddy from the smell of melted cheese and frying tortilla, she bit down on a habanero chilli pepper and her tears took her by surprise. She realized how much she missed Cancún.

She tried to teach her mother the fundamentals of book-keeping.

'You see?' she said. 'You add up all these numbers here and enter the figure here. Okay?'

'No,' said Catalina. 'You're going to have to do it for me.'

'Mama!'

It wouldn't take a certificate from night school to see that there was something inherently wrong with the accounts of the apparent temping agency, but Esmé had a certificate so she could see it quicker than most. Nobody paid any tax, of any kind. No employee deductions, just a constant flow of money from one account to the next, accumulating slowly and being siphoned off, one massive cash transaction at a time. Most of the money came from credit-card payments, crossed to Mexico and back; none of it was declared. Balancing the expenditure was a simple but highly illegal matter of cross-charging mortgage payments and small business loans from various other limited companies that would eventually be cleaned overseas.

She tackled Carlos about it. 'You don't need a book-keeper,' she said. 'You need an accountant. You could be in a lot of trouble. You're in a mess. Either it was unintentional and you just don't know what you're doing, or you planned to run a cash export business for tax-free profit.

Also, I don't want to know what it is, but there's no way your business is an employment agency.'

'I don't want an accountant,' he said. 'I want you, I trust you. Let me send you to school. It won't take long, a smart girl like you; then you'll have the work visa, the experience and the education. You could have it all.'

Esmé looked down at the rows of figures and felt dizzy. 'That's not what I came for,' she said. 'I came to help my mother.'

'Then help her. Stay a little bit longer, just a few weeks. Teach her. I don't think Catalina is capable of doing it without you, I see that now. Perhaps it is not right, her and me.'

It was a very subtle threat. Catalina was increasingly devoted to Carlos. If he ended things between them she would be devastated.

'She thinks you're going to ask her to marry you,' said Esmé.

'That would have to depend.'

'On what?'

'Your mother has many special skills,' said Carlos, and Esmé's stomach churned. 'But I am a businessman; any wife of mine would have to bring more than something I could buy on a street corner for the price of a parking ticket.'

'My brother was right about you,' she said. 'You're a dick.'

'And your mother loves me.'

Gradually Esmé took over responsibility for Carlos's

personal accounts and the limited paperwork of his business interests.

'You need more employee insurance,' she said. 'The personal liability isn't enough.'

'I like to keep things simple,' he said.

'You need to declare a banker's draft over ten thousand euros when you leave the country,' she said.

'It slipped my mind.'

Her mother took on the day-to-day welfare of the employment agency girls, because they were all girls, and only an idiot could fail to see what was going on beneath their noses. And Esmé was no idiot.

The time came when she had to voice what she had known for some time. She wondered how long her mother had known.

'He's running hookers,' said Esmé. 'Your boyfriend is a pimp, a very successful pimp.'

Catalina lit another cigarette and tucked up her feet. They were sitting on a bench in a thin strip of park that crept down to the train station. The sun was out but it was such a thin sun. She could tilt her head to catch it directly like a spotlight, but still the chill in her cheeks remained. She waited for her mother to say something. Had she known all along?

'Escorts,' said Catalina.

'Prostitutes.'

'What?' said Catalina, at breaking point. 'What is it that you want from me? These are healthy young women, some of them are beautiful; they are not short of options.

169

He's not hurting anyone, Esmé. He won't stop if I leave him. These girls need someone like me to take care of them. That's why I'm here.'

'Did you know? Before we came out here, did you know that this was what he would be getting you into?'

Catalina narrowed her eyes and drew deeply on her cigarette. 'I didn't know,' she said. 'I swear. But if you ask me would I still have come, then maybe yes, probably yes.'

'Would you have let me come with you?'

'Esmé, your whole life you did pretty much whatever you wanted. I can't see that I would have had much say in the matter.'

'I didn't want to marry Miguel.'

'You made it clear you would marry the first boy to ask you if it meant getting away from me.'

Was she right? It sounded right. But had she really been so stupid to think that marriage would bring her freedom?

Catalina ground out her cigarette with the heel of her shoe, and wrapped her coat tighter around herself. When a woman rushed past them with a pushchair, Catalina was the only one who really noticed her. 'When you were a baby,' she said, 'I thought you would have an easier life than me, and you have had so much, but you still want to leave. Just like I did.'

The clouds shifted and the pale sun was lost. The wind gusted and the leaves flurried around their feet. Her mother never spoke about her past. Like every other family in Cancún, their roots did not go deep. One good storm could rip them out.

170

'It took three days for the train to get to Cancún,' Catalina said. 'The stinking train with no air and dead chickens by my feet. Ray was too big for me to carry, but the only place that he would sleep was in my arms and I kept praying to San Cristóbal and thinking I was doing the right thing.' Her eyes misted over and she winced as if she was back there. 'Maybe I would have been better off staying in Veracruz, just like my mother said.'

Esmé looked sideways at her mother just as the damp air started to bite at their cheeks with tiny raindrops. 'Am I supposed to feel sorry for you?'

'Sorry for me?' said Catalina, and she sounded weary. 'Why would you be sorry for me? I'm in London, England, haven't you heard?'

The cigarette was finished; it was getting cold.

'So what are you going to do?' asked Catalina. 'You're going to tell the police about Carlos? Are you going to tell them about me?'

'No,' said Esmé, 'of course not.'

'And you won't start in on Carlos? He's been good to us, Esmé.'

The terrifying thing was that her mother still didn't see him as a danger. His criminality didn't extend to her because she shared his bed. Esmé would be afraid to do anything much to Carlos now except stay out of his way.

13

Megan wanted to arrive on Des Amparados looking like just another Cancún tourist. It had been over twenty years. She knew it was unlikely that the house would be sitting there empty, ready for her to move into and install cable television. What if there was nothing there? She had been dreaming about this since she was eleven years old. What if there was everything? She dressed in her cutest summer dress and her trusty old boots, slathering on coconut oil to make her skin supple and sweet scented. Her hair was growing longer so she clipped the front part back out of her eyes and rubbed on plenty of sunscreen. She toned down what was left of her rock-chick attitude with less eye make-up and a big smile.

'You look lovely,' said Ray as she got downstairs. 'Where are you going?' It had been several days since their dinner date. He had taken her dancing afterwards and the tequila and the salsa had combined to leave her quivering with lust, but to her dismay he had kissed her hand at her front door and said goodnight. Her hand, for God's sake, like she was the Pope or something.

'I thought I'd check out some of the islands in the bay,' she said. 'Get out of the city for a while.'

'Great. I'll come with you,' he said. He was already calling Miguel out of the kitchen and gathering up his keys.

'I wanted some time to myself.'

'You're not the only one who needs to get out of the city, you know. It's my day off. Don't you want to spend more time with me?'

'Sure. But I have some things planned.'

'I won't get in your way,' he said. 'Come on, it'll be fun. I can drive us to the ferry, I can buy you lunch. Let me.'

'Okay,' she said. 'But there's stuff I want to do in the afternoon that you probably won't be interested in.' She couldn't have him tagging along to Des Amparados: that would mean explaining the whole situation and there was nobody who knew the whole story, not even Connor, no matter what he might think.

'Things like what?'

'Bird-watching,' she said.

Ray laughed. 'You're right, I'll skip that part.'

He pushed open the bar and gathered up a few dirty coffee cups, crossing the space with a long, loping stride; then he was in front of her, helping her to her feet and offering her his arm. She giggled, and took it.

They caught the ferry to Isla Mujeres, the biggest and most developed island in the chain. It was only twenty minutes away but it felt far removed from the hustle of Cancún, with sleepy streets that meandered through a low-key downtown before merging with sandy tracks that led off to the beach in every direction. They had a

173

delicious lunch of pulled pork tacos and crunchy chop salad at a buzzy restaurant overlooking the water, the smell of barbecue drawing in a hungry crowd.

'You enjoyed yourself the other night with me?' he said, licking the juices from his fingertips and eyeing up her leftovers.

'I had a brilliant time,' she said, truthfully. 'Did you?'

'Of course,' he said. 'What? What did I say?'

'In England, if I had a good time like that, you'd probably try and kiss me or something.'

'You are upset because I didn't try to kiss you?'

'Not *upset*,' she said.

'A little bit upset? You want me to kiss you now?'

She shrugged. 'No, I'm eating.'

He laughed. 'I like you, Megan. Relax.'

She tried.

In the afternoon, when he was starting to get sleepy and would no doubt doze happily in the sun for an hour or two, she told him she was going on a boat trip to see some birds. Then she went down to the marina by the best hotel in town.

She found plenty of tourist boats, catering to people who wanted to snorkel and fish, and she asked the bored-looking skipper of a little boat if he would take her to Des Amparados for a few hours and then bring her back. He didn't ask for too much money and she didn't negotiate. By now her nerves were jangling and she found everything disproportionately funny. The boat guy was wearing a T-shirt that said Bimbo on it, and even though she knew it was the logo of a widely available sliced loaf, she still thought it was hilarious.

The waves slapped the prow of the flimsy panga and she felt wide awake and ready. Isla Mujeres fell away behind them and the waves reached higher as the open ocean fought back. They drew closer to the island and all she could make out was the coconut forest, and then they rounded a point and out of nowhere there was a sliver of sand and a shallow anchorage.

She was here.

It felt as though there should be trumpets heralding her arrival, but instead, as the boat's engine cut out, there was nothing but silence, as soft as the first snow in winter, which put her at ease.

She took off her shoes, threw herself over the edge of the boat into the gently sloping shallows. The ripples from the splash undulated as far as the beach. Wet sand oozed between her toes and a tiny white fish nipped her ankles in twelve inches of crystal-clear water. Why had she waited so long? What had she been so afraid of? It was quiet enough to hear her own thoughts and they weren't frightening at all.

'Are there any houses?' she asked him. 'Anything like that?'

'I don't know. Perhaps.' He shook his head and made the sign of the cross. '*Fantasmas*,' he said.

She laughed at the thought of ghosts being anything other than benign in a place as peaceful as this, and gave him half his money as agreed, as well as a meatball sandwich she had brought with her as a sweetener. He didn't look grateful enough for the sandwich. 'I'll be back in an hour or so,' she said, making sure that she had her own sandwich and plenty of water as well as her average-tourist disguise of straw cowboy hat and sunnies. She walked down the beach. East, her mum had said, and so east she went, with the warm sun at her back.

It was a challenging scramble up the headland to the next bay – for a while she picked her way over rocks and climbed steadily. She spotted a shortcut lower down and she took it. It was risky – at times she was clinging between handholds and ledges – but she ignored the dangerous fall below her as best she could. When she finally got to the top she slumped to her knees, her adrenalin drained, but she was rewarded with a sweeping view across to the open ocean to the east, which took away what little breath she had left. The clouds stretched out until they were too distant to see, and the light wrapped everything in a skein of cotton-wool mist. The end of the world.

If you had to, then this was a fine place to die. No wonder he had loved it.

She dragged her eyes away from the horizon to the descent directly ahead and she saw, a few hundred yards away, an orchard of lemon trees and, far behind them, up on the low, raw stone bluff that came next, what looked like a small white house. The steady thump of her heart rose to a scamper. That was the house. It had to be.

She resisted the urge to run, and instead walked across to the edge of the orchard, looking all the while for a path through. She found none and, stopping briefly to touch the cool dark trunk of a lemon tree, she walked into the shade and started to pick her way down through the heavily scented boughs. There were lime trees, too, some still in blossom. Wild thyme twisted through the rusting irrigation system. Her feet crunched across the dry leaves as if she was walking on fragile seashells.

At the lowest point of the valley the trees thinned, but then picked up again at the other side. Further still she found half a dozen neatly pruned avocado trees, the fruit hanging heavy on each long stem, and then she took a few more steps and she was out into the scorching sunlight once more and standing in a well-tended vegetable plot.

She would have to tell Boatman Bimbo that no ghost alive could make a garden sing like this one. There were chilli peppers in abundance, tomato plants so productive that they reminded her of the raspberry fields in Gallywood where she used to pick fruit with her mum. There were neat rows of herbs and lettuces, and a wide swathe of courgette plants with their shocking yellow flowers.

'Can I help you? This is private property.'

She almost walked into his broad naked chest and was so startled that she actually screamed. She registered his polite smile and his American accent.

'Hi!' she said. 'Hi! I'm so sorry, I didn't know. There are no signs.'

'Signs tend to make people curious. The climb usually puts people off.'

'Not me,' she said cheerfully.

'No.' He was wearing baggy denims cut off just under the knee, and a tatty pair of Havaianas flip-flops. He could do with a haircut. Americans: she might have known.

'So you live here?'

A small line appeared between his eyes. 'Like I said, it's private property, ma'am.'

True, perhaps, but he hadn't actually asked her to leave yet. 'What an incredible place you have,' she gushed. 'Amazing! Have you been here long? The garden must have taken so much work. Do you do it all yourself?'

'It's my father's garden,' he said.

'You live here with your father?'

'You ask a lot of questions.'

'Do I?'

His polite smile stretched up to his big brown eyes and he scratched his unshaven chin. 'He likes showing people his garden,' he said at last. 'You're not the only one that ever made it over the hill, you know.'

On the short walk to the house she found out that his name was Luis, he came from Arizona, his father was called Hector.

'That's amazing,' she said. 'I've never met anybody from America before.' This was a lie. Without intending to, her voice became a little more clipped and she spoke the way her mother had always wanted her to speak, believing it to be charming.

'Then you obviously haven't been in Cancún very long,' he said.

'Probably not as long as you.'

'I'm not in Cancún,' he said.

'Near enough.'

'A million miles away.' By anyone's standard, Luis was a good-looking guy. But Megan's standards weren't about looks. Even if this pretty boy played guitar, she'd bet her last hundred dollars that he'd play acoustic. No edge.

'Hey Dad,' he called as they rounded the house. Finally she saw the tantalizing uninterrupted view once more and sitting on a verdant porch admiring it was a man with mud beneath his fingernails, teasing a limp chilli plant along a slender cane. 'Dad? We have company.'

'Megan,' she said, sticking out her hand. 'Megan Watkins.'

'Hector.' He was so deeply tanned she thought that he must spend every moment of the day outside. His beard was thick but neat and she couldn't guess how old he was. Anywhere between forty and seventy. He looked like plenty of other Cancún gringos, Americans who had decided that the Mexican lifestyle suited them better than the pace of life 'up north', but there was a beguiling calmness in his grey-green eyes, almost lost in the shadows of his battered canvas sun hat.

'Megan was saying how much she liked your yard; thought I'd let her tell you herself.'

'It's a bit more than a yard,' she said.

'He's being a jackass,' said Hector, and looked down at her milky hands and settled for touching the brim of his hat. 'Much obliged, ma'am.'

'You're welcome, it's a beauty.'

'You like to garden?'

'I like to eat,' she said. 'I could have eaten some of those tomatoes straight off the vine.'

He smiled. 'That's when they taste the best. Help yourself.'

This was the right place. She was sure of it. A sense of belonging rushed up through her bare soles and the quivers of excitement made her need a wee. She brought her bladder back under control and smiled.

'Tell me something about the island,' she said.

179

'What do you want to know?'

'The name,' she said, picking something at random, because she didn't want to pile in with her real questions. 'What do you know about the name?'

'It's a mistranslation of an old colonial Spanish name, *Desamparado*. It means "abandoned".'

She smiled, agreeably taken, and so he continued.

'There was once a Spanish captain, a pirate, who found the kisses of another man on his girl. The shipmates banded together and refused to name the seducer. He had to hold a silver dagger to the first throat and draw blood before his girl cried out for him to stop. She said that she had kissed each and every one of them and he could not kill them all, for how would they sail home?'

'What happened?' said Megan.

'He abandoned her here to die.'

She shuddered. 'Are you trying to scare me away?' she said.

'Perhaps,' he said. 'Are you afraid?'

'I should leave,' she said. 'I've been here long enough. I have a man with a boat waiting for me: he probably has better things to do. I'm so sorry to have bothered you. It was good to meet you.'

'You can come back and visit,' he said. 'Don't be scared.'

'Maybe I will.' She started to walk away but turned back.

'One more thing, am I allowed on the beach, or do you own that too?'

'I don't own this house,' said Hector. 'Or the garden, not really. I'm just the caretaker.'

'Who owns it?'

'One of your very own.'

'Sorry?'

'An Englishman.'

Back on Isla Mujeres Ray said they should watch the sunset and so he took her down to Playa Norte and they found one of the double wooden swings outside Buho's where they drank beer from the bottle, their feet trailing in the sand, and looked towards Cancún where the sun was spilling pink all over the sky. She told him that her bird-watching trip to Isla Contoy had been a dream come true. Ray was at best only half listening, which made lying so much easier. They watched some college kids down on the beach, intoxicated by the buzz of legal drinking, dancing to the strum of someone's guitar and shrieking with laughter every once in a while.

Ray seemed content to watch the sky and listen to the music, leaving her with her thoughts.

The Englishman. It had to be her father, it just had to be. So there would be no island to inherit, just a shiftless father to track down if she felt like it. And the truth was that she did not. Why should she care to find him? She wanted to tell Connor and listen to what he had to say about it all. But why was she thinking of Connor when she had a man right here beside her? Why was she thinking of her father when he had walked out on her? She looked sideways at Ray. His glorious profile was strong in the sunset, his crazy hair framing it so that he looked like an album cover. Back home she didn't know any guy

181

who would take the time to watch the sunset like that, as if it was important enough to care about. Right there and then she decided to trust him. 'There's something I haven't told you,' she said.

Ray dragged his eyes away from a bikini babe on the beach who was the loudest of them all and laced his fingers through Megan's.

'My dad used to live near here.'

'No shit, really?' he said quickly, then again, a lot more slowly. 'Really?'

She nodded. 'That's where I was. I wasn't bird-watching.'

'You weren't?' His smile said fine, but his eyes glowered under the surface and she saw that he would be a different person if she ever got him angry.

'I'm sorry I lied. It was personal. I was told that he'd died. I was also told he had a house here and I wanted to make sure that it really existed.'

'And it does?'

'It does, Ray, and it's beautiful.' She told him about the beach and the views and the garden. She told him about the way the terrace curled around so that you could always find some shade and shelter, even up there on the bluff.

'Who lives there now?'

'That's the thing. This guy said he's the caretaker, that the place is owned by an Englishman. You think he means my father?'

'No,' he said. 'Your father is dead.'

'But what if he isn't?'

Ray shook his head. 'Isn't it far more likely that the house is now owned by a different Englishman?'

'I'm going to find out.'

182

Ray looked at her through his eyelashes, his eyes half closed. He had a sexy smile. 'Are you sure you didn't just come up with this plan so that you can stay here now that you are falling in love with me?'

She rolled her eyes. 'I'm sure, Ray. Chill.' She liked how relaxed it was; it took the edge off her nerves. The island had been beautiful; she must try and focus on that instead of constantly looking forward to the next step and what to do tomorrow and the day after that.

He interlaced his fingers with hers again, clasping her hand as if they were about to arm-wrestle. His hand was very dark brown against hers and briefly she liked the way they looked together. She tilted her head to one side so that it lay on his shoulder and she let out a deep breath, hoping that looking at the ocean might calm her thoughts, but all that happened was that she felt a long way from home. 'You are sad,' he said.

'A little,' she admitted.

'You didn't like what you found?'

'I did,' she said. 'I liked it a lot. Have you ever been somewhere that just feels good, no bullshit; just makes you feel good on the inside?'

'You make me feel good on the inside,' he said.

'Seriously,' she said, swatting at him. 'It's like my whole life I have been looking for a place where I belong, you know?'

'I belong here,' he said. 'I have never been anywhere else.'

'What do you mean?'

'I came to Cancún when I was six years old. I have never left.'

'Really?'

'When you live in paradise, where is it that you would wish to go?'

She could not conceive of it. 'But don't you ever wonder what else is out there for you?'

'It's what's in here that counts,' he said, patting his heart.

'But that's . . . it's so corny. Is that what you really believe? What if there is a better place, a place where you feel more yourself, a place where you are happier?'

He considered what she was saying. Down on the beach, the guitar music started up again and it was perfect for the laid-back island vibe. 'I am happy here,' he said. 'If you saw what I see, what I grew up with. Every day, all day long, the planes land and bring people here. They save all year for a week in the sun, maybe two, and they eat too much and drink too much and lie around in the sun, and sure maybe they are happy, maybe they are having the time of their lives, but then they have to go home and the happiness fades, and they wait for a whole year to be happy again. I will never understand tourists.'

'You're saying I shouldn't go home?'

'I am saying people should find a place where they are happy and stay there.'

He turned sideways on their swing and looped an arm around her waist, scooting over so that they were pressed up next to each other. He placed his hands on her shoulders and then ran one of them down the side of her arm to come to rest on her hip, all the while staring into her eyes in the gathering darkness. The bar was getting busy; she could feel people pushing in around them and some music started playing behind the bar, quietly at first but rising in volume abruptly. Someone whooped, and out of the corner of her eye she could see some other people start to dance barefoot on the sand, but mostly she could see Ray's face in front of hers, his eyes dark and serious, and knew that he was about to kiss her. She trembled.

'I wanted to kiss you before,' he said. 'But that's not how we do it in Mexico.'

'How do you do it in Mexico?' she whispered.

'Like this.'

He pressed his lips down on hers, firmly, as if staking ownership, but not urgently. His hand traced a pattern across her back until he was pressing into the base of her spine and her back arched under his touch so that every inch of her was touching him. Their legs became entwined, his chest was crushed up against hers and both of his arms were wrapped around her. She reached up to tangle her arms around his neck, taking big handfuls of his glossy hair and tugging it so that he moaned slightly and bit down gently on her lower lip. His lips parted and he started exploring her mouth with his tongue and she pushed herself into him further. The swing they were sitting on rocked back and forth, and they rocked with it and in the shadows it was impossible to see where he ended and where she began. He broke away just long enough for her to breathe, and for him to push his hair from his face, and then he was kissing her again and she melded into him once more, letting the fireworks between her legs fizzle all the way out to her fingertips where they gripped onto him and pulled him even closer into her, wanting to feel him all over her.

'We should get a room,' she murmured, when his hand played with the hem of her little dress, leaving a fiery trail across the skin of her thighs.

He pulled back. 'Don't talk that way,' he said.

'Excuse me?'

'I do the chasing, okay? Don't be a slut.'

She jerked back as if he had punched her. 'What did you just call me?'

'I didn't call you anything. It's just that a man needs to feel like a man, and if you lie down and spread your legs, then it's too easy. Do you not like the way I kiss you?' he said, leaning in and taking a strong, deliberate kiss. Her spine turned to jelly.

'You kiss like the devil,' she said.

'That's good?'

'Very good.'

'So relax. Are you like the American girls that party for Spring Break and try and hook up with as many guys as they can?'

'Of course not,' she said, but she remembered a holiday with some university friends when she had done exactly that. She couldn't remember why it had been so important to feel desired and she couldn't recall any of the three holiday romances she'd had that year being particularly satisfying on any level.

'Kiss me again, Ray,' she said. 'Kiss me and tell me to shut up.'

Later on they had some food. Tiny flaking corn discs spread with black bean paste, scattered with lettuce and crumbly white cheese like feta. Chicken cooked in a stew and served with floury tortillas to mop up the rich, peanut mole sauce.

'This is the kind of food you should serve at the bar,' she said.

'We don't do food.'

'You should. People like to wander around downtown and they want a snack that isn't Subway or McDonald's.'

He shook his head and chewed his chicken. 'We can't compete with the *mercados*.'

'You're not trying to compete with them.'

'Good, because I can't.'

'You're competing with the other knife and fork places. You're a restaurant, not a street cart.'

'We're a bar.'

'With potential.'

'You sound like my sister,' he said.

'She sounds smart.'

'She is. Always looking for a way to turn a buck. When we were kids she saw lemonade stands in a Charlie Brown comic book and set up a little table with plastic cups and a jug of *agua fresca*. You have *agua fresca*? Esmé, that's her name. She makes hers with lime and cucumber and mint.'

'Sounds delicious.'

'But a bar is for drinking beer and liquor, not messing around with lemonade.'

'It's your bar,' she said. 'You can make it whatever you want it to be.'

'I want it to be the best bar in Downtown Cancún.'

'Then let me help you.' The bonfire on the beach had

died away and she could see out to the sea. She scanned the horizon for the black shadow of Des Amparados but it was too dark now. Would he want a daughter, her father? Would he want a daughter like her?

'What time's the last ferry back to town?' she said.

'I know a place we can stay.'

She knew that blocking out uncomfortable thoughts about absent fathers and empty islands with reckless, hungry sex was destructive, but when she lay back naked across crisp white hotel sheets and Ray found the sweet spot inside her that made her buck and moan beneath him, every single thought shut down until all she could do was scream and let go.

14

In the dark depths of heartbreak, Claudia found the most unexpected ray of light.

It was Lucy who guessed. She saw that Claudia's appetite was not the mean appetite of despair, and spotted that her fatigue and mild nausea were the kind associated with something else altogether. She pressed a pregnancy test into her daughter's hand and poured herself a stiff gin and tonic while she waited outside the bathroom and contemplated becoming a grandmother. Claudia was so young. Her natural shyness and her pale blond hair meant that she could almost pass for a teenager still. Lucy shuddered and felt very old.

In the cold, clean bathroom, Claudia felt shock pierce the cloud of numbness she had dragged around since that awful day when her sky had caved in under the weight of humiliation and heartbreak. She felt the gentle fingers of hope reach out to wipe away her tears and point towards a brighter future. She felt a flash of pure joy.

She was having David's baby. She would be the mother of his child. A part of him was inside her now and would be with her forever.

She wanted to tell him at once.

They had not spoken at all. He had smashed her life and then he had changed his number, Camille – her friend – had done the same.

'It was the money,' she had wept to her mother long into the night. 'He just wanted money and Camille has more money than I do.'

'Darling, you weren't to blame. He must be very charming.'

'He didn't love me.'

'No,' said Lucy, 'he didn't. He lied to you, but in a way that makes it easier, doesn't it? A liar can't be helped.'

If her mother knew that laced through the misery was a sincere wish that she had been wealthy enough to keep hold of him, then surely she would have been ashamed. And Claudia was ashamed enough for both of them.

She was able to extract his new telephone number at last from Mika. She had found it so incredibly difficult not to think about him constantly, not to speak to him at all, and simply being able to hear his voice would feel like a rest-stop after a long and arduous journey. Either pictures of David had stopped appearing in *La Crónica* or her friends had decided to stop telling her about them. Not knowing what to expect, she telephoned the new number.

One way or another they would be forced to deal with it and move forward instead of stagnating in the miserable depths as he had forced her to do. Perhaps when they spoke, things would make sense again, and when he heard this news, everything would have to change.

Perhaps – a secret wish that she would never dare to even whisper – things could go back to the way they were.

'You broke my heart you know,' she said, instead of hello. 'I was humiliated. I never wanted to speak to you again. That's why I didn't call.'

'What changed?'

She savoured the moment, breathing in the power of the bomb she was able to drop on him. 'I'm having a baby,' she said. 'Your baby.'

'Our baby.'

'My baby.'

The words curled comfortably into her mouth. The idea of having a baby: it felt like something she could do, something she should do. It couldn't ruin her life – her life was already ruined. To be bound to him like this gave her an enormous sense of relief.

She braced herself and waited for him to tell her how an unplanned love child would ruin his political career and his new relationship, to turn this around and make it her fault, perhaps even to demand that she had an abortion. A shiver of anticipation ran through her. They would argue, and then what?

'Congratulations,' he said.

'That's it?'

She heard his slow intake of breath and knew he wanted to swear but was holding back. 'What is it that you want me to say?' His impatience was palpable.

'I don't know, maybe you could say something about being a father for the first time. Are you shocked? Worried? You could ask how I feel.'

'How do you feel?'

191

She bit down hard on her lower lip. He didn't care. This didn't change anything. She was offering herself up as a victim again, only this time it was worse. A thought occurred to her. Was she there watching all this, the new wife? Was he making that wind-up-the-call gesture that he used to do? Had they slipped together into the sensual coexistence that she missed so much? The arrow of pain that pierced her chest was so true it made her double up in a silent scream as she lost him all over again.

'Will you tell her?'

'Who?'

'Your wife.'

'Why would I do that?'

'What if she reads about it in the newspaper?' Her voice dropped to a whisper. 'It would kill her.'

'I very much doubt it.'

Her control folded. She felt her chest spasm and the cold tears slide down her face. She could not speak. The unbearable tension in her body was the only thing keeping her on her feet. She could see his face in front of her, could hear the beats of the first tango when he took her in his arms. But still it was his voice telling her all of those feelings should be over now, with the same tired inflection and his way of slicing to the meat of things as if anything else was just a waste of time.

'I thought that you should know. It felt like the right thing to do,' she said at last.

'You are very thoughtful,' he said, and it felt as restrained as a kiss on the hand. 'I expect you will also tell me when the bastard is born?'

Claudia paused just long enough to let his nastiness bounce off her resolve. 'You know what, David?' she said. 'You're heartless. Don't talk to me like this. You can kiss off everything and not even look back, not even feel bad, not even say sorry. And maybe that's your right, what's past is past, but this *bastard* is not even born yet and already you've written it off. I won't have you talking so dismissively. It's not fair, how dare you?'

'Do you need money?'

'Ha! What will you do? Ask Camille?'

'If necessary. Although then I would probably have to tell her about the pregnancy.'

'Surely you could just lie?'

'I never lie, Claudia. I told you that the first day I met you.'

That first time she saw him when he appeared to her like some kind of golden God and she had never looked back. Not until it was over.

Claudia saw her mother standing in the doorway watching her cry. She turned her face away but she heard her footsteps walking closer, over the sound of her own ragged breaths pleading into David's icy silence. 'You can't . . .' she said, 'you must . . .'

Then her mother's hand was on her shoulder and her voice was as soft and calm as a pond. 'Put the phone down, darling,' said Lucy. 'Stop talking and put the phone down.'

Claudia did as she was told, turned around and flung herself into her mother, nuzzling into her shoulder and letting the sobs just come for a while. Lucy stroked her

193

hair and told her not to cry and that everything was going to be okay. They would work it out.

A few weeks later, Claudia and Lucy drove up to the family house in Oxfordshire. Her grandmother was not there – she spent most of her time in Scotland now with her latest husband and their countless dogs – but she had left them keys for one of the estate cottages and had told Lucy that Claudia could live there for as long as she liked. They picked their way through the poky cottage, throwing open curtains and shaking off dustsheets, forcing open windows that had swollen closed. The back kitchen led out into a small garden, riotous with foxgloves and poppies in long grass.

'You said you wanted some space,' said Lucy. 'A few weeks might be all you need, but if you decide to stay here you can have the baby at Beard Mill and we'll go from there. Is that okay?'

'Are you trying to get rid of me?' asked Claudia.

'Not for the reasons you think.'

'For any reason?'

'Because you said that you wanted some space. How's this for space?' The view from the cottage garden spread down into the woods and beyond that over the county and towards Warwickshire. The sun was warm on her face. Claudia was reminded of holidays she had spent in this part of the world, of picnics in the woods and sledging after church on Christmas Day. How could she look the poor women of Mexico City in the face again when she was the recipient of so much comfort and charity she did not deserve?

'I can't go back to Mexico,' she said. 'Never. It's too humiliating.'

'I know,' said Lucy. 'Believe me I know.'

Claudia settled into the cottage and went about the business of getting through the day with a slothful apathy. She knew that it was important to take care of herself and she tried to feed her constant hunger with things that were good for her and for the baby, but mostly she ate steaks and salad, with buttery potatoes baked in their jackets, the same thing every night; leftovers for lunch, nothing for breakfast except tea, made in the pot, which she drank constantly. She felt very alone, although as her prenatal checks passed without incident and she started to feel the baby's movements, she realized that she was not alone at all, just lonely. In Mexico City she had been surrounded by twenty million people and felt alone all the same. Until David.

Although eventually the heartache dulled, as everyone had said it would, it was replaced by a secret hope that she didn't share with a soul, a hope that at some point in the future David would realize his mistake and come back to her. If anyone had asked her she would have denied that this was what she wanted, she would have said that she was over him, but she would have been lying.

She barely left the cottage. Her skin started to look bad, and when her mother commented on it, she blamed it on pregnancy hormones. She let the summer pass by outside while she stayed behind the small windows and panicked about her future. She bought a book about pregnancy and babies and it was so neurotic that it turned her insomniac for several days until at last she left it out for the charity shop and decided not to read any more such books for a while.

'Have you decided what you want to do?' asked Lucy.

'I'm having the baby here,' she said. 'At home.'

'Don't be absurd.'

'I can, it's allowed. A midwife will come here to help me. I can use the spare bedroom at the front.'

'I spoke to Beard Mill, just in case. They have the space, and darling I can take care of the costs.'

Claudia picked at her nails. She had been trying to grow tomatoes in the garden to force herself into the fresh air. Mud was deep beneath her fingernails like a bizarre French manicure; she could smell the tomato plants on them.

'I never had you down as some kind of hippy,' said Lucy.

'What do you mean?'

'Having a baby at home is such a – I don't know – earthy thing to do.'

'It seems the easiest option,' said Claudia. 'Why would I want to go anywhere when I'm in labour? Let them come to us.' She had been to the NHS hospital in Banbury for her scans and, given the chance to avoid those sterile corridors and forced social interactions, she put her name down for home birth there and then. Her pregnancy was expected to be straightforward. When the booking midwife had described her as an 'excellent candidate', she had felt proud of herself for the first time in months. Her mother had never given her any perspective on this pregnancy other than that it was another sort of failure.

'Do you want me here?' asked Lucy. 'You know, when the time comes?'

'God no,' said Claudia.

'Thank you, darling,' said Lucy. 'Although, of course if you change your mind . . .' She winked and then shuddered.

To the surprise of them both, their relationship seemed to thrive out here in the country. They rarely saw eye to eye but their differences could rub along nicely in the open where there was plenty of room for all kinds of opinions. Her mother must feel it too: why else would she come back on her next visit with good sheets for the guest room and state that if Claudia was determined to give birth like a peasant, she should at least be lying on Egyptian cotton.

Claudia felt angry still, all the time. She raised her new grumpy personality like a shield when forced to pay the milkman or the boy who came to deal with the falling leaves from the plum tree in the garden.

Christmas came and went. There would be no sledging this year. She was so big that she could barely sit down and everybody said, the various shopkeepers and strangers of the village who saw fit to comment, that she must be having a bouncing baby boy. And one night in spring, with a frost dusting the landscape like ash, a bouncing baby boy was exactly what she had.

Her son was born after a tiring twenty-four-hour labour onto her crisp clean sheets. He looked nothing like either of his parents, he just looked like a baby, and she assumed that the waves of love she had expected to feel would come later when she wasn't so exhausted.

'Hello,' she whispered.

When Lucy arrived a few hours later she took the baby up into her arms with none of Claudia's hesitation and had never looked so much like a mother.

'Have you thought of what you might call him?' she asked.

'Maybe Danny, Daniel. Would you be okay with that?'

'Sweetheart, anything other than David would be wonderful. I assumed you would want to call him after his father. I'm delighted that you don't.'

She didn't tell her mother that David was what she had planned to call a boy at first, except when she'd peered into his unfocused eyes for the first time, it was not his father that she thought of, but her own. 'Daniel,' she said. 'Daniel Stewart. Stewart after Pappy.'

'He'll be over the moon.'

'I must call him,' said Claudia.

'And David, will you call him too?'

Claudia looked down at the sleeping baby and knew at once that he would be better off if she stopped thinking about David now and moved on. 'I don't think I will,' said Claudia. 'He'll work it out if he cares enough to remember.'

'And if he doesn't?'

'Then Daniel is one more child growing up without his father. It doesn't always have to be a disaster.'

The unspoken agreement was that the worst of their own disastrous relationship was behind them.

The first few months were very hard. Despite the best efforts of her mother to offset feelings of loneliness by forcing old family friends to call in on her and offer their congratulations, Claudia was always happier when they left. Then, when it was just her and Daniel, she could retreat back into the bedroom where they mostly lived and sink into her inadequacy as she fed him all through the night just so they could both get back to sleep again. She lied to everyone, including her own mother, when they asked if he was a good sleeper, because the truth was that he might well be a good sleeper if she let him sleep in his own cot, but by now she had grown so used to his tiny form warm beside her, the ease of feeding him without leaving the cosy confines of their nest, that she kept putting off the move.

It was as if she was living two separate lives: in one she sat and chattered with people she barely knew, let strangers hold Daniel and smiled while she poured the tea; and in the other one she never slept, and lived a world of milk, shit and the flickering light of a muted television.

After a while her mother insisted that she employ a nanny a couple of afternoons a week. She found her a nice Scottish girl, who Claudia hired even though every sighting of this capable, maternal force made her feel pathetic that she couldn't cope on her own. She was managing perfectly well. The baby was clothed and healthy, fed and burped. What more did anyone want?

Underneath her bed, in a box with the postcard from Las Vegas, was a chart of the sailing waters around Cancún. She could not look at it without feeling overwhelming despair. What good did it do her to know the name of a place on the other side of the world where her father's footprints had once fallen? It was a shred of information that might as well float away on the tide. Wherever he was he would not want her. He never had.

One night, when baby Daniel would not stop crying – relentless wails of unspecified anguish that her milk and rock-a-bye arms did nothing to abate, she called David in Mexico City one more time and simply put the phone close to their child's bawling mouth. She was too exhausted to do anything more. After a few seconds she took the phone back again but David had already hung up. Of course he had, she thought, looking down at her angry little squawk. Who wouldn't?

She rocked him back and forth, back and forth.

Her own father had never been given the chance to hold her. Her mother said that she had tried to find him but it was easy to imagine that she hadn't tried particularly hard. He did not know that she existed.

Might it have been better, she mused, if she had never met David? Ignorance is bliss. Now that she knew how heartbreak feels, would she still choose the love he gave her? Putting aside everything she had learnt about herself at the Women's Centre and all the friends she had made there, was she glad that she had known David and loved him? Even now?

She decided yes.

And finally baby Daniel's head lolled onto her arm and

200

he fell into an exhausted sleep. The silence rushed back in like a roll of tide and carried with it a sense of purpose. If her father was still alive, she would find him. She would let him know he had a family.

Every so often, her mother insisted that she make the torturous sortie into London, but Claudia always found an excuse not to. Lucy said it was important for Claudia not to lose touch with reality completely, but Claudia felt as if the real world was no longer relevant. She had been to the toddler group in a nearby village and then spent the rest of the afternoon crying at the thought of ever having to see those women again, well-meaning women who were killing her with their kindness. It was hard to stay grumpy in the face of such barefaced enthusiasm.

'Will you be renting here very long?' they all asked innocently, not knowing that the very question threw up a hundred more about what she was doing, where she was going and how she wanted to live. She didn't tell them she was connected to the prominent family at the big house. She remembered from a bad experience at the local youth club nearby that this did not endear her to people. She never went back to youth club, and this only reinforced the perception that she was a bit of a snob. She would not be going back to toddler group either.

'Dinner at Cecconi's,' said her mother. 'You have to get out and engage with civilization.'

'What about Daniel?' He was fast approaching the age that she had been when her mother flew the coop, and she was starting to understand how Lucy must have felt when she crawled out from under the responsibility. To be able to say, 'Dinner sounds fabulous, why not?' To be free. But she conveniently forgot that dinner with her mother had long been an ordeal, with or without the added complication of a baby. And that her mother was never happy, responsibilities or no responsibilities. And when she tried to put herself in her mother's position and imagined leaving him, there was something tugging on her heartstrings that went far beyond a sense of responsibility. Knowing that her mother had not felt that strong connection, or had felt it and ignored it, made her wonder what she had done wrong.

'Bring the nanny,' said Lucy.

'She doesn't work weekends.'

'Are you sure? Have you asked her? I'm sure she'd be thrilled to earn an extra fifty quid.'

Claudia ran out of excuses.

The nanny immediately said yes, though she negotiated her pay up to seventy pounds. In next to no time, Claudia was sitting in a good restaurant wearing a pretty dress, confident that Daniel was asleep and safe in Pimlico. It seemed almost a shame to wreck the atmosphere by telling her mother of her plans.

'I'm thinking of taking a holiday,' she said.

Her mother nodded. 'You should leave Daniel with me,' she said immediately. 'Have a proper break, recharge.'

'I don't mean a weekend in Lausanne. I'm talking about a few weeks – months, even.'

'That's okay,' said Lucy. 'Try some of my crab.'

'I'm not leaving Daniel with you for a month!'

'Whatever you like,' said Lucy. 'I'm here if you need me.'

'Is that supposed to be a joke?'

'What?' Lucy reluctantly stopped eating her crab salad when she realized her daughter was furious.

'You had a baby once,' said Claudia, 'and you abandoned me, so if you think I'd let Daniel stay with you so you can work through whatever sense of guilt you might still be nurturing, then forget it.'

'I was trying to be helpful,' said Lucy softly. She pushed her plate aside even though she had not finished. She no longer had an appetite. 'I believe that's what grandmothers do.'

'And what about what mothers do?'

'I did what I had to do. One day maybe you'll understand.'

'I'm going to Mexico,' said Claudia. 'I want to find out what happened to my father.'

'Don't be ridiculous, you can't go to Mexico.'

'Sawyer told me the name of the island where he owned a house. Did you know that my father owned a house?'

'Sawyer had no right to tell you that.'

'You had no right not to.'

'You can't go to Mexico, it's too dangerous.'

Claudia felt radiant. The joy of defying her mother was making her glow. The more objections that Lucy threw in front of her plans, the more she wanted to smash them out of the way and proceed.

'You can't take a small child to the opposite side of the world on a whisper, and believe me when I tell you this, Claudia: it's a fool's errand. Danny Featherbow has been gone a long time.'

'Then I'll go to Las Vegas.'

203

'And do what?'

'I have to do something, don't you see? I have to. I can't rot in a cottage up there and hope that the answers come to me. I have to go out there into the world and ask the right questions.'

'You would have to take security, and an extra nanny for Daniel, a night nanny. You will need a place to stay, access to money and basic services. It's not feasible.'

'No nannies. And security? Are you mad?'

'You are a wealthy woman travelling in one of the most troubled countries of the world. Of course you need to take security.'

'I have looked at the sailing charts. Des Amparados is within shouting distance of the Hard Rock Café. It's hardly the wilds.'

Lucy looked genuinely stricken. 'Don't be flippant about this, Claudia. I am trying to protect you. Go without a nanny if you wish, but you simply must take a bodyguard of some kind. You could hire Sawyer.'

'Sawyer? Now I know you're being ridiculous.'

'Not at all. He's army trained, ex-military – private security is his thing now. Let me call him.'

'Absolutely not,' said Claudia.

'You're determined to go?'

Claudia nodded.

'And you won't leave Daniel with me?'

She shook her head. 'The nanny starts a new job on Monday. I've booked the flights: we leave in four days.'

Lucy said nothing, staring at her daughter as if she was hoping for her to say something else. Claudia thought she saw a wash of tears mist her mother's eyes, but then

204

Lucy took a deep breath and the candlelight shifted, and Claudia assumed it was a trick of the light.

Lucy caught the attention of a passing waiter. 'Two shots of Herradura, the Suprema,' she said.

'Tequila?'

'I think it's appropriate, don't you?'

When the shot glass came, Lucy stopped her daughter from slamming it down in one. 'This is an *ultra anejo*, aged in oak caskets for five years. You sip it, slowly.' Lucy swirled her glass as if it was a fine cognac. 'Think of a cactus under the hot desert sun, year after year, those lethal spikes warding off the elements, all so that you and I can sit here in this fine London establishment and savour the sun's glory in every sip.' She raised her glass. 'I wish you would reconsider Mexico,' she said. 'But even though you think I don't know you well, I know you well enough to see my stubborn streak running through you a mile wide. So I'm not going to beg you not to go. I'm just begging you to be vigilant.' She raised her glass. 'Be careful, that's all.'

Claudia raised her own glass and they toasted each other. 'I will.'

The following evening Claudia was driving back to her cottage, having said goodbye to the nanny when they dropped her off in town. Daniel was asleep in the back of the car and she was alone with her thoughts. The landscape looked particularly beautiful, as if taunting her for leaving it all behind. She had the strangest sense that she would never be coming back, even though she would leave most of her things in the cottage. She did not know what she would find in Mexico; she would never tell anyone how terrified she was that she would find nothing at all. It felt like a new beginning.

The road was icy beneath the car and on her right there was a steep drop down over the frosted fields of three counties, darkening in the fast-fading light, which made her press her foot down on the accelerator a little harder so that she could get home and light a fire before the chill really took hold. She still had so much to do.

She did not see the deer leap from the woods and straight in front of her until it was too late to do much except brake and pray. It was a young deer, probably no more than a year, and before Claudia's eyes snapped shut in terror, she saw him quake with a fear that mirrored her own, as the car took a lazy, uncontrolled spin across the winding road. Her foot was hard on the brake but having no effect. There was a sickening crunch as metal smashed through hard bone and then mercifully, finally, the car smacked up against the trees, having spun in a complete circle to come back to the safe side of the road and the woods.

Her eyes whipped to the backseat, and when she saw that Daniel had slept through the entire episode, she smiled with relief. Her hands on the wheel were shaking and she rested her head on the back of them so that they would stop trembling. Her engine had cut out so she started it again and her headlights carved through the blackness of the first trees to pick out the deer, bucking and lurching on the forest floor, half his head caved

206

in as if he had been stoned. She felt sick. She checked on Daniel, still sleeping, and cautiously stepped out of the car.

The chill was shocking, like diving into cold water, and her misty breath caught the diffused light of the moon from behind the high cloud. There was no wind tonight to take her breath away and it sparkled as it hung in the air. When she breathed out again, it was as if she was surrounded by fog.

She approached the stricken deer in a daze. His plaintive bleats sounded alien in the silence of the shadowy woods. She could see the trail of blood on the road where he had dragged himself into the safety of the tall oaks; she could see white gunk that she realized might be his brain and she gagged violently.

'*Out of the way.*'

She was firmly pushed aside as he marched past her.

'Sawyer?' she said incredulously.

In his right hand he held a pistol. He pressed the gun into what was left of the deer's head and pulled the trigger.

The shot echoed across the field and a pair of roosting pheasants was startled into the sky.

'Sawyer?' she said again. 'Were you following me?'

'Your mother sent me,' he said. 'I'm to take care of you. I understand we're going to Mexico.'

Lucy was having a light lunch in the atrium at the Landmark Hotel at Marylebone when Claudia burst into the hush and marched across the room to confront her.

'How could you?' she demanded.

Lucy apologized to her companion, a woman her own age who smiled with sickening insincerity, and ushered Claudia into one of the quiet spaces near the hotel lobby. 'Where's Daniel?' she asked.

'In a room upstairs, I brought the nanny.'

'This is about Sawyer? I told you I didn't want you going to Mexico without protection.'

'And I told you there was no way I was going to pay Sawyer Stone to look after me. He's obnoxious, he's cavalier. Don't you understand? I have to do this on my own.'

'You are not paying him,' said Lucy firmly. 'I am. Just as you are not paying for your ticket, or for your accommodation, or for your entire life, for that matter.'

'You had no right.'

'I have every right,' she said. 'I'm your mother.'

'When it suits you.'

'I am always your mother, Claudia. Like it or not.'

'So that's it? I have to have Sawyer watching my back or you'll cut me off?'

'Yes,' she said. 'That's it.'

Claudia glared at her. Lucy glared right back.

'I hope I find my father,' said Claudia.

'You're setting yourself up for an enormous disappointment.'

'He can't be any worse than you.'

15

Esmé and her mother were both trapped. Carlos controlled how much money they had, where they went, how
they lived. It was worse than being with Miguel.

'He loves me,' said Catalina.

Carlos didn't love her; he kept her stashed here to keep
the house and the books, and be a warm body in the
bed if he stopped by. Esmé felt responsible. She was the
one who had pushed for them to come out here. But that
was before she knew that her mother was falling in love
with a pimp who took young foreign girls, dazed from an
interview with a so-called temp agency, and put them to
work on their backs.

'He's a pig,' said Esmé. 'You watch him. Just watch
him paw at me when he says hello. He's a creep.'

'Tonight could be the night, Esmé.'

Her mother still thought there was a possibility of a
marriage proposal. Esmé didn't have the heart to question her about the pale stripe on her boyfriend's ring finger that made her suspect he might already be married.
Catalina would refuse to listen.

'We have to get out of here,' said Esmé.

'And do what? What did you think it was going to be

like, exactly? I don't have it so bad, Esmé. I have a place to live and a job.' Thanks mostly to the efforts of Esmé and her mother, the women that worked for Carlos were luckier than many in their position. They knew they could call Catalina if things with a trick turned nasty and Catalina would swiftly despatch a muscle on loan from Carlos. But too many girls put up with pretty much anything to avoid causing trouble, so very low was their sense of worth, so scared were they of the debt Carlos told them all they needed to repay him for their travel and the squalid rooms he let them have for nothing out of the goodness of his heart.

Esmé changed tack. 'You could go to Madrid,' she said. 'I met this Spanish girl at the cinema last night and she—'

'I like it here.'

Esmé shook her head vehemently. 'Nobody could like it here. This house, the smell of it makes me feel sick.'

Catalina's eyes flashed with brewing fury. 'It has been weeks, Esmé. Longer than you said. Isn't it time you went home?'

'I don't want to leave you,' said Esmé. 'Not with him.'

Catalina shrugged and spritzed herself with a cloud of perfume that was supposed to be Guerlain but smelt like sour milk. A gift from Carlos, no doubt. A cheap knock-off of the thing that it was supposed to be. 'Come on, let's go, we'll be late.'

'He's not picking us up?'

'When does he ever?'

The meal was delicious but the company was painful. She didn't know why he had insisted that Esmé come with them tonight, but was glad of the chance to watch out for her mother as Carlos kept plying them both with cheap champagne. Catalina was soon rolling. After dinner they took a cab to a nightclub where everybody knew Carlos and they drank lots of white wine.

'You can hold your drink better than your mother,' said Carlos, nodding towards Catalina, who was snoozing in the corner of their booth.

'I don't get drunk,' said Esmé. 'I've tried. My brother Ray says it's because I won't let go.'

'Have you tried drugs?'

She shook her head, not fooled by his overly casual tone. She wondered if her mother had taken something and that was why she was pretty much out of it. The music in this club was relentless and Carlos had to lean very close to her to make himself heard.

'I want to talk to you,' he said. 'How would you like to earn three thousand dollars?'

She stalled. 'American dollars?'

'What? Yeah, of course.'

'Doing what?'

'Surely you can guess?' Carlos poured her another glass of white wine and she hoped that this would be the one that tipped her over into oblivion because unless she was very much mistaken her mother's boyfriend was asking her to have sex for money. 'You don't have to decide tonight,' he said. 'But a friend of mine is coming into town next weekend and he has asked me to make arrangements. Speaks Spanish, not a freak.'

'Does my mother know you are asking me this?'

'You must know by now that you are a beautiful girl,

Esmé, and with the accent and your amazing skin . . .' He looked her up and down. 'Was your father white?'

'He was a tourist having a holiday romance.'

'I could make you a lot of money,' he said. 'You think I haven't known that from the minute I met you? Since the first time I saw your picture?' His hand brushed the bare skin at the hem of her skirt and she jumped back violently and spilt her glass, the white wine flooding the table and dripping onto the floor.

With a snap of his fingers Carlos was able to summon one of the waiting staff to take care of the mess.

'We should go,' she said. 'I need to get her home.' She shuffled over to sit beside her mother and roused her from her light sleep. 'Come on,' she said. 'Let's go.' She turned to Carlos who seemed amused by this sudden flurry of activity. 'Are you going to call us a cab?'

He helped her with her drunken mother and hailed a black cab on the street. 'Think about what I said, okay? If not this time, then maybe next time, no pressure.'

'You're not coming with us?' she said, relieved when he shook his head no.

'You shouldn't let her drink so much,' he said. Then he walked back into the club and didn't look back.

'He's a real prince, your boyfriend, Ma,' she said, but her mother was snoozing again and didn't say anything.

That night in bed, lying awake and thinking about the options available to her, a third option opened up. She could tell Carlos that she was willing to sleep with his friend. Then take the money and run.

The next day she told him she would do it. And she made plans for their escape.

She needed to persuade Catalina to leave with her. She could see the road ahead for her mother and it was terrifying. After giving it some thought, she decided to try and shock her into action at the very last minute, hoping that the element of surprise would be on her side.

She waited until everything was arranged – the time, the place, the price – and then she confronted her mother for the final time.

'We're going,' she said bluntly. 'Right now. Carlos is trying to recruit me and I'm scared of what will happen to me if I stay, and I'm scared of what will happen to you if I don't. So we're going. Okay? It'll be fun.'

The sigh that escaped from Catalina's lips carried no regrets, only sadness. Slowly and deliberately she crossed the room to embrace her only daughter.

'I'm staying,' she said and burst into tears.

Esmé stamped her foot impatiently. 'Did you hear what I said? He tried to recruit me. Your boyfriend is hoping to pimp me out. There is a man waiting for me in a hotel room.' Catalina didn't say anything, just carried on crying, and Esmé fought with her urge to run and comfort her. 'Is that what you want for me? For us.'

'Just go,' said Catalina. 'I never asked you to come with me.'

'Please, Mama? At least for a little while. You need to get away from him so that you can see things as they really are.'

'Isn't that what you told Miguel? Just for a little while? To clear your head?'

'No,' said Esmé. 'I told him that I was worried about my mother.'

Esmé crossed to the bedroom, pulled the suitcase from the top of the wardrobe and started packing Catalina's things.

'Stop it,' said Catalina, pressing her hands to the side of her head as if she had a migraine. 'What the hell are you doing?'

'I'll make sure we get to Madrid,' she said, 'and from there perhaps Barcelona or another beach town. Maybe it will remind us of home.'

'If you miss home so badly, why don't you go back? Why do you hate Mexico so much?'

'Why do you?'

Catalina appeared to give the question thought. 'Because of the disappointment. Because of everything that happened to me there, I suppose.'

'I hate it because of everything that *didn't* happen to me. Married at sixteen, no college, no adventure, no money of my own.'

'You ever think maybe Mexico is not to blame for the way you feel?' Catalina pushed back her long dark hair. She had cried away most of her make-up and she was once again the simple straight-talking Mexican woman she had been before he found her. 'Maybe you are running away from problems that you can't leave behind.'

'And you're not?'

'I left a part of myself buried in Cancún. Some good, some bad. Everyone I once was. Carlos is a wicked man, but I have known him to be kind, and I do believe he loves me. And I think these girls need someone like me here watching their backs. There are worse things to be in life than a prostitute.'

She walked to the safe, unlocked the combination and handed Esmé her passport.

Esmé fought back tears of her own. She pushed her nails into the soft flesh of her palm and focused on that pain instead of the pain in her heart. 'I love you so much, Mama. I don't think I can make it without you.'

'Don't say that,' said Catalina. 'I have brought you nothing but trouble.'

'You're my mother; you have given me love. It is enough.' She had a sudden memory of her mother teaching her how to swim in the crystal-clear waters of a beach somewhere, holding her for hours until she learnt to trust the natural buoyancy of her body and was finally able to let go. Her mother had screamed with delight.

Catalina pressed her hands on either side of her daughter's face, as if committing her face to memory to last her a long time.

'I have to tell you something,' said Catalina urgently.

'What?'

'There is an island, Des Amparados,' she said. 'Do you know it?'

'I think so. You can't get a ferry there, though.'

'A long time ago, the night I met your father, I buried some money there – a lot of money.' She spoke fast, as if afraid that the words would stop coming if she did not get them out.

'Whose money?'

215

'Your father's money,' said Catalina. 'There is a small temple to Ixchel on the edge of the beach at Des Amparados, the third stone from the end. The money was in a cotton bag, which may have rotted away, I suppose, but inside there was a plastic cash envelope. It will still be okay.'

'And you've left it there all this time?'

'I thought that I would see him again one day, and that I could give it back to him, but he disappeared, he just disappeared. Nobody knew where he had gone. Nobody had even heard his name.'

'What was his name?'

Catalina smiled. 'Danny. His name was Danny. I never told you that? At least that's what he said. I guess that he might have been lying about some things. After a while, when I didn't see him, I didn't want to go back. I didn't want to take his money. Not without his love.' She glanced around the apartment, paid for solely by Carlos. 'And now look at me.'

'You could earn your own money,' said Esmé.

'It's too late for me,' said Catalina. 'Don't worry about me. But that money is yours, Esmé, it is your father's money. There's thousands of dollars. It should be yours.'

'I can earn my own money too.'

She could not be sure, but she thought she saw something like pride cross her mother's face and she wondered if they would ever see each other again. 'I can't stay,' she said.

'I know.'

'Is there anything I can say to make you change your mind?' When her mother shook her head, she couldn't even look Esmé in the eye. 'Then do what's good for you,' said Esmé, 'and don't tell him you knew I was planning to leave.'

'But where will you go?'

'Anywhere but here.'

Esmé walked through the vast atrium of the Landmark Hotel and wondered if she looked like a prostitute. She was wearing a charity shop dress and had pinned her hair up at the front, letting the rest of it swing down in luxurious waves towards the small of her back. Her shoes were expensive, on loan from her mother, and her neckline was modest. But she was sporting a slash of fierce red lipstick that glared at anyone who dared to look at her. Even though she had no intention of going through with anything, Esmé still felt imaginary eyes on her as she walked to the elevator.

Upstairs she padded along the carpets until she found the room number that Carlos had given her. Then she knocked.

'Esmé?'

She wished there and then that she had thought to use a fake name. 'Hello.'

'Come in and shut the door.'

She stood awkwardly in the corner of the room whilst the man – old enough to be her father, grey haired with a fat face the colour of raw pork – bent over his computer and tapped a few keys. The bed in the room was unmade and she noticed the sheets needed washing. It made her think of all the other rooms in this hotel and whether a drama was being played out in each of them, or if some of them had occupants for whom life was a simple process. She thought about the rooms that were empty, calm and serene. She thought of anything she could to avoid thinking about the room in which she stood.

When he turned back to her a full five minutes later, he seemed surprised.

'Take off your dress,' he said, loosening his tie. He had a strange accent that she found hard to understand.

'Aren't you forgetting something?' she said.

'I have a condom.'

'There's a matter of three thousand dollars.'

'It's five and I gave it to your pimp.'

'He's not my pimp.'

'Boyfriend, whatever. Take off your dress.'

She wanted to punch the wall. How could she have been so stupid? All the reassurances Carlos had given her – that she would be safe and that she could back out whenever she wanted; she could keep all the money – not once did she think to confirm where the money would change hands. Of course Carlos had pocketed it, of course he had. She wondered briefly how much of that five thousand would have made it to her, if any at all. He would probably think that her sense of shame would hold back her sense of entitlement. She had seen this lifestyle break several women over the last few months, taking from them the last bit of fight they had left. Carlos depended on it to stay afloat.

Like her mother, she had stupidly believed herself capable of some special arrangement with Carlos by virtue of their personal relationship, when the truth was that he saw her as just another whore.

She was more like her mother than she had ever imagined.

'There's been a mistake,' she said, readying herself to flee the room, checking the latch – on – and recalling the way back to the elevator. She took a couple of steps towards the door.

'Take off your fucking dress,' he said.

He was on her within two strides, ripping the thin silk straps of the forty-year-old fabric, and pushing her towards the bed.

She tried to sidestep him but he blocked her way. 'I'll scream rape,' she said. She hated the way that her voice cracked and weakened her threat.

'Nobody gives a shit.'

He pushed her half onto the bed. His body weight felt massive. If she had wanted to scream she would not have been able to, because it felt as if he was crushing her, lungs first. She was trapped. Pointlessly she kicked out at him and one of her shoes flew off. She heard it land somewhere near her head and strained to reach it with her free arm, her fingers stretching until they got hold. It wasn't much, but it was something, and her grateful fingers curled around it like a hand to hold, making a nasty weapon out of the sexy heel.

On top of her, he forced her legs apart with a mean thrust of his thigh and held her by her jaw as he dry-humped her skirt around her waist.

She slammed the heel of her shoe into the soft flesh beneath his cheekbone and he yowled like a savaged dog. '*Bitch*!' he screamed.

She pushed her right knee hard into his stomach and

his body weight shifted just enough to let her slip from beneath him and scrabble to her feet.

He rose up, clutching the side of his face and spitting blood onto the bed. 'My bloody teeth, you crazy whore.' She moved fast: *door, latch, hallway, run.*

She left behind her shoe and lurched awkwardly on one heel, not daring to stop and remove it.

But he wasn't coming after her. When she got to the elevators she looked back to judge if she would be better off taking the stairs, and she caught a glimpse of him, the back of his head as he stepped back into his room. One more stain on his sheets.

Who would he call next? Carlos? The police?

All she had in her bag was her passport and a return ticket to Cancún.

She thought of the buried treasure, a legacy from the father she never knew, and felt a needle of hope push into the mess of panic and paranoia in her head. Hope was all that she had left.

Soon she was on a plane back to Mexico. Back to a husband she no longer loved, leaving a mother in need of her prayers. This wasn't hope: this was despair.

16

If Sawyer wanted to come to Mexico with her so badly, then let him. God knows what her mother was paying him, but as long as he stayed out of her way then what did she care?

She would just ignore him. She was sure that he was used to women becoming putty in his strong, well-shaped hands. They would no doubt find the combination of a military fit body and that silent glower sexy as hell – to them he would be like Mr Darcy packing a handgun; but she wasn't some damsel in distress that needed taking care of, and he could look at her with those forbidding eyes just as much as he wanted: she would *not* be intimidated. No sir. She hadn't forgiven him for being so rude when they first met. Just because he was on the payroll, he needn't think she would forget how pitiful he had made her feel.

It wasn't even the first time Claudia had been protected. When she was a teenager, the political situation in Mexico had been unstable. Unemployment had been soaring, and kidnappings were often a way of making quick money. Nowadays Mexico City was as safe as most other major capital cities, and it was the border town drug cartels that fought their own battles for control, often with bloody results, but back then she remembered everybody being tense all the time. Her grandfather's house had constantly been filled with his rich friends, debating how best to weather the economic storm. Every time she left the house she was accompanied by a stern and sour man whose name she had forgotten. She remembered now how impossible it is to avoid someone when they are being paid to protect you.

'Nice of my mother to spring for a business-class fare,' she said. Daniel was fast asleep in his skycot. She tucked his blankets around him a little tighter.

'I suppose she thought you would appreciate the company,' said Sawyer.

Claudia popped on an eye mask and reclined her seat.

She awoke somewhere over the Atlantic, desperate to use the bathroom. She thought at first that Sawyer was asleep, but the moment she touched his arm he turned to face her and, with a whispered exchange, a few muted shuffles and the brush of limbs, she moved past him, leaving him to watch Daniel sleeping under the dim cabin lights.

She locked the toilet door and the fluorescent light came on automatically. She recoiled from her own haggard image and ran her tongue across her teeth in an effort to refresh her mouth. Glancing back to her seat when she was finished, she saw no reason to rush back, and slipped instead to the galley where a stewardess broke away from her magazine long enough to fix her a strong gin and tonic with lots of ice. There was a jug of water with plastic cups, so she drank one of those too. If Daniel cried she would still be able to hear him in the eerie hush of a night plane, so she lingered a while, enjoying standing tall after sleeping in her seat.

She took another glance at Sawyer and wondered what he thought of her. He had been unfailingly polite, but she still caught him smirking sometimes, as if underneath his thick skin he was laughing at her.

After he'd shot the deer her legs had given way and he had caught her. He'd left his car on the side of the road and driven them both home. He'd slept in the spare room. The next morning she'd woken before dawn to see his car parked in front of the cottage. He must have hiked seven miles in the winter darkness to retrieve it. He had known her all her life but she barely knew him at all. He was here now. She might as well make good use of him.

She went back to the galley and fetched them both a drink.

'G and T?' she said, slipping back into her seat and passing him his drink.

'I thought you were ignoring me.'

'I was but I'm bored.'

'I don't drink,' he said.

'Never?'

'Not when I'm on a job.'

They kept their voices down low. It felt as if they were the only two people on the aeroplane who were talking. The rest of the passengers were either asleep or plugged into the in-flight entertainment, or both.

She poured the contents of one glass into another to make hers a double. 'I'll be squiffy if I drink all of this.'

'I'll look after you,' he said, and there it was again: the smirk, the laughter. She was gripped by an urge to see him laugh for real, to see him throw back his head and laugh from his guts, to let loose.

'Did Lucy include that in the job specs?'

'She asked me to look after you and make sure that you didn't come to any harm.'

'She's quite the expert at delegating parental responsibility,' said Claudia.

'You're over twenty-one. Why does she have any responsibility at all?'

'She's running a deficit.'

'Sooner or later you have to let that shit go,' said Sawyer.

'So now you're my therapist? Is she paying you extra?'

'I apologize,' he said, and he seemed genuine. 'Let's get into it. I have extensive PSD experience, that's personal security detail.'

'I know what it is,' she snapped.

He threw her a sideways glance. 'Perhaps it might be better if you told me what kind of working relationship you envisage.'

'Relationship?'

'For want of a better word.'

'One where you don't get on my nerves,' she said.

'Goes with the territory,' he said. 'You know what? Let me have some of that.' He crooked his finger and she passed him her drink. He touched the rim of the glass to his lips quickly, took a swift, biting sip and then passed it back to her, holding her eyes for a fraction longer than necessary.

'Now I'm guessing that Mexico isn't an arbitrary holiday choice. We're going back to Des Amparados?'

'I want to find out what happened.'

'Okay, you want me to help?'

'Do you speak Spanish?'

'Some. There was a Columbian guy on my PSD in Iraq.'

'When you were in service?'

'Private. I went back the second time around, like a lot of my guys did. There are plenty of rich men looking to rent their own armies in the Middle East. They call it security, but it's the same thing. People are still trying to kill you.'

'So why do you do it?'

'The money, of course. Why else?'

'Did you ever save anyone's life?'

To her intense gratification, he laughed out loud, and it was a good, hearty laugh, just as she had hoped. It lifted all the shadows of his face and changed the way he looked at her, as if he had just noticed something about her that intrigued him. 'That's a new one,' he said.

'What do you mean?'

'Normally people ask me if I've ever killed anyone.'

'I don't want to know,' said Claudia. 'I prefer happy endings.'

'But there's only one real ending though, right? And I've seen all sorts – it's rarely happy.'

'But I believe in fate, don't you?' She held up a warning palm. 'Don't smirk,' she added, and then because he did, she had to say it again. 'I said, don't smirk.'

225

'It's involuntary.'

'Well, stop it.'

'Hey, it's fate.'

She tried to intimidate him with one of her fiercest looks but he raised his eyebrows and his smirk turned into a self-satisfied grin.

'For an older man you act like a bloody teenager.'

'Come on, Claudia. Don't hold it against me. Don't you know that anything that happens in the sky stays in the sky?

'If it happens on a plane it doesn't count.'

'Right.'

A bullet of excitement pinballed across her body and took her by surprise. The gin and tonic buzz was clouding her judgement. This was Sawyer; she was supposed to be ignoring him.

The hotel was horrid, a gigantic edifice of hedonism where everything on the room service menu came with melted cheese. Her room overlooked the pool, and when Daniel finally fell asleep around midnight they were still doling out margaritas and bad nachos to guests who only knew how to converse by shouting and squealing. They were all American. Children raced around, hysterical with tiredness. This wasn't what she was expecting. She knew plenty of people who vacationed in the Yucatán, and they had never mentioned the children's pool or the five-dollar margarita specials and karaoke. She should have asked Camille Lepage where she stayed when she came over for Christmas with her family, but of course she was no longer speaking to Camille. Presumably if Camille came here again, she would bring her husband. She would love to see David cope in a place like this. She had never seen him drink a margarita in all the months they were together. She wondered if he had changed since he married into money.

There was a soft knock on the interconnecting door.

'He asleep?'

Sawyer had showered and changed his clothes. He looked as crisp as ironed bedlinen, while she was still wearing her clothes from the plane. She tugged at her blond ponytail and wondered what she looked like.

'Would you like me to watch him for half an hour while you take a long shower?'

'You don't have to,' she said. 'That's not what you signed up for.'

He dismissed her protests. 'So you don't have to worry. Go on, I know you ladies like to check out the freebies in the bathroom. They have good stuff. Go.'

'I would love to.'

She took longer than she meant to and was liberal with the hotel products, lingering in front of the bathroom mirror to tidy her eyebrows and exfoliate her lips and double up on body moisturizer – all the things that she hadn't found the time to do lately. She used the blow-dryer. She told herself that it had nothing to do with Sawyer sitting in her bedroom waiting.

She wrapped the hotel robe more tightly around herself and pushed open the door. The air-conditioned room felt cool after the damp, steamy bathroom, and her gleaming skin tingled.

227

The news was on television with the sound down low and Sawyer was stretched out across her bed, his bare feet a couple of inches over the end. 'Better?' he said, and stood up.

'Much,' she said, 'thank you.'

'So this is goodnight then. Do you have a plan for tomorrow?'

'City Hall in the morning; then in the afternoon we go to the island and see what's what.'

'Okay.' Sawyer pressed his lips together and nodded a few times, but he looked as if he wanted to say something. 'What? You have a better idea?' she said. 'There's no point in waiting around.'

'You're fearless,' he said.

'Just like my mother?' she said.

'That isn't what I was going to say at all. You're nothing like Lucy. She lives in constant fear, haven't you noticed?'

'Fear of what?'

'Fear that people will see her for who she really is. Why do you think she has never settled down and got married? She fell in love with Guy and then with Leo, and either of them would have married her too. But she didn't think that anyone could ever truly love her.'

'Why not?'

'Because she pretends to be something she is not.'

His was one of the few friendships in Lucy's life that had been constant, despite the ever-present drama. 'What?' said Claudia. 'What does she pretend to be?'

'Lucy pretends to be happy.'

The way he spoke about her with such sincere affection

gave Claudia grounds to suspect that Lucy and Sawyer had been intimate, and suddenly she passionately did not want that to be the case. He sensed her suspicions.

'Lucy's not my type,' he said. 'Never was. Also she's too old for me. Best don't tell her I said that.'

Claudia giggled. 'Goodnight, Sawyer.'

'Yeah,' he said. 'Goodnight.'

There was a lacklustre protest camp outside City Hall in Downtown Cancún. A collection of young people and tents, a few placards, but none of them were held aloft. They had the appearance of activists on a tea break in a pretend shantytown. She had seen far worse living conditions in Mexico City. She read one of the signs: they were protesting about police corruption. No wonder it looked as if they had been here for a long time. Corruption was a fact of life in Mexico. The most prominent people in town were commonly known to be the most dangerous.

The white curves of the municipal building were drab, and some ill-advised pink detailing in the paint job did nothing to improve the impression of a battle-weary old ruin. The line was already long and reached the entire length of the terracotta forecourt, despite the fact that they didn't open for another twenty minutes. Judging by the disproportionately high number of tiny babies, most of the locals were here to register births. She should have brought Daniel. He liked seeing other babies. But the hotel had fantastic babysitters and a crèche. Hopefully this wouldn't take too long.

'What now?' said Sawyer.

229

'We wait.'

On the phone from England she had been able to ascertain that if Danny Featherbow had died here in Yucatán then it would be a matter of public record and a copy of his death certificate would be easy to obtain in person.

Sawyer was a head and a half taller than anyone else in the queue and she could feel curious eyes upon them. Who were these pale-faced people lining up with the young mothers of Cancún? Were they in the right place?

Someone approached them, a woman around her own age; in halting English she asked if she could help them. In flawless Spanish, Claudia said that she was here for a death certificate for her father who had died in Mexico, and within seconds she was surrounded by the babble of sympathetic strangers, local women offering condolences as if he had died just recently and offering up babies for her praise. 'Yes,' she said repeatedly, 'a beautiful baby, *preciosa*.'

They thought Sawyer was her husband. She told them he was a family friend and a couple of them started to flirt with him. A woman not much older than her was making obvious eyes at him and offering to show him around the city, and Claudia could barely concentrate on the old woman asking for her life story.

'Tell us about your father,' she urged, and because it was easier than the truth, Claudia made up a story about an accident, leaving out details that she said she did not know.

Out of the corner of her eye she saw the young woman give up on flirting with Sawyer and was pleased.

By the time the line started moving forward, the queue behind them stretched around two corners. Some people had brought food. Some people had brought chairs. The entire forecourt resembled a picnic in the park.

She asked for her father's death certificate.

The clerk behind the desk went back to his supervisor to check, and while he was gone Claudia's vision narrowed and she started to dread the clerk walking back with a piece of paper that would confirm that she had nothing left to search for. Just as she was on the verge of a full-blown panic attack, the man came back empty-handed and Claudia could breathe again. They had no record of the death of Danny Featherbow. The man was patient but realistic. Even if they did not know the exact date, a simple computer search would have produced a result.

He was sorry, said the clerk.

'Don't worry,' said Claudia, smiling inappropriately. 'You have been very helpful.'

It was still early. The taxi took them to the port where she found a boat to take them to Des Amparados.

'Why do you keep looking at me like I'm crazy?' she said, as Sawyer climbed into the panga beside her.

'Do I?' he said. 'It's just something Lucy said.'

'What?'

'She said you were shy.'

'She doesn't really know me very well,' said Claudia.

'Perhaps because you are too shy around her?'

'Maybe.' She shot him a sideways glance. 'Can we drop it?'

'No problem.'

The fisherman who took them across to the island had never been there before. He did not speak English and usually stayed away from the tourists because they scared him. He did not know to drop tourists in the anchorage to south, where the white sand beach would satisfy and the rocky headland would dissuade all but the most intrepid from wider exploration. Instead he motored into the mangrove shallows of a deserted coconut farm, the densely planted palms up to their waists in seawater like the ghosts of drowned trees.

He cut back on the engine and they floated into the shade.

A shrieking bird made her teeth clench. 'There's nothing here?'

The fisherman shrugged.

'You've been here before, Sawyer: are we in the right place?'

He scratched his head and looked around him doubtfully. 'I don't know. There was more beach; there was always a beach wherever we went. Are you sure this is Des Amparados?'

The fisherman was sure.

'Was it a hurricane?' She had heard that the sand on Cancún's white beaches all had to be replaced after Hurricane Wilma dragged tons of it into the water. Perhaps the same had happened here, but there was nobody who cared enough to fix the erosion. They drifted past a palm, close enough to touch, and she reached out her hand, but it was slimy in the damp shadows and she shuddered.

The murky water was starting to trouble her. Her skin felt itchy and her throat tight. She started to feel invisible creatures crawling over her and wafted away mosquitoes that weren't really there. Out of the gloom rose a grey concrete building, and near it stood a storage shed with a transformer on the top, the thick cables all snapped and twisted. The jungle had reclaimed much of the building, and where it had crumbled into the water, metal pilings – now beginning to rust – thrust into the open air.

The beginning of a road stretched into the distance but soon became badly overgrown. It was clear that nobody had been here for many years. The boat glided to a complete stop and the fisherman looked at her expectantly. She glanced at Sawyer, who seemed sceptical but entirely at ease.

'I suppose we should go back,' said Claudia, her gaze fixed on the road. There could be all kinds of things in there, things that could sting her or scare her or eat her alive. It would be best to go back to the hotel and rethink her entire strategy. She could hire a private investigator. If there was nothing to be learned here in Mexico, then she could go to Las Vegas.

The road was overgrown just a few yards from where they were. Surely within moments it would prove to be impassable?

But what if it wasn't? What might she find at the end? It would be silly to come all this way and not at least look a little further.

They pulled up beside an intact piling and the fisherman held up a rope and questioned her with a single eyebrow.

'Come on, Sawyer,' she said. 'Earn your money.' She climbed out onto the concrete walkway before she could change her mind and headed off in the direction of the road. She was reminded what her mother said about courage: that if you act as if you have courage, then courage shall be yours.

Claudia was surprised by the body's ability to fool the brain. Lucy was right: simply by walking with a confident stride, she was able to convince herself that she was not afraid of what lay ahead. The dark and the green of it all reminded her of the deep, dark woods of fairytales, and she searched her childhood memories for one of those that hadn't ended badly. Soon, though, the road opened out into a disused irrigation system and there was more concrete underfoot and the going was much easier; then the road banked sharply upwards and they found themselves walking largely unhindered above the worst of the vegetation.

She noticed Sawyer kept glancing back the way they had come. 'Are you worried the boat will go without us?'

'No, I want to make sure we're not going in a big circle.'

She hadn't actually thought of that. 'Are we?'

'The road follows the curve of the reservoir, but I'm hoping up ahead there will be a spur which will take us east, otherwise we'll start to come back on ourselves.'

'What reservoir?'

He pointed down at the wide hollow in the ground on either side of them. 'It's an old reservoir,' he said. 'You didn't see the pipes?'

This was stupid. They were walking into the unknown, and for what? She carried on putting one foot in front of another, but she had lost her appetite for adventure. Her feet were hurting and she wanted to be back at the hotel with Daniel.

'Here,' said Sawyer. 'Good.'

Ahead of them, the road broke into two.

'Why is that good?'

'It's a small island. If we head east, we should hit the other side fairly soon.'

'Or what?'

'Or we won't. Either way it won't be far.'

It felt to her as if they were walking for miles and miles, so perhaps they had a different idea about what constituted far, but eventually she heard the roar of the ocean.

'Is that what I think it is?' she said. She stood still for a while and listened to the churning water. She peered eastward but there was nothing to see.

'And look . . .' Up ahead, the road swerved to the right and climbed to the top of a hill where there was a small white house. 'That's the place,' he said. 'I remember.' He looked back the way they had come, as if trying to get his bearing and dredge up further details from his memories.

He snapped his head back when he heard her shouting. She was walking way ahead of him. 'Hello?' she shouted. 'Is anyone there?'

Sawyer chased her down. 'Hey, don't do that. Tread carefully, okay?'

There was movement at the house and an old man shambled out onto the terrace. He looked down at them and yelled, 'This is private property.'

'I'd just like to ask you a few questions,' she said.

'Are you the police?'

'No,' she said, close enough now to speak in a normal voice. She could see his deeply tanned face beneath his beard, a silver-hooped earring with a white stone dangling from it. 'I'm just looking for information about someone who used to live here.'

'Who's that?'

'Danny Featherbow.'

'Never heard of him.'

'He used to own the place.'

'Sorry, can't help you.'

'You're sure?'

'Frankly I'm not inclined to answer questions from folk who turn up uninvited.'

Sawyer stepped forward. 'The young lady has come a long way, sir.'

'I appreciate that, I do, but Danny Featherbow is not a name I know.'

Another dead end. Perhaps her mother was right: this entire trip was a fool's errand. She was running after a man who had run away for a reason, whatever that was. Either that or he was dead, but because this was Mexico, and things being the way they were here, he had died just as her mother had been told, but the death had not been properly recorded. It wasn't right to take her frustration out on this old-timer who was probably sick of day-trippers ripping up his solitude. She turned away and caught sight of his view.

The ocean, the three limestone rocks out in the water.

'Please excuse the intrusion,' she said. 'We'll be going. Thank you for your time.'

She started to walk away slowly, her sense of defeat dragging her feet.

'One more thing?' Sawyer wasn't ready to quit. 'We moored by the old coconut farm, but there's another anchorage, isn't there? There must be.'

The old-timer hesitated, but then jerked his head over the bluff behind him. 'South.'

'A beach.'

'I suppose.'

'And you never heard of Danny Featherbow?'

'Afraid not.'

'Then we'll trouble you no longer. Come on, babe.'

They walked away, at a much faster pace than they had approached. Claudia waited until they were out of earshot and then looked at him for an explanation. 'Babe?' she said.

'I thought it would be better for him to think we were a couple rather than—'

'A rich bitch and her bodyguard?'

'Exactly.'

'Why do you care what he thinks?'

'Because he's lying.'

'Lying about what?'

'He knew your father.'

'What makes you so sure?'

'I remember him. I remember his earring, it's a shark's tooth.'

She shuddered. 'Ugh. So why would he lie?'

'I don't know, but his name is Hector.'

'Hector?'

'If this is the last place that anyone saw Danny Feather-bow alive, then my guess is that that man, Hector, would have been the last one to see him.'

17

It was another Saturday night at the bar and the place was packed. Two-dollar beer and guacamole special. The guacamole that Megan made from scratch with her secret ingredient; the guacamole beloved of Mexicans and tourists alike, but particularly beloved, it must be said, of the loyal brigade of retired Americans that had made Cancún their home and made Esmeralda's their local bar of choice.

'Esmeralda's?' said Megan, when Ray and Miguel had unveiled the new sign. 'I thought we said Ray's?'

'No way,' said Miguel.

'She's my sister,' said Ray.

'And she always hated this bar, so it's kind of funny,' said Miguel.

'She's going to be so pissed,' said Ray, and the two guys snickered and high-fived like a couple of juiced-up teens.

'We should vote on it,' said Ray. 'Miguel?'

'Yes.'

'Megan?'

It was the first time they had asked her to vote on

anything. Usually they just went ahead and did it anyway, ordering the new coffee cups or measuring out the requesón cheese for the Danish pastries without her approval, moving quickly to make every one of her ideas for the bar a reality, but not spending much time on the detail.

'I like the detail,' she said. 'It's where the devil is.'

'You don't like the coffee cups, angel?'

'They're fine,' she said. And it was true that the two guys were showing an unlikely instinct for implementing her vision. There was so much to do that she had to let some of it go. Finally, a project. She hadn't enjoyed herself this much since she had to organise a festival-slash-birthday for her boyfriend, that little drummer boy, what was his name again? She shocked herself by forgetting him so quickly. Ray was the perfect rebound guy: good looking but not sharp enough to pierce her heart. And it helped that Saturday nights were always busy.

She picked her way through the crowd with an armful of empty glasses. The music was loud, a mixture of classic rock and indie gems, and as ever there was a dance-like movement in her step. There were still a hundred things to be done before the bar was exactly how she wanted it, but they could all wait for a while because it was the weekend.

Okay, so she was a glorified barmaid, but so what? So she wasn't using her degree? Who cares? She was happy. She could turn up for work in denim hot pants and a vintage halterneck and nobody blinked. She liked it when they were so busy that she didn't get to sit down. She liked it when her feet were sore at the end of a long night and Ray gave her a foot rub while Miguel cashed up.

'Megan,' yelled Ray from behind the bar. 'Phone call for you.'

'For me?'

'Hey, Megan,' someone shouted. 'Is there no band tonight?'

'I don't know, Bobby, did you bring your tambourine?'

People laughed and she glowed, lighting up the room as she passed by.

Megan had tapped into the ex-pat community as a big potential market. There was a huge happy crowd that clustered around the American-owned bars near Punta Sam where they showed Monday Night Football and had Miller on tap. But she was convinced that nobody uproots to retire in a foreign country in the hope of finding football and pale ale. So they still went to Punta Sam on Monday nights, but the rest of the week a lot of them came to her and her perfect margaritas, her tapas-inspired bar food, her live music three times a week and the two guys that helped her to make the place something special in downtown Cancún.

Eventually, of course, Ray had been forced to pay her a wage. Miguel had insisted upon it, but Ray said he was going to do it anyway, and as usual they fought about who wanted to please Megan the most.

When Ray passed her the phone, he stole a kiss and grabbed her in a way that he knew would make her slap him away.

She turned away from him, feigning annoyance, and took the call, but the music was too loud so she couldn't hear the person on the other end of the line. Laughing, she tried to pull the phone into the kitchen, but it wouldn't reach, so she crouched down on the floor and covered up her other ear. 'You'll have to shout,' she said.

'*Connor, it's Connor! Can you hear me?*'

'Connor?'

Back in the bar there was a cheer as the band turned up – late – and started plugging their kit into the corner they cleared of tables and called a stage. Miguel was shouting for another batch of guacamole, and there were people waiting to be served.

'Connor,' she said. 'Where did you get this number?'

'Your mum.'

'How is she?'

'You should call her and ask her. Do you even know she got engaged?'

'Piss off. Did you phone just to give me a hard time?'

'I'm in Cancún.'

'What was that? Sorry? Say it again, the music . . . Did you just say you're in Cancún. Here? My Cancún?'

'You've been here less than a year and it's yours already?'

'Connor!'

'Will you pick me up from the airport?'

'No. Are you crazy? Get a cab, don't pay more than fifteen dollars, have the guy bring you to Esmeralda's on Palmera.'

'All right,' he said, and he sounded pumped, as if getting on a plane to Mexico was the most exciting thing he had ever done. 'And Megan?'

'Yeah?'

'I can't wait to see you.'

She put down the phone and stayed curled up on the floor for a little while until Miguel yelled for more

242

guacamole and she remembered where she was. She pushed through the door into the kitchen in a daze, washed her hands and reached for some of the avocados, peeled them and crushed them in her fists so that the ripe jade flesh oozed out between her fingers and chunky nuggets fell into the bowl.

She had never made guacamole for Connor. A thousand bowls here but never one for him. He probably didn't even know she could cook and she was a great cook now.

He didn't know about Ray.

She whizzed up the tomatoes and onions with lime juice and salt, and added that to the bowl.

Miguel yelled from outside. 'Megan, *chica*, I have to have guacamole now or things will turn nasty.'

There was no secret ingredient. She just said that to add mystery.

'Here,' she said, adding a big pile of crispy *chicarones*, just like the pork scratchings in the pubs back home, and pushing the plate at him. 'You think you'll need more?'

'The same again,' he said. 'You okay?'

'Sure, why?'

'You look as if you have seen a ghost. Who was on the phone?'

'Old boyfriend,' she said. 'Surprise visit. What do you think Ray will say?'

Miguel pulled a face. 'Nothing good. Do you have to tell him?'

'You think maybe I can just sneak him in and hide him in my room?'

'He can't sleep in your room.'

243

'I hadn't even thought of that.'

For the next hour she flinched every time somebody new walked in the door. She avoided Ray, figuring that if she didn't have an opportunity to tell him, then she couldn't be blamed for keeping it quiet. She found herself stealing away for five minutes, even though the bar was packed, to check her face and make sure she didn't have lumps of guacamole hardening in her hair. She thought about make-up but it was much too late for that. She hadn't worn any for weeks.

Besides, this was Connor. He'd seen her through emo phases and acne, since when was she in the habit of putting on make-up for Connor? And she knew she looked great. All those months of sunshine had turned her skin a gorgeous honey. She'd kept her dark hair quite short, but not as short as it had been, and because she was constantly dipping in and out of the sea it was choppy and raw, perfectly offsetting her doll-like features and ruby-red lips.

She thought about the last time she saw Connor. He had kissed her outside the pub and their relationship had balanced for a moment on the edge of being something more. She remembered thinking that she shouldn't lead him on when her flight was booked, but then his kiss had overwhelmed her and she had been unable to think of anything at all except how good it felt to be kissed by him and how much she was going to miss him while she was gone.

'Everything okay?' Ray startled her in the hallway and she backed up into a pile of beer crates that almost fell.

'Sure,' she said, finding her feet. 'Sure.' She kissed him, hard.

'What was that for?'

'A friend of mine from England is coming to visit, a guy friend – that's okay, right?'

'You were sleeping with this guy friend?' said Ray, hooking his arms around her waist and clasping his hands behind her back. He was acting like he was joking around, but Megan could tell from the way he wouldn't meet her eyes that it bothered him.

'Never,' she said. 'We're just friends.'

'He knows you're my woman?'

'If he doesn't, I'll tell him.'

'You'd better.'

When eventually Connor walked in through the door, she was so tightly coiled that she bounded across the bar in a single leap. His face made her heart skip a beat. His sandy brown hair was a disaster, as usual. He was still wearing his sunglasses and she had to wait before he pushed them back and she was rewarded with the steady, sincere gaze of his soft blue eyes. She hugged him, feeling Ray's eyes burn into her as she did so. Connor looked around the bar.

'Do you work here?' he said. 'Or live here, or what?'

'Both!' she said, and laughed. Oh, how she laughed, a staccato cackle as harsh as cheap tequila. Until he looked at her strangely and she stopped laughing because it wasn't that funny. 'It's so incredible that you're here. Why didn't you tell me you were coming?' She wanted to touch him to believe that he was real, but she could see Ray behind the bar, watching her every move.

'I wanted to surprise you.'

'You have.

'I have something for you,' said Connor. 'A present.'

He reached into the side pocket of his rucksack and took out a small brown paper bag folded in four. It was feather-light and she didn't know what it could be. 'I was going to give it you when you came back but . . .'

'I don't know if I'm coming back,' said Megan, unfolding the bag. 'I like it here.'

Out tumbled a necklace, her necklace – the gold star and the opal moon. 'What the . . . ? Connor, what is this?'

'I went down to the shop on the high street the morning after you left. I know how much you loved it and I didn't want it to go to someone who would stash it in the bottom of a jewellery box and forget about it. I missed you, Meg.'

She ran her fingers across the smooth stone, like holding the hand of an old friend. 'Thank you,' she said. 'Really, thank you. I do love it. I can't believe it. That's so thoughtful of you. It's the nicest gift I ever had.'

'That's because I didn't choose it.'

'Neither did I,' she said.

'Here,' he said, 'let me.'

She turned around so that he could fasten it behind her neck. She felt his fingers linger there when he was done and she didn't turn back.

His fingertips stroked the base of her neck very slowly. 'Your hair is getting long,' he said.

She turned back to face him, her thoughts colliding. 'Connor, I . . .'

Then suddenly Ray was upon her, slinging his arm around her shoulder in an unmistakably territorial move. Connor took a giant step back.

'Hey babe,' said Ray. 'Want to give me some help

behind the bar?' He thrust a hand towards Connor. 'I'm Ramon, Megan's boyfriend.'

'Connor,' he said, and then, after a confused pause so brief that nobody noticed except her, 'Megan's buddy from back home.'

'Good to meet you,' he said. 'Mind if I steal her away?'

'He just got here,' said Megan. 'Give me a few minutes.'

'Sweetheart, the kitchen, now, let's go.' She didn't like it when he talked to her like that, and it was worse that he did it in front of Connor.

Ray pulled Megan into the kitchen so fast that she was almost swept off her feet as she tried to keep up with him. In the kitchen he found a quiet corner by the walk-in refrigerator and bent over her to speak softly into her ear.

'Don't humiliate me in my own place, okay?'

'Humiliate you?'

'I saw him, with the necklace.'

'It's mine,' she said. 'From a long time ago. I forgot it, that's all. He brought it back to me.'

'It's pretty,' he said, tracing the moon with his finger-tips, hot on her throat where he touched her.

'I suppose.'

'Where's he going to sleep tonight?'

'Can I stay with you? Then he can have my room.'

'How long is he staying?'

'He just got here. I don't know. What's the matter? You love it when I stay over.' She took a step closer to him and slid her hand beneath the waistband at the back of his jeans. 'Don't be mad, okay? I didn't know he was coming.' She stretched up onto her toes but as she closed her eyes to kiss him it was Connor's face that she saw.

Ray pulled her into him and kissed her passionately then murmured into her ear. 'The thought of another man sleeping in your bed.'

'It's not like I'll be in it,' she snapped. Then, 'I'm sorry, I don't know what else to suggest. I can stay over?'

He nodded and released her, but his eyes were still dark and stormy and she left the kitchen feeling as though she had done something wrong.

Had Connor really come all this way just to give her a necklace? She was enjoying herself with Ray, she loved Mexico and the bar; it finally felt as if she was on the right track. The last thing she needed was Connor turning up and reminding her that not everything she had left behind in England was bad.

She watched Connor for a second. He had struck up a conversation with one of her regulars, and she enjoyed the familiar contours of his lively face, and yet his presence here in her new life was jarring, like a drunk in the middle of the afternoon, and it made her feel jumpy.

'How's it going?' she said, walking back to his table.

She knew that Ray was behind the bar, watching her, staring at her, and she took pains not to touch Connor or to flirt with him and it felt stilted and horrible. Poor Connor looked tired and utterly confused.

'You have a boyfriend,' he said.

'Ray? Yeah, I do.'

'I didn't know that.'

'Would you have come?'

He stared at her and didn't answer straight away. 'You look great, by the way,' he said. 'You look amazing. I didn't get a chance to say that. I didn't get the chance to say a lot of things.'

'Like what?'

He laughed wearily. 'I can't do this, Megan. I won't make a play for another guy's girl. You know me better than that.'

'I would have told you if you'd asked,' she said.

'Maybe I just didn't want to know. It's not your fault.' His eyes were glazed, though whether with sadness or fatigue she could not tell.

A huge table of Americans arrived and ordered margaritas all round. She heard a snatch of Blondie and realized that Ray was playing one of her favourite songs. She glanced at him behind the bar, chatting with the newcomers, in his element making new friends and US dollars. He saw her acknowledge the music and he grinned, pointing her out to his customers so that – in the midst of this terrifying conversation with Connor – she was forced to smile and wave, feeling more awkward than she ever had in this bar and feeling a flash of resentment towards Connor and his unannounced visit.

'Does this place ever close?' asked Connor.

'Only when it empties,' she said. 'Come on, let's get you to bed.'

He cocked an eyebrow. To her horror she felt a blush burn across her cheeks and stammered out the sleeping solution she had conceived. 'You can have my room,' she said. 'And I'll stay at Ray's.'

It felt strange to be saying goodnight instead of crawling

249

into bed with him. He kissed her on the forehead and she felt her heart sink and sigh. He had pulled the shutters closed – shutters which had been open since the day she moved in – and she remembered how he always found it hard to sleep if there was a sliver of light in the room. She wondered how he would feel about the stark Mexican sunrise she loved so much.

'Stay,' he murmured into her hair. His voice was heavy with fatigue.

'I can't,' she whispered, and she tried to ignore the deep seam of longing that rose in her, so different to the sparky thrill she felt when she thought of Ray. What would happen, she wondered, if she were to slip beneath the sheets beside him and tell him how much she had thought about him while she had been gone?

And she slipped away.

As she climbed the stairs to the small apartment that Ray had once shared with his mother, she could hear the deep thump of angry rock music coming from behind his door. It wasn't locked and she pushed her way in to see Ray laying spread-eagled in the middle of the floor, a half-smoked cigarette smouldering in the ashtray next to him, the lights down low and the bass from the stereo making the ground tremble beneath her feet. When she lay down next to him he didn't move, and when she curled into him his chest was as hard as stone.

The hostility rose from him like steam and she wondered how long they were expected to lie there in silence. 'If you're going to be angry,' she said, 'we should go to bed.' She gave him a lingering kiss and pulled him to his feet, unfastening the clasp at the neck of her draping halterneck top and letting it fall to the floor as he followed behind her.

He didn't say a word, he didn't have to. She let him work out all his frustrations on her stirred-up body until at last he was clinging to her, wet with sweat, calling out her name and making it sound as if she was forgiven.

They watched the moon rise over the city and she lit his cigarettes for him, one after another.

'You should move in,' he said.

'Here?'

'I can't see that ma's coming back. I don't like to think of you sleeping over there at the bar. It doesn't look good.'

'Can I think about it?'

'It doesn't have to be a big deal.'

Later on they made love again and Megan paused on top of him, gripping him with the muscles of her thighs and holding him tight inside her. 'Tell me you love me,' she whispered. 'Please. Tell me you love me.'

'Don't stop,' he begged.

'Tell me,' she said, twisting down onto him exquisitely slowly and watching his face contort with longing.

'I love you,' he said, as he lost control.

It was enough.

The next day Megan took Connor to the small port at Playa Linda, he stood back while she chatted with one of the fisherman there for a while before, to Connor's astonishment, they commandeered his boat and set off across the water.

'The fisherman used to take me himself,' she said, 'but after a while it felt like a waste of his time. It's cheaper for me this way too.'

'And you're okay?' he said, gripping the side of the boat so tightly that she could see his knuckles turning white. 'You can drive it and everything?'

'Drive it? Yes, Con, I can drive the boat!' She swerved a couple of times and giggled when he paled.

'Where are we going?' said Connor.

'Shopping,' she said.

She was glad to impress him with the way that she handled a boat, if only because back in England she had so rarely done anything remarkable. It was a good feeling to be proud of something, even if it was only a stupid old boat. It reminded her of one summer holiday when they were kids, and they'd been allowed off on their own in a pedalo. They went round in circles because Connor's legs were twice as strong as Megan's. Sparrow legs, he'd called her, for a whole summer, and every time he did it she despaired that he would ever see her in the way that she was starting to see him. She wanted to kiss him on the mouth and make sense of all the curious changes in her feelings. But then when they went back to school, Connor had gone to the cinema with Lesley Flinch and twelve-year-old Megan had been heartbroken.

'Hey,' she said, shouting over the noise of the boat engine so that he could hear her. 'What happened to Lesley Flinch?'

'Who?'

'From school, you remember? You went out with her for a while.'

'Did I? I must have been trying to make you jealous.'

'Very funny.'

Connor had girls falling over him at school. Handsome, captain of the football team. He was in the running for head boy until he got into trouble for skipping school to go on a protest march with his mum, and even this helped his status as a schoolboy hero, with everyone except for Megan. 'With your mum?' she'd said when she heard. 'Tragic.'

They were friends because their parents were friends, At school she ignored him. He didn't speak to her either; he was too busy fending off the attentions of the most popular girls in school. But one summer, the summer after the pedalo and Lesley Flinch, he had kissed her in the woods in France while their parents hiked up ahead, and family holidays became a lot more interesting.

She cut across the western shore of Des Amparados so that he could get a good look. The water here was so clear that you could see all the way to the bottom of the sea and sometimes, if you cut out the engine and drifted for a while, you would see a lobster scuttle across the pebbled seabed.

They rounded the southern point, and curved into the bay smoothly. He helped her haul the boat onto the sand. Cancún felt very far away all of a sudden, as if they were marooned alone together, far from sight.

'This is the place, isn't it?' he said, understanding immediately, 'the place you came to find?'

She nodded. Her eyes glowed. She had never brought Ray here, and if he wondered where she found the most succulent avocados for the menu at Esmeralda's, then he never asked.

'It's beautiful,' said Connor. 'I mean, look at it. How can somewhere so close to that – ' he waved his arm back towards the city of Cancún – 'remain so untouched?'

'There's not enough water, that's the problem,' said Megan. 'There was a coconut farm here once, but after they built Cancún there were a few years of drought and the reservoir dried up, the harvest failed, and after that they must have decided there were easier ways to make money across the water.'

'And who owns it?'

'I'm trying to find out. Mexican red tape. And the caretaker, Hector, he says he isn't exactly sure. He gets paid, he doesn't ask too many questions.'

'You think he's lying?'

'No,' she said. She looked up and was surprised. It wasn't like Connor to be suspicious. She was usually the doubter; he was too trusting. 'Why would you say that?'

'I don't know. You seemed hell-bent on claiming your legacy and now . . .'

'Wait until you see what he's done with the place. Hector's incredible. The house is his now, more than it could ever be mine. You'll understand. He's been a good friend to me.' She paused. 'I haven't told him,' she said. 'I haven't told him about Danny Featherbow and who he is to me. You understand?'

'The old guy lives here on his own?'

'His son is here a lot. Luis, action-man type. But he's away right now.'

'Action-man type?'

'You know: fit, American, keen, stupidly handsome.'

254

'Sounds like a prick,' deadpanned Connor.

'I think you'd like him. He was an alcoholic, I think. Or a druggie or something, until Hector came looking for him and turned his life around.'

'Whatever. I'm just glad he's not here. I don't think it would do my ego any good right now to stand next to a guy like that. It's pretty fragile.'

'Why?'

'Come off it, Megan. I feel like an idiot. Are we just not going to talk about it? I don't know what I expected, but I know that I missed you and now you're with that dude who looks exactly like a Latino version of every bad boyfriend you ever had.'

'I didn't ask you to come,' she said.

He winced. 'Nice, Megs. Sorry if I'm messing up your *Coyote Ugly* fantasy. I didn't realize working behind a bar was a your big dream.'

'Nobody said it was a big dream. You can have small dreams too, you know.'

'Maybe,' said Connor. 'But why would you want to?'

The ground rose steadily and they slowed. Conversation ceased as they picked their footholds with increasing care. Near the top it seemed easier to crawl, almost, than try to stay upright. She was used to the climb after all these months, but Connor struggled, his city-soft body scraping over the coarse ground. Every time she looked back he made a big show of acting as if he wasn't scared of the drop beneath them, that he wasn't struggling with the heavy going. 'You okay?' she said.

His face was grave. 'What if you fell, Megan? You do this on your own?' He kicked out a stone that had got lodged in his shoe, pausing for breath, bewildered and fazed. 'I don't want you to.'

'You can't tell me what to do,' she said.

'No, you'll leave that to your boyfriend.'

She didn't want to get drawn into it, and she ignored him until they crested the rise and a small white house revealed itself.

'Look,' she said. 'Can you see it?'

Connor trailed after her in wonder, down into the orchard in the valley and the garden on the other side, amazed, just as she had been when she saw it for the first time.

Her pace slowed as she picked the dangling avocados from their long slender stalks. Her eyes sparkled, as dazzling as the silver sky above. On Des Amparados something happened to Megan that she couldn't explain. She became a better version of herself, as if she had been poured into a filter so that all her insecurities could be leached out and she was as close to perfect as a girl like her could get. It was the way she used to feel around Connor if they stayed up and talked all night. She had never stayed up all night and talked with Ray. Talking was not his strong suit.

There was a new crop of tomatoes turning from russet-orange to red – she could smell them from ten yards away – and she swooped down on the vines as Connor imagined another woman her age might gleefully pounce on a bargain at a shoe sale. She placed them in her bag with a reverent tenderness, popping one into his mouth with her fingers. The explosion of sweetness was so intense that it blew away any erotic undertones of the gesture. 'Bloody hell,' he said.

'That's what a tomato is supposed to taste like,' she said. 'Mexico's gift to the world.'

They climbed up to the house and she called out for Hector but the place was deserted. Pools of shade were everywhere, making the house feel like an oasis. From time to time the breeze carried the sound and scent of the ocean. 'What now?' he said.

'We wait,' she replied. 'He won't have gone far.'

'How long?'

'Why? You have somewhere that you have to be? This is Mexico, Connor. Relax.'

He looked at her sideways, a frown rippling his calm. 'What?'

'Nothing.' His smile was back in place and so perhaps she had imagined the friction burn. She could still feel tension, though: faint like a bad odour that lingers.

'Connor? What did I say?'

'You, of all people, telling someone to relax, that's all.'

'Look at me,' she said, sitting down on the floor at the edge of the porch so that her legs dangled over the edge. She leant back on her elbows. 'Don't I look relaxed to you?'

'You look great,' he said. 'You look like you belong here. But you look like someone who is relaxing, and that's a different thing all together. I'll bet your mind is still racing; I'll bet you're still thinking a hundred things all at once.' He picked up a stone and threw it into the garden, aiming for an old watering can and missing it by several feet.

She felt the muscles in her body tense one by one and her good mood floated away; there was nothing she could do to catch it. She pictured it drifting off into the sky like a silver balloon, leaving her miserable. 'I can't believe you came all the way here just to make me feel bad.'

'I don't mean to make you feel bad, Megan.' He reached out and touched her necklace. 'That's not what I want.'

He moved towards her, looming close, and she knew he was about to kiss her.

'Please don't,' she said, shaking her head and moving backwards one sure step at time, her eyes pleading with him to take it back. 'I have a boyfriend. You met him.'

'End it.'

'For you? No.'

'You don't love him.'

'You don't know that.'

'Why are you shouting?'

She hadn't realized that she was, but now that he mentioned it she stopped to catch her breath, and when it came it came ragged.

'Don't you understand?' she said. 'You think that you and I are going to get together, and then what? I'm not going to marry my childhood sweetheart. My mum did that and look how it worked out for her.'

'She once told my mum that leaving Danny Featherbow was the worst mistake she ever made. She wasn't clever enough to stick with her childhood sweetheart. That's not going to happen with you.' He grinned and she saw how he saw her, like an inevitability, and she hated how trapped that made her feel.

'Mum's doing okay,' said Megan. 'She just got engaged.'

'And if you had any kind of relationship with her, you wouldn't have needed me to tell you that. What is it with you and getting close to people? I thought this trip was supposed to help you with your father issues.'

'I don't have father issues,' she said.

'I don't mean to be cruel,' said Connor. 'But ha ha.'

She turned away from him then because she didn't want him to see that he had hurt her. She pretended that she was looking at the view.

His voice softened. 'I wasn't asking you to marry me,' he said. 'But you can't run around with bad boys forever. Sooner or later you have to try having a real relationship.'

'We kiss every summer and occasionally at Christmas and once outside a pub. I don't know what we had, but it wasn't a real relationship.'

She took some pesos from her pocket, folding the bills in half and tucking them into a seashell by the door.

'You're angry,' he said.

'Let's go,' she replied. She walked off without him, passing through the herb beds without smelling them, striding briskly through the avocado trees and lemons, without caring if she mashed overripe fruit beneath her stamping feet. She had to restrain herself from running. Connor made her feel all scratchy and uncomfortable, and even though Hector was most likely only down at the opposite end of the property fixing something, she no longer wanted to wait for him. She no longer wanted to introduce him to Connor, nor did she want to sit for the rest of the afternoon listening to Hector's stories and pretending everything was okay.

Unable to contain herself she spun around to confront him. 'I didn't invite you,' she said. 'You turn up and you say these stupid things . . .'

'Stupid? I'm trying to tell you that I love you.'

'*Stop it!*' she snapped. 'Just shut up, Connor, shut up, shut up.' She struggled with the clasp of her necklace and then gathered it in her hand and held it out to him. 'Here. Take it. I don't want it.'

'It's your necklace, Megan. Keep it.'

'I don't want you to think that it means something. You're my oldest friend, Connor. Can't that be enough?'

He took the necklace and searched her face for a chink in her armour, a way past the wall she had built up so meticulously around herself, but she closed her eyes and put her hands over her ears like a child.

'You love me too,' he said. 'This is all because you're scared. And it's okay to be scared. But I won't wait forever.'

When Ray answered his door her eyes were as pink and puffy as marshmallows and she looked younger. Without the confident half-smirk, she did not have an expression that sat comfortably on her face, so she was blank, numb. The fire in her eyes had gone.

'I want to move in,' she said.

Connor was right. She was scared. She did not deserve a good guy like him. She didn't know how to love like that. She didn't know how to love him back. She wanted to be with him, but it wouldn't last and one of them would get hurt. It was better this way.

He had been able to change his flight and so right now he would be on his way back to England. Her heart ached for him already. It felt pounded flat.

'Come inside,' said Ray.

He pushed the door closed behind her and followed her into the bedroom. She lay on the bed, emotionally exhausted but determined to spend the rest of the night doing the only thing she could think of to banish all thoughts of Connor from her mind.

Ray was the lucky beneficiary of her passionate revenge.

18

Sawyer came into the hotel room just as Claudia was slamming down the phone. She turned towards him, startled, and quickly tried to regain her composure, but she was obviously upset.

'Your mother?' he said.

'I couldn't reach her. Sardinia apparently. I should have known. She spends every summer cruising the Mediterranean on expensive yachts that belong to other people. She must have jumped on a plane the moment I left. She probably couldn't wait to get rid of me.'

Sawyer nodded sympathetically and pulled out a chair so that she could sit down. She felt almost unbearably tired. He didn't say anything and she was glad, because of course she was grateful for every material thing that her mother gave her, but they didn't make up for her absence when it really mattered, and this was another of those times that it really mattered.

'She's useless,' said Claudia bitterly. 'How can I ask her about this Hector person if she's off getting her heart broken on some rich guy's sailboat? I just wish she was there for me, that's all. But she makes me feel so . . . inconvenient.'

'It can't have been easy having a mother like Lucy.'

'Exactly. You know what she's like.'

'But it seems like she came through in the last year or so, with the baby and everything?'

Claudia paused for thought. It was true that Lucy had found them a place to live, found her a nanny, insisted that Claudia kept her head above water during the most testing times, even if that meant a dinner in London. The trouble was that Claudia had been so consumed by heart-break and the demands of motherhood that she had barely noticed Lucy rising to an occasion. Even those things that Lucy had objected to at first – things like a home birth and this trip to Mexico – had worked out in the end.

'I suppose,' said Claudia.

'So she's not entirely useless?'

'Not entirely, no.'

She smiled tentatively and so did he, and when their eyes met she was surprised by how much warmth there was behind his, and saw that he wasn't quite as hard as he liked to make out. He cared about Lucy, that much was obvious. But the way that he was looking at Claudia now made her nerve endings spark and her heart flutter with something that felt inappropriate, given that he was supposed to be her bodyguard and was almost twenty years older than her. She found herself wondering how his solid masculinity would translate in the bedroom and felt a crimson blush steal across her pale cheeks.

'So what now?' she said, trying to bend the conversation onto something less personal.

'I'm having a friend in the States run a background check on Hector.'

'Meanwhile, let's go back to city hall and try and find out who owns the place.'

They stood in line again, asking this time for the land registry details of Des Amparados.

They had to wait for a long time and she grew bored. 'Tell me what you'd rather be doing right now,' she said.

'Rather than standing in line with you?' he said, as if there was very little that would be better.

She grinned. 'If you were here on your own, what would you do?'

She wanted to picture him without the sense of duty that he wore like a harness, stopping him from letting go.

'I'd have my motorcycle. I'd cruise up and down the coast for a while and then, after it got really dark, I'd go out into the desert with my bike and look at the stars. Maybe camp out, maybe not.'

'You have a motorbike?'

'A vintage Indian. 1947. My pride and joy. I've had her since I was seventeen.'

'What colour is it?'

He threw her a look loaded with mock scorn. 'That's such a girl question. Red: bright, chilli-pepper red. The 1947s were all red.' He smiled, reminiscing like a nostalgic father. 'It's been a long time since she was in the desert. She's been all over the world.'

'Where is it, um, *she* now?'

'In a dark garage in Shoreditch.'

'I hope she's okay,' said Claudia, humouring him, but he didn't pick up on the joke.

'Thanks,' he said, nodding tightly. 'Me too. So yeah, that's what I'd do, I'd ride my motorbike, but seeing as how that's not possible, I think perhaps I'll stay here with you. Deal?'

'Deal.'

She was glad that she'd asked him what was important to him, and was amused by the answer. He walked around like a man who carried all his cards close to his chest, and just by finding out his one secret passion she felt closer to him.

It wasn't until she was almost at the front of the line that it occurred to her to wonder why feeling close to him was important.

They would not give the land registry details to her, no matter how much she begged. After a few fruitless minutes, Sawyer stepped forward. He spoke to the clerk in hushed tones and the next thing she knew they were both being ushered down a corridor, into an empty office and told to wait.

'What did you say to him?'

'I gave him three hundred US dollars.'

'When?' She had been with him the whole time, and she hadn't seen any money change hands.

'Does it matter?'

'Corruption is destroying this country. I can't be a part of this. We should go.'

'Don't be so naïve. Mexico doesn't have exclusivity on corruption. You want the information or not?'

'Not like this.'

'Then let's go.'

But before they could, the clerk returned with a

cardboard file. In it, amongst pages of names and dates and figures, was a copy of the bank trust transfer, a form that had been filled in neatly, naming Hector Spinoza as the new beneficiary, signed and dated by Danny Featherbow.

Seeing his signature in front of her like that made her giddy. She reached out to trace the letters.

'It's just a photocopy,' said Sawyer. 'Where's the original?'

The clerk cast an anxious look towards the door, keen to dispatch these foreigners before his boss realized and asked for a share of the spoils. 'With the bank.'

She gripped the top of his arm so tightly that her nails left little imprints in the flesh when he shook her off. 'I see it,' said Sawyer. 'Hector. He was lying.'

'No,' whispered Claudia. 'The handwriting. Look.' She drew the Las Vegas postcard from her pocket. The handwriting was identical.

'You owe me three hundred dollars,' he said.

Claudia was impatient. To be so close to the truth about her father was intoxicating. She fancied that she could feel his spirit calling to her when she stared at the moon and stars. It felt as if this was something she was meant to do, as if unravelling the circumstances around his disappearance was a reason to live.

He was alive. Or had been. The postcard proved it.

She gathered up Daniel in her arms as soon as she saw him, determined that she would love him in a way that both her parents had utterly failed to do. She had a mother whose idea of devotion was paying for a bodyguard and a father who sent one postcard in twenty years and signed it with love.

'We shouldn't go back,' said Sawyer. 'That Hector fellow could be very dangerous. I don't like it.'

'Stop telling me what to do. What if he's the only person who knows where my father is?'

Sawyer was drinking coffee on her terrace. He looked up, his face soft with compassion. 'Your father is long gone, Claudia. If he's not dead, he might as well be.'

'What about this?' She thrust the postcard into his field of vision. A postcard that was soft at the edges from where she'd rubbed her fingers across it night after night, like worry beads or a rosary.

'What about it? Las Vegas is where people go when they don't want to be found.'

'He wants to be found. I feel it, okay? I just *know*.'

Sawyer rubbed his thumbs against his temples. 'You just know?'

'It's called intuition. If you had any you might realize that you are not welcome here. I don't need your protection and I sure as hell don't need your advice.' Her cheeks reddened and she resisted the urge to apologize. Instead she used fussing with her son as an excuse to avoid Sawyer's penetrating stare. She didn't like the way he looked at her; it was like being naked. And the frisson of excitement she felt at being seen like that was unexpected.

She missed David. Sawyer had none of David's charm, none of his passion. In the week that he had been here she had not once seen him make the time to look at the stars, when he ate he didn't savour the taste, when he spoke he chose his words for their brevity not their poetry. She hated the way that he looked at her as if he could see straight through her. She knew he thought her quest was silly and would come to nothing. Most of all she hated that she didn't know how to get his respect.

'Are you angry?' he said.

'I'm fine. I just want to get back to the island.'

'But you'll wait until we hear about the background check on Hector Spinoza?'

'I don't want to.'

'I'm supposed to keep you safe,' he said. 'And that's exactly what I'm going to do.'

'You seem to think I'm some fragile little thing and I'm not. I can take care of myself.'

'Can I tell you what I think?' he said.

'No.'

'I think you want to believe in your father because you are lonely.'

'Lonely? With you breathing down my back all day?'

'There's a big difference between being alone and being lonely.'

'Thank you, Oprah, I'll bear that in mind.' She ignored him and turned the pages of her newspaper, looking for her horoscope. It didn't say anything helpful, though, and she wanted to read Sawyer's in case his was more illuminating, but she wasn't in the mood to ask him his sign. An Aries, probably – one of the pushy, dominant ones anyway. The silence that groaned between them was uncomfortable. It felt as if he was watching her, but when she looked up she saw that he was fiddling with his mobile phone.

'Girlfriend?' she said.

He put the phone down on the table and looked at her with all the weary patience of a parent humouring a young child. 'What are our plans today?'

'*Our* plans?'

'As long as your mother is paying me then, yes, I'm afraid you're stuck with me.'

'I didn't ask her to hire you, you know,' she said. 'How about you go and check into a different hotel? I'll do my thing and then we'll tell Lucy we had a wonderful time together.'

'Or you can stop being a brat and let me do my job.'

'A brat?'

'You think you're the first rich kid I had to look after?'

'You think I'm a kid?' she shot back.

'You used to live in Mexico City, is that right?'

His casual use of the past tense was startling. Until he said it out loud, she had harboured a secret place at the back of her mind that thought she was just taking a break. But he was right. She used to live there. And now she lived in a cottage thousands of miles away and she really wasn't sure how much longer she wanted to stay there. Sometimes she wished that she could take Daniel and live on the moon.

'Yes, I lived in Mexico City, so what?'

'Let me tell you a story about a guy I know who worked in Mexico City. He was a negotiator, you know, the guy they send in to stop the kidnappers from killing you? A girl, younger than you, she was out shopping with her mother – their father was a rich guy, petrochemicals I think – and somewhere between Mazaryk Avenue and Dumas they got them both. They were thrown in the back of a car and for seven days they were kept in the back of a boarded-up garage in Tepito. After five days they cut off the little girl's hand. Not her finger. Not her ear or something, or her big toe. Her hand. And they sent it, along with a photograph of her mother holding it up to a camera. Her own daughter's hand. They wanted six million pesos. They agreed three. The daughter came back, minus the hand, but the mother never made it. I guess probably they should have paid the whole six.'

'Is that a true story?'

He nodded.

'Then it doesn't sound as if your friend was very good at his job.' She flicked the pages of her newspaper, trying to stop her hands from trembling and thinking about this thin vulnerability of her own wrists.

Sawyer yanked the newspaper away from her and she was thrilled by the crack in his smooth surface. Her breath quickened, her pupils dilated, and as she glared at him she flicked back her golden hair. Their faces were close enough to smell the coffee that lingered on his lips. 'Your mother is trying to protect you,' he said.

'You don't know anything about my mother and me.'

'I've known her for more than twenty years; I think I know her pretty well. And I've known you for less than six months and I'm fairly sure I've got your number.'

'Is that right?'

'Beautiful, spoilt, lost. You think you're independent because you've been raised by nannies and not parents, but every penny in your pocket was given to you by someone else. I bet you've never done an honest day's work in your life.'

270

'This time last year I was helping teenage mothers get tested for HIV and teaching slum kids how to speak English.'

'Why? Because you genuinely cared about them, or because giving to charity is all you can do to ward off the demons that come with being born rich?'

She slammed a fist down on the table. 'It can be for both,' she yelled. 'It *should* be for both. I didn't write a cheque, you know. I didn't buy a table at a society ball. I got my hands dirty.'

He raised an eyebrow, shook his head a fraction, and folded her newspaper before passing it back. She could tell there was plenty he wanted to say and his silence was infuriating. She snapped, picking up the nearest thing to hand, which happened to be his mobile phone, and throwing it at him. It would have hit him in the face but he reached out and caught it in mid-air. 'Stupid girl,' he snarled.

He jumped up from the table and stood over her. She faced up to him and they glared at each other for a long, charged moment. He was so close that she could hear the sound of his breath and smell the crisp linen smell of his soap. She could see the thin line of sweat break on his forehead as his hands curled into fists and then relaxed again. Her skin tingled and she felt all stirred up and giddy, like an angry wasp under a champagne glass.

'You're fired,' she said. 'And if you carry on following me around, I'll call the police.'

She took Daniel and headed straight down to the port, where the small pleasure cruisers waited to take tourists out to look for birds and fishes. 'Not today,' they said, over and over. 'Not in this weather.' They pointed out at the horizon. The water was as flat as glass, a thick grey line marking the border between sky and sea. 'There's a storm coming. A big one.'

Eventually she found someone willing to take them across to Des Amparados. For a price, of course. She was starting to understand that everything in Mexico could be bought or sold and she wondered how she had managed to live so long without noticing that no rarely means no at all.

Daniel woke up when the boat smashed into the first of the big waves. And Claudia was afraid she had made a terrible mistake.

19

Esmé did not like being carried on the water. She loved many things about the sea: the lullaby sound it made, the briny tang that carried on the air for miles around, and most of all she loved the way all her problems floated away if she looked at the waves for long enough, but the one thing she avoided if she could was the feel of it beneath her, knowing that the ocean could destroy her in a single moment of unpredictably. She'd grown up in Cancún where stories of fishermen drowning or boats that went out and never came back were a part of life. Her stomach churned with nerves and the rise and fall of white spray. She felt out of control and she hated that. The wind was up and she wished that she had picked another day, any other day, to see if what her mother had told her was true. She vowed that as soon as she was done with this crazy mission, she would stay off the water as long as she could.

The island made her skin crawl. She had heard the ghost stories and she crossed herself when she made land, hoping that if the phantoms were watching her, then they would not mind the intrusion.

It had not been an easy decision to come.

Arriving back in Cancún she had taken some time to think things through.

Given a chance to reflect on what her mother had promised, she had realized it was unlikely to be true. Or at least there was a good chance that money buried twenty years back would have been found a long time ago. But there was something else deep inside her where the root of her stubbornness took hold. Taking his money would be admitting that she could not make it on her own.

And perhaps she could not. What then?

The small Mayan temple looked like a heap of stones until she got close enough to see how strong the little structure had stood against the ravages of nature and time. Ixchel, Mother Goddess of the moon and fertility. Was she supposed to feel in touch with her higher feminine self? She just wanted to check things out and get back to the mainland as quickly as she could. She knelt down on the coarse sand and peered inside, squeamish. The air smelt different in there, damp and rich, and she rooted around in the place her mother had told her to dig and prepared for a disappointment. Even if her mother was getting things straight in her head, this promised stash of ready money would surely have been looted years before.

My father's legacy, she thought. Ha. His legacy was the pale skin that marked her out as different back at school, and the infernal freckles that she had always loathed. Aged about nine years old, she had tried to bleach them away with a bottle of something she'd found under the kitchen sink, but it hadn't worked and the liquid had burnt her skin so badly that she could still see the scars under certain light. Nobody else could see them, not even Miguel, though he had spent enough time staring at her face, kissing her with his eyes wide open.

She hadn't seen him yet. She hadn't been home. From the airport she'd taken the bus that went in the other direction. It made being back here again feel less like a personal failure.

She was staying with a waitress she barely knew in Puerto Juarez who worked two crappy jobs to make ends meet and was happy to rent out the couch in her horrid little apartment. She didn't know if she could find it within herself to take the giant step back into her old life. Every night she lay awake, wondering what to do for the best, frozen by indecision, her night fears plagued with hesitancy and regret. She wasn't ready to go back to Miguel, she wasn't ready to go backwards; who could say, perhaps if this gift from Daddy Dearest wasn't a figment of her mother's hopeful imagination, she would not have to. So finally she came.

Her digging became more frantic; the wisp of hope trailed out of reach.

There was nothing here. She threw a handful of sand against the wall of the temple in anger. One more fantasy of her mother's that didn't pan out. Of course it didn't. She was a fool to have come back to Mexico after finally breaking free. She should have kept on running. She could have gone to Madrid, or Paris. Instead she was here with her head stuck inside a dark hole, digging around in the dirt for something that—

Wait.

The third stone from the end came away in her hand so easily that she was scared the entire structure would collapse onto her and she would die there, half buried in old stones, her ass and her legs hanging out the back, waiting for someone to come to this backwater and discover her sacrificed body. But the rest of the temple wall held true and she scrabbled in the sandy earth, excitement mounting, small pebbles lodging painfully under her fingernails, until her hand touched a shred of fabric that fell apart in her hands as she dragged it to the surface, until what was left was a small plastic bag crammed with American dollars. More money than she had ever seen.

Thank you, Mother.

Thank you, Father.

She started to laugh. The unfamiliar sound of her own laughter shocked her. She counted the notes quickly; not enough to make her rich but enough to make her happy. She laughed so hard that she could feel it in her chest and at the bridge of her stupid, freckled nose. All this time, all those months of hard work, all those sheets and towels she had washed and dried under the hot sun, she had in her hands more than she could have made in a year. All hers. Money meant choices, money meant freedom.

Thank you, Ixchel.

She said a little prayer to all three of them. Now all she needed to do was get back to the mainland and consider her next move.

Then she heard a shout and scrambled to her feet.

'Hey! You there. Hey, yes, you. What are you doing here?'

A young woman was striding down the beach towards her. Esmé thrust the pouch of money down the waistband of her blue jeans but not quickly enough. The stranger's sharp eyes saw the movement. 'What is that? What have you got there?'

'Nothing. What?'

'This is private property.'

'No it isn't.'

The fierce expression on the young woman's face faltered. 'You have no right to be here.'

'There are no private beaches in Cancún,' said Esmé. 'I have just as much right to be here as you.'

'The temple is protected.'

'You think I am stealing a temple?' Amusement flickered over her face and she thought she saw a glimmer of it mirrored in the face of the stranger, the beginning of a smile. It felt as if she was sharing a joke with a friend she had not made yet. 'For my garden perhaps? I could paint it gold and turn it into a fountain?'

She wondered what this young woman was doing here, throwing her weight around as if she owned the place. Perhaps she did. She clearly wasn't Mexican, but she was dressed as if she was working outdoors with her arms and legs covered and grubby hands.

'I'm Esmé,' she said. 'Who are you?'

'What are you doing here?'

'My father left something here,' she said truthfully. 'I came to collect it.'

'I'm Megan. Is it money?'

'I'm not telling you.'

'I saw it. It's money.'

'Nice to meet you, Megan. You live here?'

She shook her head. 'I have friends,' she said, and waved vaguely behind her to the east. She gave in to her curiosity. 'Why would he leave money here for you?' she said.

'My mother buried it,' said Esmé. 'It's a family thing. Private.' She echoed Megan's earlier word with a defiant stare, her hands on her hips, and then looked around. She no longer wanted to get off the island as much as she wanted to annoy this foreigner. How dare she tell her, Esmé, born and raised across the water, where she could and could not go? 'It's very beautiful. I think I'm going to take a walk.' She enjoyed the crease of annoyance that folded between Megan's flashing eyes. 'If that's okay with you, of course.'

Megan shook her head with momentary displeasure and then smiled insincerely. 'Look out for scorpions,' she said.

'In the middle of the day?' said Esmé. 'You tourists do say the funniest things.'

'What makes you think I'm a tourist?'

'Bad Spanish and too much attitude.' She swept her long dark hair over her shoulder and stalked away, unsure of where she was going but insolently deciding to follow the direction that Megan had alluded to, if only because that would suggest that there was something to see. She sensed eyes upon her until she crested the first bluff.

When Esmé saw the house with its orchard and gardens she was amazed that a house like this could be on its own all the way out here. It didn't look abandoned but it was clear from the parched garden that nobody had watered it for some time.

Vines trailed between her feet, dried out and gasping, the little yellow flowers on the cucumber plants were browning at the tips. The lettuces were limp and the herbs going to seed. The trees were still verdant, the glossy green leaves of the avocado and the paler green of the lemons, but everything else was dead or dying and it made her sad. She climbed onto the porch of the house and sat down for a while to rest and felt the emptiness of the place creeping underneath her skin.

The snap of a twig made her look up. Megan stood there.

'Would you like to sit down?' said Megan sarcastically.

'These are your friends?' said Esmé, indicating the vacant house. 'Where are they?'

'I don't know,' she admitted. 'It's been more than a week since I last saw them. The younger one, the son Luis, he comes and goes, but I have never known Hector to leave the island. It's weird. He told me he hasn't left in years. But look at the garden, nobody's here.'

'What about the pipes?' she said. 'They are for irrigation, aren't they?'

'I can't figure out how they work. They draw the water from the well over there but I don't know how. I could ask someone from work to take a look.'

'Here in Cancún? You work?'

Megan nodded. 'Does that still make me a tourist?' she said, and the lightness in her voice washed over Esmé and made her smile.

'Let me see the pipes,' said Esmé.

Esmé twisted her hair into a knot on top of her head and followed Megan over to the well at the back of the house. Immediately Esmé could see that the system worked on the same wind-turbine and header-tank system as the well in the old neighbourhood they had lived in when she was a child.

Megan stood back, no idea how to be helpful.

Esmé dragged one of the porch chairs over to the turbine, climbed up and started to poke around. Immediately she smelt something bad.

'Pass me a bit of cloth or something?'

Megan grabbed an old rag and passed it up to her. 'Don't break anything,' she said.

Esmé rolled her eyes and leant inside between two of the sails and, battling with her squeamishness, removed the cluster of feathers and bloody bones that was once an old bird. 'Get rid of this,' she said, recoiling from the stink. The bird had been there for a few days, poor thing. She tried to turn the sails by hand but still nothing happened.

'I need a stick or something,' she said.

Megan cast her eyes around the garden and came up with a length of bamboo cane. 'Will this do?'

Esmé poked around with the stick until at last a large lump of bird shit was dislodged, the wind gusted and the sails began to turn.

Esmé hopped down and wiped her hands.

'Now what?'

'We wait. The header tank might be completely empty – it's hard to tell. But it will need a top-up at least.'

The pair of them walked a short distance to the terrace and waited in silence. It was weird. The strange sensation of sitting and doing nothing seduced Megan until at last her thoughts began to slow and soften. She stretched out in the heat and snoozed. Maybe Connor had been right; maybe she wasn't as relaxed as she liked to think she was.

'Can you smell coconut?' said Esmé, sniffing the air around her.

'I think that's me,' said Megan, wafting an arm near Esmé's nose.

Esme looked at her like she was crazy.

The air was thick and humid. Pale grey clouds snuggled up tight together and barricaded the sun.

Esmé found herself thinking about her father because if this was the kind of place that he liked, then they had nothing in common. She longed for the city, any city, a place where water flowed from taps and dead birds were only found in butcher's shops. To Esmé, and most Mexicans, the rural life was the hard life and to live in a city meant success. She didn't stop to think why most everyone she knew in the city felt like a failure. Or why she felt so disappointed in the city where she was born.

Time passed, and when the water finally began to flow, Esmé was ready. She jumped up, swollen with achievement, and fastened the end of the rubber tube to the worn-out irrigation pipes, then she twisted the stopcock. There was a gurgle of released pressure and then, as if the Goddess Ixchel herself had reached down to bring life to the land, the sprinklers came on.

'Okay,' said Megan. 'I'm impressed. How did you know how to do that?'

Esmé shrugged. 'Not all Mexicans are dumb.'

'Not all tourists are either.'

They watched the thirsty land soak up the water and

281

Megan imagined the roots in the earth slurping up their sustenance. In a day or two she would be able to see which plants had been rescued and which she should cut down and let go. 'Do you know as much about plants as you do about water pumps?'

'I know nothing about plants. Do I look like a farmer to you?'

'Me neither. I suppose I'll just have to guess.'

The longer Hector stayed away, the more worried she was that something had happened to him. Why would he leave the garden to die? She started plucking away limp brown lettuces to give their more hale cousins a chance.

Esmé looked up at the sky. After all that effort it looked as though it might rain anyway. As much as she disliked Cancún, she disliked it even more when it rained. The tourists were unhappy, so were all the people that depended on them: the bars, the restaurants and the boat trips. The only people that were pleased were the shopping malls, and most of those profits never made it into the pockets of the people who worked there for minimum wage. It would be good for the gardens, though. A sharp shower always refreshed the green spaces and kept the dust at bay. 'How did you find this place?' she asked.

Megan didn't answer straight away. She kept plucking away at the lettuces and started to doubt that any of them could be saved. She hadn't told anyone about Danny Featherbow. But there was something very easy-going about Esmé, despite her sharp tongue. Although they had only just met, and Megan wasn't even sure that she liked her that much, it felt as if she had known her for much longer. Comfortable silences were not a familiar component of her life; in fact silence was so rarely comfortable that Megan did whatever she could to avoid it, whether that was putting on music or singing out loud or talking to strangers. But with Esmé she had been silent for hours and now found that she wanted to talk. 'It belongs to my father,' she said.

'Seriously? You're kidding.'

'He came over in the late eighties, won it in a game of poker, according to my mother.'

'Where is he now?'

'Dead, I suppose.'

'You never knew your father?'

Megan shook her head. She wondered if the day would ever come when she thought of Danny instead of Alan Watkins when someone said 'father'. And she couldn't stand Alan. If only she had a picture of Danny, then it might be easier to bring his face to mind.

'I didn't either,' said Esmé.

Megan felt them becoming friends, the mesh of experience and empathy. 'It's not a good feeling.'

'No. But it's not rare in Mexico. A lot of tourists, a lot of transients, a lot of hot sun and cheap liquor.'

They were both sitting down on the edge of the porch and because they were more or less the same height, their feet reached the very edge of the sprinklers' range so that their dusty toes became speckled with flecks of water when a gust of wind sent the spray in their direction. Then a stronger gust blew the water into their faces and they spluttered.

The wind turbine whined.

They looked up. The sky above them had turned grey

and dense, charcoal clouds gathered out over the water. Beneath the storm, the sea churned angrily.

Megan gasped. 'What's happening?'

'Nothing good,' said Esmé. 'Did you see the weather report?'

'Not since I left England,' said Megan, making a joke. 'The weather in Cancún never changes.'

Esmé looked at her scornfully. 'I think you're about to see that you are wrong. This looks like a big one. Quickly, we might not have much time.'

'Until what?'

'If we hurry, we might be able to make it back to the mainland before the storm sets in.'

Esmé led the way back across the garden, Megan following behind. 'I've been in England,' Esmé said. 'I've seen your storms. You don't understand what's happening.'

'What?' said Megan, and glanced up at the sky, quickening her pace.

'In England it rains for a few hours and people call it torrential. The wind picks up and the trains stop running. The summer storms there are beautiful, refreshing. It's not like that here.'

'You're scaring me,' said Megan.

'That wasn't my intention,' said Esmé. 'But I grew up here, okay? This could get bad. You need to know that.'

The first drops of rain started to fall and Megan thought how ironic it was that on the day Esmé was here to fix the turbine, the rains came. The air was chilled and little goose bumps rose on her bare legs. The storm clouds above raced over them on their way to the mainland.

They reached the top of the rise and when they looked down at the raging sea, both girls felt sick. 'We're not going anywhere,' decided Esmé immediately. 'We should go back to the house and find decent shelter.'

Esmé had lived through two hurricanes and, unless she was very much mistaken, she was about to try and live through a third. Only this time she would not be safe at home with her mother and her brother, but stuck out here in this place with a stranger, with nothing to protect her.

At least they would be on high ground, so they would be spared the risk of flooding, but when things started flying around in the air – and by things she meant trees, walls, that kind of thing – they needed to be somewhere safe, otherwise it could get very nasty indeed.

Megan thought of the flimsy house and suddenly it reminded her of the house of twigs made by the second little pig. *He huffed and he puffed and he blew the house down.* Fear gripped her and shook her like a palm tree in gale. She felt exposed, and wished for a moment that she was back in Essex, where the most you ever needed to protect you from the weather was a good umbrella and a pair of wellington boots.

'Look,' said Esmé. 'There's someone out there.'

'What?' She looked to where Esmé was pointing and saw the little boat battling against the ferocious sea and her heart shot into her throat. 'My God.'

The boat was tossed so high it looked for a moment as if she could see air beneath it, then the wave curled and the boat was lost from sight. Both women stood frozen until the boat was revealed again by the receding water, and they felt fleeting relief.

'There's nothing we can do; nothing except pray for them,' said Esmé. 'Come on, let's go.'

'There must be something.'

'There isn't, believe me.'

'We can't just leave them there all alone.'

'You want to swim out and give them life jackets?'

'But we could call someone.'

'With what? And who? To do what?'

Megan could not rip her eyes away from the boat in peril. She took a few steps back, but Esmé grabbed her arm impatiently. 'You hear that?' she shouted, as the wind picked up and the howl tore her words to whispered shreds. 'That is your warning. Why would you ignore a warning like that?'

They stumbled back down the hill. Water was rushing in rivulets down the parched earth and, when Esmé stumbled, Megan grabbed at her arm but was angrily pushed away. 'If I fall I will fall alone,' she said. 'I won't take you down with me.'

The storm had gathered a huge amount of force in a very small space of time. Esmé was furious at herself for even contemplating fleeing. They had wasted energy climbing to the top of the bluff and now they still had to get back down again and the wind was in their faces. They should have stayed where they were. She could see the rest of the island. The old coconut trees to the north were bending so much it seemed impossible that the trunks would not snap like toothpicks.

Finally the house was close enough for them to see, and Megan was relieved that it was standing strong. It no longer looked like a house of twigs but a safe haven.

'What the hell?' murmured Esmé. She put a restraining hand on Megan's arm.

'What?' said Megan. 'What is it?'

'The door is open, there's someone there.'

'It's okay.' Megan started to run. 'Hector!' she called. 'Hector?'

They heard a strange sound, as if the wind was screaming. Esmé was the first to realize that it was a baby.

A woman appeared on the porch, rocking the small child in her arms, back and forth, his wails soaring above the rain and the gales. They were both soaked through.

'Please,' she shouted to them. 'Please help me.'

Megan and Esmé shared a look, aghast, and began to run. The sudden rain had made the garden slippery and treacherous. Megan lost her footing and landed painfully on her tailbone, crying out but getting up again.

She registered the wind ripping the carefully planted garden to pieces, but was focused on getting to the house, getting all of them out of danger. She remembered what Hector had told her about the island flooding, and had a sudden vision of the tide sweeping in and carrying them all away.

When they reached the house and saw the woman close up, they saw how pale she was, and that she was trembling violently. In a single motion the woman passed over her baby to Esmé and then her legs crumpled up beneath her. Megan tried to hold her up but she folded into a heap on the floor like a puppet with her strings cut.

'*Ay Dios!*' breathed Esmé, and murmured comfort into the baby's ear, not knowing how to hold him or what was wrong with him, and feeling helpless. She jiggled him up and down and he calmed a little bit, but then a part of the guttering collapsed under the sheer weight of the water, and the baby jerked in her arms and cried afresh.

Esmé stared into his little face and started to sing a lullaby she didn't know that she remembered.

His mother, the woman they assumed was his mother, stirred on the floor and tried to sit up. Megan was afraid that the porch would soon collapse and so she took control. She relieved Esmé of the baby and ran inside with him. She made a nest of blankets for him and left him there, his cries muted to a sleepy whimper, while she went back and asked Esmé to help her haul the mysterious woman inside. The kitchen was the oldest part of the house and, as far as she could tell, that and the storeroom next to it where they had put the baby were the most sturdy, so hooking one arm each underneath her, they half carried, half dragged her into shelter and propped her up in one of the equipale barrel chairs.

She slumped forward, her face concealed by wet hair pasted to her skin. She groaned something indistinct, wiped her hair back from her face, then gasped, sat bolt upright and said very clearly, '*Danny*!'

Megan, who had been looking in the cupboards for towels, jerked back towards her. 'Danny?'

'Daniel,' said the woman, 'my baby. Where is my baby?'

'He's in the room next door,' said Megan. 'He's stopped crying.'

'Who are you?'

'I'm Megan, this is Esmé.'

Esmé stared at the woman, seeing her clearly for the

first time, her grey eyes wide and scared, and once more she was struck by the odd sensation of seeing an old friend she did not yet know.

'I didn't know there was going to be a storm,' said Claudia, sobbing uncontrollably. 'The man that brought me here in his boat, he refused to wait even though I said I would pay him more, and I walked here but I lost my way. We were walking for hours. It felt like hours, anyway. When it started to rain, the road disappeared beneath the muddy water and I thought . . . I knew we were in trouble. I thought we would die. I couldn't find my way out and then suddenly the house was here but there was nobody, nobody to help me. Sawyer was right. I need people. I can't . . . I can't . . .'

She started to cry again.

Esmé locked eyes with Megan over Claudia's shoulder, and Megan understood. She took Claudia's arm and led her into the next room where baby Daniel was sleeping so peacefully it seemed impossible that mere minutes ago he had been howling loudly enough to drown out the wind.

Claudia's hand flew to her chest and she dropped to her knees, stroking his face, then she curled up onto the floor next to him.

Esmé dragged a blanket over both of them. 'Rest,' she said. 'We will be here. The storm will pass.'

Then they backed out of the room.

Megan flinched at a crashing sound outside. 'It's getting worse,' she said.

'In Mexico we have a saying: There is no bad thing that doesn't happen for good.'

'Meaning?'

'There's a reason. We just don't know what it is yet.'

'We need to batten the hatches or something. Board up the windows, I don't know. We can't just sit here.'

Esmé glanced at the windows. 'That's a good idea,' she said. 'We can't use the place as shelter if the windows explode. Let's go and see if that old shed has fallen apart yet. We can use the wood from that.'

They went into the small storeroom and took a tarpaulin from a pile there in case they needed it. Megan noted that there was plenty of canned food and candles. Just in case.

Unbelievably, the shed was still standing, although with every gust of wind it leant ominously to the side.

'Rip it down,' said Esmé. 'It won't last the night.'

'Are you sure?'

Esmé looked inside and came back with a crowbar and a sledgehammer. 'This side,' she said, 'and the roof, rip it down.' She nodded, and passed the sledgehammer to Megan.

They stared at each other for a moment and, despite being terrified, despite the rain that fell like a waterfall from the sky, their eyes twinkled and they both grinned through their flattened hair as they raised their tools. Megan felt her fear teeter on the edge of hysteria. But at the same time she felt alive: viscerally, seductively alive.

'One, two . . .'

'Three!'

The shed fell apart like a house of cards. The roof threatened to lift off but together they grabbed the sheets of plywood and stashed them while they worked at the walls. Megan put all her fear and frustration into every pounding blow from her sledgehammer, and Esmé had to pull her back for fear that she would reduce the wood to unusable splinters. She stopped as soon as they had half a dozen usable sheets of plywood. Megan dragged the tarpaulin over the tools that were left exposed, weighting it down with half-finished cans of paint and old concrete breezeblocks.

The wind carried a shout towards them. 'You there,' yelled a man's voice. 'Stop that.'

Megan peered into the gloom and when she saw Hector the dread lifted off her shoulders and for a moment she felt as if she was floating. His face was familiar enough to be a comfort and, besides, Hector was not the kind of man given to panic. She could almost imagine him calming the skies with one of his stoic pronouncements. She realized it might have been them she saw on the boat, decided that it definitely must have been, and was no longer worried about their fate.

Hector was here. He would know what to do. All would be well.

She called out. 'It's me, Megan, come and help us, quickly.'

'Megan? Shit, girl, what the hell are you doing?'

Luis was with him. The two men came thundering towards them, weighed down with a can of diesel and two huge plastic storage jugs of water.

'I said what are you doing?' He grabbed the sledgehammer from her and threw it to the floor. He placed both hands on her shoulders and she thought he was going to shake her. 'Get into the storm cellar, quickly.'

'But the windows . . .'

'There's a storm cellar?' Esmé turned accusingly towards Megan. 'We don't need to worry about the windows. Come on.'

'I didn't know,' said Megan, shouting above the wind.

Behind them Luis was staring dismally at what was left of the shed. 'What were you thinking?'

'I was trying to help.'

'Come on. When the worst of it is passed, we'll come back up and see what's left. Who's this?'

'My friend,' said Megan, if only because it was the fastest explanation.

Luis did not wait for an introduction but dragged Esmé off with him to gather what they might need for a few hours in the storm cellar.

Hector and Megan were left together. She embraced him without thinking and felt him stiffen in her arms, unused to physical contact, not knowing how to comfort her. But she held on tight because it was what she needed and eventually she felt him soften in her lock and his awkward pats on her back became more like the strokes that she wanted. It was only a few seconds but when they pulled apart he looked dazed and she wondered how long it had been since the old man felt affection. She resolved to hug him more often. If they lived through this.

'There's a woman with a baby in the kitchen,' said Megan.

Hector glared at her with mock sternness. 'You've been having a party here while I've been gone?' She loved him for making jokes. Except when they got back to the house he clearly recognized Claudia, and Megan wondered what the story was between the two of them.

Claudia and Danny were curled around each other in their nest of blankets, but the moment that she saw him, Claudia gasped and staggered to her feet. The baby was sleeping through the chaos, a little half-frown on his face that wavered with every steady breath.

Claudia pulled herself upright and pointed a finger at Hector. She no longer looked like the weak little teardrop she had when Megan first saw her; she was in control now and there was a streak of fire in her gaze that was quite forbidding. She was, Megan realized with shock, rather beautiful, and yet at the same time she looked a lot like Megan herself. The same eyes and the same bee-sting mouth.

'You,' said Claudia, her pointed finger just inches from Hector's heart. 'You lied to me. You said you were the caretaker.'

'He is,' said Megan.

'That's a lie. He owns this house,' said Claudia. 'I've seen the proof. So I'm asking you again, sir, with all the respect that I can. What happened to Danny Featherbow?'

Megan, who had been jumping from foot to foot with nervous anticipation, eager to move on, froze in place. She saw again the similarities between this young woman and herself. Looking into her eyes was like seeing her own eyes reflected back at her. Her mind clicked together the pieces of information like a jigsaw, but still the picture was not yet clear. 'What did you say?' It might have been the rain and the wind distorting the words, but she could have sworn she heard the name of her father escape from this stranger's oddly familiar lips.

'He knows something. I can see it. What happened to my father?' she demanded. 'I have a right to know.'

Megan hadn't moved. The wind screamed and the roof above her rattled. 'Danny Featherbow can't be your father,' she said.

'Why not?'

'Because he's mine.'

They stared at each other for a long moment and then turned to Hector, searching for a way past the confusion that blurred the one truth. They were sisters.

'Into the storm cellar,' said Hector. 'I'll tell you everything I know.'

20

Esmé had always believed in love at first sight, but she'd thought it was something that happened to other people, hopeless romantics who believed their endings could be happy and that all the great love songs were true. Love at first sight was not the same as love everlasting. But in the face of Luis Spinoza she saw both.

She had been faithful to Miguel for all the years of their marriage. In her whole life he was the only one she had kissed. She prized her loyalty, never straying, even though she had long understood that she was not in love. She knew another woman, a Mexican woman, who took a new lover every year to numb the pain of her unfulfilling marriage, and Esmé quietly congratulated herself on her ability to stay faithful under the same circumstances. But now she was faced with the awful truth. She had never been tempted. And that wasn't the same as being true.

Luis mistook her dazed expression for terror.

'We'll be okay,' he said.

She believed him. She would believe anything that he said.

He had the most touchable skin she had ever seen. It looked as if it would taste like the dark sweetness of burnt honey. She wanted to bury her face in the downy hairs at the nape of his neck and lose herself in the scent of him. Together they collected a few things from around the house, blankets mainly. They didn't talk. They didn't have to. When he looked at her she saw his strong features glaze over with longing. She melted under his gaze as if she were a piece of chocolate in the tropical sun, oozing into a silken nugget of stolen indulgence. She kept touching her own hair, her face, running her hands across her arms, and she noticed that he was doing the same, both of them seeking to satisfy the sudden craving they had to touch and to be touched. She pictured him gently laying her down in a field of long green grass, far from here, where everything was peaceful and they were alone.

'Luis,' she said. She wasn't calling him to her or asking him a question. She just wanted to feel his name in her mouth, to curl her lips around the kiss at the beginning of it and the sharp whistle at the end. He looked up and she blushed scarlet, afraid that he could read her carnal thoughts.

'We should hurry,' he said. 'This house is not a strong house. Parts of it will not be here when this is over.' He touched his palm to the door frame, as if blessing the whitewashed walls.

She thought of the thousands of dollars buried deep in her clothes, her ticket out of this place once more, this place she had wanted to leave her entire life. Except now that she had found Luis she knew she had to stay.

Hector led Megan, Claudia and baby Daniel behind the house. Claudia was burning with suspicion but had revived enough to see that safety was her immediate priority: safety for herself and for her son.

'It will be okay,' said Hector. 'The storm will pass. Do you know the story of the Mayan god of storms, Hurakan?'

'Hurricane?' said Megan, and glanced up at the sky.

Hector nodded. 'It's where the word comes from. A good word for the Mayans to leave behind them. When all the world was water, the mighty God Hurakan sat above the world in the heavens and invoked the earth until land rose out of the sea. It was a great triumph. But the first race of man to walk on the earth was selfish, led by his own desires and not by love. So in his rage Hurakan sent a Great Flood down to mankind to wash away the greed.'

There was a path cut into the trees and it took them higher.

Hector carried on with his story. 'When they built Cancún here, the Mayans said that modern man was trying to be Hurakan and would be punished for his arrogance. A few years after the resort opened, Hurricane Gilbert caused so much destruction they practically had to start all over again.'

'You think we are being punished for our sins?' said Claudia scornfully. She knew that she should be scared, but somewhere on the arduous journey to make it to this place, her fear had left her, and in its place was a sense of pride and determination.

'Perhaps we all are,' said Hector.

The storm cellar was built on the highest part of the smallholding and reached via a metal trapdoor and a short wooden ladder. When Esmé peered inside, she saw the flickering light of a dozen candles but could not hear any voices.

'Megan?'

'In here.'

She wondered why they were all sitting in silence. 'What's going on?' she said. 'Did something happen?'

Luis followed her down and they saw Megan sitting with Hector and Claudia, the baby nuzzling into Claudia's shoulder.

'Your father,' said Megan. 'The one who left you the money. What was his name?'

'My father?' Esmé was confused. 'Why?'

'Do you know his name?'

'Danny,' said Esmé. 'His name was Danny. But that's all I know. My mother told me his name was Danny.'

Claudia and Megan shared a look. Hector groaned the word of God and put his palms to the sides of his face. 'You are sisters,' said Hector. 'All three of you. Corn, squash and beans.'

Luis slammed the trapdoor shut above them and the sound of the wind was at last muffled.

'Corn, squash and beans is what the three sisters means to a Mexican,' Hector explained. 'The staples of the ancestors. The lifeblood of a country. Each of them the perfect complement of the other. If you have corn, squash and beans you can live well and be happy.'

Megan, Esmé and Claudia exchanged quick, furtive glances, as if they were competitors at the start of some epic battle.

Hector spoke into the silence and told them about

298

Danny Featherbow. How he came to the island a winner, with a wife; how he turned to Catalina in heartbreak and how, when he found Lucy, it looked for a while as though he could be happy.

Luis turned from one sister to the next, seeing the family resemblance immediately: they must be Danny's grey eyes, that must be his quick, supple mouth.

Esmé's hand drifted to her money. She did not intend to share it.

Claudia could not understand why the other two were not dancing around her in joy, why they were not all embracing and laughing, picking up the family ties that had come unravelled and marvelling over their new sisters, their nephew. There should be an outpouring of love, an expression of regret for years lost, facing forward to a shared future. But there was none of this; only the flicker of tension and suspicion and the occasional howl from above.

Hector finished talking and fell silent.

Luis had issues with Megan. 'All this time,' he said, pointing his finger and quivering with anger, 'you've been coming here and pretending to be a friend to my father. We trusted you.'

Megan reached out for Hector's arm, but he recoiled with an expression of hurt that made her want to hug him again and make him understand that truly she had not meant any harm. A man not given to friendship had allowed himself to trust her and been betrayed. She understood why a person would keep the world at arm's length and so she understood why he had gone back into himself, to that place he had been when she first met him, that place far away from the risk of love. And knowing that he had genuinely cared about her only made it worse.

'I was going to tell you,' she said. 'I came here because my mother told me about this house and, as far as we knew, it still belonged to him, to Danny, and I thought that perhaps there was a way it could belong to me. I've never owned anything, I've never had a place that felt like it was mine, and I suppose the idea that out there was a place in the world I would feel safe . . .'

Luis trembled with barely suppressed rage. 'If you think for one second—'

'But,' said Megan hastily, 'then I met you both. I spent some time here and I saw that it doesn't matter what the official line is,' – here she shot a glance at Claudia – 'this place belongs to you, Hector. Only you. You have made it your own.'

Esmé listened to this little speech and as she did so her hand snaked a few inches across the bench where she sat, until her fingertips found those of Luis. It was as if her hand moved independently of her will, seeking out the hand it was born to hold. He responded and their hands stretched into each other, their fingers intertwining, and his touch gave her instant comfort.

Esmé could not take it all in. She had a brother she couldn't stand, a mother she could never forgive, a husband she didn't love, and now what? Two sisters that she did not know, did not wish to know, who were here looking for a father whose name she'd had in her memory for less than a month. And if the pair of them were searching so hard for Danny that they had crossed the world and yet still had not found him, then in all likelihood they never would. So they were family. So what?

The hand that held hers was not the hand of her husband. So what did that make her?

Claudia spoke in a whisper. 'What was he like?'

'Danny?' said Hector, and Claudia nodded. 'He was complicated, but he didn't know that, and he expected life to be simple. But life is not simple, it is never simple, and when things went wrong for him he couldn't cope.'

'So he just ran away?' said Megan.

'Who among us has never run away?' said Hector.

Was that where it came from, Megan wondered, her insatiable desire to escape?

'I have to know,' said Claudia. 'We all do.' She looked at the women on either side of her and tried to see them as more than strangers. Surely this desire for answers would be something that they all shared? 'What happened to him?'

'He disappeared. Nobody ever saw him again. Some people say he died here. There was trouble the summer that he came, big trouble: a man was shot and killed.'

'Danny?'

'By the time the police came, there was nothing to find except rumours and false accusations. This was drug country back then, cocaine alley, and Danny found himself in the middle of it. I think either he was killed or he threw himself off those rocks up there and let the sea take him to his heartbroken oblivion. I don't know for sure. But in my heart I do believe that Danny Featherbow is dead.'

'But why?' said Claudia.

301

'Because if he was alive, he would have come back. And I am sorry, so sorry, because he wasn't a bad person, he was my friend.'

The baby stirred and rubbed sleepy fists into his eyes, the grey eyes that looked like his mother's, that looked like his aunts'.

'You named him Daniel?' said Megan, touching his tiny feet and feeling an unexpected stirring of long-buried affection.

'After his grandfather,' said Claudia.

Esmé felt her heart crack open and let in some light. She turned to Luis and saw that he was staring at her as if he had seen the bloom of love cross her face and make her radiant. She wondered again what had possessed her when she agreed to marry Miguel all those years ago, having never felt, not once, the way she felt under Luis's gaze.

I didn't know, she excused herself. *I didn't know it could feel like this.*

The connection between them was as fine and as magical as an early morning cobweb, and just as insubstantial. And yet it pulled her inexorably towards the path that she must take. She could no longer be married. Not now that she knew.

'There's something else,' said Hector.

It looked as if there were tears in the corners of his soft eyes, but surely that must be a trick of the candlelight?

'Danny gave this place to me,' he said. 'He didn't love it any more and this is a place that deserves to be loved, that demands to be loved, you must have felt that. It is deep in the soil here, that longing. I took it from him. But

302

I promised him that after I was gone from this earth, it would go to his children.'

Megan, Esmé and Claudia drew in the implications of what he was saying. One day this would all be theirs to share if they wanted it. Every grain of sand, every rock, every sunset.

'After he disappeared, after I believed him dead, I thought that was the end of it. He had nobody. I thought that I would leave it to my own children, to you Luis, but now everything has changed.'

'I'm not after the house,' said Luis. 'I told you that a long time ago. I just wanted to get to know my dad.'

Hector's gaze was proud and full of love. Luis was relaxed but Hector was uncharacteristically emotional.

'So it will belong to you, you girls. That's the right thing to do. It can be yours right now if that is what you want.'

'What do you mean?' said Megan.

'For many years the name of this house has been Featherbow,' he said. 'And so it shall remain.' He smiled wanly. 'I am only the caretaker.'

Hector told them more of what he could remember, how Danny had fallen in love with Mexico, how he had loved each of their mothers in his way and how his time here had been filled with every emotion under the cruel sun, how despite his heartbreak he had been alive.

Megan was enraptured. With each passing hour it felt as if she was regaining Hector's trust, that they were friends again. Only on the brink of losing him had she realized how important he was to her.

'Where have you been?' said Megan. 'These last few days, where did you go?'

Hector frowned. 'I had to get away, an emergency. But I saw the weather report and I turned around and came back. This island is my home, Megan, and if this was the end for her, then I wanted to be here. I had to be here. Nothing is more important than that.'

She wanted to ask him more about what had finally drawn him away from this place that he'd said he would never leave, but she didn't want to rock the life raft on which their shipwrecked friendship was still afloat. He was private. She could respect that. He was back now and that was all that mattered.

On the other side of the room Claudia, who was quiet with her sleeping son, listened in on Megan and Hector's conversation and wondered why Hector had felt he had to leave in such a hurry. Was it after she'd come and started asking questions? She could see that Megan cared about the old man, and it was plain to all of them that Esmé was wrapped up in some crazy flirtation with the young American, but Claudia refused to be distracted from the truth she had come here to find, and as far as she was concerned Hector's answers were far from satisfactory. She knew that if Sawyer was here he would be peering into all the holes in Hector's explanation and asking for them to be filled. A man was shot? How did he know? Was he one of the people who fled before the police came? Was he wrapped up in the criminal element of the island's past? Drugs? Perhaps worse, perhaps murder?

Was Hector offering the island to divert them from a darker truth? She was certain he knew more than he was telling. She felt it in her soul.

In her mind she heard Sawyer's voice teasing her.

I just know.

Eventually everybody fell quiet and tried to sleep. Esmé could not shake the sensation of Luis being so close to her; there was an energy humming gently between them that made her feel safe, as she was caught in his force field, protected from harm. She felt slumber steal in to claim her tired mind. She closed her eyes and in the dark shadows cast by the flickering candle he traced the contours of her face and, in the last fragile moment just before she fell asleep, she thought she felt his lips brush against hers, as soft as a spider's dance, but before she could fasten onto the sensation she lost herself to sleep.

Only one man lay awake. He had not slept well for almost thirty years, and tonight was no exception. In the pitch-black silence of the storm cellar, his thoughts were with the house above and whether it would last the night. He tried to pick out the individual breaths of each of the sleeping girls, these precious girls who had come to him for answers, but they harmonized, like the softest lullaby, and still he could not sleep.

In the morning the storm had passed.

21

It was the first time that Megan really understood the expression 'burst into tears'. She had read it many times, friends had said it, she had even on occasion seen it happen, notably to her mother, but when she saw what had become of Featherbow she felt a swell build from deep within her that she was powerless to stop. The emotion burst out from her like a raging torrent through a dam. She did not cry often, and the ferocity of her tears took her by surprise. Everywhere she looked there was a fresh devastation.

The core of the house had stood more or less firm, just as Luis predicted, but the palapa roof on each of the wings had been ripped clean away and the east-facing wall had vanished, so that they could all look directly into the simple bedroom where Hector slept, the bed incongruously neat, but exposed so crudely that it felt like a violation and she had to avert her eyes. Debris had gathered in the corners, banked up against the house like snowdrifts, beautiful wooden furniture was destroyed; that which remained intact was swollen with rainwater. The house and the gardens looked more like an earthquake had passed through or a bomb had been dropped. Wires hung from the places where the walls used to be. The wraparound porch had collapsed, a tangled mess of wooden struts and trailing plants, dangerous raw edges and angles. Only the view remained the same. As the sky cleared it seemed impossible that nature had wreaked such havoc.

Worst of all was the garden. Dozens of avocado and citrus trees had been ripped from the ground to lie dying, their roots out in the open, slopping in the brown sludge left by the downpour. The ground had not been able to absorb the water fast enough and rivers of rain had rushed through the vegetable plots where it had pulled and torn at the roots of the delicate crops, gathering momentum and flotsam, so that where there had once been a flourishing garden there was a lake of mud and a few desperate-looking plants left to drown.

It was a mess.

Esmé thought about Cancún and what this had done to her city. She remembered how the last hurricane had been strong enough to take all the sand from the beaches, reclaiming it for the seabed. The sand never came back. They had to shift tons of it up from the beaches down in the south of the state. But the city had recovered. Would Featherbow recover too, or was this the end? The house had done well to withstand all the changes that Cancún had seen over the years. If this was its time, then perhaps that was the way it should be.

Claudia looked at the sea and wondered where she had found the guts to come out here all alone and how angry Sawyer would be when he caught up with her. Her son gurgled happily on her hip. She tried to remember the house as it had been but found that she could not. She had been so caught up in her own drama that she had never really looked at it properly, and she found herself mourning something that she had never taken the time to know. Megan was obviously distraught but Claudia found that she just couldn't care as deeply as all that. Nobody was hurt. It was only a house.

Luis started to sluice out the kitchen but after a minute slumped back against the wall, acknowledging the futility of the task and not knowing how to begin to make it right. He looked anxiously at his father.

Hector was pale and silent. Trancelike he picked his way towards the house and plucked the medallion of St Joseph from the door frame.

One by one they turned to him to take their lead. It was his life's work that lay in ruins before them. But still he said nothing, his mind seemed absent, and privately each of them worried that the shock was too much for the old man's system to take and they were looking at the beginning of his breakdown.

Megan's sobs subsided. 'What can we do?' she said. 'Hector, I'm so, so sorry.'

His gaze fell on each of them individually, their scared, tired faces. His thumb rubbed the face of the medallion clean and then he repositioned it on the nail that was hammered into the door frame many years ago when Featherbow was just a house and not a home.

'Is everyone okay?' he said.

They nodded, turning to each other for reassurance, and the women felt a bond between the three of them starting to form.

'Then let's go,' he said. 'Grab a broom, grab a trash bag, save only what is worth saving. The rest we can burn.'

Luis slapped his father on the shoulder. 'We should make a pile of building materials we can reuse. We need to get a roof of some kind sorted soon in case it rains again.'

'There are those tarpaulins in the storeroom,' said Esmé. 'Perhaps we can use them.'

'I'll dig some drainage channels in the garden and check the well,' said Megan. 'The turbine is still standing at least.'

'I need to keep an eye on Daniel,' said Claudia. 'But let me get started on the kitchen and we'll see what we can rescue for lunch. We'll need to eat.'

The old man felt love bloom in his heart as he watched the young people go to their tasks. There had been too many lonely times here.

After what happened . . .

He shut his eyes to the memory, the truth that he had not told them, and closed his hand tightly around St Joseph and prayed for forgiveness.

Claudia watched him.

She saw how eager the others were to please him. She pretended that she too was driven by a need to make things right for Hector, but she did not trust him. She did not trust him at all.

Luis sidled up to Esmé, his arms laden down with loose branches as he took them to the patch they had designated for their bonfire. As he touched her she flinched.

'Are you okay?' he said.

'I'm fine.' She smiled blandly. She remembered the seductive energy that had passed between them down in the cellar and she knew that if she allowed it to then the energy could overwhelm her again. Falling in love was not part of her plan to finally be independent. She hadn't walked out on her husband, and then her mother, just to get trapped under the spell of another man. No matter how frantically her insides twisted at the thought of being close to him. That twisting itself repulsed her. It made her feel weak. Stepping out of the storm cellar had cleared her head.

Luis pulled back his hand and eyed her quizzically. 'Have I done something wrong?'

'What could you have done wrong?' she said, and tried to forget that moment last night in the darkness when she thought that he had kissed her.

'I don't know, it's just that I thought . . .' He shook his head, as though he was trying to shake off an idea. 'It doesn't matter.'

She hadn't noticed the way the sun could pick out a dozen different shades of chestnut in his hair, which the gloomy skies and the dark cellar had hidden. She recalled Megan saying that he'd been a drunk or a druggie or something, and thought he looked very well on it. He looked as if he could lift her up in a single swipe, lift her up and . . .

She walked away from him before her thoughts got out of hand. She could feel his eyes burning a hole in her back.

She found Claudia in the kitchen, mopping up the

310

water that had found its way inside, sweeping up broken glass and other bits of wreckage. Claudia didn't notice her at first and didn't see how her every move was being scrutinized until she looked up and was surprised by the look of intense concentration on Esmé's face.

'What is it?' asked Claudia.

'You really think that's true? We're sisters? Half-sisters, I mean.'

Claudia looked outside to check that they weren't being overheard. She saw Megan with Hector, piling bashed crates on top of the bonfire together. Luis was walking off in the direction of the beach, probably to check if their boat had survived the night. 'I'm not sure I believe everything he says, but I think we're sisters, yes. I can see a resemblance, can't you?'

'I suppose.'

'The dates match up. He even knew your mother's name.'

'True.'

'When I first spoke to you, I felt something, like we had met in another life or something, like it was fate,' said Claudia.

Esmé rolled her eyes. 'You believe in all that?'

'What else would bring us all together like this?'

'We all have our reasons for being here. I came here for money. You came looking for Danny. It sounds as if Megan was looking for her father's legacy, her birthright.'

'You mean property? The house?'

'I suppose.'

Claudia looked out at Hector and Megan. He was holding out his hand to help her over some rough ground near the orchard, or what was left of it. 'But a few months later and he has her right where he wants her. She would never take this house from him.'

'You don't like him?'

'He lied to me the first time I met him,' said Claudia. 'He told me that he'd never heard of Danny Featherbow. Now he tells us he is dead or disappeared, a man was shot right here on the island, and yet he had enough time to go to the bank and sign over the bank trust so that Hector now owns the house and all the land? It doesn't add up. Besides, I know Danny didn't die here.'

'How do you know?'

Claudia found her bag and carefully took out the postcard from the pages of her journal. 'I saw his handwriting on the forms at the town hall. It's a match; this is him. This postcard was sent long after he left this place. Dead men don't send postcards.'

By mid-afternoon Hector was exhausted. They had all worked hard, but Hector had pushed himself beyond what was practical and this, coupled with the shock of seeing his life's work reduced to little more than the sort of house that the immigrant workers lived in on the outskirts of town, had rendered him useless. They all watched him stumble over a patch of rough ground by the well and it was Megan who insisted that he had some rest.

'Did you sleep at all last night?' she said.

'What if something had happened?' he said. 'Somebody needed to keep watch.'

It had already been decided that Luis would give up his room for Hector as his roof was easier to patch and the old man deserved a decent bed. After a long morning, in the heat of the late afternoon sun, he ate a few mouthfuls of soup and then made his excuses and left for his siesta.

'Thank you,' he said, reaching for the words to express his emotions and failing. He placed his hand over his heart and they heard him regardless.

The rest of them drank cooled hibiscus tea in the shade on what was left of the terrace.

'Daniel and I will take the little storeroom tonight if that's all right with all of you,' said Claudia. 'The mattress from your father's room has dried out in the sun. There's plenty of linen.'

'Fit for a princess,' said Megan.

'Excuse me? What's that supposed to mean?' said Claudia.

'It doesn't mean anything,' said Megan, although the truth was that she was intimidated by Claudia's grace and by Esmé's beauty, and also by the fact that the two girls seemed to have bonded while she wasn't looking. She had meant it exactly as Claudia had understood it. As a sideswipe to Claudia's obvious privilege. Typical Megan Watkins luck, to find two long-lost sisters who made her feel insecure. One rich, the other beautiful.

'Won't anybody be missing you?' asked Esmé.

'Maybe. I don't care,' said Claudia. Tiny pinpricks of guilt stabbed the back of her neck and made her shudder. Sawyer would be furious.

The women continued to laze in the shade while indefatigable Luis loaded more wood onto the bonfire at the end of the garden. He had taken his shirt off and was ridiculously easy to watch.

'You two seem to have started something,' said Claudia, reaching out her toe to gently poke Esmé.

'What?' said Esmé, blushing. 'Don't talk stupid.'

'Please,' said Claudia. 'It's obvious. It's charming.'

'I'm married,' said Esmé.

Claudia and Megan shared a look. The sparks flew between Esmé and Luis so powerfully that you could almost see them; they burnt with a ferocity that made being around them feel awkward. 'Really?' said Claudia.

Esmé nodded and held up her left hand to show the wedding ring that neither of them had noticed up until now. 'Seven years almost.'

'Maybe you have the itch.'

'Perhaps.'

'Where's your husband?' asked Claudia.

'He runs a bar with my brother downtown. I've been away. They don't know I'm back.'

'But you've been back for weeks,' said Claudia.

'I don't think I can face them. A future there, I just don't want it. The bar won't last, not with the pair of them in charge. They'll drink the profits and do nothing to improve the place. They can barely improve themselves. It's nearby. I suppose I lost my nerve. I don't know what to say to him. To either of them.'

Here on the island it was easy for Esmé to forget that she had certain responsibilities. Perhaps she could live here forever. Weave flowers through her hair and dance under the stars, never to return. Maybe that was real independence, the kind that had nothing to do with money or a place of your own. Freedom of the soul. She thought about expressing this sentiment to her new sisters, but decided that would give them an unrealistic idea of who she really was. She was practical. Unrealistic dreams like that were for little girls and foolish women. She was neither.

'I will go and see him when we're done here,' she resolved. 'As soon as we're back on the mainland. I think I'm just scared.' She looked sideways to see if her admission of fear elicited pity, but all she saw in their faces was sympathy. Which was unexpectedly comforting.

'I do care about him,' she confessed. 'I worry about them. My brother, Ray, used to run around with a bad crowd, and some of those boys have grown up to be pretty powerful figures, but criminal, you know? Ray lets people take advantage of him. Always has. If the bar fails, there will be nothing left for him to do but join them.'

'Your brother's called Ray?' said Megan.

'Ramon.'

'And Esmé? Is that short for something too?'

'Esmeralda.'

There was a moment, no more, when Megan could have asked her to confirm what she knew – that the bar she worked at was the same one Esmé spoke of. Instead she recoiled, stunned into silence by Esmé's admission. Perhaps she could even have provided some reassurance, told Esmé that her husband missed her, but that he would survive, that they had renamed the bar after her and that they were doing just fine. But she had met enough Mexican women to know how protective they were over their families. It was likely that Esmé would not approve

315

of Megan's close relationship with hers. So she let the moment pass. But as soon as she did she regretted it, because it felt as if she was telling a lie of some kind and it was too late to backtrack.

Esmé didn't notice Megan's silence, or if she did she didn't find it unusual. She stared at Luis in a kind of reverie, from which she had to shake herself free. She tore her eyes away from him and turned back to the others.

'Show her the postcard,' she prompted.

'What postcard?' said Megan, and Claudia passed over the postcard from Danny.

'Wow,' said Megan. 'Is this really from him?

Claudia nodded. Megan looked at Esmé who shrugged. 'I think so,' she said.

'But what does it prove?'

'It proves he's still alive.'

'So we don't get the house?' said Megan. She hadn't meant it to come out so callously. As she swept up and cleared away today, she hadn't been able to prevent her imagination planting a tree here, or hanging a hammock there. Maybe positioning a hot tub to take advantage of the best views. 'Sorry.'

'Are you really as heartless as you seem, or is it just an act?' said Claudia. She felt as if she could easily cry but she held herself back from it. She sensed that neither Megan nor Esmé would be much comfort. Instead she gazed down at Daniel and held out a fern to tickle him with, marvelling at the way his little fingers reached out and grabbed it, no matter how quickly she pulled it away. 'I want him to be alive. You both should want him to be alive. I don't know how you can be so, so . . . cavalier.'

316

'I made it this far without him,' said Esmé. 'I can manage, thanks.'

'Me too,' said Megan.

Claudia looked at them in disbelief. 'Then why are you here? I mean, really. You can tell me it's about money, or a house, but you must feel it.'

'What?'

'The sense of belonging somewhere that comes with walking in the footprints of your forefathers; the feeling of history, of peace. Grace.'

Esmé snorted but Megan held back her scorn. Claudia was right. She had felt something. Grace was as good a way of describing it as any. 'I think I know what you mean, maybe,' she said. 'But what good is a postcard from Las Vegas? None of us know the first thing about Las Vegas.'

'I do,' said Luis, who had returned with a bucket of salvaged limes.

'You do?' said Esmé.

'I used to live there. It's where Hector found me. We'd been in touch a little bit by letter when I was young, nothing really. But then I quit college, I left home and I wound up in Vegas. I guess my mum was worried about me. It seemed like a good time for my father to step up. And he did, he really did. He told me about this island, he thought it would be a good spot to clean myself up. I was a big drinker then. So he brought me back here with him. I haven't been back for almost ten years. But I knew Vegas pretty good. I knew a lot of people. What is that you want to find?'

'We think maybe that's where Danny Featherbow ended up,' said Claudia.

'It's possible. A lot of people do. And he played cards, didn't he?'

He wiped the back of his sweaty palms against his chest, leaving a streak of mud, and then started to squeeze the juice from the limes into a plastic jug. 'Does anyone want a margarita?'

'*Me*,' said all three sisters at once. They smiled tentatively at each other.

'Please,' added Claudia and the other two laughed.

'Well, that's one thing we have in common,' said Esmé.

'One more thing,' corrected Megan.

Claudia gazed at her postcard in a way that reminded Esmé of a mother looking at a photograph of her child. 'You're not seriously suggesting we go and look for him in Las Vegas?' said Esmé.

'Why not?' said Claudia. 'I can pay, we can all go.'

'It's a ridiculous idea,' said Esmé. 'There must be a million people in Las Vegas. Besides which, you're talking about twenty years ago. It would be like trying to find a star on a moonless night.'

'A needle in a haystack,' added Megan.

'We know he played poker,' said Claudia. 'Maybe he won something; maybe people will remember him.'

'I'm with Esmé. It's not a good idea.'

'Then what else do you suggest that we do?'

'What else? Why do we have to do anything? Even if you find him one day, what then? You don't know anything about him, none of us do. Claudia, he might not be a good person. How do you know he will be half the man you want him to be?'

Claudia looked at the waves out at sea, close to despair.

If these women did not share her desire, then who would? Perhaps she was wrong to want it so badly.

'I don't understand you, either of you. Don't you care? This is your father. I want to go to Las Vegas. I have to, even if only because I believe that he was once there too. I want us all to go to Las Vegas together. Why am I the only one who wants to find out the truth?'

'The truth can be painful.'

'I won't have you make me feel like a fool for wanting to believe in something, in someone. I am not a fool. I am not a fool to believe in love.'

Esmé reached out her hand. 'We're not saying that.'

'Get off me,' Claudia snapped. 'Fine, if you don't give a damn, that's fine. But my life has changed in so many ways since I started ignoring what I was supposed to do and followed my instincts, and my instincts are telling me that the next piece to this puzzle is in Las Vegas. Who's with me?'

There was a noise from the sky above and she broke off, confused, looking around her for the source.

'What the hell?' muttered Luis, looking up.

A helicopter was above them.

'Is that thing going to land?'

Luis got to his feet. The air around them started to move and the roar from the helicopter blades got louder as it began its descent. Baby Daniel looked on in wonder. Instinctively Claudia gathered her child to her, shielding her eyes from the sun.

Esmé's hair was whipped back from her face.

Megan hoped they would still get to have the margaritas.

The whump of the blades slowed down and the helicopter landed perfectly about fifty yards away, behind the place where the remains of the shed stood.

'Oh my God,' said Claudia, looking closely at the pilot in his leather flight jacket. 'I know who's flying that thing. It's Sawyer.'

'Who's Sawyer?' said Megan. She looked at Esmé, who shrugged.

Sawyer was grim-faced in the pilot seat. He yanked off his earphones. 'Get in,' he yelled.

Claudia looked back at Esmé and Megan with dismay.

'I said, *get in!*'

'No,' yelled Claudia. 'I fired you.'

'Lucy's here.'

'Mother? Where?'

'Here, in Cancún. Will you just get in the damn chopper?'

She stood her ground and within a few moments she realized that Esmé and Megan were standing beside her. 'Who *is* this guy?' said Esmé.

'He's my . . . look, he's just a friend, okay?' said Claudia.

'A friend you say?' said Megan.

'Claudia, please,' yelled Sawyer.

'He's cute,' said Esmé. Claudia looked at her in amazement, stunned by their reactions. 'Well, he is,' said Esmé defensively.

'That,' said Megan, admiring the helicopter, 'is one sweet ride.'

'I have to go,' said Claudia, with incredulous resignation. 'I don't want to.' Tears welled up in her eyes and she faced her sisters for guidance. Watching her come close to

320

tears as her hope drained away was like watching a kid find out about Santa Claus.

'Then don't,' said Megan.

'You don't understand. My mother is here. It's over.'

22

'It's over, Claudia. Whatever silly little dream you were following, it ends now, you understand?' Lucy was containing an icy fury that made her rigid with tension. 'What were you *thinking*?'

Claudia was standing ineffectively while two chambermaids packed up her mother's things. When they'd finished doing that, they would start on hers and Daniel's belongings, ready for their flight back to England.

Her mother had brought a letter with her. A letter from David.

Or more accurately from his lawyer.

In the letter it had been made clear to Claudia that unless she provided a stable home for baby Daniel, then his father, David, would be forced to seek custody. The letter cited her tender age and her habit of crossing international borders without the approval of the child's natural father as grounds.

'How convenient for you,' said Claudia. 'How much did you have to pay him to send a letter like this?'

'I didn't pay him anything,' said Lucy. 'I swear.'

'He didn't even call me to find out if Daniel had been

born, and now all of a sudden he wants custody? He can't have it. I doubt he even wants it, not really.'

Sawyer lurked in the background. She wondered how much trouble he was in for letting them out of his sight.

'Des Amparados is a dangerous place. David may have a point.'

'You said you didn't even remember Des Amparados,' protested Claudia.

'Did I? Yes, I did. But Sawyer has reminded me of a few things. It's a drugs corridor; this is Mexico. You're lucky you didn't get shot. You never should have come to this godforsaken corner of the world. I never should have let you.'

'*Let* me?'

'When you have your own money, feel free to make your own choices, but until then, you do as you're told.'

Claudia squealed in frustration and marched out of the room into her adjoining room and slammed the door behind her. She left Daniel with his grandmother – let her look after him for a while if she was so bloody concerned. She was well aware that she was behaving like a spoilt brat, but she was too frustrated to care. For years she had wished for a mother who would show an interest in her life, and now finally her mother was getting involved and it was hideous.

Was she, as her mother had spent the last hour or more telling her, and the letter from David's lawyers alleged, being fundamentally selfish? Would it be best if she were to stop dreaming altogether and focus on what was really important – her child?

Without going to Las Vegas, even if Megan and Esmé

were right and it was a fool's errand, her search felt incomplete. Without that kind of closure, she wasn't sure if she would be content to return to Oxfordshire with Daniel and try to build a life. But there was no hope of being allowed to travel anywhere now but home. And home, for the time being, was a cottage in England.

And where was Sawyer in all of this? He had barely spoken to her and she knew he was angry with her for walking out on him, but she was angry with him too, for all the horrible things he had said, for dragging her mother out here; and though she knew that Sawyer was the one person who would be able to calm her down, he was also the last person that she wanted to speak to. When she looked at him she felt a sort of confused fury and didn't know whether she wanted to hit him or hold him.

She heard a muffled knock from next door and then the sound of raised voices coming from that room, than the sharp rat-a-tat-tat of knuckles on her own bedroom door. She got up from the bed, curious. And there in the doorway stood Esmé.

'Hi!' she said, all breezy and blasé, as if there was nothing unexpected at all about this unannounced visit. 'Ready?'

'For what?'

'For Vegas, silly. You're not even packed!' Esmé grabbed a bag from the bottom of the wardrobe. 'You don't need much,' she said. 'It's just a couple of days. Quickly, Claude, the flight leaves in a few hours.'

'Claudia?' Her mother's chilly tones struck a note of reason. She stood in the doorway, bearing Daniel uncomfortably on her slim hip. The child grabbed at her blond hair and yanked it with glee. 'What's going on?' said Lucy.

Claudia looked from her mother to Esmé and back again. 'You'll come?' she said. 'To Vegas, really?'

Esmé nodded. 'It's only over when we say it is,' she said.

'Las Vegas? Absolutely not,' said Lucy firmly.

'Hi, I'm Esmé.' She held out her hand, and Lucy, with her good breeding and her spare hand, shook it.

'Where's Megan?' asked Claudia.

'She had to get back to work. She seemed fairly stressed out about it: perhaps she's afraid she'd lose her job. Hurry up, Luis is waiting.'

'Luis is coming?' said Claudia.

'He knows the best places. It'll be fun,' said Esmé firmly. 'And please take that look off your face. There is nothing going on between Luis and me.'

Claudia slumped. 'I don't think I can.' She explained to Esmé about the letter from David. 'I think he's bluffing,' she said, with a sour look towards Lucy, 'but how can I take the risk?'

'I always think if you're already in trouble you might as well stay there,' said Esmé. 'What can he do? Send another letter?'

Claudia weighed up Las Vegas against David's threat. She looked across the room at her mother and thought she saw there a trace of guilt. And that was enough to decide her. 'I'm calling his bluff,' she said, and added some of Daniel's things to the bag that Esmé had thrown onto the bed.

Esmé cheered and whisked the baby away from Lucy in such a swift motion that Lucy couldn't stop her. Daniel gurgled happily and tried to grab hold of Esme's nose. Bubbles of laughter lodged themselves in Claudia's throat like gas and she watched the disbelief bloom on her mother's face, avoiding her eyes for fear that she would burst out laughing and that her mother would think she was mocking her – she wasn't, it was just that the thrill of defying her was growing addictive. She saw a flash of another life, one where she was as feisty as Esmé.

'And just how do you intend to pay for this jaunt off into the sunset?' said Lucy, pulling herself tall and trying to sound as if she still had the situation under control.

'Don't worry,' said Esmé. 'I recently came into a little money and I've decided to use it for this. I think it's important. It's important to Claudia.'

Lucy looked at her daughter and saw the determination on her face, saw that this whole summer might just be the best thing that had ever happened to her daughter. Saw that she had failed. 'Sawyer will go with you,' she said. And Claudia knew that she had won.

'Yeah?' said Esmé. 'Well, he's paying for himself.'

Sawyer and Claudia locked eyes. It felt odd after all their time alone to be surrounded by people. There were things she needed to say to him. She wanted him to know how angry she was that he had involved her mother. In that moment when he looked at her she felt a surge of confidence. 'Let's do it,' she said.

The four of them, plus Daniel, were out of the hotel room before Lucy had time to gather her thoughts into a convincing argument against them leaving. Claudia kissed her cheek and told her that she would be back in a couple of days.

'And then we go home,' said Lucy.

'And then we go home.

Luis was double parked outside in his beat-up old Volvo. He honked his horn and started his engine when he caught sight of them.

'Do you think we have a hope of finding Danny?' said Claudia.

'No chance,' said Esmé. 'But I know you want to, I know you really want to, and what the hell, we've come this far, right?'

'I'll pay you back,' said Claudia.

'Don't worry about it,' said Esmé, patting the stack of notes she had dug out of the sand on the island. 'This road trip's on Daddy.'

23

Las Vegas makes an impression on all who visit, but there was a clear division in the hire car along gender lines in terms of impact. Luis had spent some lonely years in Las Vegas and was far from enthusiastic, while Sawyer, who was driving, couldn't have cared less. Meanwhile Claudia was thrilled by the razzmatazz and Esmé was playing it cool but slightly awestruck as they crawled along The Strip in the car that Claudia had insisted on christening Big Blue on account of its size and colour. Imitations of Paris, New York and Venice sat alongside towering silver skyscrapers and advertising hoardings the size of cruise ships. People were happily walking up and down the famous strip all day long, dipping in and out of bars and casinos that didn't care what time it was. 'I grew up in Cancún,' said Esmé. 'This whole place is like Dady'O on a Saturday night.' As if to prove her point, a cackle of raucous college kids spilled off the sidewalk and into the street in front of them, causing Sawyer to lean heavily on the car horn and the biggest guy in the college crowd to extend his middle finger.

'You could kill him with a single blow to the neck, right?' said Luis.

'Of course I could,' said Sawyer, 'but when the cops came I'd blame it on you.'

The rollercoaster outside New York, New York thundered past and they could hear people screaming in happy terror.

Claudia saw the live pirate show outside Treasure Island and wondered if they would be able to go there later. Daniel was propped up in his car seat next to her, his little head flicking backwards comically when his eye was caught by a flashy bit of neon or a bright colour, and neon brights happened about every ten seconds. She tore her eyes away from him in time to see a hotel with a waterfall outside and the looming black pyramid of the Luxor.

As happened so often these days, she tried putting herself in her father's mindset. This would be the perfect place to get lost.

If only Sawyer wasn't with them. He was being jovial enough, but the tension between them was upsetting her balance. Since her return from the island he had taken a giant step backwards and the connection she had felt to him had been severed. Once upon a time, people might have mistaken them for a couple; now, because of the way he was holding himself and the physical distance he kept from her – even the way he was dressed, in a smart shirt and dark trousers, it felt obvious that he was staff. She didn't like it. She wondered if he was trying to punish her for running away from him.

'Where are we staying?' she said, leaning into the front of the car and hoping it might be Excalibur with its fairy-tale castle.

'Fremont Street.'

'Not on The Strip?' said Esmé, her disappointment plain. Luis caught her eye in the mirror and winked. 'I mean, anywhere is fine,' she said.

'Most of these hotels weren't even here a decade ago,' said Luis. 'They knock them down and build them up again, hire a whole new staff. We'd have no hope of finding anybody unless they won the World Series Poker, and if he'd done that then even I would have heard of Danny Featherbow.'

'You seriously think we'll have any luck downtown?' asked Sawyer. 'Where do you start to find someone in a city like this?'

'You ask around,' he said. 'That's how my father found me.'

They checked into the Golden Gate Hotel and Casino just as the sun was setting. It was a creaking old place with a strange layout and miles of gloomy corridors that gave Esmé the creeps. Her room looked out on Fremont Street itself, a crazy electric walkway of light and sound that made you feel as if you were strolling through an enormous video arcade. She could see the signs for Glitter Gulch and Golden Goose, thousand of bulbs twinkling in the all-year-round Christmas parade of downtown Vegas. The night was starting to get cooler, but people were still wandering around in shorts and vests as if they were down at the beach.

She unpacked a few things and thought about all the people she knew that held the dream of coming to America as the most precious life they could imagine. She

330

wondered if they would change their minds if they saw this particular part of it. She was glad they were only here for a couple of days. She was in the cheapest room they had, but it still felt luxurious after her time sleeping on her friend's couch and camping out on Des Amparados. The bed was on the small side but it was a double. Which felt unnecessary. It made her think of Luis. The more time she spent with him the more exhausting it became to resist the magnetic pull he had on her body. Her fingers were constantly reaching out for him and a few days here, in the city of sin, would keep her in a state of constant excitement which would build itself into a frenzy over time. What would happen if she gave in to temptation?

She looked down at the thin gold band on her ring finger and slowly and deliberately twisted it off, then hid it from sight and went to meet Luis.

She found him at Du-Par's eating pancakes and looking miserable.

'What's wrong?'

'This used to be the Bay City Diner,' he said. 'My favourite place in town. I'm in mourning. The whole way here I was dreaming about their steak special.'

'How are the pancakes?'

'Fantastic,' he said. 'Best I've ever had.'

'So what's the problem?'

'Too much is different.'

'Are you worried you'll get dragged back into your old ways?'

He looked grim. 'Don't tempt me. Look around you.' Du-Par's was crammed with people getting ready to have a good time. 'I live with my old man on a desert island.

You have any idea how much trouble I'd get into if I let myself go?'

She tried to stop picturing whether his six-foot-three frame would fit into her double bed and thought that she knew exactly what he meant by trouble.

She barely knew him. For years her marriage had anaesthetized her to the possibility of these feelings and she now saw that romance could be irrevocably true. This was the kind of thing for which it was worth trading in your independence, because you were trading up. Her fingertips tingled and the skin on her face felt hot, as if she had just drunk a strong margarita.

'Are we waiting for Claudia and Sawyer?'

'She wanted Daniel to get some rest, start fresh tomorrow. Tonight it's just you and me.'

Claudia gazed down at her sleeping son and silently apologized for dragging him around the world before his first birthday. But really, what was the alternative? After a lifetime of bitterness towards her own mother, she couldn't exactly leave him behind just the same. She closed the door to his little bedroom and investigated the rest of her junior suite. The tub in the bathroom was on the small side but she decided to have a long soak and an early night. She was beginning to understand that unless she found a reliable babysitter, there would be a lot of long soaks and early nights in her future. She poured in the entire contents of the small bottle of shower gel that the hotel provided to try and make it feel more luxurious, and was just about to step in when there was a gentle knock at the door. She pulled on a robe and opened the door. Sawyer leant against her door frame and peered inside.

'He's sleeping?'

'Out like a light,' she said.

He came into the room and closed the door behind him. He had undone the top buttons on his shirt and his feet were bare, just like they had been the first time she'd seen him.

'You okay? You need anything?'

'I need sleep.'

'Got ya,' he said. 'I just wanted to see if you were okay.'

'I'm all set,' she said. But he didn't leave.

Sawyer rubbed the five o'clock shadow on his chin. 'I know you're mad at me,' he said. 'I knew you would have gone to the island. It was obvious. And then the storm came. I had to call your mother. That's what someone doing my job is obligated to do at that point.'

'It's what you were *obligated* to do?'

'Yes.'

'And whatever I want doesn't come into it?'

'No. I was scared, Claudia, okay? It was my fault you ran away. I said some pretty nasty things and I didn't mean any of them.'

'Then why did you say them?'

'I don't know. You confuse me. Sometimes, even when we argue, it kind of feels as if you might like me and maybe I get freaked out. I'm supposed to be looking out for the bad guy, Claudia. You understand? That's my job right now. I can't go getting all distracted by how beautiful you are when you're angry.'

'So this is all my fault? Our argument, the hurricane,

333

the letter from Daniel's father telling me what a crap mother I am? I brought it all on myself?'

'In a way, yes.'

Blood rushed to her face and her cheeks blazed. 'In what way exactly?'

'You're selfish,' he said. 'But that's only because you don't believe anybody cares about what you do. And they do, they care very much. People were worried about you,' he said.

'I suppose by people you mean my mother? She really has you wrapped around her little finger, hasn't she?'

'I don't mean Lucy, you idiot, I mean me. *I* was worried about you.'

'Because you felt *obligated*?'

'Will you cut it out? I'm trying to tell you something.' He grabbed her and silenced her with a long, slow kiss on the mouth. She pulled back, stunned, and slapped him sharply around the face. The noise echoed like a whip crack in the shadowy old hotel room.

He stopped kissing her immediately and pulled back. 'I don't think you really mean that,' he said, and he kissed her again.

'How dare you,' she said, her voice no more than a low whisper. The touch of his lips sent her reeling.

'We shouldn't be doing this,' he said. But even as he said it he was walking her backwards, like in a waltz, towards the hotel bed.

'Why not?' She started undoing the remaining buttons on his shirt.

'There's nobody looking out for the bad guy,' he said. He slipped his hands underneath the neck of her robe and

334

as she untied the belt he slipped it off her and it fell to the floor. She shivered.

He took his hands and placed them on the side of her breasts, smoothing his palms down over her sides, past the dip of her waist and over the swell of her hips until they came to rest under her arse. She wrapped her legs around his waist as he lifted her up onto him as if she weighed nothing at all. She ran her hands across his impossibly broad back and gripped him tighter as they fell, locked together, onto her bed.

He divested himself of his remaining clothing and when they were both naked he paused for a moment and stared at her in a way that made her feel gorgeous. In time his hands roamed across every inch of her body and he kissed her in places she hadn't even known she longed to be kissed.

She cried out as he rocked inside her and when it was over he whispered her name over and over again like a prayer, losing himself for a long moment in the sweaty afterglow of lust.

Luis and Esmé walked from one bar to another looking for people that Luis used to know, but they didn't have much luck. He found a barman who had heard of a dancer he knew, and a dancer who had heard of a dealer. He found a gambler that he remembered but didn't remember him, he found a waitress who thought she had waited on him in Fat Eddie's until they compared dates and they didn't match up. The hotel where he worked was still there but he didn't recognize a single person.

They ended up back at Du-Par's and ordered coffee.

She was starting to see how hopeless it was, looking for a trail that had been cold for so many years. She was tired of saying the same name over and over and getting the same blank look in reply, and she was wondering why they were here. Luis had started the evening full of fun and optimism, looking forward to the challenge, but as the night wore on, a bitter edge to him was sharpening and bringing them both down.

The number of drunks and homeless people in the area had risen slowly as the evening progressed, and she began to see some of the downtown sleaze that gave this area its dubious reputation. She was glad that Claudia and Daniel were stashed away upstairs. Megan had been right with what she said about Claudia: she was something of a princess.

'This town is too fast,' said Luis, sipping his coffee and watching a police officer confront a crazy old guy who might have been essentially harmless but was scaring a couple of young girls who looked as if they had wandered in straight from the wholesome fields of the Midwest. 'It moves around,' he said. 'And it moves on.'

'You did.'

'People come here to shop now,' he said. 'And to see a show. That's the craziest thing I ever heard. Gaming, girls and liquor, that's what Las Vegas is supposed to be about, not shopping malls and Broadway shows. Since when do the casino owners want you sitting in a theatre watching Elton John play piano all night when you should be throwing your money away on the gaming floor?'

'They can make two hundred and fifty bucks a seat,' she said. 'I guess they must think it's good business.'

'A family resort,' said Luis. 'That's what that guy at Caesar's said, right? Did you ever hear anything so fucking stupid?'

'Things change,' said Esmé. 'If they didn't I guess you'd still be living here.'

'If things didn't change I'd be dead.'

She wasn't sure what to say. She shredded a paper napkin between her fingers and watched the storm gather in his eyes.

'I used to get up in the middle of the afternoon and start drinking, kidding myself that it wasn't a problem because at least it wasn't morning. But it was morning to me so the only person I was lying to was myself.'

'I don't get it.' '

'I liked working the graveyard shift,' he explained. 'Midnight till six. I'd check people into their rooms, or send up room service, and they never noticed that I was out of my head. Because they were too. Then I'd ride the bus down to The Strip catch up with the last few players at the tables. Sink a few more beers.'

Esmé noticed that he gripped the edge of the table as if he was afraid he might fall off his seat. He wasn't very old even now, older than her maybe by ten years or so, but she did the mental arithmetic and figured that this must have happened when he was very young.

'There is a particular kind of gambler who plays at breakfast,' he said. 'He's had a good night maybe, but not great, he's drunk himself sober and he's lost all track of time; he's lost all track of everything. Nothing matters, not really, not any more. They were my kind of people. Vegas is great for finding people you can drink with, and that's not the same thing as finding friends, not nearly the same.'

'So what happened?'

'Dad happened. Hector.' He knocked back the last of his coffee as if it was a shot and rubbed the back of his hand across his mouth. 'He wrote to my mother in Boulder, she wrote back, told him to forget about me. But he kept writing. I replied. We got to know each other a bit, I guess, but when I stopped replying he wrote to my mother again and she told him I'd moved out, moved to Vegas. Told him that I'd stolen everything I could carry and maxed out her credit card too.' He saw Esmé trying to hide her shock. 'Yeah, I did,' he confirmed.

Esmé added dark and shade to the picture of Luis he had painted in her mind.

'She told him she was done with me, and I don't blame her. But Hector, well, he hadn't even started.'

'Started with what?'

'With being a parent.'

He paid the check and they walked out together into the mayhem of the casino, into the unique Las Vegas cocktail of hilarity and despair. The revellers were easy to spot, loud and amused; so too were the mini-breakers and the budget travellers. But amongst them were scattered the lost souls, with their open wallets and empty hearts.

'That was me,' said Luis, pointing at a young guy, college aged, pounding coins into the slot machines and sipping constantly from a double measure with a straw. 'The slots were my cover. I pretended that gambling was my thing, but that wasn't what I liked about Vegas. What

338

I liked about Vegas, what plenty of people like, is there's always someone worse than you. More drunk, more dumb, more fucked. Someone you can point to and say, "See? I'm not so bad," and feel safe.'

'Hector found you?' she said.

'I think he was here for a while before he did. He followed my trail. I started off working at one of the bigger hotels down on The Strip, but I lost that job and then another, until I found a place up here where I could keep my head down and make enough money for rent and beer. I didn't care about much else.'

A jubilant cheer went up from one of the craps tables and Esmé craned her neck to see a huge fat guy try and lift his equally fat wife to celebrate their win.

'And then one day a buddy of mine said some guy had been asking after me down at the Bay City Diner. Nobody had told him where I was because that's what you did: you looked after your buddies. They probably thought I owed him money. But he must have understood that was the way it worked in Vegas because he just told anyone who knew me that he'd be there every night from eight until midnight and I should stop by and say hello. But I didn't go, not for weeks.'

'Why not?'

'It's simple. I knew he'd make me stop drinking. And I didn't want to stop drinking. I was twenty-two. I didn't have a problem, I just liked a beer. This was Vegas. But people kept telling me that he was showing up there, every night, just like he said. So of course, eventually, I had to go.' They reached the entrance to the casino and stepped out onto Fremont Street. The frontage was crammed with people, caught between being inside and out, and Luis and Esmé had to move closer together to keep moving. 'We left Las Vegas the same night.'

Suddenly all the lights on the Fremont Street casinos went dark and the music cut out. Esmé span around, confused. At first she thought it was a power cut and there was an eerie moment of quiet gloom. Luis tucked his arm around her shoulders and tilted her chin with his other hand. 'Look up,' he said. The domed roof above them, which Esmé had taken for a sunshade, burst into an explosion of sound and colour. It was a screen, a giant screen, a million LED lights stretching the length of three entire city blocks, playing a fantastical montage of stars that became snow that became cracks of ice and eventually a singing and dancing spectacular, and Esmé started to laugh because for all her protestations that Las Vegas was like Cancún in high season, they had nothing like this in Cancún. It finished, and all of Fremont Street hollered and cheered for precisely three seconds and they went back to the business of having a good time.

They both turned when they heard the voice. 'Luis? Is that you?'

A woman of around forty was standing on the street next to them, wearing a waitressing outfit and a pair of bright pink high-top sneakers. She clapped her hands together and grinned so hard that her shoulders almost touched her ears. She was short and she looked fun.

'Margot? Jesus, Margot you look great.'

'I look like shit, thank you very much for lying. I ran into Paul, he spoke to a dancer down at the Golden Nugget who said you were back in town.'

'Esmé, this is Margot, my favourite waitress in Vegas.'

'If I'm your favourite, you're a really mean tipper.'

'Give me a break,' he said. 'I was no trouble.'

'That's true,' she said. 'One steak dinner a day and not too many refills. You want to buy me a cup of coffee and tell me all about it?'

A cup of coffee and a slice of pie later, Margot came up with something. 'Do you remember Tosca, the Italian guy? He works down in archives at Caesar's Palace now. They had that no-limit open in the late nineties, he could tell you if your guy ever showed up to play there. It was a cash game but you still needed a member's card. It's a long shot and, honey, don't take this the wrong way, but your whole mission sounds a bit like shooting for the moon.'

'We know,' said Esmé. 'But my sister, she really wanted to check it out. This Tosca guy sounds like a lead, that's all she wants, really – to be able to say she's tried.'

'Where is she now?'

'Upstairs in the hotel,' said Esmé. 'She has a little boy.'

'How old?'

'Almost one I guess.'

'You got a picture?'

'Me?' said Esmé. 'Why would I have a picture?'

'Sometimes aunts do, you know. I used to carry a picture of my niece everywhere until she got real ugly.'

Esmé snapped her head around to Luis, her eyes wide with delighted mirth.

'Still as charming as ever, Margot,' he said. 'There's just one problem.'

'What's that?'

'I don't know anyone called Tosca, never did.'

Margot shrugged. 'It's Vegas, honey. Who can remember everyone? Tell him you guys are old friends and he'll believe it. Slip him a fifty and he'll pretty much do whatever you want.'

'Tosca. Got it. Thanks, Margot, you're a diamond.'

'Damn straight,' she said, and wandered off into the crazy Las Vegas night.

Claudia wondered if Esmé could tell that things had changed between her and Sawyer. It wasn't as if he was holding her hand in public or anything, but surely it was obvious that they had spent all of last night naked and entwined. She didn't feel tired; in fact she felt more awake than she had for months. She felt sparks between her legs every time she caught Sawyer staring at her, and he was staring at her a lot, as if he couldn't believe his luck. She felt invincible. She loved the feel of his eyes constantly on her. Then Esmé told them about the lead they had uncovered the night before and she was so invigorated that she felt as though she could have flown the two miles down to The Strip from Fremont Street, but instead she piled into the car with the others and tried to rein in her wildest dreams. Yet in her mind's eye she saw Danny Featherbow sitting at one of the tables in Caesar's Palace. He would look up when they walked across the room. His eyes would meet hers and he would know, he would just know.

He would shake Sawyer's hand like a real father would, and they would all live happily ever after.

'What are you thinking?' said Sawyer, seeing that she was lost in a daydream that was making her smile.

342

'Nothing,' she said, enjoying the zing that coursed through her when his hand brushed against hers. She dropped her voice to a whisper and pressed her palm against his. 'Come over again tonight.'

'I've been waiting all morning for you to say that,' he said, and his voice made her squirm pleasantly inside.

At Caesar's Palace, Tosca pretended to remember Luis, just as Margot had said he would, and after a few minutes of small talk about the good old days, he agreed to comb through the archives on his break and meet up with them later.

'How much did you slip him?' said Sawyer as they watched him walk away.

'A fifty. You think I should have given him more?'

'Wait and see if he finds anything.'

Babies and children were allowed to pass through the casino but not to loiter, so Claudia took Daniel down to see the sharks in the Aquarium at Mandalay Bay. Sawyer followed them like a shadow.

'What do you want to do?' asked Luis. 'We could grab something to eat, maybe at the Palms or somewhere high up so that you can see the view. We could just walk around a little bit. Or, I don't know, go shopping?'

'Shopping, Luis? Really? I thought you said Las Vegas should be all about gaming, girls and liquor?' She took a bunch of twenties out of her purse and waved them at him. 'Let's play!' Her eyes twinkled.

'Don't flash your money on The Strip. Are you crazy?' But he was grinning as he hustled her cash back inside the safe confines of her purse. 'Stupid tourists.'

They played blackjack and Esmé came out slightly ahead, but she soon bored of Luis's insistence that she play strategically, which meant hitting only until she reached seventeen, twelve if the dealer had a low up-card.

'You made money, didn't you?'

'But where's the risk?'

She lost a lot of money on the roulette table, but made some of it back playing black or red, which wasn't as exciting. Then Luis tried to explain the rules of craps but she couldn't follow them.

'Hey buddy,' said a guy at the table. 'You mind if your girlfriend kisses the dice here?'

'I would *love* to kiss the dice!' said Esmé, sidestepping both Luis and the assumption about their relationship.

She kissed the dice and threw them for him. He seemed very pleased and the dealer pushed over a lot of chips, but she still wasn't clear exactly why. She accepted his hug and his twenty-dollar chip gracefully, and then looked around to see what else she could spend it on.

'Tosca should be back any minute,' said Luis. 'Maybe you should wait.'

'I don't want to wait,' she joked. 'I want to win.'

'Do you play poker?' he asked.

'Never learnt,' she said.

'I could teach you,' he said. 'Not now, we don't have enough time and the poker room of a casino on The Strip is not a great place to learn the basics. But maybe when we get back to Cancún, if you'd like me to, I could show you some stuff, the rules and whatever. Maybe we could come back to Vegas one day. Or, you know, I've always wanted to go to Atlantic City: they say the ocean there is beautiful.'

'I'm married,' she said.

He broke off from his tentative plans for some kind of future together with a snap as clean as a brittle bone. 'You're what?'

'My husband lives in Cancún. We got married when I was sixteen.'

He searched her face for some sign that she was joking, or lying, for reasons that he could not understand. But he saw that she was telling him now because she saw the path that he was on and could not let him go further down it without knowing the truth.

'Do the others know. Claudia and Megan? Does Sawyer know?'

She nodded. 'I don't want to be married. I never really did.'

'Those guys must be killing themselves laughing every time they see the way I look at you.'

'How do you look at me?' she whispered, tipping up her face so that there was no more than a breath of air between them.

'Like I can't look away.'

The slot machines shrieked their jangling tunes, the piped music competed with the loud voices of a thousand tourists and a hundred touts, the electronic billboards promised every wonder of the world for less than the price of your soul, but when Luis kissed Esmé in the daylight, she heard only the voices of the better angels in her mind telling her that this, this wonder, this could not be wrong.

They broke apart and he thought about apologizing, but how could he be sorry when kissing her was all that

345

he had wanted to do since the moment he'd first laid eyes on her?

'*Guys!*' Claudia came barrelling towards them, ignoring the dirty looks she got from gamblers who didn't want a baby stroller to ruin their buzz, or the illusion of night-time that the windowless casinos perpetuated. 'I *love* Vegas!' She was holding a forty-ounce slushy and propped on the back of the stroller was a stuffed bear larger than the baby within it. 'Any news?'

'There he is now,' said Sawyer, spotting him a hundred yards away, picking through the crowds towards them.

'How did you see him all the way over there?'

'It's my job,' said Sawyer.

Tosca had something for them. He revealed it with typically Vegas flourish, stringing out a long story that took in the history of No-limit Texas Hold'em on the famous Strip. But eventually he got to the point and pulled a computer printout from his back pocket, pointing at a name from the final poker table in the 2004 Barcadi Classic.

'Danny Featherbow,' he said, and stood back, his arms open wide like a magician at the end of the trick.

'Did he win?' asked Esmé.

'Fifth. Walked away with a little over ten Gs. Pretty good for Caesar's.'

Claudia burnt fiercely with triumph. She took the piece of paper from Tosca and studied it as though she expected to see something more. 'Can I keep this?'

'Sure,' he said, and glanced at Luis, who nodded discreetly and palmed him another fifty when they shook hands and said goodbye.

'Nice to see you again after all this time,' said Tosca.

'Great to catch up,' said Luis. He wondered if Tosca would remember him for real if he ever saw him again.

Claudia was marvelling over the sheet of paper as though it was a holy scripture. 'This is amazing!' she said. 'What now? What next?'

Esmé knew she had to be the voice of reason. 'There's nothing there to go on, Claudia,' she said, as gently as she could. 'We know he was alive, that's all.'

'But we could take this to the police, or a private detective. It proves he didn't die on Des Amparados. It proves your father was wrong,' she said, turning to Luis and unable to keep the tone of accusation from her voice. 'Either he was wrong or he was lying.'

'Don't go to the police,' said Luis.

'What is it?' said Esmé. 'What's wrong?'

'Just promise me you won't go to the police.'

'What?' said Claudia with indignation. 'No, I won't promise that.'

He turned to Esmé. 'What made him come looking for me?' he said. 'That's what I can't stop thinking about. What made Hector seek me out after so many years? Did something happen? Did something happen with Danny?'

Claudia folded the piece of paper and tucked it right next to the postcard, feeling that she had a growing body of evidence and that Hector had been lying to all of them from the very beginning. 'Let's go back, then,' she said. 'Let's go back to Des Amparados and ask him.'

24

At Esmeralda's they greeted Megan as if she had been gone for months, not days. Ray ran out from behind the bar and kissed her, the regulars whooped and told them to get a room, at the same time as shouting out hi and asking where she had been.

'I have a life, you know,' she kidded. 'A life beyond frying pork rinds for you guys.'

'You okay,' said Ray, nuzzling into her hair. 'I was worried, we all were.'

'That's quite a welcome,' she said.

'We missed you.'

'I missed you too.' It was not a lie. She had missed him. She just was not sure how much. She wanted to figure out some things, given the events of the last few days, and with Esmé safely out of town, this seemed like the perfect opportunity. She didn't think they would find anything in Las Vegas and she knew that Esmé didn't think they would either, but they could both see that it was something Claudia needed to work through for the sake of her own sanity, and much like Esmé, Megan couldn't stand it when someone told her no. Helping Claudia stand up to her mother felt like a very sisterly thing to do.

'Megan?' said one of her regulars. 'Can you tell Miguel the secret ingredient in the guacamole in case something happens to you?'

'And can you get your ass in the kitchen and make a batch?' said someone else, she couldn't quite see who.

'Watch your mouth,' admonished Ray in the general direction of the comment.

'Chill, Ray,' she said. 'I'm on it.' After the time she'd had, she felt like squishing some avocados.

Miguel was in the kitchen. 'Hey,' he said.

'Hey.'

She could see why a tiger like Esmé might find life with a teddy bear like Miguel less than challenging, and yet she still felt sorry for him. It made her feel awkward to know that his wife had been just a few miles away.

'How was it here?' she said. 'Okay?'

'The windows rattled,' he said. 'But nothing major.'

'Good job you put up those storm shutters, huh?'

'Yeah,' he said modestly, for they could both remember the protests from Ray about the expense. 'I suppose.'

In all this time, the closest she had ever seen him come to flirting with another woman was the friendly way he was with her. He wasn't like Ray, sweet-talking any woman that walked into the bar. Although Ray would insist that it was all in the name of repeat business.

On impulse she kissed him on the cheek.

'What was that for?' he said.

'No reason,' she said. 'Just glad to see you.'

Ray crashed through the kitchen door. 'Big order, new

349

table, *puerco pibil*, *chiles en nogado*, plus the mixed plate. Okay? And don't forget the guac for the guys.'

Megan and Miguel got to work. Megan ground the walnuts for the sauce to go with the roasted chillies, Miguel unwrapped the banana leaves from around the pork leg that had been soaking all last night in a bath of orange juice and ancho chilli paste and then roasting slowly all day in their oven. The smells drove her wild. It was good to be back.

The following evening, Ray was in a bad mood. Miguel had cut out early because he needed to retrieve his truck from a friend in Los Corales, but Ray had a long-standing engagement with a supplier who had promised to cut their bill for imported liquor in half. 'The guy has a limited warehouse, babe, I'd hate for him to cut a deal with someone else.'

'Leave me here,' said Megan. 'I'll be fine.'

'You're sure?'

'It's a Monday,' she said. They were never busy on Mondays. If she was lucky she would even be able to switch the television over to something that wasn't sport.

He had never left her in the bar all alone before. He was hesitant to do so this time, but eventually he did, and the bar was fairly empty, so Megan took the opportunity to clean things up behind the beer trays, to polish the glasses and to dust off the rows of tequila bottles they kept stacked behind the bar. After the revamp they had pulled off over on Des Amparados, making this little bar gleam was a piece of cake.

350

She was so intent on her work that she barely registered when the last set of customers paid up and left. It was a surprise to look up and see that she had the entire place to herself.

She pounced on the remote control and found MTV.

She was in the kitchen, fixing herself a coffee and bowl of coconut ice cream, when she heard them come in.

'One moment!' she yelled, and emerged with a welcoming grin, expecting that maybe some of the Americans had tired of the scene down at Punta Sam and decided to finish up their night over here.

Four men. Locals. All on the large side. None of them smiling.

Three of them came to the bar but a third stationed himself by the door in a way that instantly put her on her guard.

'Get Ray,' said one of them.

'He'll be back in a little while,' she said. 'What can I get you to drink?'

'I don't want a drink. I want to speak to Ray. Where's Miguel?'

'Out,' she said. 'Can I take a message?'

He looked at his buddies and laughed. 'So there's nobody here but you?'

'They're on their way back,' she lied. Warning bells were going off in her head. She saw the man at the door turn the latch and the bells turned into sirens, her internal alarm screaming of the danger she could be in.

'What's your name, honey?' said the man.

'Megan.'

'American?'

'English.'

'You're the one Ray's been talking about?'

She hoped not. The idea of Ray telling this guy, whose breath smelt of pork rinds and garlic, anything about her made her stomach turn.

'Depends what he said.' Perhaps if she added a little levity to the situation, things would stay under her control. She was good at getting people on her side: just look at how she could make an entire bar full of customers stay all night on a Saturday. Hadn't she turned this little saloon into one of the best places to be downtown?

'He said you're a good lay.'

She kept her smile steady. 'Yep. That would be me.'

The guy grinned, but it wasn't a nice grin. It didn't make her feel any better. 'You seen Esmeralda around here lately?'

She shook her head.

'What about the mother, Catalina? You seen her?'

She shook her head again, this time truthfully. 'I never met her.'

'She was with a buddy of mine, Carlos. Maybe you know him?'

'I'm just a tourist,' said Megan. 'I don't know anybody.'

'Esmé and Catalina were both with Carlos, you know? Working for him, I guess.' He exchanged a loaded look with his two heavies and they laughed. 'But then they skipped out. Esmé first back home, we thought, and then Catalina to Madrid. And Carlos is a little angry about losing both of them one after another like that. Plenty angry, as it happens. You see, Carlos figures they owe

352

him, and seeing as how he can't find the ladies, he's asked me to collect from Ray.'

'Ray's not here,' said Megan. Her eyes flicked from the ringleader, to the heavies, to the guy at the door. She knew that she didn't stand a chance against all four of them. Nobody would.

'How much is in that cash register there?' he said.

'Not much,' she said. 'It's a Monday. We don't do good business on a Monday.'

'Pretty good the rest of the time though, right? I told Carlos all about it. Word is you guys are running a fairly slick little operation down here, pulling down big money on the weekends.'

'We do okay.'

'So good that maybe you think you don't need guys like me looking out for you any more?' He made the smallest nod to his left.

Before she could do anything about it, the largest of the men took two giant strides until he was behind the bar next to her and then he lifted her clean off her feet.

'What the hell?' she yelled, and kicked out with her legs. His left arm was wrapped tightly around her, pinning her arms to her side. He clamped his right hand over her mouth and he walked back over to his boss until Megan was eyeball to eyeball with him.

'I changed my mind,' he said. 'You can take a message. Tell your boyfriend that we came looking for his slut sister and his thieving mother. Tell him I stole his cash register. I wrecked his bar. And then I cut up his pretty little girlfriend's face. You got that, honey?' She saw the glint of a knife in his hand and felt the cool blade tickle against her cheek. 'You tell him Carlos is real proud of his success.'

Megan wanted to speak, but with the hand over her mouth it was impossible. Besides, what would she say? The adrenalin pumping round her body was making her dizzy. Her feet flailed in the open air. The skin of her face, so proudly tanned, felt paper thin; she wondered how quickly she would bleed and how much it would hurt. In her peripheral vision she saw one of the two remaining men open the drawer of the cash register, then yank the entire console from the counter. The last man took a baseball bat to the bottles behind the bar. With an enormous crash the air was filled with the sharp scent of alcohol and Megan's resolve liquefied. She thought that she might pee.

'I'll tell you what,' said the ringleader. 'Maybe you and I will make a deal, okay?'

She glared at him, her grey eyes paling with the glaze of her terrified tears and exposing her tough-girl attitude for what it was. She tried to think of something else, and what came to mind was Connor and how safe she would be wrapped up in his arms.

'You tell me where the rest of my money is and maybe you get to keep your face, okay?

It just so happened that Ray didn't like to go to the bank Mondays. He said it was too busy; he couldn't stand waiting in line. Megan had offered to go for him once but he had vetoed that idea the moment she'd voiced it, and so their weekend takings always sat in a lockbox in the storeroom until Tuesday, when the lines at the bank were shorter and Ray could bring himself to go. She flinched as the glasses were swept from the shelves and the brute holding her up chuckled and removed his hand from her mouth.

'It's a Monday,' she said. 'Everything is in the cash register.'

'There's nothing else?'

'No.'

'Don't lie to me, honey. A guy like Ray likes to keep a little something on hand. You want to tell me, or you want to keep your teeth?'

She said nothing.

'It won't be me,' he said. 'I'll get Nico here to do it.' He jerked his thumb towards the guy with baseball bat, who smiled amiably as if he had been asked to help her push-start her car.

The bar was insured. She knew that. She had heard Ray complain often enough about the cost of the premiums, and argue with Miguel over the necessity of cover. Her breath came to her in tight little pants and she remembered everything she had heard about organized crime in Mexico. She looked up at the clock. It was getting to that time when the regulars might stop in. The longer these thugs lurked in the bar, the closer she was getting to putting others in danger.

What would Ray want her to do? She saw Nico and his buddy making for the kitchen, where they could cause plenty of havoc. The insurance would cover the lost cash. The time it would take to restore the bar and kitchen to working order would eat into their profits.

'Let me check,' she said.

'I can't hear you?'

'In the storeroom,' she said. 'There's a cashbox in the storeroom.'

'Go get it,' he said, nodding at her captor to release her.

Her legs trembled as her feet touched the floor and she longed for a moment to be back in Essex. In her childhood bedroom, with the warning light on her bookshelf to save her from harm. She walked over to the storeroom. What if she gave him the money and he cut her anyway?

The stainless-steel box was on a high shelf and she felt his salacious eyes on her exposed tattooed torso as she stretched for it.

'Where's the key?'

'I don't know.'

'You lying to me, honey?'

'I really don't know,' she said. 'Please, just take it and go. Tell your guys to leave my kitchen alone.'

'Does Ray keep you happy?'

'What?'

'Ramon. Does he keep you happy? You know what they say about Mexican guys that sleep with gringos?'

She shook her head. The fight drained out of her. The cashbox was the last bargaining chip she had. She watched him sheathe his knife but it brought her no relief. She was standing in a storeroom with her back to the wall. There was nowhere to run to. He took a step forward and she wondered if it was worth trying to fight him off if he came any closer, or if she should just submit; go limp beneath him and let him do whatever it took to stay alive.

'A real man can handle a Mexican woman. These fools

who screw tourists like you are only halfway there.' He grabbed the cashbox from her hand and pushed his palm into her chest so that she stumbled backwards until she sat down on an upturned crate. 'You tell your boyfriend to get his house in order, okay? You tell him that from Carlos.'

He walked away and slammed the door closed. She heard the sound of something being dragged up against the outside and when she tried it the door wouldn't open. She sat back down again, as tight as the skin of a drum, trembling violently when she heard an enormous crash that she guessed was the huge old mirror on the wall behind the bar, and then nothing, silence.

By the time Ray came back she had slipped into a state of shock and when he yelled her name and scraped the barrier away from the door, she screamed.

'What the hell, Megan?' he said. 'What's happened?'

She bit down so hard on her lip that it started to bleed.

'Hey,' he said, 'stop it. Are you okay? Listen to me, are you okay?'

She nodded maniacally. When she tried to speak her voice came out croaky, as if she had just woken up; she had to clear her throat and start again. 'Did they wreck everything?' she said.

'Not everything,' he said. 'Almost. Can you tell me what happened?' He slipped his arm around her and led her out of the closet. She looked around her as if expecting to get jumped. He sat next to her in one of the booths at the back of the bar. 'The closed sign is on the

357

door. I thought you'd shut up shop and gone home. Who was it?'

'A guy came in asking for you, he didn't tell me his name. He said he was here on behalf of Carlos. He had three other guys with him.'

Ray shook his head. 'This doesn't sound right. Are you lying to me?'

She snapped out of her daze. 'He knew you,' she said. 'He knew Miguel. He even knew me, said you'd talked about me. It was something to do with Esmé and your mother.' The pitch of her voice climbed and wavered. She second-guessed herself. It had been Carlos, right? That's what he said.

'One of the guys with him was called Nico,' she added.

Ray looked at the ruined bar in despair. 'What did he say?'

'He said Carlos wants you to get your house in order. Ray, he took the cashbox. With all the money from the weekend.'

'How did he know where it was?'

'I told him.'

'You told him?'

'He had a knife in my face, his guys were smashing up the bar, they were about to start smashing up the kitchen. I was scared, Ray, I was really scared.'

'So you told him where to find the money?'

'He asked.'

Ray pulled his hands through his perfect hair. 'Jesus.' He stood up and started picking up the shards of mirrored glass from the floor with his bare hands. He didn't speak to her again and she sat there uncomfortably, wondering why he was not calling the police, or at least calling her sweetheart. He muttered to himself while he fetched a broom and a plastic bin from the kitchen and she grew nervous. It was as if he expected her to apologize, and so after a few minutes she did.

'I'm sorry. I really thought he was going to hurt me. I was pretty scared. I was terrified.'

'You seem fine now.'

'Ray . . . I . . . why are you being so cold?'

He stopped sweeping up and faced her, leaning on the handle of the broom. 'The first time I ever leave you on your own and the entire weekend takings go missing? You don't think that's a bit of a coincidence?'

'They knew you wouldn't be here. They were looking for money.'

'I thought you said they asked for me?'

'They did.' Her mind tripped over itself to remember things more clearly.

'Why would they ask for me if they already knew I wasn't here?'

'Wait.' She was confused. Was he accusing her of something? Was it possible that he thought she was a part of this? 'Ray, if you're suggesting what I think you're suggesting . . . I love this bar; nobody loves this bar more than me. You know how hard I work. Why would I do that? Why would you even *think* I would do that?'

'You tell me. You must have heard me talking about Carlos and remembered the name.'

'Ray!' She was stunned. 'Come on, I know this a shock but seriously, come on.'

His gaze was steady and analytical. For a moment, no

more than a split second really, he softened, and then the warmth was gone and he closed himself off from her as surely as a set of steel shutters over a pane of glass, and she could no longer see the man that she thought he was.

It took her back, not to the trauma of a few hours previously, but back to the day she found out who her real father was, the terrible feeling of being the stupid person in the room, the only one who hadn't seen what was going on. The one who had been fooled.

'This is low, Ray,' she said. 'This is bad. You want me to swear? Okay, I swear.' But even as she said it, she knew that it was over between them, even if he turned around and said he was sorry. Even if he walked into the kitchen and came back with a cup of hot chocolate with a ribbon of chilli, just the way she liked it, even then she knew they could never go back.

'I trusted you,' he said.

'No, you didn't,' she said incredulously. 'I'm just another gringo, right? You were happy to have me pull this bar up to where it is now. Cheap labour. Was that funny? Getting cheap labour from a gringo girl like me? Did it make you feel good? I told him no, Ray, I told him no, even with his knife in my face I told him no. I did that for you, for us, for the bar. You don't believe me, fine. At least now I know the truth about you and me.'

Just then Miguel arrived back, swinging the keys to his truck and whistling. He stopped short when he saw the mess in the bar. 'Megan,' he said, and scanned the bar, seeing her at once, and ran to her side. 'Are you okay? What happened? Do you need to go to the hospital? Ray, what the hell, man?'

'Tell him, Ray,' said Megan. 'Tell him how I screwed you over.'

She stood up and walked over to the worst of the carnage, spotting a surviving bottle of Don Julio, her favourite. She picked it up and flipped it in her hand like a flashy cocktail bartender or a gunslinger. She crossed back to Miguel by the door and kissed him on the cheek. Then she walked out with the tequila in her hand and hoped she had the strength not to look back.

25

They were tired when they got back from Las Vegas. Tired, but at the same time exhilarated. Luis picked up his car at the airport, dropped them off at the hotel and sped off into the night with Esmé. Claudia looked at Sawyer shyly. It would be strange adapting to the new shape of their relationship, and they were both wondering what Lucy would make of it, but too nervous to discuss this with each other. He kissed her once in the elevator on the way up to their rooms, and had one hand on the stroller while he did so, but he put a decent distance between them when they walked into Lucy's suite. They hadn't discussed what to say.

As it turned out, they needn't have worried.

Lucy was sitting at an easy chair in her picture window taking afternoon tea with David, her ex, David, as if it was the most natural thing in the world.

'What is he doing here?' hissed Claudia.

'You're back,' said Lucy.

'Evidently,' said Claudia. She felt Sawyer take a step closer, his chest automatically pumped out, and she loved him for that.

'Claudia,' said David formally, as if they hadn't once been as intimate as it was possible to be.

'I'd like you to leave.'

'Who's this?' he asked, instinctively sensing Sawyer's threatening presence as a smooth operator like David always could.

'This is Sawyer,' said Claudia, and she reached out for his hand. Sawyer took it. Something flickered across Lucy's face that might have been surprise, but she effortlessly swept over this new development and answered Claudia's original question.

'David is here on the advice of his lawyer, darling.'

Claudia could tell from the slight catch in her voice that Lucy was not as relaxed with the situation as she was pretending to be.

'You look well,' said David. 'I must say I was rather surprised that you'd left the country again without my permission.'

'Since when do I need your permission?'

He regarded her with barely concealed amusement, and she realized what a familiar expression this was for him and wondered why this air of constant condescension had never annoyed her up until now. His tone crawled under her skin and she wanted to rip it out like a deer tick. 'Under Mexican law, an unmarried mother needs the permission of the baby's father to travel with him. They didn't stop you at the border?'

'I told them you were dead,' she said viciously. 'I told them I was a widow.'

'You lied,' he said. He walked towards them so he could look at Daniel, who was kicking away quite happily in his stroller. 'You could get into quite a lot of trouble for that,' he said.

'What is it that you want, David?'

'You did get my letter, I take it?'

'I assumed that someone had paid you to threaten me,' she said, shooting a malicious look towards Lucy and feeling triumphant when at last she had the good grace to look embarrassed. 'Oh mother, you swore you didn't give him any money.'

'She didn't.'

'You don't want to be a father.'

'I could give a baby a stable home,' he said. 'I'm standing for the federal district; there is some concern about Camille's values – a baby could be advantageous.'

'You want Daniel to be a political asset? You go to hell. And what do you mean, Camille's *values*? Married life not working out quite the way you expected? Is your wife sleeping around? You must be completely mad to think I would ever let my son be with you.'

'Our son.'

'Mine,' said Claudia. 'And if you think I'm wrong, then I'm happy to allow the lawyers to decide. It'll be big news in Mexico City, maybe even national. I'll make sure it is. We'll see how leaving a young girl pregnant and alone plays with the values of voters, shall we? And there's a few things I know about Camille too. I might even have photographs. Don't test me, David, because I'll make sure every news outlet in Mexico City knows what a scumbag you are.'

David glanced across at Lucy. There was a pronounced pause. Daniel started to cry and Sawyer scooped him up out of his stroller. David was still looking at Lucy. He seemed flustered and very uncomfortable.

'Why are you looking at her?' said Claudia. 'Do you need her to tell you what to say next?'

David started to pull on his jacket. 'This is nuts,' he said. 'I did what you wanted, Lucy, and I'm keeping the money.'

He marched past Daniel without even looking and out of the door. It slammed behind him and Claudia was overcome with relief. She fell against Sawyer's reassuring form and took a breath.

'Are you okay?' said Sawyer.

Claudia whirled about to confront her mother. 'You swore you didn't give him any money.'

'I didn't,' said Lucy, ashamed. 'It was your grandfather. I asked him to make a donation.'

'But why?' said Claudia. 'Why is it so important to you?'

'I want you to stop looking for your father.'

'Why?'

'Because I don't think you will like what you find.'

After they pulled away from the hotel, Luis asked Esmé where he should take her and she didn't know what to say. The couch of her waitress friend in Puerto Juarez did not call to her.

'There's a bar on Palerma,' she said. 'Downtown. I think I need to speak to my husband. It's time.'

'You're sure?'

'I kissed you,' she said simply. 'The conversation is already overdue.'

'You want me to come with you?'

'That's not a good idea.'

'You want me to wait?'

She shook her head. 'I'll be okay. I'll meet you tomorrow outside their hotel. We'll have breakfast together and we can figure out what we're going to do next.'

'About what?' he said.

'About everything.'

After a while they pulled up outside the bar. '*Esmeralda's*,' she read. 'Is that supposed to be a joke?'

Miguel had been working all through the night and into the next day to get the bar open for business again tonight. He had tried to find Megan, to apologize to her; maybe even Ray might apologize because now that he had heard the whole story from him, Megan's explanation sounded feasible, given that he remembered the name Carlos, and when he reminded Ray then Ray remembered him too. But he did not know where Megan would have gone, and the few places he was able to try turned up nothing. One thing bothered him about the story, though. If Esmé had skipped out on Carlos, where was she now?

'Miguel?'

He turned around and it felt as if his thoughts alone had conjured her. She was as beautiful as she had always been – more perhaps, because it had been so long, but her eyes were very sad and he knew what she was going to say before she told him.

'You came back to me,' he said.

She nodded.

'But you're not going to stay?'

366

'We were too young to get married,' she said.

He walked up to her and took both her hands in his. 'I couldn't believe it when you said you'd marry me,' he said. 'A girl like you, with a guy like me.'

'You're a decent guy, Miguel. I really am sorry.'

'I missed you,' he said. 'But the sky didn't cave in or anything like that. I'll make it okay on my own. I know you always thought I was pretty dumb, but the bar's doing well now, you know?' He looked around. He had done his best but the smashed mirror still needed to be cleaned up and one of the wooden tables was broken where it had taken a pounding from a baseball bat. 'Or at least it was.'

'What happened?' she said, and he told her. When he got to the part about Catalina skipping out on Carlos too, perhaps being safe Madrid, she was happy and knew that her mother would be in touch – perhaps there was already a letter waiting for her somewhere. For once she wanted to go back to her own apartment, even if only to pick up her post.

'This girl,' she said, when he was finished, knowing there was something familiar about the British tourist he described. 'What was her name?'

'Megan,' he said. 'She quit. You'd have liked her. You need a place to stay? Her room's upstairs, it's available. It's the one that smells like coconut oil.'

'I think I know her,' said Esmé, smiling. She grabbed a broom and a trash bag and helped him to clear up the mess.

In a hotel room about seven miles to the east, Claudia was refusing to have anything further to do with Lucy.

'She's a lying *bitch*,' she yelled from her standoff in the bedroom, hoping that her mother could hear her.

Sawyer covered Daniel's ears. He was growing very fond of the little boy and had known when David was threatening to take him that he would have fought him off every step of the way, with his fists if he had to. 'Maybe she's lying,' he said, diplomatically. 'But why don't you let me talk to her and try to find out why? Do you trust me?'

'Of course I do.'

'Then get some rest. It's late. Daniel will be awake again in a few hours and we can take it from there.' He kissed her slowly and she felt her tension drain away and decided to close her eyes for just a few minutes.

When she was asleep, Sawyer left the room, gently closing the door behind him, and called room service to order a bottle of Lucy's favourite Sancerre and two glasses.

When it arrived, he padded along the corridor to Lucy's room and knocked sharply on her door. She opened it almost immediately. Her blond hair was wild, as if she had been tearing at it, and he pictured her pacing up and down in her hotel room on her own. Not for the first time, he wondered what it was she was trying to hide. She was his oldest friend and he had never seen her so spooked.

'Drinks?' he said, just as if it was twenty years ago and they were young and stupid.

He waited until she had a couple of sips but found that he didn't want to wait any longer than that. 'What is it, Luce? Why don't you tell me? You know the truth always comes out in the end.'

'Not this time,' she said.

'Is it something to do with the old guy, Hector?'

Her head snapped up at the mention of his name. 'What do you know about Hector?'

'I met him.'

'What do you mean you met him? When? Where?'

'A week ago. On Des Amparados. You remember him?'

Lucy had gone terribly pale. She looked as if she might throw up or faint. 'That's impossible,' she said. 'Hector left the island a long time ago.'

'Is that right?' said Sawyer. 'Well, guess what? He's back.'

26

Megan spent an uncomfortable night on a bench near Punta Sam. She had everything she owned in a backpack yet again. A couple of Mexican taxi drivers approached her but they backed off quickly when she snarled at them. The knife in her face was all she could see when she closed her eyes, and so she did not sleep at all.

The moment that it was light enough to take the boat out, Megan went straight back to Des Amparados, where she found Hector all alone, kneeling in the garden, potting tomato and courgette seeds in dozens of neat rows in some freshly cleared soil. She liked that he still didn't have a proper roof on his house but he was already getting the seed beds established. She admired his priorities. He didn't see her straight away so she watched him for a little while, and gradually the slow, repetitive nature of his task calmed the fears that last night's events had left her with, fears that had felt in the small hours of the morning as if they would never go away.

When at last he looked up, he didn't seem the slightest bit surprised to see Megan standing there watching him.

'Pass me the twine?' he said, and she did, watching him

snap a length of it between his teeth as if it was as soft as a strand of spaghetti. He marked out the line that he had just planted and stood up, wiping his muddy hands down the front of his old blue jeans, and declared it lunchtime.

Hector crossed over to the crude outdoor kitchen he had rigged up, with a pan of steaming liquid over a twig fire, and he ladled two huge bowls of simmering rice soup, rich with chicken stock, and scattered it with chopped lettuce. He warmed some torn stale tortillas in the empty pan with tomatoes, salt and a slug of golden oil that filled the air with a waft of garlic when he stirred and immediately made Megan feel a little bit better.

He placed a bowl in her hands and the pan of chilaquiles on the floor between them. 'Eat,' he said. 'Eat and tell me.'

So she told him what had happened at the bar. He sat through her story and in the retelling some of the fears came back, but as long as she looked into Hector's eyes, they did not overwhelm her. She felt safe.

'Why would Ray think me capable of something like that?' she said. 'That's what I don't understand.'

'I think I do,' said Hector. 'But I don't know if you're going to like it.'

'Try me.'

'He knew that you were hiding something from him.'

Megan was still perplexed. 'Hiding something? What?'

'The fact that you don't love him, you never did. A guy like Ray, he has grown up with a mother who adored him. That was his idea of love, an unconditional acceptance. With you he has to work a little and maybe he always wondered why. You just gave him a reason.'

'But that's stupid,' said Megan. 'I was crazy about him.'

'Is it? I know you're scared of love, Megan. More scared than you are of anything. And who can blame you? Your mother lied to you; the man you thought was your father lied too. Love doesn't exist, right? And if it does then it ends. Have you ever been in love, really in love?'

Connor loved me. 'Once perhaps,' she said. 'Have you?'

'Once,' he said.

Last night, with a knife to her throat, Connor had been all she'd been able to think of. Not for him to save her, or to say goodbye when she thought that she might die; not even to comfort her when she was locked in the cupboard not knowing if they would be back; but simply so that she could right a wrong.

She had lied when she told him goodbye. She had lied when she said she did not want him.

'I have to go back to England,' she said, the only way forward opening out like a path. She saw Connor's clear eyes and hoped that she wasn't too late for the chance to let him love her. She would try to love him back.

She felt Hector tense beside her and followed his gaze to a set of figures approaching them at speed. They were backlit by the mid-morning sun and it took her a moment to distinguish Esmé's stride and Claudia's graceful gait, flanked on either side by Sawyer and Luis.

'Who's that?' she said, meaning the fifth person in the middle. Slight and slender. A woman who walked as if she was a single chord away from dance.

'Lucy,' whispered Hector.

He stood up. Megan held his hand.

'Move away from him, Megan,' said Esmé. Next to her, Luis contained so much fury that it was coming off him in waves.

'Hector?' said Megan, noticing that his face had gone as pale as ash. He dropped her hand, and his arm reached out towards Luis in a gesture of infinite mercy.

'*I'm sorry*,' he whispered, and she didn't know if he was saying it to her, to Luis, or to himself.

'What's going on?' said Megan. 'Claudia? What's happened?'

'Ask him,' said Claudia, jerking her thumb towards Hector. 'Ask him for an explanation. Start by asking him his name. The man standing next to you is not Hector Spinoza.'

'Who are you?' said Luis, and his eyes contained only confusion and despair.

Megan turned to Claudia and the woman who must be Claudia's mother. 'How do you know?' she asked.

'Because Hector Spinoza is dead,' said Claudia.

'But how do you know?'

Lucy stepped forward. 'Because I killed him.'

'*What?*' Megan felt dizzy. Her eyes darted from Hector to Luis to Esmé, waiting for someone to tell her that this was a joke, or test, or something other than the truth.

'Hector died twenty-three years ago, right where you're standing,' said Claudia. 'We got back from Las Vegas last night and the moment Sawyer mentioned Hector's name, my mother knew she had to tell us, didn't you?'

But Lucy was not listening. She kept walking, one step after another. Her eyes were locked onto the face of the man who claimed to be Hector and she moved with a single purpose, as if an unseen force that emanated from him was pulling her forward. She stopped just a few inches away and put her hands on the sides of his face, seeing past the deep suntan and the lines, past the beard, past the woes that he carried on his timeworn face and she looked deep into his sad grey eyes.

'*Danny*,' she said, her voice softened by wonder. 'Is it really you?'

27

Cancún, 1989

'Oh, for fuck's sake Lucy, lighten up.' Leo lit yet another cigarette and flicked the just-burned match in the direction of the weeping woman. He ignored the dirty look that Sawyer threw his way. Sawyer was eighteen: what did he know about women? Lucy was always losing her heart to some guy or another. True, she hadn't been quite this bad before, but her crush on Danny Featherbow wouldn't last beyond the summer. They never did. 'If this guy doesn't show up in the next ten minutes, we're starting to pack up anyway.'

The yacht was stern aside at the coconut farm loading dock where they stood, held fast by a couple of lines, waiting patiently to be loaded up and take them on to Florida. The wind was perfect and they should make it to Key West in a few days.

'I can't wait to get out of this place,' said Guy. 'I have a bad feeling about this.'

'I want to stay,' whispered Lucy.

'Don't be absurd,' said Leo. 'Christ, you'd think you'd never been laid properly before.'

'I think I could be in love with him; this could be it for me. What if I'm running away from my own future?'

'Too bad, sweetheart, it's your boat and we need it to get the hell out of here.'

It was a ridiculous, romantic notion. What kind of future would they have? She liked her stupid, complicated life exactly the way it was. Didn't she?

They waited. Lucy knew that they were all nervous. This was the biggest deal any of them had got close to, and it was far too close for comfort. It wasn't the same any more, Leo had said. Years ago, when there was nothing here, it was romantic laced with a hint of danger; now that there were ten thousand tourists a few miles away, and a city with a police force, it was dangerous with a hint of romance. They had all agreed that this would be the last time.

'Ah fuck it,' said Guy. 'Sawyer, start getting the ramp ready to load the bike.'

Sawyer stroked his gleaming Indian motorbike, a gift so beloved he had refused to leave it behind. They had sailed across the Atlantic with the thing strapped down on the foredeck, double wrapped in tarpaulin in case of salt water damage, with Guy and Leo bitching all the time about how it threw the weight of the boat off balance. But they all loved having it to play with when they were on land.

Just then the tan pick-up rounded the corner and the men they had been waiting for climbed out. They did not look happy.

'What's happening?' said Lucy, as the men exchanged heated Spanish.

'I don't know,' said Sawyer, and they both stood there while a blazing row erupted, catching the odd word here and there, like police and jail and bad; very, very bad.

At last Guy thought to translate events for them. 'The boat was intercepted,' he said. 'Coastguard. It's not going to happen.'

'It was that fucking Hector chap,' said Leo.

'Hector?' said Lucy. 'No, surely not?'

'You heard him,' said Leo. 'Sanctimonious little do-gooder with his Catholic values and all that shite. Probably thinks he owns the place. *Shit!*' He kicked the back tyre of the motorbike.

'Hey, man, relax,' cautioned Sawyer.

'Don't you dare tell me to relax. I had thirty Gs stacked up on this deal and now I'm just supposed to relax, am I?'

He turned back to the Mexicans and told them something that immediately galvanized them into action. They traded furious conversation. She caught the name Hector. She saw Leo point in the direction of the house that it had been almost impossible for her to leave, no matter how much she had tried to play down her emotions in front of Danny.

'Leo?' said Lucy, a chill of apprehension making her shiver. 'Leo, what did you say to them?'

The two men climbed back into their pick-up and Lucy saw the glint of gunmetal tucked into the back of each waistband, and her warm, sun-kissed skin turned icy as the blood beneath it turned cold.

'Leo? Leo, talk to me.'

'Come on,' said Leo. 'Let's get out of here.'

The Mexicans started up the truck and with a spray of

grit and sand they started off down the road that led all the way to back to Featherbow.

'Where are they going? Leo, my God, what did you tell them?'

'I told them to check in on the old man if they wanted to know who grassed them up.'

'Leo, why? You have no proof that it was him.'

'Come on, Lucy, get real. You want me to let them think that it was me? You saw what he was like at breakfast. He's lived here for a while; these consignments are pretty regular, he must have known we were waiting for something.'

'But Danny's there,' she pleaded.

'I'm sure they won't hurt Danny,' said Sawyer, placing a comforting hand on her shoulder.

'He'll get involved,' said Lucy desperately. 'You don't know him like I do. If he sees Hector in trouble, he won't be able to stop himself.'

'They're just going to scare him, Lucy,' said Guy. 'Calm down.'

'Scare him? Scare him? How do you know that? This is Mexico, Guy, and you're talking about an old man, a drifter, with nobody to miss him. This is Mexico, not Mayfair. They won't waste their time scaring him: they'll shoot him.'

Leo shrugged, and raised his eyes at Guy who returned the look. They brushed off Lucy's outrage. 'He's not so old. He can take care of himself. But, like you said, there's nobody to miss him,' said Leo.

Quicker than any of them could move to stop her, Lucy darted across and plucked the keys for the motorbike off the table. Sawyer was distracted setting up the ramp to wheel the bike on board, and by the time he'd turned around, Lucy was astride the bike, starting up the engine. 'Lucy,' he yelled above the powerful bike. 'Don't be bloody ridiculous.'

She was as good on the bike as any of them. She had ridden all day through the mountains when they were in Venezuela; the others might moan about the bike being on the yacht, but Lucy adored it. She knocked back the kickstand with her bare foot, opened the throttle and was gone.

She didn't want to go too fast. If she came off there, she was wearing nothing to protect her – no helmet, no boots, no gloves; and yet she couldn't help pushing the bike to the very edge of what was safe. She had to get to Featherbow and warn Danny. It didn't take very long at all to travel the mile or so along the tarmac access road, and when she was almost there she heard something that might have been a gunshot, but the wind whipped the sound away before she could be sure.

The pick-up was parked in front of the gardens, on a patch of dirty gravel that passed for a driveway, but there was no sign of anybody about. She cut the engine and jumped from the bike, running into Hector's *cabaña* and finding it empty.

Where was everyone?

She was about to leave and walk across to Featherbow to find Danny, when she saw the unmistakably menacing muzzle of a revolver poking out from underneath the kitchen table. Her heart raced, and then she almost laughed when she realized there was nobody holding the gun. It was lying on the floor, apparently discarded.

Cautiously she crept towards it, looking over her shoulder repeatedly, until she was close enough to pick it up.

The touch of her hand was controlled and measured, but the weight of the gun surprised her and she took a step back, knocking over one of the kitchen stools, which crashed to the floor.

She spun round in the direction of the noise. Just then there was a sudden movement to her left and a man jumped out at her, roaring it seemed, and all she saw was the gun in his hand.

She pulled the trigger.

It was a lucky shot. Straight to the side of his neck. Fatal. Unlucky. Unlucky for him.

It was Hector. He fell in a heap on the floor in front of her.

She screamed.

The blood pumped out of the wound in his neck onto the reed matting that covered the floor of the *cabaña* and his body spasmed violently, his legs kicking out at nothing, his arms reaching for an impossible lifeline that did not come. She dropped the revolver and a wash of bile filled her throat and her mouth and she retched.

'*Lucy!*' She only registered Danny's voice with the tiny part of her that was not coping with the trauma of what she had done. It felt like several minutes before she was able to look in his direction and see the horror on his face. 'My God, Lucy, what have you done?'

She didn't answer. She could not speak.

Hector stopped quaking and was still.

Danny rushed to his body but they both knew there

380

was no hope. He ripped off his own shirt and stuffed it into the wound, but the bullet had ripped through Hector's carotid artery and he was already dead.

There was the sound of running footsteps, the slam of a truck's doors and the tan pick-up reversed noisily and then tore away back where it had come from.

'Lucy,' said Danny. 'What happened?'

'There was a gun,' she said. 'On the floor. I don't . . . Is he . . . ?' But she already knew the answer. 'We have to call the police,' she said.

'The police? I don't think that's a good idea.'

'But we must. I killed him, Danny.' The shock fell on her like a cannonball and she started to sob. 'I killed him.'

'Don't cry,' he said. 'Let me think.'

He forced himself to focus. Hector was a drifter. Nobody would be looking for him, not for a very long time, if ever. The murder weapon must belong to one of the men who had fled the scene. Perhaps there was a struggle; those first two shots he had heard, perhaps those had been from Hector defending himself.

'Do you think they saw you?'

'I don't know,' said Lucy.

The police would sooner believe that foot soldiers of a drug cartel had killed Hector than a young English rose, particularly since she had shot him with their gun. He had to believe that – even if they had seen Lucy pull the trigger – they wouldn't say a word in order to protect themselves. Except what if they did? Lucy could go to prison for a very long time. So could he.

'Listen to me,' he said. She stared at him and he wanted with all his heart to make that anguish in her eyes disappear. 'It will be okay. You hear me? Everything is going to be okay.'

They threw the gun into the ocean and Danny told Lucy that she must leave the island and never come back. He told her that he would do the same.

'You should leave Mexico,' he said. 'As soon as you can.'

She nodded. The tears streamed down her face. They hadn't stopped; she wondered if they ever would.

'I heard your scream,' he said. 'I had my face in the dirt and I heard a gunshot and your scream. And I have never been so scared. But you know what? I hoped it was you. I hoped you had come back for me.'

'I came back to save you,' she said. 'But I am afraid that I have ruined your life.'

'But you came back,' he said.

'Will I ever see you again?'

He shook his head and told her to hurry before her friends came looking for her. He kissed the tears from her cheeks and then she was gone.

That night he buried Hector's body in the rough ground close to the beach where he first met her. The moon hung heavy in the sky, as if it was suspended on an invisible thread that could snap at any minute and send the moon crashing down to earth to explode into a million pearl teardrops. He stood above the unmarked grave and said every prayer he could remember, to deliver Lucy from the

382

guilt and shame he knew she would be running from for the rest of her life.

In the years to come he tried to forget what he had seen on Des Amparados, but he kept with him two things that belonged to Hector: a photograph of an unsmiling boy with an address written on the back, and a silver earring with a shark's tooth, which he pushed through the soft, bleeding flesh of his earlobe. He travelled the continent hoping to find peace. He drifted, as he thought Hector must have drifted, doing odd jobs to earn enough money for a very simple life on the outskirts of society. He played some cards. He won some money. He kept moving. But peace never came. Eventually he found his way back to Des Amparados, where the coconut farm had long since been abandoned but where Featherbow still stood.

And the truth was buried along with the man he used to be.

28

After so many years of silence, Danny Featherbow wished that Lucy had shouted his name and not whispered it. With the truth came an enormous release, as if the bad memories were gushing from his body in the way that the blood had ebbed from Hector all those years ago.

'You lied,' said Esmé. 'You told us that Danny Featherbow was dead. You lied to us all.'

'I panicked,' said Danny. 'To all intents and purposes Danny died a long time ago. I didn't know. I didn't know about any of you.'

'But we came looking for you,' said Megan. 'Why didn't you say something?'

'How?' he said. 'How could I have said it? What words could I use? Would you have understood? Do you understand now?'

He was looking directly at Luis, who was staring at him with a scathing expression of dismay. 'I don't,' said Luis. 'I don't understand at all.' He turned sharply and walked away towards the cliffs. Esmé reached out for him as he passed. 'Get off me. I need to be by myself.'

'Let him be,' said Danny softly. 'I think I can guess where he is going.'

Megan moved aside to allow Claudia to step into the paternal embrace that she had been waiting for and searching for. More than any of them, Claudia had believed in this moment. That it could be. If such faith was to be rewarded, then the moment should be hers and hers alone.

Claudia waited for the sign, the sign that all was well in her world at last now that she had found her father, but it did not come. It was a nice embrace, a hug really, but she was still the same girl, it changed precisely nothing. She wondered if baby Daniel was all right with his jolly Puerto Rican babysitter and momentarily wished that her baby was here to see his grandparents together. She glanced at her mother who had stayed tight to Danny's side. A fragment of sympathy for Lucy slipped beneath her bitter disappointment.

'It's okay,' said Claudia. 'We're going to be okay.'

'The greatest regret in my life,' said Lucy, 'is not that I had to leave you in Mexico, but that I could never tell you all about your father.' Her eyes were bright with unshed tears.

'But why?'

Sawyer was quick to comprehend what they had done. 'They killed a man,' he said. 'You leave the country, you leave no trace, you forget you ever knew each other.'

'And now?' said Claudia.

'Now? I don't know.' Sawyer took her into his arms and she closed her eyes briefly against the brilliant glare of the sun. 'Perhaps enough time has passed and people will be able to forgive.'

'All those stories you told about him,' said Megan, 'about the Danny we had been looking for, all the time you were talking about yourself.'

Danny nodded, shame casting a shadow of regret across his face. 'I told you the good things. The parts that I thought you would want to hear. I couldn't tell you the whole truth, you would hate me for the things I did, for the father I never was.'

'It was an accident,' said Megan softly.

Claudia reached for her mother's hand and nodded in silent agreement.

'The truth finds a way out in the end,' said Esmé. 'In Mexico we say: If you breed crows, one day they will take out your eyes.' Her beautiful face was clouded with great sadness and she knew that she could not forgive Danny as quickly as the others.

Luis climbed down to the beach that Danny had described and knew that he was close to the place where his father was buried. He sank down to his knees and wept. None of it made sense. He had credited his father with turning his life around, and now not only was the man a stranger to him, but he was also complicit in his real father's murder. For the first time in almost ten years, he wanted a drink. He wanted to go out and get absolutely wasted, annihilated beyond reason, so that he didn't have to take all this on board. His hot tears fell onto the earth of his father's grave and he longed for something to make sense to him, something strong enough to resist the seductive call of his worst vice.

When at last he stood up, he saw Danny approaching him.

'Get away from me,' he said. But Danny kept walking towards him with strong, determined strides.

For one awful moment, Luis thought that he was about to embrace him, and that he was supposed to forgive him.

'I would like to say I'm sorry,' said Danny. 'But I'm not.'

'Why?' said Luis. 'Why did you do it? Why did you lie to me?'

'Your father loved you,' said Danny. 'He told me that he did. He told me that the only regret in his life was not being a father to you. What happened here, what happened to him, it changed me. I had to try and help him. Do something to try and make it right. For me. And for Lucy, too. Can you understand that? And when I found out you were in trouble . . .'

Luis forced his eyes closed, but they didn't erase the memory of the things that Danny had seen when he found Luis at rock bottom and dragged him upwards, and kept him up, never letting him go under again.

'I know what it's like,' said Danny. 'I know the pull of addiction. For me it was gambling, for you it was drink. My addiction cost me my marriage. What would yours have cost you in the end?'

'But why did you have to lie to me? Why couldn't you have just been a friend?'

'Would you have listened? Or would you have gone straight to the police? It was an accident. A terrible accident. I couldn't be Danny, not any more, not after what happened. So I was Hector. And you want to know the real reason why?'

387

'The truth?'

'He had so much of it right. Your father knew a few things about the way to live a life, and I thought maybe if I could live that life, and if you could live like that, then maybe God, or whoever else it matters to, could forgive me for what I had done.'

'I can't stay here,' said Luis.

'I know. And that's the one thing I am truly sorry about. I only ever wanted good things for you, son.'

On the top of the cliff, Esmé appeared, framed by the fierce noon light, her hair crazy in the sea breeze, her beauty taking his breath away. Luis did not know quite what would happen next. He didn't know if he could ever forgive the man in front of him. He could spend a long time running from his past, but he knew without question that his future lay with the woman walking down the hill towards him.

Esmé and Luis left the island together there and then and they didn't come back to Cancún for many years.

He was right about his future.

'Didn't you get lonely, Danny?' asked Megan. The rest of them stayed on the island until sunset. Lucy stayed fixed to Danny's side, her hand clasping his. It was almost time to leave.

'I felt free,' he said. 'Except I forgot one thing. You can never be truly free, not unless you are willing to give up on love. And that's the difference between freedom and loneliness. Loneliness means you still believe in love.'

Megan's thoughts drifted to Connor and the first time

he'd told her that he loved her. She remembered him telling her that what they had together was a big deal, a forever thing. Why had she found it so hard to believe him, yet she had been suckered in by Ray's smooth words and wicked ways? How could she have been so wrong?

She had to go and see if real love was still out there waiting for her.

'I'll come back,' she said, gathering her things and kissing Claudia and the baby, saying goodbye to Sawyer and Lucy. She hugged Danny fiercely. 'Soon.'

'This is your house now,' he said. 'If you ever find yourself lonely.'

'Hey,' she said, something occurring to her. 'Are you still technically married to Mum, to Harriet?'

'God, I don't know. Maybe.'

'I probably ought to tell her,' said Megan. 'I heard she just got engaged.'

She found a flight to take her back to England the very next day. She just hoped that Connor would still be waiting.

'Let's go home,' said Sawyer. Daniel was snoozing at her feet and the sun was slipping away from Des Amparados in a gentle wash of candy pink.

Sawyer tilted her head so that he could kiss her on the lips. 'Where's home?' she said.

'I'm not sure. Let's go back to the hotel and work it out together. We need to let the dust settle here. And I think we should leave those two alone.'

Danny and Lucy could barely keep their hands off each other.

As they pulled away from the island, she watched Sawyer with Daniel and thought it odd that she had found a father, she had found two sisters, but the family she had been looking for so hard was hers to create all along. All she needed was love.

'What now?' said Lucy. She stared into Danny Featherbow's eyes, hardly daring to believe any of it. She was too old to find love. She had given up.

'Just this,' he said, dropping kisses all over her face. 'More of this.'

A single tear slipped down her cheek and Danny smudged it with his thumb. 'What is it?' he said. 'Why are you crying?'

'I forgot how beautiful it is here.'

'Will you stay?' he said.

'Here? With you? What about the past? Luis might go to the police.'

'I don't think he will.'

'Still, it might get complicated. It might be the most stupid idea you ever had.'

'So, is that a yes?'

She laughed and she thought that maybe she could live here with him. She could keep the real world at bay for a few more years: it would be easy in a place like this. Claudia would like it if they could try to be some kind of family.

'I thought about you every day,' he said.

'Honestly?'

He nodded.

Darkness was falling and with it came the first stars. They dragged a rug down onto the sand and they lay watching as the sky popped with the twinkling light of a million stars. They made love beneath a slice of silver moon. These two belonged with each other. They always had.

Megan had known where they kept the spare key for Connor's house for as long as she could remember. She found it under the flowerpot and let herself in, just as the last star was fading from the sky. She tiptoed upstairs to his bedroom, touching only the edges of the stairs with her toes so they did not creak, the way that they had to do years ago when they didn't want their parents in the front room to hear them and to ask why they were going upstairs.

Outside his door she paused and, after a moment's hesitation, she pushed it open and slipped inside.

It was warm and very dark in the bedroom. She stumbled against a chair and it rattled against the wall. 'Connor?' she whispered.

'Megan?' came the reply, almost immediately. 'What are you doing here?'

The sound of his voice was enough to make her happy. For a while neither of them spoke and she wondered if he could tell that she was smiling. 'I'm so sorry,' she said eventually, into the darkness. 'You were right. I'm scared. And you know that, because you know me better than anyone, and yet somehow you still love me. At least, I hope you do.'

He snapped on the light. They were both momentarily blinded and then, as her eyes adjusted, she saw that he was wearing her necklace on a piece of black leather around his neck.

'I always loved you, Megan.'

She felt tears brimming in her eyes. She slipped out of her shoes and crawled into bed with him.

'Always?' she said.

'Always will.'

'Let's go to sleep,' she said. 'It's early.'